S0-DUU-873

A Garland Series

The
Flowering of the Novel

Representative Mid-Eighteenth Century Fiction 1740-1775

A Collection of 121 Titles

Oriental Anecdotes

Or, the History of Haroun Alrachid

Marianne, Dame de Fauques

Two Volumes
Reprinted in One

Garland Publishing, Inc., New York & London

1974

Bibliographical note:

this facsimile has been made from a copy in the
Library of the University of California
(PQ1982.F107.1764)

Library of Congress Cataloging in Publication Data

Fauques, Marianne Agnès Pillement, dame de, d. 1773.
Oriental anecdotes.

(The Flowering of the novel)
Reprint of the 1764 ed. printed for P. Wilson,
J. Potts, A. M'Culloh, and J. Williams, Dublin.
1. Hārūn al-Rashīd, caliph, 763 ca.--809--Fiction.
I. Title.
PZ3.F2750r20 [PQ1982.F8] 843'.5 74-19079
ISBN 0-8240-1166-X

Printed in the United States of America

ORIENTAL

ANECDOTES:

OR,

THE HISTORY OF

HAROUN ALRACHID.

In TWO VOLUMES.

VOL. I.

DUBLIN:

Printed for PETER WILSON, JAMES POTTS,
ALEX. M'CULLOH, and JAM. WILLIAMS.

M,DCC,LXIV.

Advertisement.

THere is perhaps not in history an æra more curious and interesting than that in which those great personages, Charlemagne in the West, the Empress Irene and Haroun Alrachid in the East, gave law to the greatest part of the then known world. They were characters made up of great virtues and great vices. Their public glory did not a little suffer by their domestic foibles, and even by their crimes. But of the three, Haroun Alrachid, equal as to the distance of the time, seems, by the remoteness of his country, being more oriental, and by the greater difference of the Asiatic manner and customs, to have more excited the European curiosity. The merit then of the Author of the following production is not only to have assembled all the scattered passages relating to the life of a prince so famous in the Eastern Country, as to be to this instant the favourite subject of those histories, tales, and novels, by retailing which in the coffee-houses of Damascus, and other towns of the Turkish empire, numbers get a livelihood; but to have thrown that compilation into the most agreeable form of entertainment for the making itself be read; by divesting the bottom of the story of all the gross absurdities so greedily swallowed in the East, of inchantments, genii, and other the like embellishments of the Arabian and Turkish tales, and by making it less unnatural, giving it a better relish; and yet retaining enough of the oriental air and manner to distinguish it from the common insipid run of French romances; of which all the characters are, without regard to propriety, drawn in the French fashion of *Messieurs* and *Mesdames*.

There is also an uncommon circumstance to be mentioned in favour of this work, that, by its being a translation from an unpublished original, it has the merit, if not of originality, at least of novelty.

As to the original author, who is a Lady, it might perhaps suffice to observe that she is already advantageously known in the literary world, by productions in more than one kind of writing. The King of Prussia himself, in the midst of all the occupations of a war, in which he was making head singly against an union of the greatest powers in Europe, vouchsafed to express, by letter to her, his sense of her merit. But even her private history has something uncommonly curious in it. Madam de Fauques de la Cepeds, for that is her real name, forced, in her tender years, by a cruel parent, into a convent at Avignon her place of birth, and there to take her vows, she, on the death of her persecutor and unnatural oppressor, had the courage to appeal to the court of Rome against the violence which had been done her, and obtained so authentic a sentence in her favour, of the nullity of her vows, that she procured her liberty, and her due share of fortune from the co-heirs.

It was there that she casually became acquainted with the young Chevalier, by whom, it is said, she had a son, lately dead. Without warranting the truth of this report, it is not at least unfair to observe that she has touched on the incident of her knowledge of him, with great delicacy, in her memorial against Mr. Celesia, late minister to our court from the republic of Genoa.

I happened (says she) *to be in my own country at the time when an Illustrious and unfortunate personage*

nage had chosen it for his asylum. I had partaken in the general esteem and concern inspired by merit and misfortune.

Upon my having acquainted, in confidence, Mr. Celesia with this, he triumphed, and built upon it projects of hurting or of frightening me.

But how little does he know the greatness of heart of a King who generously protects even the subjects of an enemy armed against him, if he can believe that that King, more revered yet for the qualities of his soul than for the splendor of the throne, would stoop to search into my heart, to punish me for sentiments which every thing had authorised, for sentiments that cannot at present weaken the duty which my confidence in his protection has imposed on me, nor my gratitude for that beneficent protection? Mem. p. 156.

Certainly if this Lady had made Mr. Celesia her confident of nothing *more* than her having only known and pitied the young Chevalier, at Avignon, he had not much to build on either to hurt or frighten her with an information against her, had he even been capable of it. Her adventures however with Mr. Celesia here, where she had taken refuge against certain disagreeable circumstances in France, are of too complicated a nature to be particularised. It can only be in a summary way mentioned, that it appears from her memorial, that she cohabited with him, under the sanction of a written promise of marriage, which was afterwards wrested from her by violence, and that she complained of having been deserted in favour of a young English Lady whom Mr. Celesia married, and, on being recalled from his employ, took to Genoa with him. It is not for any one unacquainted with his motives, and means of defence to pronounce decisively one way or other ; but so much is certain, that, in that memorial above referred to, she has pleaded her cause with exquisite ad-

 dress,

dreſs, written, as it is, with all that energy and pathos, which it is only for feelings to inſpire to ſo much wit as ſhe undoubtedly has; for, when ſhe firſt arrived at Paris from Avignon, ſhe aſtoniſhed the *beaux eſprits* of that capital, not only with the livelineſs of her imagination, but the delicacy of her expreſſion, which had nothing of the provincial in it. M. Fontenelle, and many other great judges, admired and praiſed her genius. Some misfortunes however into which ſhe fell, thro' that exceſs of paſſions which ſeems to be too common a viſitation on extraordinary talents, perhaps ſo ordained for the conſolation of thoſe who have none, brought her to this hoſpitable country, where one would wiſh her to meet with the greater indulgence for her being a woman well-born, a ſtranger, not perhaps over happy, and of a literary merit ſo rare in thoſe of her ſex.

HISTORY

OF THE REIGN OF

HAROUN ALRACHID.

PART I.

THE Arabs had for four years carried on a successful war against the Eastern empire, when the Calif Haroun Alrachid gave the command of his troops to his favourite and first Vizir Giafar; in the choice of whom he was equally happy and prudent. Giafar was descended from the illustrious family of the Bermicides, renowned in the annals of the Arabs for their many accomplishments and virtues: he added to the charms of a most graceful person, every qualification requisite in the agreeable companion, the hero, and the philosopher.

THE Empress Irene was greatly alarmed at Giafar's promotion to this dignity, as she dreaded the most fatal consequences from his known abilities: for since she had frequently by her artifice, either raised animosity amongst the Calif's Generals, or gained them over to her own intereſt, ſhe depended more upon her intrigues than her troops. She always avoided any ſtep that might prove deciſive, was obſtinate when ſhe ought to have been complying, and ſubmitted when ſhe ought to have been reſolute; in ſhort, her conduct was ſo inconſiſtent, that it was difficult to gueſs whether peace or war was the object of her councils.

It was impoſſible ſuch a wild irregular method of proceeding could be ſucceſsful againſt a Prince, incapable of conſenting to a diſhonourable accommodation; and her impoveriſhed ſubjects dreaded utter ruin from the folly and caprice of an obſtinate woman.

The rapid progreſs of Giafar's arms was of the utmoſt ſervice to the Greeks, as it convinced Irene of the inutility of theſe little trifling ſchemes, upon which ſhe had hitherto entirely depended.—The mortification of being obliged to ſue for peace, did not prevent her from entertaining an eſteem, or even a more tender paſſion, for her conqueror. She did not ſend her miniſters to treat with Giafar, but voluntarily opened the gates of Conſtantinople to that generous victor, whoſe humanity made even the vanquiſhed inſenſible of their misfortunes.

As Irene had always given full ſcope to her paſſions, ſhe did not endeavour to ſuppreſs her affection for her conqueror; even the conſideration of his being an Infidel did not leſſen her eſteem. But Giafar having never experienced the power of love, did not perceive the Empreſs's inclination, and aſcribed her endeavours to entertain and oblige him to policy. For the great freedom and gallantry which prevailed in the court of Haroun, prevented his being led into a ſnare by civility and complaiſance; and the Arabs magnificence, taſte, and delicacy, being their eſtabliſhed characteriſtics, are

are proof againſt all ſuch attempts. The Greeks had not yet attained this ſummit of politeneſs, which is the produce of all-creative love, that gradually refines and ſoftens the tempers of men.

Giafar was moſt ſumptuouſly entertained, during the ſhort interval it was neceſſary for him to await the arrival of the Calif's inſtructions with reſpect to the treaty of peace; an interval Irene wiſhed might be prolonged to eternity; and her ſubjects, wearied out with the fatigues of a tedious war, were in great hopes of a laſting peace, and joined with pleaſure in the public rejoicings, which upon this occaſion were very ſplendid, and in which Chriſtians and Mahometans were mixed together, without any appearance of that rancour and animoſity which the common people of different perſuaſions are generally ſubject to.

Irene was the only unhappy perſon amidſt this general joy, who, though ſhe had loſt ſome of the charms of youth, was ſtill beautiful; for a diſpoſition to love and oblige, has the inexpreſſible power of making beauty in ſome degree triumph over time. And as it was in her power to exalt the object of her affection to the higheſt dignity, love or ambition had procured her admirers from every court in Europe; even Charlemain had ſolicited ſuch an honourable and advantageous alliance, which would have again united the Eaſtern and Weſtern empires. But Irene's hatred to the confinement of an indiſſoluble connection, was equal to her thirſt for pleaſure; and therefore ſhe artfully turned the addreſſes of her admirers to her own advantage, and favourably received the tender of their affections, without engaging her own. Her behaviour would have been deſpiſed in private life, but ſovereignty alters the nature of things; and as it can do it with impunity, looks upon it as its prerogative, to dispense with reason and justice.

Though many of her lovers, seeing through her artifice, had shook off their chains, it did not give her the least concern; for a disposition that is more amorous than delicate, is not ruffled by such accidents. Her conduct would have been censured by many, if her high station, instead of increasing the number of her calumniators, had not made them afraid to divulge their sentiments.

It was not at all surprising that the Empress, the motive of whose actions was always pleasure, should fix her affections upon Giafar; for as an unsurmountable obstacle prevented the presenting of her hand together with her heart, she was in no danger of losing him, as she had done the rest of her ambitious admirers, by a refusal of marriage; and she flattered herself with the hopes of an union, free from those canker-worms of love, interest and ambition. But Giafar was so much engaged in business, that he did not perceive the impression he had made on the heart of Irene, who, dreading his departure, used every method to delay it.

Being one day alone with Giafar, she could not help expressing herself in such terms as made him at last sensible of her inclination; and when he answered her warm interrogatories, with that coldness as if they had been common chat, she could not refrain expressing her emotion by a sigh; and ashamed of having discovered her weakness with so little success, she changed the subject of discourse, and blushing said, "I cannot, Sir, help "reflecting on the folly and unreasonableness of a "general prejudice: even I myself, till this moment, judged it impossible for an Infidel to be "master of those accomplishments which are so "conspicuous in you; and I always looked upon "the

" the encomiums beſtowed on the Calif Haroun
" Alrachid, as abſurdities propagated by his cre-
" dulous ſubjects."

I am ſurpriſed, replied Giafar, that the Empreſs Irene ſhould be capable of ſuch a prejudice, and glad that it is in my power to remove it. I will venture to affirm, that we entertain more favourable ſentiments of you Chriſtians. We do indeed in our turn call you Infidels, through that natural propenſity all men have to deſpiſe thoſe of different perſuaſions. But though we judge your religion too ſevere to admit of an abſolute unlimited obedience, yet we believe that honour and virtue are as attainable by you as ourſelves. Though I think I may ſay, without prejudice, that we excel in theſe reſpects, as the principal view of our religion is the good of ſociety, free from thoſe cramping injunctions that are prejudicial to it.

The fame of Charlemain does not in the leaſt obſcure that of the Calif my maſter; Oſmaide his mother, and the Princeſs Zobeide, may have as noble minds as the Empreſs Irene. I hope, replied ſhe, for their own happineſs, they have not, as the confinement of a ſeraglio would be inſupportable: Can prejudice, can cuſtom, make a great ſoul love reſtraint? Alas! the leaſt ſhadow of it is ſo intolerable, that! . . . . . But breaking off, ſhe ſaid, I have only been informed in general of the Calif's great abilities; a particular detail from a perſon of your undoubted veracity will entirely diſpel all my doubts; and I hope the pleaſure of convincing me, will be a ſufficient ſatisfaction for your trouble. Yes, Madam, replied he, and I am greatly obliged to you for this requeſt, as it gives me a double pleaſure, that of obeying your commands, and of enumerating the many virtues of a maſter whom I adore.

Haroun

Haroun is the fifth Calif of the houfe of Abaf-fides; he began his reign at Bagdad in the hundred and feventieth year of the Hegyra; he is celebrated for his valour, and his exemplary piety and equity have procured him the title of Alrachid, that is, the Juft. Nature has fhowered her choiceft gifts upon him, and Fortune, by being always his friend, has given them the higheft luftre; he is the protector and pattern of his fubjects, who fear and adore him; he is mafter of that difficult art of tempering feverity with mildnefs, and of being eafy and familiar without leffening his dignity. He infures the allegiance of his fubjects, by taking care to relieve their diftreffes, and fupply their wants: being fupreme both in civil and religious affairs, he endeavours to prevent error, but never punifhes it. The paffions of hatred, rage, and ambition, never reigned in his heart; and though he has fubmitted to the foft bondage of love, he did not become its flave; for he has fuch command over himfelf, that he readily quits the moft enticing pleafures when they feem to threaten any dangerous confequences. It is the grand view of the Mahometan religion, to fupprefs the violence of that too often fatal paffion; for by allowing a multiplicity of wives, it greatly diminifhes that warmth of conftitution which generally attends a confinement to one.

As my father Jahia was prime Vizir to the Calif Mahadi, he placed me in my infancy with the two young Princes Hadi and Haroun. The moft exact conformity of tafte and manners, was what firft attached me to the latter; and he in return had fo fincere a regard for me, that he treated me as his equal, and not as his fubject, a circumftance of no fmall importance to true friendfhip; neither did I always confider him as my Prince, as fuch a reflection might have weakened my attachment, and prevented

prevented an unlimited confidence. In our infancy we had the ſame education, and delighted in the ſame ſports and amuſements; and as we advanced in life, and our reaſon together with our paſſions began to dawn, I was the companion of his pleaſures and ſtudies; and particularly admired in him an uncommon greatneſs of ſoul, which rendered him incapable of being guilty of a mean action on any conſideration.

Oſmaide very juſtly gave Haroun the preference to her elder ſon Hadi, and as ſhe had great influence over the Calif Mahadi, endeavoured to perſuade him to invert the order of ſucceſſion in favour of Haroun's great abilities, and the public utility; and when he could not, by all the arguments he could uſe, divert his mother from this attempt, he deſired me to ſolicit my father's intereſt, in order to baffle her deſigns. I exerted my utmoſt efforts in this affair, reflecting, that if we could defeat Oſmaide's intention, Haroun would acquire that ſolid glory that always accompanies noble and generous actions, at the expence only of a ſcandalous uſurped royalty. And I muſt acknowledge, that, if I have any accompliſhments, they are more owing to his example than my own natural diſpoſition. I could enumerate many incidents of his youth, which even then ſtrongly preſaged that clemency and greatneſs of ſoul which have ſo diſtinguiſhed his riper years: one of the moſt remarkable was as follows.

Being one day hunting in the foreſt of Bagdad, Haroun, who loved rural ſimplicity, which is a novelty to Princes, quitted the chace; and as he and I were wandering about, we perceived an Arab, who ſeemed to labour under ſome ſevere calamity. That perſon, ſaid Haroun, might probably be freed from the anxiety which ſo dejects him; I will enquire if it be in my power to re-

lieve

lieve him. So ſaying, he rode up to him, and aſked with great affection and tenderneſs the cauſe of his affliction? To which the Arab replied, with ſome warmth, How can you aſk ſuch a queſtion? Who can diſpaſſionately behold the throne of Ali in the poſſeſſion of thoſe baſe uſurpers the Abaſſides? and who can ſuppreſs his indignation, when he ſees our ſhame and deſpair perpetuated by the fruitfulneſs of that upſtart infamous family? Haroun, without being the leaſt affected by ſuch falſe and injurious aſperſions, aſked him, if he knew who he was? And when the other replied in the negative, he told him, that he was Haroun the ſon of the Calif Mahadi. The Arab endeavouring to conceal the uneaſineſs this information gave him, aſked in return if he knew him? I am, ſaid he, of the family of Allah, all whoſe deſcendants are fools one day in ſeven, and this happens to be the day that I labour under that unhappy infirmity. Haroun ſmiled at the Arab's anſwer; and preſenting him with a rich diamond, ſaid, Friend, I hope that trifle will cure your folly: if it has any effect, come without any fear or apprehenſion to court, and I will endeavour by future favours to complete your recovery.

When we parted from the Arab, I told Haroun, that I was not ſo ſurpriſed at his preſence of mind, as at the others inſolence; for which I could ſcarce reſtrain myſelf from puniſhing him. You would, my dear Giafar, replied he, have acted very imprudently; the man was probably ſenſible of his error, by aſcribing it to his folly, and it was my duty to complete his converſion, if poſſible, by kind and generous treatment; which will recal undutiful and prejudiced ſubjects to their allegiance, when ſeverity will have no effect; for as independence is a natural principle, mankind look upon ſovereignty as an inſupportable yoke; and even the moſt

moſt ſenſible part of them, though convinced of its utility, frequently ridicule the pomp and pageantry of royalty. I very well remember a piece of inſtruction given the Calif Mahadi on this ſubject.

Being one day greatly fatigued with the chace, and ſeparated from his attendants by a violent ſtorm, he perceived in the thickeſt part of the foreſt whither he had retired for ſhelter, an old man ſitting at the door of his cottage; and going up to him, aſked for ſome refreſhment: the old man gave him ſome wine, which though very indifferent, my father, from his exceſſive thirſt, thought moſt excellent; and ſaid to him, you have highly obliged one of the principal perſonages belonging to the Calif's court. Scarce had he uttered theſe words, when his hoſt ran into his cot, and brought a pitcher of wine conſiderably better than the firſt. Mahadi having taſted it, ſaid to him, Friend, I am nearly related to the Calif. The old man went in a ſecond time, and returned with ſome wine greatly ſuperior to both the other. Hey day! ſaid my father, as you are ſo generous, I will own to you that I am the Calif. The old man immediately ſnatched up his pitcher and fled. In vain Mahadi called to him to ſtop; he purſued, and coming up with him, deſired to know the reaſon of his leaving him ſo abruptly. The reaſon, replied the old man, is very evident; you enhanced your titles and dignity, in proportion as you thought you could impoſe upon my credulity, and at laſt told me that you are God's vicegerent; and if I had ſtaid longer, you would probably have told me that you were God himſelf. I fled therefore to prevent you uttering ſuch blaſphemy, and myſelf from being dazzled by the ſplendor of your dignity; moreover, I had a mind to inform you, that the more a man leſſens thoſe he converſes with, by intimating

intimating his own importance, the more unlikely he is to obtain their aſſiſtance, the want of which ought to inform him, that all men are by nature equal. I was obliged by the laws of hoſpitality to have a reſpect to the dignity of my gueſt ; but duty ceaſes when it becomes impracticable. Mahadi was ſo far from being offended with the freedom of the old man's juſt and rational obſervation, that he loaded him with favours.

Haroun added to this narration many judicious remarks, becoming his great abilities, and conformable to the conſtant tenor of his behavionr.

At the death of Mahadi, his eldeſt ſon Hadi aſcended the throne, which he enjoyed but two years, and was ſucceeded by Haroun, who, as he had been, during his brother's reign, a bright example of allegiance to his ſubjects, became now by his prudent adminiſtration a model for Princes ; and his great abilities, of which I had been the firſt admirer, became now the aſtoniſhment of the whole world.

Though the Calif Mahadi was a juſt and religious Prince, and ſo zealous for the obſervation of the laws, that no perſon during his reign dared commit any flagrant act of oppreſſion ; yet his circumſpection did not extend ſo far as it ought to have done ; for he overlooked minuter affairs, to the prejudice of the loweſt claſs of his ſubjects, whoſe oppreſſion was concealed by their obſcurity, and whoſe complaints were obſtructed by their poverty.

Accordingly Haroun obſerved to me, that ſince in the day of the Lord, the complaints of the meaneſt of his ſubjects would be of equal weight with thoſe of the rich and noble ; it was, his duty to inſpect theſe ſmaller concerns of government, to liſten to the remonſtrances of the loweſt of his people, and redreſs their grievances ; otherwiſe, inſtead

inſtead of being rewarded as an impartial adminiſtrator of juſtice, he ſhould be puniſhed for partiality and negligence.

The new Calif honoured me with the poſt of Prime Vizir, which my father deſired to quit, in order to paſs the evening of his life in retirement; and he ſhewed great judgment in the choice of all the other officers of ſtate, whoſe proceedings he ſuperintended with the utmoſt circumſpection. He frequently in the duſk of the evening, attended only by his firſt eunuch Meſrour and myſelf, walked in diſguiſe through the ſtreets of Bagdad, and took particular notice of every occurrence. One evening as we paſſed by a moſque, when the congregation were coming out from prayers, we heard two men at the door talking with great warmth; we ſtopped to liſten, and as the duſk prevented their obſerving us, they continued their diſcourſe. "Yes, ſaid "one of them, I have ſuffered the moſt flagrant "oppreſſion, in the reign of a Prince renowned for "his equity and piety; the corrupt judge hath "not only violated ſecrecy, which ought to have "been ſacred to his profeſſion, he hath not only "refuſed me juſtice, but hath treated me with "the moſt baſe and unmerited partiality. I have "complained to the Prime Vizir Giafar; but tho' he "is looked upon as the father of the people, the patron "of the unhappy, the protector of the injured,—he "has not vouchſafed to liſten to my remonſtrance." Here their diſcourſe ended, and each of them went his way: upon which the Calif ſaid to me with great auſterity, "Follow them, and bring thy "accuſers before me to-morrow, that thou mayeſt "receive due puniſhment if it ſhall appear thou haſt "been negligent in the execution of thy office." I obeyed his commands, who finding, after a ſtrict examination into the affair, that I had been impoſed

upon

upon with respect to the injured complainant, forgave me, after severely reprimanding my credulity.

As to the corrupt Judge, his baseness and partiality were too flagrant to admit of any alleviation, not even, that this was the first time he had been guilty of such iniquitous and oppressive decisions. This Judge was one of the most famous Cadys of Bagdad, who had acquired great reputation, by some pretended generous and equitable determinations; and though he had not ability to discern innocence from guilt, by those evident marks which appear in the countenance of the accused, yet his court was crowded more than any other. The Calif ordered an exact inquiry to be made into all his decrees, which were found to be most scandalously unjust in all cases, where the poor and wretched could be secretly sacrificed to an opulent and powerful adversary. Haroun expressed a very just and becoming resentment upon this discovery; and after reflecting what punishment to inflict on the Judge, he thought that any common chastisement would not imprint on the minds of his subjects a lasting abhorrence of his crime; and even the most shocking torture, as it could be but of short duration, would be soon forgot. At last he resolved on a very particular and affecting method of punishment, whose impressions would not soon be obliterated. He ordered it to be publickly proclaimed through the city, and engraved in large characters over the door of the Cady, "That all "the advocates of injustice, who wanted partial "decisions, might repair to the corrupt judge."

The greatest villains endeavour to conceal themselves by a mask of honesty and integrity, which if they happen to drop, they become incapable of further mischief. Thus the court of the corrupt Judge was immediately forsaken by all his clients, and himself despised; instead of being crouded with

with busineſs, not a perſon came nea. him, which gave him the tormenting opportunity of reflecting on his own villainy.

Irene could not any longer refrain interrupting Giafar's narration, ſaying, Really the Calif ought to be an example to all Princes, for he ſeems to be ſomething more than man ; but, continued ſhe with a ſmile, has he in no action ſhewn himſelf to be only a mere mortal ? He may gratify ſome foibles, without tarniſhing his many and great accompliſhments : conceal them not from me, and as you have excited my admiration, let me be intereſted in his conduct ; for a tender concern, if properly founded, is the moſt acceptable panegyric.——Yes, Madam, replied Giafar, the Calif has experienced the force of that paſſion you hint at, which is a neceſſary ingredient in our nature ; but inſtead of ſullying his glory by any exceſs, or improper purſuit, he has, by curbing his inclination, given a higher luſtre to his other virtues. I have hinted before, that the paſſions, which are the tyrants of moſt men, are entirely his vaſſals : this I could prove by a number of his actions, which ought to be inſcribed on the wings of Fame ; but an inſtance or two that happened in the war he has lately ſo glorioulſy put an end to, may ſuffice.

The greateſt part of the Princes of Aſia, being conquered by the ſucceſſors of Mahomet, are become tributary, or rather vaſſals, to the throne of Ali. It is cuſtomary to accompany their annual payment, with a preſent of whatever is moſt curious or valuable in their reſpective dominions ; and the Monarchs of the faithful always receive from the Kings of Circaſſia, thoſe beautiful damſels that are the delicious ornaments of their ſeraglios. The eunuchs who conduct theſe fair ſlaves, are eſcorted by a Captain of the guard, with a ſufficient number of troops.

Gioher,

Gioher, an officer of character, and remarkable for his valour, going one year on this account to Aſtracan, ſent an expreſs to the Calif, that Zinebi, King of Circaſſia, had not only refuſed paying his tribute, and ſending his annual preſent, but had alſo ſhamefully driven him out of his dominions, and was making all poſſible preparations to ſupport his revolt. Haroun immmediately aſſembled a body of troops ſufficient to ſuppreſs Zinebi, and gave the command to Gioher, who gained two battles, and took ſeveral towns; and having ſubdued the greateſt part of Circaſſia, and forced Zinebi to fly his dominions, thought himſelf ſure of a compleat conqueſt, when he was informed, that that Prince had entered into an alliance with Mirgehan and Aſſelan, monarchs of Segeſtan and Zagatay; and that their troops being united, formed an army greatly ſuperior to his, which made forced marches to attack him.

Haroun being informed of his ſituation, marched immediately at the head of his beſt troops, and took me for his companion in this expedition.—We found the enemy encamped upon the banks of the Volga, who, though they were much ſuperior to us, expreſſed great conſternation when they underſtood that Haroun commanded in perſon; and the Calif having paſſed the river by a bridge of boats, they retired in great diſorder. We were greatly aſtoniſhed at this unexpected retreat, of which we could not gueſs the motive; but a priſoner of rank informed us, that Zinebi, deſpairing of ſucceſs, as his two allies were ſeized with a panic, had retired; but by reaſoning with them on the ſhame and diſhonour of ſuch behaviour, he had prevailed on them to return, and they were preparing to attack us within three days. As this delay ſeemed to Haroun ſuſpicious, his prudence put a check upon his courage; he croſſed the river again,

again, and entrenched himſelf in his camp ; and though he was impatient to engage and conquer his adverſary, reſolved to wait for him in this advantageous ſituation.

Gioher, knowing that the Calif always gave a favourable audience to the advice of his Generals, endeavoured, but in vain, to perſuade him that it would be the moſt prudent ſtep to purſue the rebels. He was however ſoon convinced of the Calif's ſuperior judgment ; for another priſoner ſoon after informed us, that it was the King of Circaſſia that adviſed their retreat, flattering himſelf that Haroun would quit the banks of the Volga to purſue them ; and as in that caſe he would be obliged to paſs through foreſts and defiles he was unacquainted with, it would be an eaſy matter to ſurround him, after cutting off his retreat, by deſtroying the bridge.

During this delay, Haroun, perceiving a caſtle at ſome diſtance from the camp, ſent me with a detachment to take it. The beſieged defended themſelves beyond what could have been expected ; and when I was preparing to ſtorm it, two ladies in mourning opened the gates, which were immediately ſhut after them : upon their arrival at my tent, the eldeſt of them, addreſſing herſelf to me, deſired I would conduct her to the Calif, for ſhe would deliver the keys of the caſtle to no one elſe, which, being no longer defenſible, ſhe judged it moſt prudent, to avoid any further effuſion of blood. I ordered one of my officers to conduct the ladies to the Calif, as I could not quit the ſiege myſelf, without endangering my ſucceſs, if what they ſaid ſhould prove only a ſtratagem. The Calif gave them a moſt gracious reception, and taking off their veils in reſpect to his dignity, he was ſtruck with the amazing beauty of the younger ; and though the other had paſſed the bloom

of

of youth, yet her noble air, and majeſtic deportment, could not fail to excite admiration, who, addreſſing herſelf to the Calif, ſaid, " My name, moſt noble Prince, is Elmaze ; I am wife to Zinebi's prime Vizir Huſſeyn, and this is my daughter Zeinib : the precipitate retreat of the army prevented our following them ; this indeed did not give us much concern, as we judged the caſtle impregnable ; but nothing can reſiſt your victorious arms. Receive the keys of the fort you have conquered, and excuſe your ſlaves for a reſiſtance we were obliged to make by the expreſs command of Zinebi. I hope the grief ſo evident in our countenances and dreſs, will vouch for our ſincerity."— Having thus ſpoke, the beautiful Zeinib took the keys of the caſtle from a ſlave that attended her, and preſented them to the Calif with ſuch a grace, and enchanting expreſſion of countenance, as entirely captivated him ; and receiving them, he ſaid, " Madam, I accept theſe, not as due to conqueſt, but as a preſent which preſages further ſucceſs : the pleaſure I receive from my firſt victory makes me hope a moſt favourable iſſue to this enterprize ; but thoſe that ſurrender before they are conquered, have a right to propoſe terms ; be pleaſed, moſt charming Zeinib, to ſignify your pleaſure, and it ſhall be immediately complied with."—The ſlave, replied ſhe, is at his maſter's diſpoſal, and muſt not conſult his own inclination.—Alas, Madam, ſaid the Calif, with great tenderneſs ! he, to whom you give the title of Maſter, is not ſo free as yourſelf, it is but too evident that your beauty has enſlaved him. I will myſelf reconduct you to the caſtle, and the troops I ſhall place for your defence ſhall be abſolutely at your command ; only let me beg of you, not to depart from thence till the fate of the two armies be determined.—Your generoſity, returned

returned Zeinib, overpowers me; and Elmaze interrupting her, said, I ſwear that the daughter of Huſſeyn ſhall not, without your leave, quit the place you ſhall appoint for her reſidence.

The Calif, attended by his guard, came to the caſtle: Elmaze was conducted by my brother Mahomed, and Haroun waited upon the charming Zeinib; at the ſame time he informed his principal officers, that he would fix his head quarters there, until the enemy appeared. This order ſeemed very agreeable to Elmaze, but had a different effect on Zeinib, whoſe ſorrowful dejected countenance ſtrongly intimated the agitation of her heart; and when ſhe thought Elmaze could not hear her, ſhe whiſpered to the Calif: Sir, your ſlaves have it not in their power to entertain ſuch a gueſt ſuiting his dignity; we have ſcarce common neceſſaries, and our cooks are greatly inferior to thoſe of your Majeſty. Upon this Haroun immediately gave orders for his own domeſtics to attend him, and provide every thing ſuiting the luxury of an Eaſtern monarch: theſe directions diſperſed that gloom that before clouded the countenance of the beautiful Zeinib. We took poſſeſſion of the caſtle, which though greatly inferior to the meaneſt of the Calif's palaces, was preferred by him to any place he had ever ſeen, for the company of Zeinib made every thing agreeable, every thing charming.

I ſoon perceived the Calif's affection for his fair priſoner; which gave me great pleaſure, as nothing but love was wanting to complete his happineſs. I approved of his intention of offering his hand and heart to the beautiful Zeinib, concerning whom he expreſſed himſelf without any reſerve, and acquainted me with his minuteſt actions and intentions. The relation he gave me of Zeinib's requeſt, that he might be attended by his own ſervants,

vants, and her concern on that affair, raiſed a ſuſpicion I judged proper to communicate to him. Do you not perceive, ſaid I, in the uneaſineſs of Zeinib, the ſtruggles of a ſoul that recoils the thoughts of a baſe action; and in the joy and ſatisfaction of Elmaze, that ſome fatal project is formed againſt your life? Theſe ladies are probably appointed to execute ſome horrid plot; honour and virtue raiſe commotions in the ſimple and innocent heart of Zeinib, while Elmaze is proof againſt ſuch ſuggeſtions; for baſe wicked minds, do not readily liſten to the checks of conſcience, which are the ſafeſt guardians of unſullied innocence.

Haroun acknowledged, that there was ſome foundation for my ſuſpicion, which was ſhortly confirmed by the flight of ſome of Elmaze's favourite domeſtics, and the chargin and confuſion of the reſt; ſo that I more diligently ſuperintended the Calif's ſecurity.—Zeinib became more dear to him by the intimation ſhe had given of this affair; but the fear of alarming her for her mother's ſafety, prevented his making thoſe acknowledgements which were due to her generoſity. He contented himſelf with informing her, that he intended to offer her his hand, and thought the joy and gratitude ſhe expreſſed on this occaſion ſincere; and who could imagine that ſhe ſhould be unaffected by ſuch an honourable propoſal, and inſenſible to the addreſſes of the moſt amiable Prince in the univerſe?

Zeinib's wit and ſprightlineſs were equal to her beauty, ſo that the Calif quitted her agreeable company with reluctance upon the appearance of the enemy, at the approach of whom the two armies immediately engaged.———Fortune, or rather the ſword of Haroun, decided the day in our favour; he encouraged his ſoldiers more by his example

than

than harangues; he slew a great number of the enemy, and amongst them the King of Segestan, and took the Prince of Zagatay prisoner. In short, Zinebi, having lost two thirds of his army, beat a retreat, and retired to his camp. The Calif resolved to follow and attack him the next day; but in the mean time, that unfortunate Prince sent his Vizir Husseyn to solicit his pardon, and beg a truce. Haroun could refuse nothing to the father of the charming Zeinib: moreover, his noble mind enjoyed more sensible pleasure in pardoning a suppliant enemy than in conquering him.

The truce being agreed to, the Calif dedicated his first leisure moments to an affectionate and paternal ease, both of his own subjects, and the enemy who were his prisoners; intending afterwards to indulge his passion in the conversation of the beautiful Zeinib. But how was he thunderstruck, when he neither found her nor Elmaze in the castle! and repented, when too late, his having placed so much confidence in them. The commanding officer excused himself by the orders the Calif had given him, punctually to observe the commands of the two ladies. Sir, said he, after the battle, a young gentleman (whose noble intrepid deportment claimed the utmost respect, notwithstanding the discomposure of his dress, which was besmeared with blood and dust) came to the castle, attended by some of your own troops. Elmaze commanded me to admit him, and told me afterwards, that he came by your order to conduct her and Zeinib to the camp, and desired me to take care of her domestics during her absence. How was it possible for me to foresee their design? How could I imagine, that after the extraordinary favours you had conferred upon them, and the solemn oath they had taken, not to leave the castle without your orders, they wou'd endeavour to efcape, even though you had juft defeated their army, and intended raifing them to the moft exalted dignity?

While the officer thus fpoke, Haroun ftood in fullen filence; he could not prevent fome fparks of refentment kindling in his breaft againft the perfon whofe credulity had occafioned the lofs of his miftrefs; but he fuppreffed them, reflecting, that the orders he himfelf had given, fufficiently excufed him; and he quitted the caftle without fpeaking to any of the women Elmaze had left there.

He returned to his camp in great anxiety; and paffing through a fmall wood, he was furrounded by a number of Zinebi's foldiers, or more properly affaffins. Haroun, relying on the fufpenfion of arms, was attended by a very fmall guard, and would have even left me behind him in the camp, if my good genius had not prompted me to accompany him.—We defended our Prince with all the courage and refolution that could be expected from the moft loyal and affectionate fubjects; but the great fuperiority of the affaffins made us defpair of fuccefs. Many of our company being flain, there remained but eight, which few formed themfelves in the beft manner they could to protect their Sovereign; but it was impoffible they fhould be able to make a long refiftance. In fhort, his only refource was in his own valour, and our defpair; when on a fudden we heard the approach of a large body of horfe, and a general chear, "Health and "profperity to the fucceffor of our Holy Prophet, "and confufion to all his enemies!" The troops of Zinebi were inftantly overpowered; and Mahomed, who commanded ours, came to the Calif's affiftance the moment he fell from his horfe, which was killed under him: he informed him that a deferter had acquainted Gioher with the ambufcade, who immediately difpatched him to our affiftance,

and

and inſtantly himſelf attacked the camp of the treacherous Circaſſian. The Calif called for another horſe, and made all haſte to join the army: his preſence gave freſh ſpirits to his troops, whoſe concern for the fate of their Prince had ſo weakened their courage, that they began to give ground. He rallied and led them on again, and gained a total victory, cutting Zinebi's whole army to pieces; who, though he uſed his utmoſt endeavour to die bravely in the field, was taken priſoner, and conducted to the Calif's tent.

Upon ſeeing the King of Circaſſia, Haroun could not forbear expreſſing himſelf with great, though becoming warmth: Approach, unhappy wretch, ſaid he, and receive at the feet of thy conqueror a ſentence which cannot be too ſevere, as it is impoſſible to invent a puniſhment adequate to thy crimes. Thou haſt even blackened rebellion by the baſeſt treachery; thou haſt violated the moſt ſacred ties, the laws of honour and of nations. I could have forgiven thee an attempt upon my life, if it had been ſuch a one as became a Prince; but now I think it my duty to puniſh thee as an aſſaſſin, guilty of a crime a Barbarian would have ſcorned, and which will be an indelible ſtain on the title of Muſſulman.——Thou thyſelf, replied Zinebi, with a haughty air, art the cauſe of my baſeneſs; I was not inſenſible of my ſcandalous attempt, but I thought I could not act amiſs, while I imitated the example of the ſupreme commander of the Faithful. Though this ſarcaſm greatly incenſed all that were preſent, and called for the Calif's warmeſt reſentment; yet he ſuppreſſed his indignation, and ſaid coolly, What behaviour of mine authoriſes thy treachery? The moſt flagrant injuſtice and unparalleled cruelty, replied the other. When Gioher came to demand your tribute, which I always punctually paid with due ſubmiſſion, he thought proper to uſe the moſt inſolent threats; and not content with the beautiful damſels I had provided for him, he had the impudence to demand my own daughter; and, upon my refuſal, he ſwore he would take her by force, and make her one of the meaneſt ſlaves in your ſeraglio. This inſolence obliged me to drive him out of my dominions; but, returning at the head of your troops, he defeated me, and, abuſing the power victory gave him, he diſcarded all ſenſe of humanity; for having taken a fort in which I had placed my wives and children, he firſt delivered them to the brutality of his troops, and then ordered them to be maſſacred in his preſence, ſaying, they were not worthy to be your ſlaves. Could I ſuppoſe a man whom you honoured with your eſteem and confidence, acted otherwiſe than by your orders? Could I uſe any ceremony towards a perſon who could give ſuch orders? Could I, in ſhort, confine myſelf to the laws of honour, humanity, or religion, in oppoſing an enemy who had ſhewed no regard to ſuch obligations, though it was his duty to have given an example of juſtice, moderation, and compaſſion?

The Calif was greatly affected by this information: he caſt a look of moſt violent reſentment at Gioher, who, acknowledging the crimes laid to his charge, threw himſelf at his feet in great confuſion, and endeavoured to excuſe himſelf, by his zeal for his ſervice. Cruel and barbarous zeal, replied the Calif! Here he ſtopped, his indignation ſuppreſſing his utterance; and covering his face with his hand, he ſunk down upon his ſopha, his faculties being overcome by this ſurpriſing and ſhocking narrative. The Calif's ſituation greatly affected all that were preſent: upon recovering himſelf, his eyes ſparkled with indignation, and he ſaid to Gioher, in an accent that would have ſtruck

terror

terror into the moſt undaunted heart, Thou then art my real aſſaſſin ! and I wiſh this may be thy only crime. But even this has caſt ſuch a ſtain upon my glory as the moſt exemplary puniſhment cannot wipe off, and which, if I had fallen a victim to that reſentment thou hadſt given ſo juſt an occaſion for, would have been an eternal blemiſh on my fame. Take him away, continued he, and let him die the cruelleſt of deaths ; the diſgrace he has brought upon me, the innocent blood he has occaſioned to be ſhed, the miſery into which he has plunged this unhappy Prince, exclude all compaſſion : make him a laſting example to all, who abuſe their Sovereign's confidence, and who by their oppreſſion and falſe zeal become the worſt of traitors.—And you, my friend, added he, offering his hand to Zinebi, obliterate as far as may be poſſible, thoſe afflictions this wretch has occaſioned ; and pardon me for being concerned in this ſhocking affair, ſince I readily excuſe your imprudence in concealing from me the true ſtate of the caſe : you cannot but be ſenſible of the errors and miſtakes attendant on royalty, from which the wiſeſt of Princes are not exempted. Let us be friends, accept of your liberty and kingdom ; I wiſh I could by my own blood expiate that of your ſubjects and family : however, I will for the future excuſe that fatal tribute which has been the cauſe of our mutual unhappineſs.

The unfortunate Monarch of Circaſſia was deeply affected by theſe humane generous offers : he fixed his eyes upon the Calif with a mixture of grief, ſurpriſe, and gratitude in his countenance, and burſting into tears, he fell down at his feet, and in a faultering accent, ſaid, Alas ! moſt victorious hero, and worthy ſucceſſor of our Holy Prophet ! I wiſh I could enjoy the pardon you ſo kindly vouchſafe to offer me ! I wiſh I could dedicate to your ſervice the ſucceeding years of a long life, and diſtinguiſh each by a tribute of gratitude! But death this moment hovers over me; the dread of falling a victim to your reſentment and revenge, made me ſhorten my days; and notwithſtanding the vigilance of thoſe who took off my armour, I found an opportunity to take ſome poiſon, for life became inſupportable under ſuch a load of miſery; and, as an aggravation of my juſt doom, I am going to quit it when I ſhould be glad to prolong my days in order to copy your virtues! Alas! you are not acquainted with all my crimes!——Forgive them, moſt noble commander of the Faithful!——Deliver me from thoſe evil ſpirits that are ready to ſeize me!——Having thus ſpoke, he fell into violent convulſions, which however were ſomewhat abated by the remedies that were applied; and as it was impoſſible to ſave his life, the Calif took this opportunity to alleviate the horrors of his laſt moments by ſome wholeſome religious admonitions: but the unhappy Zinebi, not being able to ſpeak, could only expreſs by his looks the comfort his inſtructions gave him. The poiſon at laſt overcame him; and the Calif ſeeing him expire, could not forbear expreſſing his grief in the ſtrongeſt manner: he rent his garments, and ſaid, Alas, my brother! why did you diſpute my juſtice and clemency, eſpecially when you had ſo good a title to both? May your ſoul enjoy in theſe unknown regions whither it is gone, that tranquillity, to which the remembrance of your misfortunes will for ever make me a ſtranger.

Haroun mourned three days for the death of Zinebi, whom he interred in a moſt magnificent manner. He could not help looking upon himſelf as the author of thoſe enormities Gioher had committed,

mitted, and refused seeing any company, that he might give the freer vent to his grief.

Mahomed alarmed at the Calif's melancholy, came to inform me of it, notwithstanding the miserable situation I was in. For in the skirmish that happened in the wood, I had, in defending my master, received a great many wounds, which during the fury of the action I did not perceive; but seeing him out of danger, necessity and despair no longer supported my spirits. I lay stretched upon the ground covered with wounds, and bathed in blood, and they carried me to the castle Elmaze had just quitted. As soon as I recovered my understanding, I enquired after Haroun; and they informed me in general, that he was safe and victorious, fearing I should be too much affected by a detail of particulars. In short, the Calif engrossed all my thoughts, and I was anxious for him as my bosom-friend, rather than my Prince. I reflected on the uneasiness he must be under for the loss of Zeinib, and resolved to examine and intimidate the domestics of Elmaze; but, on enquiry, the commandant of the castle informed me, that having intelligence of Zinebi's treachery, he went to the Calif's assistance, and at his return found all the Circassians fled. This information disturbed me so much that it increased my malady. Judge, Madam, by the faint idea I have given you of my extreme regard for Haroun, how sensibly I was affected by my brother's intelligence. I immediately ordered myself to be put in a litter, and carried to the Calif's tent. On seeing me, he threw off that gloom occasioned by his grief, and received me most graciously; affectionately returning that tender concern I expressed on seeing him in that melancholy situation. He was displeased at my endangering my life, by quitting that repose so necessary to my recovery; he censured my imprudence, and I, in return, took the liberty to cenſure his immoderate concern, which I at laſt ſomewhat mitigated ; for true friendſhip has alone the power of ſoftening affliction.

As ſoon as I was perfectly recovered, the Calif prepared to return to Bagdad, and gave the government of Circaſſia to Mahomed. I was ſurpriſed that he never mentioned Zeinib, nor made any ſearch after her. This indeed I had privately done, but to no purpoſe ; and I durſt not ſpeak on this ſubject, knowing it dangerous to open the wounds of love, without balſam to heal them. Haroun perceived my diſquietude, and in order to relieve me, ſaid, I plainly ſee, my dear Giafar, you think I am unhappy by the loſs of Zeinib ; will you believe me, when I aſſure you that the moſt ardent love is ſunk into a cold indifference? Sir, replied I, I by no means diſpute what you ſay ; and after having by turns ſubdued the paſſions of hatred, revenge, and even pity ; after ſincerely lamenting the death of an enemy, whom another's crimes could not entirely juſtify ; after delivering up to juſtice a ſubject, who, though criminal, might have by his great abilities and loyalty excited your compaſſion ; in ſhort, after acting in every reſpect as ſomething more than mortal, you have crowned all by this victory over love. But I am afraid your heart does not ſincerely join in this laſt triumph, and that is the occaſion of my anxiety.—Well then, ſaid he, with a ſmile, I muſt undeceive you ; for ſhould I ſuffer you to continue in this miſtake, it would be a violation of that cordial friendſhip which has cemented our hearts ; a bleſſing, prejudice and paſſion ſeldom ſuffers princes to enjoy. You muſt know then, that my ſoul lothes a baſe villainous action, and abhors its author ; and ſhould even Zeinib be guilty of ingratitude and treachery, ſhe would be inſtantly expelled

expelled that heart of which ſhe was before ſole miſtreſs. Her beauty ſo ſtrongly impreſſed upon my mind, and which might have pleaded in her favour, would be immediately effaced. She is therefore at preſent as odious to me, as before ſhe was dear; and, though I ſhould be glad to ſee her, it would be to puniſh her treachery, and not to breathe thoſe ſentiments of love, which ſhe has forfeited by her perfidious behaviour. Oaths are an obligation God himſelf has appointed for the protection and ſecurity of man; and promiſes ſealed with his tremendous name, ought not to be lightly and wantonly broke, as thoſe that accept them, look upon him as guarantee for the performance. The violator of his oath therefore muſt be hated both by God and man; and Princes cannot therefore too ſtrongly enforce the execution of the laws enacted againſt this blackeſt of crimes. A perſon ſhould be careful not inconſiderately to engage himſelf; but whoever confirms his promiſe by an oath, becomes infamous, if he does not religiouſly obſerve it, how much ſoever it may be to his own prejudice. In ſhort, I aſſure you, ſuch is my abhorrence of this crime, that if the Lord, in his wrath, ſhould permit even Giafar to be guilty of it, I would with pleaſure paſs ſentence on my dear friend; and as, by ſuch an act, he would become an object of diſguſt and horror, I could ſee his blood ſprinkled upon me. Alas, Sir, ſaid I, interrupting him, preſent not ſuch a ſhocking image to my mind! For though my heart aſſures me that I ſhall never be guilty of this baſeſt of crimes, I cannot help being deeply affected by what you ſay. The Calif perceiving that the warmth with which he had expreſſed himſelf, and the producing me as an example, had made me turn pale, dropped the ſubject, and preſently, by his eaſy and friendly conversation, entirely dissipated my involuntary anxiety.

Soon after our return to Bagdad, Haroun married the Princess Zobeide. Love was not his motive to this union; for though Zobeide was very beautiful, and of an illustrious family, though she was even nearly related to the Calif, yet it was the reputation of her wisdom and exemplary pie:y that alone raised her to this high station. Haroun entertained that solid and respectful affection for her, which is a surer foundation for happiness in the married state, than a more violent passion, which is gradually extinguished by its own heat. Zobeide, on the contrary, was ardently in love with the Calif, which rendered her uneasy and jealous; and though she took great care to conceal her anxiety from her husband, by a mask of ease and chearfulness, yet he at last discovered her weakness, but let it pass unnoticed: for to speak the truth, he had given more occasion for such suspicions, than became a Prince of his justice and humanity.

He observed that Zobeide concealed those of her slaves, whose beauty might make any dangerous impression, and let him only see such, whose persons were by no means captivating. Any other Prince would have resented such a finesse, as it deprived him of the pleasure of viewing beautiful objects; but Haroun chose to take no notice of it; and he had not as yet, amongst all his own slaves, though selected from the most beautiful women in Asia, found one that rivaled Zobeide in his affections.

It happened one night in the summer, that the Calif not being able to compose himself to sleep, arose and went privately to Zobeide's apartment, whose chamber was only separated by a partition of gauze. He went in; but finding the Princess asleep, and unwilling to disturb her repose, he retired;

retired; and as he was returning to his own apartment, he heard two women talking with ſome earneſtneſs in a cloſet, though he could not diſtinguiſh what they ſaid, as they ſpoke ſoftly for fear of diſturbing their miſtreſs. Upon going up to them, he was greatly ſurpriſed at the graceful and majeſtic mien of one of them; and though, upon perceiving the Calif, ſhe had thrown her veil over her head, yet her diſhabille diſcovered charms ſufficient to excite his paſſion. He inſtantly ſeized her in his arms, and endeavoured to pull off her veil, in order to have a full view of her beauty; but ſhe was ſo alarmed by this attempt, that ſhe ſprung from his embrace, and fled into another cloſet adjoining to Zobeide's chamber. The darkneſs of this place prevented the Calif's gratifying his curioſity by a ſight of her beauty, but did not cool his deſires. He ſeized, and cloſely embraced the object of his ſudden and irreſiſtible tranſport, who exerted her utmoſt efforts to get from him; and though pulling off her veil was now of no ſervice, as to viewing her charms, yet it gave him the opportunity of copiouſly enjoying the nectar of her lips. The ſlave, aſtoniſhed at the rapidity of the Calif's embraces, endeavoured to check them by reſiſtance, but was at laſt, contrary to her inclination, forced to ſpeak. Alas, Sir, ſaid ſhe, in a faultering and breathleſs accent, occaſioned by her fear and ſurprize, plunge not your unhappy Princeſs into the depth of miſery! Your ſeraglio abounds with ſlaves greatly ſuperior to me in beauty, and Zobeide is only jealous of her own.—She is faſt aſleep, interrupted the Calif, but if your voice would make as ſtrong an impreſſion on her ears, as it does on my heart, ſhe will awake before I could wiſh; ceaſe then any further reſiſtance. Do you, replied the ſlave, ceaſe to importune me to betray my miſtreſs's honour, as I will inſtantly

inſtantly awake her by my cries; but, continued ſhe, ſeeing her threats were ineffectual, ſhe may awake every moment, and I beſeech you, by all you love, have compaſſion on my fears! To-morrow after mid-day ſervice, I will meet you in the honey-ſuckle grove, and there you ſhall be happy if it be in my power to make you ſo: juſtify not by a violent impatience thoſe dire ſuſpicions, which but this evening ſo greatly diſquieted Zobeide.

Haroun ſatisfied by this promiſe, and fearful of alarming his ſpouſe, for whom he had a great eſteem, agreed to defer his imaginary pleaſure till the time appointed; but the ferment of his heart made him a ſtranger to the ſoft embraces of ſleep; his mind was entirely occupied by the imperfect image of this half-ſeen beauty; he fancied he diſcovered ſomething reſembling Zeinib, which greatly aſtoniſhed him; and by that violent agitation and diſcompoſure of mind, which he had been free from ever ſince the loſs of his firſt love, he plainly perceived that he was again become the ſlave of the little blind deity. However, he comforted himſelf with the hopes of meeting with a heart more worthy of his own; and by ruminating on the happineſs he flattered himſelf with enjoying, he ſhortened thoſe moments his impatience would otherwiſe have made tedious.

The Calif flew to the grove at the hour of aſſignation, where he waited a long while to no purpoſe. At laſt, extremely diſappointed and chagrined, he went to viſit Zobeide, who, notwithſtanding the maſk of chearfulneſs he endeavoured to put on, was greatly alarmed at the uneaſineſs that appeared in his countenance; for the leaſt alteration in a beautiful face is preſently diſcovered, which in a more ordinary one might have paſſed unobſerved. Zobeide, in order to diſpel the Calif's melancholy,

choly, ordered her women to perform a concert in the ſalon adjoining, which was only ſeparated by a curtain. Scarce had Haroun begun to liſten to the harmonious ſounds, when a ſurpriſing and inchanting voice removed his preſent diſquietude, though only to involve him in freſh anxiety; he was ſtruck with aſtoniſhment when he heard a female ſing the following air.

The tim'rous nymph, at dead of night,
May promiſe lover in her fright,
She'll with his wiſh comply;
But when reliev'd by chearing day,
Herſelf ſecure ſhe can ſurvey,
Off fear and promiſe fly.

Not even the preſence of Zobeide could prevent his inſiſting to ſee the perſon that ſung; and behold it was the individual Zeinib! that Zeinib whom he thought he deteſted, and by whoſe charms he had unknowingly been captivated. But ſuch is the Calif's greatneſs of ſoul, that even love could not for a moment ſuſpend the dictates of honour; his eyes ſparkled with rage, and he ſaid, Is it you? Are you come here to receive the reward of your perfidy? I aſſure you your beauty ſhall not protect you; for though it has made a ſecond impreſſion on my heart, it was owing to my being ignorant of the baſe ſoul that animated the object of my tranſport. Zeinib was greatly aſtoniſhed at theſe expreſſions, and with a countenance of ſorrow, rather than fear, threw herſelf at his feet, and ſaid, Let me not, dear Sir, feel the weight of your indignation, as the unhappy daughter of Zinebi already bends under a complication of diſtreſs; I ſhould inſtantly expire with ſhame and grief, if I had been guilty of treachery to the moſt humane and generous of monarchs. Are you, interrupted the Calif,

Calif, the daughter of the unhappy Prince of Circassia, and can you prove your innocence ? I am, replied she, and can prove my innocence, if you will be pleased to hear your slave in her own defence. Proceed then, Madam, said the Calif, raising her up, proceed without fear ; but, upon perceiving her diffident, he added, let not the presence of Zobeide be any check upon you, for truth has not so much to dread from any other person, as from him, who will be as severe when a judge, as he was before ardent when a lover. It is not, Sir, said she, the dread of your equitable decision that occasions the confusion you observe in me ; your justice is rather my support, and I will instantly obey your commands.

My father, the King of Circassia, committed the care of my infancy to Elmaze, wife of Hussеyn his Prime Vizir, who brought me up with all the tenderness of a parent. Her affectionate care of my infancy strongly attached me to her, and an inestimable present she made my heart in my riper years, laid me under the strongest ties of gratitude and friendship. As Elmaze was a native of Zagatay, she formed a design of marrying me to Ahmed, heir to the throne of that kingdom. She gained my father's consent ; and the young Prince being her nephew, she desired he might be educated with me under her inspection ; and this request was also readily complied with. I, as it were, sucked in love in my very infancy, before it was possible I should be either acquainted with it or myself. Love was the first sensation of my heart ; and Ahmed was the object of this infant passion. I shall ever remember the happy hours I have spent in the indulgences of an innocent affection, notwithstanding my future disappointment has plunged me into the deepest abyss of misery.

We

We were arrived at the eve of accomplishing our happiness, when Gioher basely commenced that bloody war, which entirely destroyed the fair prospect. I escaped that cruel fate of the rest of my father's family, which would justify treason, by being with Elmaze, fortune reserving me for greater calamities. I would pass in silence that horrid plot, if I had not been informed, that my father intended giving you an account of it, but was prevented by the hand of death. It was by his orders that we surrendered the castle; for he flattered himself, that my faint charms would induce you to fix your quarters there, and Elmaze was prepared to give you a fatal reception. Even the thought of such a crime chilled my heart; for I reflected, that Gioher's barbarities could not justify such a shocking attempt, and therefore resolved to be guilty of disobedience to my father, rather than treason; and if honour and integrity should not, yet your person and accomplishments would have undoubtedly dictated this conduct. I assure you, Sir, that if the heart of the unhappy Zeinib had not been pre-engaged in a passion, that was become absolutely necessary to her existence, she would have made the most tender and affectionate returns to your unbounded favours; for my esteem and admiration of your virtues, and regard for your person, almost counterbalanced my love. How often have I lamented, that it was not in my power to make you happy! Far from joining in my father's prejudice and resentment, and laying our misfortunes to your charge, I could not bear to think that you were the least acquainted with them. Zinebi had forbid me to speak to you, or signify who I was; the last of which orders I was necessarily obliged to observe. But my concern for your safety demonstrates how much I interested myself in the preservation of your life: I seconded

Giafar's

Giafar's diligence and circumſpection, which the hints I had given occaſioned ; I intimidated thoſe domeſtics Elmaze had gained to her party, and was always fearful leſt they ſhould evade the vigilance of your Vizir ; for the impatience to execute a plot, which the heart has once formed and approved, is as violent as that zeal which firſt ſuggeſted it ; the traitor thinking he ſhall ſilence his remorſe, and bury his ſhame, by ſucceeding in his enterprize.

You might plainly perceive by my behaviour, how ſenſibly I was affected by the generous offer you made me of your hand ; and that I was greatly diſtreſſed by a paſſion, which though it till then was my ſole happineſs, gave me at that inſtant great uneaſineſs, as it prevented my returning your affection in the manner I could have wiſhed. I was obliged to avoid explanation, both by my father's orders, and my own fear of making you uneaſy. I did not at all doubt but the faint impreſſion my charms had made on your heart, would ſoon be effaced, and was more ſollicitous for your tranquillity, than the gratification of my own paſſion. Really, Sir, I did not expect your diſpleaſure, and you ſhall judge whether I have deſerved it.

Juſt before the deciſive battle, Ahmed found means, by deceiving the officer on guard, to come to us. Though the concern I had been in for his ſafety, greatly increaſed the pleaſure I had in ſeeing him, yet that tranſport was ſoon checked by the fatal meſſage he brought. When we are in affliction we readily believe every thing we fear, and I ſuſpected Ahmed did not reveal all he knew, and was anxious for my father's ſafety ; but his preſenting me with a letter from him, which I ſtill keep, diſperſed my apprehenſions. In this Zinebi commanded me to follow the Prince of Zagatay, in in order to avoid a fate, he ſaid, you intended me which was equally cruel with that the reſt of our family had ſuffered. He aſſured me that Elmaze's oath laid no reſtraint upon me, ſince ſhe had only engaged for the daughter of Huſſeyn, whom we really left in the caſtle. In ſhort, he laid the heavieſt imprecations upon me, if I diſobeyed his commands through the idle fear of perjury. Ahmed informed us that my father intended to take the opportunity of the truce to aſſaſſinate you, when you ſhould come to the caſtle to viſit me. So many conſiderations prevailed upon me to diſobey your orders; but on leaving the caſtle, I gave a letter to a ſoldier, which he promiſed to bring to you in the camp. In this I informed you of my departure, and the plot that was laid for your life, to preſerve which I readily gave up my own ſcruples, and even diſobeyed the commands of a parent. This intelligence undoubtedly never reached you, for I was ſoon after informed of the danger you were in: and as I had the greateſt abhorrence of this ſecond attempt, I exerted my utmoſt endeavours to render it ineffectual, and hired two ſoldiers, one of which was to alarm your camp, and the other to ſend the Governor of the caſtle immediately to your aſſiſtance. Scarce had I done this, when my father ordered me to depart with Ahmed for Cariſmia; for as the ſucceſs of his enterprize was uncertain, he did not chuſe that I ſhould be liable to the reſentment and revenge of your officers; and I was a ſtranger to his unhappy fate, until I myſelf was overwhelmed with a load of miſery.—The fear of falling into the hands of your troops, which ſwarmed all over Circaſſia, obliged us to travel by night, and conceal ourſelves in the woods by day, where Ahmed ordered a tent to be pitched for me, and uſed his utmoſt endeavours to procure me ſome repoſe, that I might be able to

ſupport

ſupport the fatigue of the journey ; but his tenderneſs and ſolicitude, which were the reſult of his
love, were ſtronger incentives to my reſolution
than any conveniences of life he could procure
me.——Ahmed was equally conſpicuous for the
beauties of his mind as thoſe of his perſon : his
goodneſs, generoſity, and every virtue of an honeſt man and noble Prince, were imprinted in his
countenance, which was the mirrour, and not the
maſk, of his ſoul. How often, in our happier
hours, have his eyes, thoſe elegant interpreters of
his heart, given me the moſt ſenſible pleaſure !
But, alas ! in our preſent diſtreſsful ſituation, I
looked in vain for thoſe chearing rays ; our mutual
internal affection was now our ſole comfort. Our
converſation always began and ended with lamenting our paſt afflictions, and dreading thoſe which
we ſuppoſed futurity had reſerve for us ; and if a
chance expreſſion of tenderneſs, which lovers, be
their ſituation ever ſo miſerable, will ſometimes
indulge, caſually interrupted our mournful accents,
it imbittered our woes by the ſweet contraſt.

We had paſſed the river Jahia, and were travelling along the coaſt of the Caſpian ſea, when I ſaid
one day to the Prince of Cariſmia : I now begin
to hope, my dear Ahmed, that I ſhall avoid that
ſevereſt of trials, the loſs of you ; we are now
near the end of our journey, and ſhall reach Zagatay before the barbarous Gioher can come and
lay it waſte, contrary to the Calif's orders. The
crown you will receive upon your arrival, will put
it in your power to propoſe terms to Haroun ; and
if you will take my advice, you ſhall go to him
with all expedition, and make a tender of that homage he ſo juſtly claims. I know his generoſity
and greatneſs of ſoul ; and inſtead of puniſhing
you for being concerned in a rebellion, for which
you have always expreſſed the greateſt abhorrence,
your

your due ſubmiſſion will be rewarded with your father's liberty ; but mine, alas, will fall a victim to his own crimes ! What can be offered in his defence, after this ſecond horrid attempt ! and am not I juſtly chargeable with his ruin ?—By no means, my dear Zeinib, replied Ahmed, even tho' your generous information, ſhould have ſaved the Calif's life, and occaſioned your father's defeat, you have nothing to reproach yourſelf with ; the vengeance of heaven is more to be dreaded than that of man. Haroun informed of thoſe barbarities that inſtigated your father to this conduct, will readily pardon all his crimes. Alas ! I wiſh you had informed that Prince who you were, and acquainted him with Gioher's cruelty ; with what irreſiſtible eloquence would the beauty and modeſty of the daughter have pleaded for an unhappy parent ? I was greatly concerned at your being interdicted this infallible method of promoting the general welfare, and ſincerely wiſhed that you would diſpenſe with your father's inſtructions in this point, even though it ſhould have occaſioned my own ruin by the reſentment of a rival—What is that you ſay, Ahmed, replied I ? I aſſure you, that you would have had nothing to fear from jealouſy, a paſſion never harboured in a noble mind ; the Calif's known equity guarantee'd your ſafety ; for it would have been an infringement of his juſtice, if he had puniſhed you for having the prior claim to my heart. Moreover, the moſt violent paſſions cannot influence a mind like his. Thus, Sir, we placed all our hopes, and all our confidence in your virtues ; thus, they were the ſole fountain of our mutual conſolation. But alas ! our future miſery rendered theſe conſiderations uſeleſs.—We were preparing to paſs the river Jaſartes, when our eſcorte was attacked by a large body of banditti ; and

though

though Ahmed performed wonders, even ſurpaſſing the exploits of the moſt renowned heroes of old, yet courage muſt always yield to numbers. His intrepidity, which would have claimed admiration and reſpect even from Barbarians, only increaſed the fury of theſe baſe villains, who were inſenſible to every thing but the mean ſordid deſire of plunder. At laſt, all our attendants being ſlain, Ahmed remained my ſole defender; and the turf, on which my fainting body ſunk down, was dyed with the blood of my lover. I was all attention to this horrid ſcene, but was ſo ſhocked, that though my honour and liberty were ſo nearly concerned, I was not able to offer up my prayers to heaven; for my own life ſeemed to flow in the purple ſtreams that guſhed from Ahmed; but on ſeeing him fall, pierced with a thouſand mortal wounds, I recovered ſufficient reſolution to endeavour to defend him: upon this, he ſaid with a faint voice, what are you doing, my dear Zeinib? Let me die without being ſhocked at the brutal behaviour of my aſſaſſins to you, let not their barbarity diſturb my laſt moments, which are ſufficiently imbittered by my not being able to defend your honour and liberty, tho' at the expence of a thouſand lives; inſtead of having this fatal moment ſoftened by your endearments, the dread of your future fate renders the king of terrors more grim and ghaſtly. Alas, replied I, almoſt diſtracted! I wiſh I could as eaſily ſave your life, as I can free you from thoſe apprehenſions which give you ſo much uneaſineſs! I aſſure you, my dear Ahmed, you ſhall not depart for the regions of peace and joy under ſuch anxiety! Nothing can ſeparate the union of our ſouls; receive this kiſs, not as a laſt farewel, but as a mark of affection from her that adores you? Turn your fainting eyes upon me, that your departing ſight may confirm to you that happineſs which I have promiſed! Having

ing thus ſaid, I plunged myſelf into the river. The banditti, buſied in ſecuring the ſpoil, gave us an opportunity for the foregoing affecting dialogue; but the noiſe I made in falling into the ſtream, checked their earneſtneſs for plunder; and ſince in loſing me, they would have been deprived of part of the ſpoil, they made all haſte to ſave me. Having leaped into the ſtream, and ſeized their prey, they no ſooner got to ſhore, than they perceived a large body of horſe approaching, upon which they inſtantly fled. He who bore me in his arms, had but juſt time to mount, and the inconvenience of carrying a perſon, in all appearance dead, ſo much retarded his flight, that he had loſt ſight of his companions. A perſon attended by two ſlaves, chanced to meet him, who, compaſſionating the ſituation I was in, ſtopped him, and ſaid, Whoever you are, I will not admit of ſuch barbarous behaviour; uſe ſome method this moment for the relief of that woman, for the leaſt delay will be fatal to her. I may do what I pleaſe with my own ſlave, replied the robber; but if you have a fancy for her, you are welcome to purchaſe her. My deliverer immediately accepted the propoſal; and as the other ſet a ſmall value upon me, becauſe he thought I was expiring, his demand was inſtantly paid, and he followed his companions.

I had been a ſtranger to theſe incidents, but that, upon recovering my ſenſes, I found myſelf in the houſe of my new maſter. How great was my ſurprize and concern to find myſelf ſtill in this mortal ſtate! Alas, my dear Ahmed, ſaid I, I have broke my promiſe! you have in vain expected me in the regions of bliſs, where I ought to have met you before now! Thoſe cruel wretches who reſcued me from the cold embraces of death, did it only to verify your ſuſpicions. But my life, which is your's alone, ſhall not be at their diſpoſal; if my affliction

affliction does not put a short period to my days, my despair will soon furnish means to get rid of this miserable being! As I thus expressed myself, a woman, whose graceful and engaging air greatly enlivened me, approached my bed. She exerted the utmost efforts of reason and religion to calm my disquietude, and informed me of the happy change of my fortune. I in return assured her, that I was not his slave who had so basely sold me, and related to her part of my misfortunes, but took care to conceal both my own family, and that of Ahmed. However, my sollicitous enquiry after the King of Circassia, gave her reason to suspect that I was greatly interested in his fate: this consideration, joined to the weak condition I was in, made her judge it most prudent to conceal the truth.

Arouya (for that was the name of this good woman, and Chapour of my deliverer) was so obliging as to go at my request to the place where I had left the body of my unhappy lover, in order to bury him. But on her return, she informed me that your troops, who were marching for Zagatay, and whose approach had occasioned the flight of the banditti, had paid this last office to the unhappy victims of those wretches cruelty. As soon as my strength would permit, I was desirous to go and water that fatal spot with my tears, which Ahmed had dyed with his blood. Arouya was so kind as to give me leave, and to accompany me: but she soon repented her compliance; for on seeing the place where I had lost all that was dear to me in this world, I fainted a second time, and was carried to Chapour's house in as deplorable a condition as before.

As all their endeavours to mitigate my grief had proved ineffectual, they carried me to a city not far distant from the country seat where they at present resided; and their kind and tender treatment

ment made me insensible of the chains of slavery. But fortune still reserved me for greater trials; I at last was informed of the unhappy fate of Zinebi; and though I thought the fountain of my tears had been exhausted, it flowed abundantly on this occasion; yet I must own that his contrition, and your generosity, somewhat alleviated my concern. I was not affected by the loss of my rank in life, as I did not in the least doubt, but your goodness, if I had been inclined to discover myself, would have amply compensated that misfortune; but all ambitious thoughts were now banished this afflicted breast. In losing Ahmed I had lost my all, even the power to wish myself happy; and that obscure life and calm retreat I now enjoyed, was the only situation that could have been tolerable: but malicious fate deprived me of this also.

Chapour was a rich Carismian merchant; his unbounded generosity frequently induced him to oblige and assist the undeserving and ungrateful, which at last proved his ruin. His affairs being greatly perplexed, suggested to him that he had a certain resource in me; but the great affection I had always expressed for him, and my frequent requests that he never would separate me from Arouya, made him abhor this project, which however his necessity at last obliged him to comply with. Arouya informed me with the utmost concern of their cruel distress; and I should have been guilty of the blackest ingratitude, if I had abused their friendship and generosity, in dissuading them from a design, which was the only means in their power to avoid absolute ruin. I was satisfied with requesting Chapour to sell me to no one but yourself; for I could not bear the thought of being in any person's possession but his, for whom alone, excepting love, I had every other sentiment of esteem. Upon our arrival at Bagdad, I was informed

formed that you had married the Princeſs Zobeide, and I judged it would be baſe in me, to run the riſque, by diſcovering myſelf, of diſturbing that happy union and your tranquillity, when it was not in my power to promote your felicity; for I perceived that Ahmed would always keep poſſeſſion of my heart, and conſequently that I never ſhould be able to give you any real ſatisfaction. I acquainted Arouya with my diſquietude, who ſoon found a method to make me eaſy; ſhe prevailed upon Chapour to offer me to the eunuch who purchaſed ſlaves for Zobeide, and aſſured me, that I might be with her without being diſcovered by you. And I ſhould, in all probability, have attained my wiſh in this reſpect, if I had not met with the daughter of Huſſeyn, who came into the ſeraglio yeſterday, and we were both of us appointed to watch with the Princeſs laſt night. As ſoon as that Lady ſaw me, ſhe burſt into the warmeſt tranſports of joy; for we had been bred up together, and had contracted the moſt inviolable friendſhip from our very infancy. We recounted to each other our reſpective misfortunes; and ſhe, far from approving my reſolution of keeping myſelf concealed, gave it the title of falſe delicacy; and I was ſtrenuouſly defending my own opinion, when you diſcovered us in the cloſet. Friendſhip often produces a blind and obſtinate zeal; and the daughter of Huſſeyn, notwithſtanding my inhibition, muſt have found means to acquaint you to-day of my being here. I was deſirous, by preventing this diſcovery, to endeavour, by my diligence and fidelity, to merit the ſummit of my wiſhes; which was, the pleaſure of ſpending my days in the ſervice of a Princeſs, whom I eſteem equally with yourſelf; and I humbly requeſt your kind aſſiſtance in gratifying this wiſh, and implore your compaſſion for the unhappy Zeinib."

It

It is impossible to describe the various sentiments that fluctuated in the breast of Haroun during this narrative; they were best expressed by the anxiety of Zobeide, whose eyes strongly reflected the agitations of that heart, which she greatly feared she should lose by so formidable a rival. She could not help expressing the greatest astonishment, when the Calif, after Zeinib had finished her defence, took the fair Circassian's hand, and kissed it with the utmost transport, and even kept his lips closely fixed to it for some moments, without being able to utter a word. At last he broke silence, and in the most passionate and tender accents, said, I now, in my turn, adorable Zeinib, beg your pardon; it is in your power to dispose of a base ungrateful Prince as you please, who accused you of perfidy, at a time when you hazarded your all for the preservation of his life! Punish him in whatever manner you chuse, except by never obliterating the remembrance of the too happy Ahmed! But, on perceiving her much affected at the uneasiness these tender expressions gave Zobeide, he checked the warm dictates of his love, and said more coolly, I assure you, Madam, you shall be rewarded for your great services; you shall live at my court, but it shall be as a Princess, and not as a slave: I am greatly indebted to your unhappy father, whose misfortunes I was, though ignorantly, concerned in; and I owe my all to the generosity of you his daughter! Let Zobeide take all my treasures to indemnify her for the loss of you! I shall not scruple the exchange; but these not being an equivalent for so precious a jewel, do you favour her with something greatly more valuable, namely, that friendship which you have already promised her; the union of your hearts is absolutely necessary to that felicity I now flatter myself with enjoying. Accept however at present that rank in life, which, though due to your birth, you have merited by your virtue. Having thus ſpoke, he preſented his hand to Zeinib, in order to conduct her into the grandeſt apartment of his palace. Zobeide, ſuppreſſing her concern, went haſtily to pay her reſpects to her rival; which ceremony was equally diſagreeable to both. As each was anxious for her own paſſion, they were mutually affected at the thought of being forced to ſhare the object of their wiſhes with another; for Zobeide muſt loſe at leaſt half of the Calif's affection, to whom Zeinib muſt grant a place in her breaſt, which was entirely poſſeſſed by the memory of Ahmed. Their reciprocal anxiety paſſed unnoticed by the Calif, who was intoxicated with love and joy, on his having found Zeinib worthy his affection. He even forgot Ahmed, or at leaſt flattered himſelf that Zeinib would prove faithleſs to his memory, in favour of an admirer, for whom ſhe acknowledged an eſteem that was but one degree diſtant from love: for our ſex is in general leſs conſtant than your's; we ſcarce care to acknowledge the influence of this virtue, which is but too evident from our frequently ſolliciting you to diſpenſe with it.

As ſoon as Haroun found himſelf alone with the fair Zeinib, he gave a looſe to the tranſports of his love; he begged a thouſand pardons for his ſuſpicions, and ſaid, Alas, how could I deſpiſe the ſole object of my moſt ardent wiſhes! How could I encourage ſuch a baſe ſurmiſe! For my heart did not countenance this error of my judgment; my paſſion was only ſmothered by ſuſpecting you guilty of perjury, and if it had proved true, would have been abſolutely extinguiſhed; but with what force did it blaze forth only on ſeeing you! And how could you, after I had given the ſtrongeſt marks of a real affection, deceive me when you had promiſed to complete my happineſs? But what do I ſay? You will

will now, I hope, look upon the obſervation of that promiſe as your duty; you ſhall ſhare my hand and my heart with Zobeide; or, if you deſpiſe this propoſal, they ſhall both be entirely your's. Make not then him the moſt miſerable of mortals, who loves you to diſtraction, and for whom you profeſs ſo great an eſteem, by a rigid fidelity Ahmed himſelf would condemn, as being an obſtacle to your own felicity.

Zeinib, greatly ſoftened by this diſcourſe, replied, I am very far, Sir, from entertaining ſuch a thought; I refuſe not the honour you are ſo kind as to offer me, if together with my hand, you will accept of a heart, which will always retain the dear image of its firſt love. But ſince it is not in my power to preſent you with the firſt and ſole poſſeſſion of my heart, I ſhould be ſorry to prevent your enjoying that agreeable ſatisfaction in Zobeide, who never entertained a paſſion for any one but yourſelf. If I am not deprived of her friendſhip by jealouſy, for which ſhe has but too juſt a foundation, we will unite our endeavours to make you happy. I muſt beg however a ſhort delay, in order to reinſtate the tranquillity of my mind, to which your agreeable converſation will greatly adminiſter; and it is your intereſt to comply with this requeſt, as it will forward the gratification of your love. Notwithſtanding all the arguments he could urge, he was obliged to grant her petition; but his compliance and tenderneſs were not rewarded as they deſerved.

The more Zeinib reflected on the Calif's great abilities and ſingular accompliſhments, the ſtronger were the charms of Ahmed revived in her mind, which recalled the cruel remembrance of his unhappy fate; and ſhe could not help accuſing herſelf of barbarity, in endeavouring to expel him her breaſt; for as he exiſted only there, ſhe thought, that in ſo doing, ſhe ſhould, as it were, aſſaſſinate him a ſecond time. The Calif always found her dejected and ſorrowful, though ſhe endeavoured to exert her ſpirits in his company. In the very height of thoſe grand feaſts, and parties of pleaſure, which he ordered for her amuſement, he was ſorry to obſerve the tears always ready to burſt from her eyes; a ſight, his violent love, joined to a tender and compaſſionate diſpoſition, rendered inſupportable; and he ſoon fell into a lowneſs of ſpirits that greatly affected his health, and alarmed the whole court. Zeinib herſelf was ſenſibly touched at the Calif's ſituation, and at laſt determined entirely to ſacrifice her own paſſion to his recovery. The daughter of Huſſeyn, who was always with her, ſtrongly enforced this compliance; and even Zobeide herſelf waited upon her with the ſame requeſt. At length ſhe got the better of her affliction, and ſeemed ardently to wiſh the arrival of the day that was fixed for her marriage to the Calif.

A few days before this wiſhed-for moment, my brother Mahomed ſent me ſome private intelligence, relating to a conſpiracy he conjectured was in agitation between the Circaſſians and ſome of the principal perſonages at court; but deſired I would enquire into the truth of his ſuſpicions, before I communicated them to the Calif. Theſe diſpatches were brought by a young Cariſmian, for whom my brother had conceived a very warm friendſhip; and the confidence he placed in him, joined to the high character he gave him, induced me to ſhew him all poſſible reſpect. After we had finiſhed the affair he came about, I made a magnificent entertainment for him; and as I had been before aſtoniſhed at his judgment and penetration in matters of buſineſs, I was now equally ſurpriſed at his agreeable and entertaining converſation in our hours of amuſement and relaxation. His juſt and fine taſte in every thing

thing I had obferved, made me fufpect he had more accomplifhments than I was as yet acquainted with: and my conjecture proved true; for befides his being compleat mafter of the lute, he had a moft enchanting voice; or at leaft I was fo charmed with it, that I refolved that Haroun fhould inftantly hear him. After the Calif had given all due commendation both to the hand and voice of the young Carifmian, he was defirous that Zobeide, who was paffionately fond of mufic, fhould enjoy the fame pleafure. Accordingly we three repaired to her apartment, where Zeinib happened then to be. As foon as the young Carifmian, who modeftly kept behind among the Calif's attendants, approached by his orders the throne of Zobeide, Zeinib gave a violent fhriek, and fainted. The Calif run in furprize to her affiftance; and the moment he took off her veil to give her air, I perceived the Carifmian turn pale, and begin to ftagger; and though I endeavoured to fupport him, he was prefently in the fame fituation with Zeinib. This fecond accident redoubled the Calif's aftonifhment; but Zeinib recovering her fpirits, cried out, Good God! what do I fee! Is that the ghoft of Ahmed come to reproach my infidelity? Or is it Ahmed himfelf, whofe life gracious heaven has miraculoufly preferved as well as my own? Upon hearing thefe charming accents, Ahmed inftantly recovered; and the two paffionate lovers, actuated folely by their mutual affection, flew eagerly into each other's arms; but this tranfport was foon checked by their refpect to the Calif's prefence, whom they feared they had offended by this freedom, and both of them threw themfelves in the moft fuppliant manner at his feet.

Punifh in whatever manner you pleafe, Sir, faid Ahmed, a Prince who pleads guilty, I was diftracted with joy at the fight of Zeinib, whofe abfence I

 felt

felt as ſenſibly to this hour, as I did that fatal day, when I judged her for ever loſt. Upon ſuch an unexpected event, it was impoſſible for me to obſerve that decorum, that became a ſlave in the preſence of his Prince. I own my imprudence deſerves to be puniſhed with death, which has been my conſtant wiſh ever ſince I was ſeparated from her, whoſe company alone could make life deſirable. But pardon Zeinib, who could not ſo eaſily reſiſt the tranſports of her ſoul; her heart is as ſtrongly attached to you as ever. Alas! why did the generous Mahomed reſcue me from the jaws of death, which the hopes of meeting Zeinib in the regions of peace and joy, made the utmoſt of my wiſhes? Why was I drawn to Bagdad by the deſire of ſeeing an unhappy father? Why did not I make myſelf known to my deliverer? Thoſe chains I then ſhould have been obliged to wear, would have prevented my interrupting her tranquillity, whoſe virtue merits the moſt conſummate felicity, and making you perhaps diſpleaſed with the moſt deſerving object of your affection! Liſten, dread Sir, to the dictates of that love which pleads her excuſe in your breaſt, and let my death alone expiate this unbecoming and involuntary tranſport!—By no means, interrupted Zeinib, the Calif will not be guilty of ſuch an act of injuſtice; as our crime was the ſame, our puniſhment ought in equity to be ſo too; and it is impoſſible you ſhould be the ſole victim of our conjoint miſdemeanor. But what do I ſay? He will rather pardon us both. I will venture to affirm, I perceive in his eyes the agitations of his generous ſoul: and, continued ſhe, addreſſing herſelf to Haroun, and bedewing his hand with her tears, I beg your compaſſion for Ahmed, which, if I have ſtill a place in your breaſt, I will endeavour to repay by a ready and chearful compliance with the utmoſt of your wiſhes; my gratitude to you ſhall equal my love for him,

him, which was greatly increafed by his fuppofed death. I fhall be lefs fcrupulous of depriving him of that exiftence he has in my breaft, when I fhall be affured, that he, through your clemency, enjoys a happy life elfewhere. Honour him alfo with your friendfhip; for his virtues, abilities, and regard for you, merit your efteem. To comfort him for the lofs of me, reftore him his dear, aged father; and then receive my hand and heart as foon as you pleafe: my gratitude will infure to you the fole pof-feffion of my affections; and, if you require it, I will even obliterate the memory of Ahmed, though at the expence of my life.

The Calif was fo far from interrupting the two preceding harangues, that one would have thought he did not even hear them, if the anxiety of the lo-vers had not been reflected from his eyes. He was filent for fome moments, which greatly affected all prefent, but upon different motives. Ahmed and Zeinib, imagined that the condition of their pardon would be, that they fhould never fee each other more; and though thefe terms were the utmoft of their wifhes, yet the thoughts of fuch a fatal in-junction gave them a moft fenfible concern. I for my part expected fome grand, noble, but too pre-cipitate determination; which I knew was moft fuit-ing the greatnefs of his foul; and was follicitous for his tranquillity, if he fhould facrifice his love to his generofity. Zobeide on the contrary dreaded, that his determination would be guided by his love.— But Haroun fatisfied none of us; he rofe with his ufual majeftic air, that infpires fear and refpect, and faid to Zobeide, I commit Zeinib, Madam, to your care; fuffer her not to fall into that me-lancholy and lownefs of fpirits, which greatly affects me. And do you, Giafar, continued he, conduct Ahmed to your palace, and fhew him all the refpect you can; not confidering him as the difturber of my repofe, but as an unfortunate Prince. Having thus faid, he quitted Zobeide's apartment, and fhut himfelf up in his own. I readily obeyed the Calif's orders; but I muft acknowledge, that the high opinion I had conceived of the abilities of Ahmed, was confiderably abated by the anxiety he occafioned the Calif, whofe happinefs I was more follicitous for than my own.

The night was pretty far advanced, when Mefrour, came to call me to wait upon the Calif, who received me very gracioufly, though with a dejected forrowful countenance, and faid, As foon as it is day, take Zeinib and conduct her to Ahmed, and reftore to him his father; and do you, taking what attendants and efcort you fhall think proper, conduct them to Zagatay. Place Zeinib upon the throne of Circaffia, and charge them to govern thofe two kingdoms with juftice and equity, and learn from my example, that the happinefs of a Prince confifts in that of his fubjects; for that God who gave him the fupreme command, requires that he fhould poftpone his own gratification to their tranquillity; that he fhould pardon the penitent, and reward the faithful. Tell them, in fhort, that they exprefs their gratitude by a prudent and impartial adminiftration. Suffer not your friendfhip to fuggeft any arguments againft this determination; nor intimate the greatnefs of the facrifice, which I am very fenfible of, by what I feel in my own breaft; but this ftep is abfolutely neceffary to the peace and tranquillity of my mind. And not to renew my forrow, and increafe the difficulty of this felf-denial, I defire you would not mention the name of Zeinib, or let me fee her any more.

Thus I was obliged to retire in filence; and greatly furprifed and affected at thefe orders, I returned to Ahmed, who expreffed the warmeft gratitude to his kind benefactor: but the generous Zeinib

Zeinib was not ſo ſenſibly affected by her own happineſs, in being in poſſeſſion of her beloved Ahmed, as at the Calif's voluntary ſacrifice of his paſſion; and was greatly concerned that ſhe was not permitted to expreſs her acknowledgments in the humbleſt manner. As for Arſelan, he affectionately embraced his ſon and Zeinib, and ardently wiſhed all happineſs to the generous author of his unexpected felicity. I placed them on their reſpective thrones; and their affection and fidelity to the Calif, and imitation of his virtues, are an ineſtimable tribute, which amply recompences that anxiety their happineſs occaſioned him. Zobeide has never ſince been diſturbed by jealouſy; ſhe has recovered the ſole poſſeſſion of the Calif's affections, who is become infinitely more dear to her by this generous heroic action. In ſhort, though Haroun is deprived of the pleaſure of gratifying a warm and real paſſion, which by many is judged the ſummit of felicity; yet he enjoys every other bleſſing of life, which he ſtrongly reflects on all about him, and by this means acquires the love of his ſubjects, and the eſteem and admiration of ſtrangers; and this faithful narration of ſome of thoſe actions, upon which his fame and happineſs are founded, will, I doubt not, inſpire you with the ſame ſentiments.

It is impoſſible, replied Irene, not to expreſs the higheſt admiration of his tranſcendent abilities; and I muſt acknowledge, that I did not think it poſſible for reaſon and virtue to have ſo ſtrong an influence over the violent paſſion of love; and I ſincerely wiſh that Haroun may never ſully that fame which he has ſo juſtly acquired, by his noble and diſintereſted behaviour. That wiſh, replied Giafar, ſo highly becoming the Empreſs Irene, will undoubtedly be accompliſhed; for as he has had the reſolution to conquer his firſt love, that paſſion can never diſturb his repoſe, or tarniſh his glory. You are miſtaken, Sir, interrupted the Empreſs, if you look upon this common obſervation as founded in reaſon and nature. Every thing by a regular progreſſion riſes to perfection; and notwithſtanding this vulgar error, a ſecond love is always more violent than the firſt. The new object finds the veſtigia of the old flame, and makes the impreſſion deeper; the warmth of deſire increaſes by habit and cuſtom, and at laſt acquires ſuch an irreſiſtible force, that baffled reaſon, which was before triumphant, is forced to ſubmit. Haroun will one time or other probably experience the truth of this obſervation. But, continued ſhe, is it poſſible, as you have aſſured me, that you can be an abſolute ſtranger to love? Has the hand of pleaſure never confined your heart in the ſoft bondage of love? I am, Madam, replied Giafar, entirely unacquainted with that agitation and ardour of a real paſſion, which conſtitutes the happineſs of lovers; but I am probably on the point of making the experiment, though, as my ſucceſs is doubtful, I ſhould gladly be excuſed. This acknowledgment, which Irene's amorous looks extracted from Giafar, gave her the higheſt ſatisfaction, as ſhe interpreted it in her own favour. Ah! dear Sir, ſaid ſhe, with a bluſh, the perſon you honour with your affection, will not uſe you cruelly! Even the common prejudice againſt your too happy country, will be no obſtacle to your happineſs; that, together with every other ſhadow of objection, muſt neceſſarily be ſurmounted by a love for your perſon and accompliſhments. This ſhe pronounced in ſuch a manner, as convinced Giafar that his addreſſes would be favourably received; but he would not encourage an inclination which was founded on ſelf-love, rather than on an eſteem for the Empreſs; though he was at preſent ignorant

norant of its principle. He was desirous first of all to conclude the peace, not thinking it safe to rely on his fidelity to his master, as he was sensible, that a person in love frequently suffers reason and duty to give way to the requests of a mistress, and that error is unavoidable where the heart is biassed by affection.

Whilst Giafar thus sacrificed his inclination to his duty; whilst he was solely intent on the honour and interest of his master, that Prince became the slave of a new flame, which, by the excess it led him into, cast such a stain upon his glory, as all his accomplishments and generous actions could never efface, and verified the prediction of Irene.

The Calif had a great respect and veneration for Osmaide his mother; and frequently postponed both his business and pleasure, in order to visit her in the old seraglio. Being there one day, and walking in the gardens which Mahadi had planted, and which Osmaide took great pleasure to embellish, he sat down in a grotto to screen himself from the scorching rays of the sun; and fell into one of those gentle slumbers which refresh the mind, without obstructing the exercise of the senses. Being in this situation, he heard a confused noise under the grotto, and saw an eunuch come out at a door, which was contrived with such art, that it had till now escaped his observation. The eunuch did not perceive the Calif, as he had placed himself in the darkest corner of the grotto; and he himself distrusted his own eyes, looking upon what he had seen to be only a dream. The fruitless search he made to find the door confirmed him in this opinion; but having at last discovered it, he burst it open, as he could not find any other method of entrance. Upon this, he discovered a staircase of white marble, over which hung a crystal lamp.

lamp. Being greatly aſtoniſhed at ſuch a ſurpri-ſing and unexpected phænomenon, he deſcended, and came into a grand apartment, which was illuminated with a great number of tapers; and in it was a bed with the curtains drawn, upon examining which, he perceived a young woman of moſt exquiſite beauty faſt aſleep. Her ſurpriſe on ſeeing the Calif when ſhe awoke, enlivened her charms; ſhe gazed at him with the utmoſt amazement, and at laſt in great confuſion, cried out, Help, Fatima, my dear Fatima, help! Upon this another woman came running into the room, who, though not ſo young and beautiful as the former, engaged the Calif's attention; [illegible] a ſpirited expreſſive countenance is generally as captivating as the moſt perfect ſymmetry of features, and bloom of complexion. Fatima was ſtruck dumb on ſeeing the Calif, who was himſelf ſo ſurprized, that he was not able able to ſpeak, and diſpel her fears. At laſt he ſaid, Speak, Madam; is what I ſee a deluſion, or the maſter-piece of nature? Explain without any heſitation this aſtoniſhing myſtery. I am the Sovereign of this place, and, whoever you are, will deliver you from this diſmal, ſolitary ſituation; for the unfortunate have always an undoubted claim to my compaſſion. This kind offer greatly encouraged Fatima, who proſtrating herſelf at his feet, ſaid, Your generoſity and humanity, Sir, ſufficiently explain who you are. Innocence always creates aſſurance, and if you deſire it, I will ſatisfy your curioſity. But I cannot proceed to my narration without the promiſe of an abſolute pardon for all thoſe that may appear guilty. I ſwear by our Holy Prophet, anſwered the Calif, that whatever is the occaſion of your being here, I will puniſh no one; proceed without fear.

After

After being harassed with a series of calamities, replied Fatima, which it is unnecessary to relate at present, I was sold to the eunuch Assad, who judged me deserving of a place in your seraglio. Instead of seeing me elated with the prospect of such an honourable situation, he found I dreaded that fate, which is the highest ambition of the rest of your slaves. He kept me some days in his own apartment, and appeared to be affected by my uneasiness; he enquired with a seeming kindness into the cause of my affliction, which I readily communicated; for a troubled mind is always open, but ought not for that reason to be the tool of artifice. I confessed to Assad that a violent, but unfortunate passion, made me abhor the thought of being your's. He listened with attention and pleasure to my narration, and frequently entertained me with his conversation, asking me many questions, which I answered with the utmost freedom.——Coming to me one day with greater gaiety and chearfulness than usual, he said, Madam, I have hitherto distrusted your sincerity, but am now convinced of my error. The women under my care have acted with so much dissimulation, that I am become perfectly acquainted with all their artifices, and can discover them through the deepest disguise. If you are desirous to avoid that fate you seem to dread, and even to regain your liberty, I will put it in your power to accomplish both, upon condition that you will for some time live in a subterraneous habitation, never visited by the chearing rays of the sun. You shall there have the care of a young Lady, who will soon appear on the stage of the world, with which you will bring her a little acquainted, but not so as to make her impatient for her appearance in public. She is at present entirely in a state of nature; and what pleasure

pleaſure will it afford a virtuous mind to form one like itſelf! I agreed to this propoſal, and was accordingly one dark night conducted to this grotto. The charming Zelia was then about twelve years old, and I was at firſt ſight captivated with her affectionate, endearing behaviour. Ah! ſaid ſhe, as ſoon as ſhe ſaw me, are you that Fatima who is to make me happy? I ſincerely wiſh that you may enjoy a longer life than my dear Repiſma did: I am now ſenſible that I was to blame, in being ſo afflicted for the loſs of her, as I have found another whom I equally eſteem.

I was greatly ſurpriſed at this ſtrange ſituation, and likewiſe at the wit of my pupil, which notwithſtanding her ſimplicity was very conſpicuous. I aſked her ſeveral queſtions which ſhe was not able to anſwer; all I could learn was, that ſhe had never ſeen any perſon but Aſſad and Repiſma, and that neither of them had informed her of her origin. I applied myſelf diligently to enlarge her underſtanding, and form her morals, in which I was ſucceſsful beyond expectation.

Zelia, beſides that ſimplicity which is a certain characteriſtic of a virtuous diſpoſition, had an extraordinary capacity; in ſhort, virtue and knowledge were in her innate. I acquainted her with nothing but what was ſuitable to her preſent ſituation, and conducible to her happineſs. Aſſad made our ſolitude the more agreeable by his conſtant attendance and engaging converſation; we liſtened to him with pleaſure; the charms of wit made us inſenſible of our darkſome ſituation; for when agreeably entertained and employed, all inconveniencies vaniſh. We had ſpent four years in this manner, when Aſſad aſſuring me that we ſhould ſoon enjoy our liberty, I endeavoured to give Zelia a more extenſive knowledge of the world; and as love had been the cauſe of all my misfortunes,

fortunes, as it is of the generality of our ſex, I deſcribed man as the moſt dangerous animal.

The Calif liſtened attentively to Fatima, and gazed with aſtoniſhment on Zelia, whoſe charms had already captivated his heart; for the imperfect account Fatima had given him, excited an aſtoniſhment and curioſity, which are often productive of love. After a long ſilence, which greatly ſurpriſed Fatima, he aroſe, and left the grotto with an eaſy unaffected chearfulneſs, and ordered his ſlaves to aſſiſt Zelia and Fatima in removing from their priſon, and to prepare a grand apartment for their reception, to which he himſelf conducted them; aſſuring Zelia, that nothing ſhould be wanting to gratify the utmoſt of her wiſhes.

Aſſad was inſtantly brought before the Calif, who generouſly offered him a full pardon, if he would diſcover the truth; but this unhappy eunuch, dreading the reſentment of his maſter, had taken poiſon, by which he expired, without giving the leaſt intelligence. Zelia was greatly affected by his death; and as he had always treated her with the utmoſt reſpect, her concern evidently ſhewed her tender diſpoſition.

This event redoubled the Calif's curioſity, which, as it is a powerful motive with all men, is more particularly ſo with Princes, whoſe abſolute ſovereignty brooks no obſtacle to their deſires. His curioſity therefore which increaſed with his love, gave him no ſmall uneaſineſs. All his endeavours to unriddle this perplexed affair proved ineffectual; and the unſatisfactory anſwers Zelia and Fatima gave to his importunate inquiries, made him deſpair of coming at the truth.

Haroun alſo began to be uneaſy for the want of an agreeable companion, and true friend; and though Giafar was at a great diſtance, and employed

ployed in a very important affair, he was ſo impatient to communicate to him the anxiety of his ſoul, that he could not perſuade himſelf to permit him to put an end to the war he had carried on againſt the Empreſs Irene, by an honourable peace. He often thought of recalling him, which would have prevented a purſuit of his ſucceſs, ſo neceſſary to the tranquillity of his ſubjects; and for whoſe happineſs, he would have formerly diſpenſed with any inconveniency. But love had now changed his diſpoſition, and reſolved to make him pay dear for his former boaſting triumphs.

Zelia was entirely employed in diſcourſing with Fatima upon her new enchanting ſituation; ſhe ſpoke the language of pure nature, which the other judged greatly ſuperior to ſtudied eloquence. Every object gave her an agreeable ſurpriſe, but not ſuch as ariſes from a ſhallow underſtanding, which dazzles, but does not inſtruct the mind; her aſtoniſhment was productive of amuſement and inſtruction. She was ſtruck with that innumerable variety of Beings which embelliſh Nature, and examined them with great attention. Having now the pleaſure of viewing them, ſhe found them greatly different from what her imagination had before repreſented; and ſhe endeavoured to range in order the general ideas of Nature ſhe had received from Fatima; but her capacity proved too weak for ſo extenſive a ſubject. The vaſt expanſe of the heavens, the ſtars the clouds, the extenſive variegated plains, what a raviſhing picture muſt all theſe afford a reaſonable being at the firſt view!

O my dear Fatima, ſaid Zelia, what inexpreſſible ſatisfaction does my new ſituation afford me, by giving me the liberty to view and contemplate nature! If it had not been for the remarkable ſingularity of my fate, the wonders I ſurvey would have

have become ere now habitual, and not have afforded that ſenſible pleaſure I at preſent enjoy. I ſhould indeed have beheld the ſame captivating objects, the brightneſs of the ſun, and the beauteous flowers that enamel the verdant plains; but it would have been before my mind was capable of that refined delight, and pleaſing ſenſation it now feels. Every thing that I ſee is a ſtronger proof than all your arguments of a ſupreme Creator, whom I devoutly thank for the felicity I at preſent enjoy. But why is not every perſon as happy as myſelf? for I think I obſerve ſome with ſorrowful and dejected countenances. Shall I become ſatiated with my preſent enjoyments? Is ſurpriſe, novelty, and aſtoniſhment, abſolutely neceſſary to our happineſs; and when habit has worn off theſe, whether will pleaſure or pain be predominant in my breaſt? You hinted to me ſomething about paſſions, which though I did not thoroughly comprehend, greatly alarms me; give me further inſtructions on that ſubject; if they are as harmleſs as man, I ſhall not in the leaſt dread them. You indeed repreſented all mankind, except Aſſad, as the moſt ſavage monſters; but I begin to entertain a better opinion of them; for what have I to dread from the Calif, who always expreſſes in his looks the greateſt ſatisfaction in my company? It is thoſe very looks, replied Fatima, that are moſt to be dreaded, for they gradually excite the paſſion of love, which at laſt proves our ruin. This, my dear Zelia, is what I intended to inform you of, when I deſcribed man as the moſt ſhocking monſter. Proceed then with your inſtructions, ſaid Zelia briſkly, for I ſhall now more eaſily comprehend your meaning, as I have the liberty to exert my faculties.

While Zelia thus expreſſed herſelf, Fatima enjoyed that ſelf-complacency, which a ſkilful artiſt

experiences

experiences when he surveys a well-finished piece; and she thus answered her pupil. You will learn more from experience than me; but, as its instructions often pass unobserved, it may be dangerous to leave you solely to such a precarious tutor. It is impossible for me at present to give you a particular account of all the passions, which are almost innumerable; some of them you will probably never be acquainted with; and others of them are in their infancy called by the softer name of desires, which various accidents frequently raise into passions. Love, jealousy, and hatred, are the most usual disturbers of a female breast; though indeed the two latter always arise from the former. But how shall I describe that agitation of the soul called love? since its causes and effects are as various as the dispositions of the human mind. The happy lover will represent this passion under the form of a most engaging deity; he will describe him with an open beautiful countenance, and as the most sincere and even ravishing companion; he will give him every charm, will crown him with roses, and put a wreath of myrtle in his hand, to denote that a series of pleasure is greatly preferable to insipid freedom. But the unhappy lover will paint him with a destructive bow, pernicious wings, and a fatal torch, which, though in appearance extinct, burns every one it touches; he will caution you to avoid this blind ungovernable passion, this excess of madness, foe to virtue, and tyrant of reason. Though this last description may shock you, yet it is undoubtedly the truest portrait. It is requisite, in order to give an exact delineation of this passion, to have felt its fatal effects; alas, how dear have I paid for my knowledge! Consider with yourself, my dear Zelia, the distressed and miserable situation of a person, who is united to a disagreeable mate, and whose mind is become the den of remorse and despair.

This

This makes her often betray that virtue, which before ſhe zealouſly eſpouſed, and precipitate herſelf into thoſe very evils ſhe moſt dreads. She may indeed caſually, through a blind paſſion for an unworthy object, enjoy a tranſient gleam of pleaſure, but all her ſtruggles for liberty will only render her ſlavery the more inſupportable. Encompaſſed with ſo many difficulties, how is it poſſible to preſerve our virtue, eſpecially when we are naturally ſo prone to vice? Jealouſy, the conſtant attendant on love, evinces this truth; it is a mortifying ſcandalous paſſion, and of the moſt fatal conſequence, as being always productive of hatred, which is the bane of ſociety. You muſt therefore ſeduloufly avoid the paſſion of love, which is generally attended by every other calamity; you muſt carefully preſerve the tranquillity of your mind, and ward off this dangerous deity; for ſhould he once get footing in your breaſt, you are probably undone. The Calif has an affection for you, which it is your duty to return, but beware it proves not poiſon in your veins; check the violence of paſſion, and ſuppreſs the warm emotions of your ſoul. You will ſoon be ſurrounded by a great number of jealous and envious rivals, let their example teach you to avoid the ſame vices. Hate not your competitors, for it is our duty to entertain ſentiments ol benevolence and humanity for every perſon. If you ſhould reign the ſole miſtreſs of the Calif's affections, you muſt expect the utmoſt efforts of envy and jealouſy; but if you only enjoy a ſhare of his heart with others, theſe tormenting adverſaries will never moleſt you.

This and ſuch like converſation was the amuſement of theſe two friends for ſome days after their firſt arrival in the ſeraglio. The Princeſs Oſmaide greatly approved their ſincere friendſhip, and expreſſed an high eſteem for Fatima, and affection for Zelia, whom ſhe always conſtantly attended, whilſt

whilſt her ſon the Calif was in the ſeraglio. This ſtrict circumſpection was far from being agreeable to an abſolute Monarch; but his reſpect for his mother made him diſpenſe with it, and even promiſe in compliance with her deſire, that Zelia ſhould ſtay for the ſpace of one moon in the old ſeraglio; but probably Oſmaide's great affection for this young beauty was the principal motive for his granting her requeſt; for we enjoy a ſelf-complacency, when the object of our affection attracts the regard of others; and though this agreeable ſenſation may ſometimes be interrupted by jealouſy, yet in the end it always proves triumphant. The Calif notwithſtanding, was ſoon weary of a reſtraint which grew every day leſs ſupportable; and one evening, after Oſmaide was retired to reſt, he ſtole privately into Zelia's apartment. He intended to have laid his abſolute commands upon her; but when he came to the trial, was ſo ſoftened, that he could only breathe forth his love; but though he put off the Sovereign, and acted the lover, yet ſhe abſolutely rejected his ſolicitations. Haroun being deeply ſmitten, was not ſo much ſurpriſed as affected by this denial; but he hoped that time would ſoften her obdurate heart, and acquainted Fatima with his caſe, who aſſured him of the affection and compliance of her fair pupil.

Fatima regarded not diſturbing the repoſe of her friend, as ſhe carried her the certain intelligence of her approaching felicity. She found her in a very melancholy poſture, with great anxiety of countenance, and ſaid, What means this uneaſineſs, my dear Zelia? Are you unhappy without acquainting me with it? I am afraid you have not that eſteem for me you formerly profeſſed.——Alas! replied Zelia, augment not my affliction by ſo cruel a charge; I never will tranſgreſs the ſacred ties of friendſhip, but Iam afraid to diſcloſe a ſecret, which

I have

I have promiſed inviolably to keep; diſcloſe it, did I ſay? It is as ſafe in your breaſt as my own, for we are both animated by the ſame ſoul! Alas, my dear Fatima, how much ſhall I now ſtand in need of your aſſiſtance! For I am afraid that I am upon the point of falling into that ſituation, which you obſerve to be the common lot of all mortals. I am uneaſy and anxious, and dread a thouſand calamities; liſten to my ſtory, and judge whether I have not ſufficient reaſon to be diſturbed.

You know Oſmaide left us very early this afternoon; ſhe retired to her chamber, and ſent for me. I inſtantly obeyed her commands, and found her reclined upon a ſopha, and very melancholy; the tears were ready to guſh from her eyes, though ſhe endeavoured to conceal them, and ſaid with great eaſe and chearfulneſs, Come hither, my Zelia. I was going to proſtrate myſelf at her feet; but ſhe prevented me, ſaying, That poſture ſuits not you; true friendſhip diſdains ſuch condeſcenſion, ariſe, my dear Zelia, come to my arms, and diſpel that horror that haraſſes my ſoul. The affectionate embraces of Oſmaide excited a ſenſation in my breaſt I was before a ſtranger to; it was not that calm ſatisfaction your care and friendſhip gives, but a more lively emotion, which I cannot deſcribe, and concerning which you have never given me the leaſt intimation. Oſmaide perceiving how much I was affected, checked the ardour of her careſſes, and fixing her eyes uyon me, ſaid, The Calif is in love with you, Zelia, and do you encourage his paſſion? Yes, Madam, replied I. Upon this ſhe ſtarted up, and walked confuſedly about the room, looking at me with ſuch indignation as chilled the very blood in my veins; to which her ſilence alſo not a little contributed. At laſt ſhe ſaid, Heaven forefend!—thou haſt ruined my project!—Zelia encourage the Calif's addreſſes! —Zelia in love!—In love, Madam, ſaid I! That is what

what I never will be; Fatima has sufficiently cautioned me on that subject. I have a regard and friendship for the Calif as my master, which I hope will give you no offence. This mitigated her passion; and seeing me greatly afflicted, she endeavoured to encourage me, and said, Be not surprised, Zelia, at the violence of my emotion: it is for you alone I am thus anxious; for the first moment I saw you, I interested myself in your fortune. I have ardently intreated our Holy Prophet, of whose power and goodness I doubt not Fatima has informed you, to shower down his choicest blessings upon you; and last night, he appeared to me in a vision, encircled with such radiance as overpowered my faculties. I threw myself at his feet, and he said, "Osmaide, "the fatal sword of justice hangs over the head of "Zelia, and her safety depends upon her refusing "to listen to the Calif's addresses." This denunciation so shocked me, that I instantly awoke, and have been ever since anxious for your safety: but I hope you will observe my advice, and make a proper return to my friendship; for I certainly merit your confidence, as I am solely intent upon your happiness. These words, together with the manner in which they were expressed, greatly affected me; for she spoke with that tender, earnest, and affectionate solicitude, which I have often observed in you. I regarded not the pretended threats of Mahomet, for you have taught me to despise such foolish superstition; but Osmaide's behaviour has occasioned apprehensions I cannot account for.

After I had greatly embarrassed her by silence, which I could not avoid, I said, I would gladly, Madam, obey your commands if it was in my power; but what will the Calif say to be rejected by his slave? He will punish me as the basest of mortals; and I wish this was all I had to dread from my compliance with your request. But I shall

ſhall likewiſe violate that duty which is due to my maſter, and which Fatima has taught me religiouſly to obſerve. I know better than Fatima, replied ſhe, the obligations of duty and virtue; of which you ſhall one day or other be convinced. But, continued ſhe with a ſigh, I hope you will think my friendſhip and affection merit this one favour; reſiſt the addreſſes of my ſon for one month, and I will afterwards leave you to your own inclination. Invent ſome plauſible excuſe for your denial, and behave to him with the utmoſt coolneſs and indifference, which will be no reſtraint upon you, as your affections are not engaged. I will inſure you from the Calif's reſentment; but acquaint him not with this my requeſt. Will you oblige me in this? Speak, my dear Zelia, for my life depends on your anſwer! What could I ſay? I was too much affected by Oſmaide's anxiety to reject ſuch a reaſonable propoſal, though I ſoon became ſenſible of the difficulty of accompliſhing my engagement. I had ſcarce returned to my own apartment when the Calif opened my door, and approached me with the air of a maſter, who thinks he honours his ſlave by his commands; but on a ſudden, by what invincible power I know not, he changed his manner, and behaved with the utmoſt deference. Upon this I recovered my ſpirits, and anſwered what he ſaid with civility and reſpect, but with an indifference that evidently affected him. I deſired he would permit me to enjoy my liberty for a while, before he inliſted me among the ſlaves of love and pleaſure. In ſhort, I exerted my utmoſt abilities, and put in practice the advice of Oſmaide, in order to deny without exaſperating; how far I ſucceeded I know not. The Calif, replied Fatima, has acquainted me with your behaviour in the moſt tender and affecting terms, and you are entirely obliged to the violence of his love for the continuance of his favour. Why did you

you make Osmaide such a rash promise? You are an absolute stranger to the wiles of courts, where the warmest friendship is frequently professed only with a view to deceive and betray. Flattery, deceit, and perfidy, which are only casually found in other places, are there necessary accomplishments; and these three vices are the sole employment of the servile attendants round a Sovereign's throne. You must know moreover, that Osmaide professes an extravagant sanctity, which is always accompanied by hypocrisy. And as she has hitherto enjoyed a despotic authority, she undoubtedly dreads you as a rival in power; for though she has disregarded all other competitors for the Calif's favour, it was owing to their being contented with the honour of amusing his private hours, without endeavouring to gain an ascendancy over him, which can only be effected by engaging his heart as you have already done. But suppose she should act with friendship and sincerity, are you obliged to sacrifice your happiness to her whimsies? Get yourself therefore absolved from this inconsiderate promise, if possible; if not, religiously observe it; and learn for the future to be more prudent. You must also second my endeavours to soften the Calif's impatience, and be careful not to excite his resentment.

Fatima's advice made Zelia suspicious and jealous of Osmaide, in which she was a few days after strongly confirmed; for the Calif informed Fatima, that Osmaide exerted her utmost endeavours to withdraw his affections from Zelia, and lessen her in his esteem: and had accordingly represented in the blackest colours, that very coldness and indifference she herself had advised, nay, obliged her to practise. The resentment, however, this behaviour excited in Zelia and Fatima, did not influence them to divulge that secret, which the former had promised Osmaide faithfully to keep; but she softened her

her refusal with every circumstance that could inflame the Calif's passion, and avoided as much as possible seeing Osmaide, who became a prey to grief and melancholy; which, as she was greatly beloved, occasioned an universal gloom in the seraglio. Zelia was not in the least enamoured with the Calif; but rational prejudice, and the servility of her sex, suffered her not to follow the dictates of her own breast. She was moreover betrayed, and those very weapons were employed against her, with which her confidence and complaisance had supplied her enemies; and who is the woman that is proof against such cogent motives? Fatima moreover encouraged that resentment which was inspired by self-love.

Friendship is more circumspect than love, and seldom so blind as to mistake vice for virtue, or deformity for beauty. But though we may reprove the vices of a friend, out of an affectionate concern that they may be prejudicial to him, yet we generally excuse, or are blind to his follies; these are reserved for the malignant censure of an enemy.

Osmaide, in endeavouring to work on the passions of her son, had increased his love; and the time was expired that Zelia had promised to resist his addresses. Haroun was transported with the joy and extasy of a most ardent lover, who is arrived at the eve of his happiness, and impatiently waits the completion of his wishes: but on the contrary, fate had in store for him a series of calamities, which could only be terminated with his life. The very day he was to be put in possession of his dear Zelia, Osmaide demanded a private interview with him. He instantly obeyed his mother's commands, who had ordered Zelia and Fatima to be called, and found her bathed in tears, and overwhelmed with sorrow. The Calif, struck with astonishment on finding Osmaide in this situation, ignorant of what

 sh

ſhe wanted, and ſeized with a fatal preſage, ſtood mute and motionleſs! As ſoon as Fatima and Zelia came, ſhe ordered her attendants to withdraw, and threw herſelf at the Calif's feet in ſuch violent agitations, as interrupted her ſpeech. Haroun in vain attempted to raiſe her up; No, my ſon, ſhe cried at laſt, in a voice broken by ſighs, no, my ſon, I will ever remain in this ſuppliant poſture; inſtantly put an end to my miſerable being, or free me from that deſpair which preys on my vitals! I intreat you for the laſt time, conquer a paſſion that I abhor! And do you, Zelia, ſupport my requeſt, as your own happineſs depends upon it!

The Calif diſengaging himſelf from his mother's embraces, ſaid, Alas! Madam, what requeſt is this? What is the meaning of this cruel obſtinacy? What have I done to make you wiſh me miſerable? I have always hitherto punctually complied with your requeſts! But love having at preſent laid his abſolute commands upon me, it is in vain for me to promiſe what you deſire, ſince it is impoſſible for me to grant it! Oſmaide riſing, replied with great indignation, Very well, indulge your criminal paſſion, and marry your ſiſter, for I aſſure you Zelia is my daughter. You have forced me to divulge this fatal ſecret, though I was reluctant to make you a ſharer in my ſhame! Good heavens! I ſink under my confuſion; and I wiſh what I at preſent ſuffer, may atone for my guilt! This declaration occaſioned a ſtrange medley of joy and grief in the company.

Haroun, thunderſtruck by this intelligence, ſunk under the weight of his ſurpriſe upon a ſopha: Zelia ran haſtily to Oſmaide, and expreſſed her duty in the ſtrongeſt terms; but this unhappy Princeſs, inſenſible of the different agitations ſhe had occaſioned, remained motionleſs and unaffected by the objects before her; for diſcloſing the foregoing ſecret, was the utmoſt effort of her faculties. Fatima was the

the first that recovered her surprise. Zelia was transported with joy on finding herself the daughter of Osmaide, and Haroun was stung with despair on discovering the object of his love to be his sister; notwithstanding they all three diligently applied themselves to recover Osmaide, who at last coming to herself, and looking affectionately on the Calif and Zelia, said, Seek not to recover me, but let my death atone for the unhappiness I have occasioned you. Listen however to the cause of my woes, which may possibly in some measure plead my excuse. Leave me, Zelia, continued she, for your affectionate caresses and tender concern will hasten my last moments; and I should be sorry to leave you, before I have acquainted you with your birth, and taught you by my example, that a wise and just Providence, sooner or later, punishes perfidy and deceit. I desire no information, replied Zelia, the utmost of my wishes is death; for I alone have been the cause of your affliction and despair. If I had implicitly followed your instructions, I had not now been anxious for your life. O fatal self-love! foolish pride! servile timidity! it is by your instigation that I have hastened the fate of my mother; but I will soon follow her, and put an end to this wretched being, whose extravagancies commenced with parricide.

Zelia's excessive concern rouzed the Calif; he ran precipitately to her, and the violence of his embraces, and unconnected discourse, were evident marks of his confusion: she pushed him from her with indignation, and the abhorrence she expressed for a criminal passion at last affected the soul of Haroun; and after casting a grim resentful look round the room, he rushed out, and retired into the most private part of his own seraglio, in order to give vent to his grief. As soon as Osmaide recovered her senses, she was tormented by the most shocking apprehensions: she ordered Fatima instantly to follow the Calif, and to persuade him to act consistent with reason and virtue. She implored heaven to shower its blessings on her two unhappy children; she ascribed to herself, Zelia's anxiety, Haroun's passion, all she then suffered, and all that might befal her hereafter, and earnestly wished death might deliver her from such a load of woe; but Fatima returning, in some measure mitigated her grief. This Lady had found the Calif in an interval when reason and remorse, which never entirely forsake a good man, had taken possession of his breast, and had made the most of this lucky accident. She had humbly, yet forcibly represented to him the disgrace his folly would bring upon him, and how shocking it was to abandon a mother and a sister to despair, for the sake of a fruitless and criminal passion; she reminded him of his former triumphs, well knowing that in exciting self-love we strengthen reason.

The Calif returned to Osmaide, and assured her that he would suppress his passion, which he then judged very practicable; for when love meets with a check, it puts on an air of indifference, and we boast of an imaginary victory, which often might be realized, by a diligent scrutiny into our own breasts. But who strives to acquire the most useful of all knowledge, the knowledge of himself? Do we not rather fly from ourselves as from a superior enemy? —Haroun moreover having already once conquered his passion, judged it easy to repeat his victory, and add fresh lustre to his glory.

The Calif's assurance, and Zelia's tenderness, entirely recovered Osmaide; and though the latter was desirous to hear her mother's history, and share in her woes, she would not urge the promised recital, lest the rehearsal of her misfortunes should make too strong an impression on a mind already depressed

pressed with sorrow. On the contrary, Haroun's curiosity would not admit of any delay; he signified his uneasiness to Fatima, who thought he distrusted Osmaide's sincerity, and accordingly acquainted her with it. Upon which this Princess saw herself obliged to clear her character by a detail of her misfortunes.

PART II.

THREE days after the fatal discovery of Zelia's parentage, Osmaide, having assembled the Calif, her daughter, and Fatima, began her promised narration as follows.

My father, Mansor Hagiana, was lineally descended from the prophet Ali: how happy should I have been in such progenitors, if I had not cast a stain on that illustrious and holy family! By his exemplary piety and virtue, my father acquired the esteem of the Calif Mahadi, who gave him the government of Yemen, and I was born at Zabith, the capital of that province.

The beauty and fertility of the country, together with the remarkable temperature of the air, has given it the name of Arabia the Happy. But, alas! this charming situation did not influence my fortune! I experienced that persons may be miserable in the happiest climes; for felicity is not connected without outward objects, an all-wise Providence having ordained that it should depend upon virtue alone, which is a plant that flourishes in every soil.

I was educated suitable to my father's dignity, who gave me early impressions of virtue and religion,

ligion, obſerving to me, that I ought to be as exemplary as I was handſome; for a depraved mind was rendered more ſhocking by a beautiful perſon; and ſince the Supreme had favoured me with his own image by giving me beauty, it was my duty to compleat the reſemblance by being virtuous. Theſe divine precepts made ſo deep an impreſſion on my heart, that even thoſe headſtrong paſſions which hurried me into a tranſgreſſion of them, have not intirely blotted them out of my memory; for the principles inſtilled in our youth are ſeldom eradicated, and prove generally the baſis of our future happineſs or miſery.

When I was fourteen years of age, Mahadi took a reſolution to make a pilgrimage to Mecca, and was deſirous that Manſor ſhould accompany him in this journey. I requeſted my father to give me leave to go with them, which he was ſo obliging as to grant; but being taken ill, I was forced to remain at Zabith with my mother. My father upon his departure enjoined us the cloſeſt retirement; he conducted us to a moſt beautiful villa at a little diſtance from the capital, and ordered us not to depart from thence until he returned. As the province of Yemen enjoys perpetual ſpring, the ground is always variegated with innumerable beautiful flowers; and the trees are ever verdant, and loaded with the moſt fragrant fruit, the country enjoying perpetual foſtering breezes. But what is moſt remarkable, the natives underſtand the value and uſe of the bleſſings of Nature, and apply them accordingly.

As they prefer a rural ſituation, their towns are only intended for ſecurity, devoid of the ornaments of architecture, a ſtudy they neglect, together with every other ſcience that tends only to ſooth the vanity of man; and the delightful gardens,

dens, with which this country abounds, conſtitute the principal pleaſure and employment of its inhabitants; that in which Manſor had placed us, being the moſt beautiful in the province, I enjoyed the utmoſt happineſs and tranquillity in this charming retreat.

Though riches multiply our wants and wiſhes, yet they enable us to give a reliſh even to trifles: it is theſe that principally call forth our ingenuity; poverty may excite induſtry, but it certainly proves an obſtacle to genius; and when we ſay it is the mother of invention, we aſcribe to it a quality it has not, for its excellence ſolely conſiſts in making us active.

I amuſed myſelf in this pleaſant retirement, in imitating the wandering life of the Arabs; and having procured ſome tents from Zabith, I ordered them every day to be pitched in a different place, and, being of various colours, they formed a very beautiful appearance. Sometimes I placed them on the banks of a murmuring rivulet, whoſe prattling current lulled me to ſleep; ſometimes, encamped in a grove of myrtle, interſperſed with roſes and jeſſamine, I indulged an innocent luxury; at another, I exchanged my flowery arbours for the ſimplicity of the verdant plains and ſhady woods; for the love of variety is deeply ingrafted in our nature, and ſhews itſelf in every ſituation of life, if not over-ruled by ſome more headſtrong paſſion.

As ſoon as my ſweet refreſhing ſlumbers were over, I was entertained with the melody of the feathered choiriſters; and, being ignorant that the ſubject of their ſong was love, I fancied they joined with me ſinging praiſes to our Holy Prophet. In ſhort, I had a full opportunity to contemplate the works of nature, which inſpired me with adoration for its great author.—Yet even in this innocent and happy retirement, the loſs of which has often given me ſincere concern, I was ſurpriſed to find a vacancy in my breaſt, and that ſomething, I knew not what, was wanting to my happineſs. I frequently uttered an involuntary ſigh, which I aſcribed to lowneſs of ſpirit; but inſtinct informed me of the contrary, without diſcovering the real cauſe of my uneaſineſs. I was indeed but too frequently ſenſible of the force of thoſe ſenſations which are coeval with our nature; for every individual is inſufficient for its own happineſs, and wants that conſolation and friendſhip which is only to be found by uniting ourſelves to an agreeable mate; but how often does fate, or the contrivance of man, oppoſe that choice to which nature and heaven direct us?

Being one day in a profound revery, I was upon the point of paſſing thoſe bounds Manſor had appointed us, and was greatly ſhocked, when I reflected that abſence of thought had almoſt made me tranſgreſs the commands of a parent. I was going to return with all haſte, when I perceived a young man ſleeping at the foot of a tree: his extraordinary beauty greatly ſurpriſed and affected me; and I ſaid to myſelf, this is undoubtedly an angel ſent by our Holy Prophet, who has been pleaſed to favour me with this charming viſion. My reflections on this unexpected ſight, were interrupted by ſeeing a ſerpent approaching the object of my wonder, which greatly alarmed me for his ſafety, and this ſenſation convinced me that he was a mere mortal. I inſtantly forgot my father's commands, and running to this fatal unknown, awoke him, and appriſed him of his danger, which he immediately avoided, and informed me that Prince Zeid was indebted to me for his life. This information gave me the moſt ſenſible pleaſure; for as I had often heard him mentioned with the higheſt

higheſt encomiums, I was overjoyed at being the happy inſtrument of his preſervation.

Zeid was renowned for his valour, generoſity, humanity, and virtue, and was greatly reſpected by the natives, who judged him worthy of the crown of Yemen, being deſcended from the Hemiarite Princes, who had for many centuries poſſeſſed the throne of Arabia the Happy. He was laviſh in his acknowledgments for the favours I had done him; and though he called it only gratitude, yet he behaved as the moſt ardent lover; my heart, at leaſt, thus interpreted his conduct, which my eyes involuntarily anſwered. Notwithſtanding this, I aſſured him he would ſee me no more; to which he replied, that he would come the next day to meet me on the ſame ſpot; and as ſoon as I could get diſengaged from my mother, I went in all haſte to him, although I had aſſured him the contrary. I will paſs over ſome circumſtances in this part of my ſtory, as their recital would be painful to me; and will only inform you in ſhort, that I enjoyed for the ſpace of a year the moſt conſummate happineſs, my felicity being founded on the pleaſures of the mind, which is not eaſily ſatiated, and foſtered by the moſt promiſing expectations.

I frequently ſaid to him, the only reaſon, my dear Zeid, why I do not return your ardour, is, that I am deſirous of preſerving my affection for you, which would be impoſſible, if you ſhould induce me to tranſgreſs the rules of duty and virtue; for then I ſhould hate even myſelf. My father will ſhortly return, and as he has a great value for you, he will undoubtedly give his conſent upon being informed of our mutual paſſion; for where can he find one more deſerving of being his ſon and my huſband? Zeid acquieſced in my opinion, though he was far from expecting ſuch a favourable event.—We frequently met in the ſame

 foreſt,

forest, under pretence of enjoying the chace; but his father having ordered him to go on business to a city at a great distance from Zabith, he informed me that I must not expect to see him for some time; and our adieu was accompanied with the tenderest expressions of affection.

Every moment after the departure of Zeid seemed an age; and while I was lamenting his absence, the arrival of my father's favourite slave drove me into despair. He brought an order from Mansor, that I should instantly set out with him for Bagdad; and the strongest intreaties I could use, instead of procuring me a respite, only excited the resentment of my mother, whom my uneasiness rendered more watchful over me, and more importunate for my speedy departure; and the only leisure moment I could find, I employed in cutting the following words on the bark of that very tree under which I first saw the charming Zeid. "When two passionate lovers are united by mutual affection, what can be so shocking as separation? Nothing, alas! except infidelity!" I durst say no more for fear of being discovered, and a woman's reputation is too valuable to be endangered for a trifle; but I took care to divulge it as much as possible at Zabith that I was going to Bagdad, thinking Zeid would hear it at his return.

My anxiety greatly affected my mother, who, by endeavouring to calm my solicitude, increased my woe. Take courage, my dear, said she, for your father's fidelity and virtue have rendered you the happiest of women; he desired indeed to inform you of this himself, but I cannot resist the pleasure of being the messenger of such welcome news. You know, continued she, that Mansor has been at Mecca with the Calif Mahadi; and after this Prince had finished his devotions to our

Great Prophet, he every day gave public audience, and granted every petition that was offered. While the Calif thus ſingalized his generoſity and devotion, Manſor employed himſelf wholly in prayer and meditation; and Mahadi, aſtoniſhed at his extraordinary ſanctity, ſaid to him, What has Manſor no favours to aſk? I ſhould be aſhamed, replied your father, to make any requeſt in the houſe of God, except for his divine favour and protection. Gracious heaven! exclaimed the Calif, I return my warmeſt acknowledgments for having found a man ſo holy, and ſo worthy of my confidence! and addreſſing himſelf to Manſor, he ſaid, We will never part; ſend for your daughter, and I will immediately make you my father by marrying her; and I ſhall think myſelf a favourite of heaven, if I can have a ſucceſſor from ſo worthy a family. Thus you ſee, Oſmaide, continued my mother, that you are deſtined to be the happieſt of women, by being married to the Prince of the Faithful. How was I thunder-ſtruck at this intelligence! The thought of never being united to the object of my love, and of even ſeeing him no more, threw me into a frenzy it is impoſſible to deſcribe! I nevertheleſs had a glimpſe of hope from the great tenderneſs of Manſor, and his ſcrupulous integrity. My mother was frequently alarmed for my life; but fate, who will not ſuffer its decrees to be reverſed, reſerved me to enhance my crimes.

I at length arrived at Bagdad, but ſo altered by my diſappointment, that my father did not think it proper to preſent me to the Calif, who, as ſoon he was informed of my arrival, was ſo impatient to ſee me, that he came to my father's houſe; and notwithſtanding my charms were greatly faded, I engaged his affections: but inſtead of being elevated with ſuch glorious conqueſt, I looked upon

power

power and ambition as bubbles, and experimentally found that the reigning paſſion extinguiſhes every other. I ſollicited that my marriage with the Calif might be poſtponed until my health was re-eſtabliſhed; and having obtained my requeſt, I employed this ſhort interval in endeavouring to prevail with Manſor, whom I acquainted with my paſſion, to prevent my doom; but all my tears and intreaties proved ineffectual.

Conſider, ſaid he, what you requeſt, and dread the indignation of that Supreme in whoſe name you ſolicit me, who always inflicts exemplary puniſhment on diſobedience; it is he who has ordained you to re-eſtabliſh the houſe of Ali on the throne of their anceſtors. By this ſtep Mahadi will make ſome atonement for a ſcandalous uſurpation, and will alſo confirm his claim with reſpect to his ſubjects, and appear leſs guilty in the ſight of the Supreme. Will you, daughter, oppoſe the divine juſtice, and by that means make him pour the fury of his anger both upon yourſelf, and the guilty object of your paſſion, who has inſtigated you to this reſiſtance?

Theſe threats, enforced by my father's abſolute commands, greatly weakened my reſolution, and at length procured my compliance. For where could I fly for redreſs? My father remained inexorable, encouraged therein by his religion; and though my mother compaſſionated my misfortune, yet ſhe had no influence, and it was impoſſible for me to avoid by flight my impending fate. Even death itſelf could not afford me an aſylum; this grim Prince may appear agreeable to the unhappy, as it is in his power to put an end to their woes, but he is always a terror to the wicked; we may in our affliction wiſh for death, but a guilty conſcience always dreads his approach. In this ſituation, I ſaid to myſelf, I am upon the

point,

point, my dear Zeid, of infringing that fidelity I have so often swore inviolably to preserve; I dreaded your inconstancy, and am myself guilty of the same crime: this consideration alone ought to put a period to my miserable existence! Neither my father's commands, nor any other motive, could have moved me to this compliance, except the dread of the Almighty's indignation, in which you would be equally involved with myself; and though it is not, alas! in my power to make my dear Zeid happy, yet I will, as far as I am able, screen him from that greatest of calamities, the vengeance of heaven! This anxiety, and these melancholy reflections, were shortly followed by the fatal sacrifice. I was married to Mahadi, and made fresh vows, which I kept no better than the former.

The magnificence of the seraglio could not efface the remembrance of my charming retirement at Zabith; and though I was surrounded with the highest decorations of art, my mind was totally occupied by the natural beauties of the groves and gardens of Yemen; I could even have given a minute detail of the situation and beauty of every flower, whose lustre had been increased by the presence of my lover; for the impressions of a sincere passion can never be obliterated.

The grandeur of the palace, and pleasures of the court, were far from affording that real solid satisfaction I enjoyed in the company of Zeid, and the forests of Zabith. In short, I was blind to every object around me, and could think of nothing but that fatal tree, where I first became one of the vassals of love, and which had been the sole witness of our last adieu, and on whose bark I had expressed my apprehensions. Thus I spent the first year of my marriage in perpetual gloom and anxiety, which would probably have put an end to my

wretched

wretched being, if my father had not supported my spirits, and assisted me in keeping on the mask. It is generally looked upon as one of the greatest afflictions attendant on love, to be obliged to put on a feigned composure of mind; whereas it is in reality of the utmost service to those who labour under that restless passion; for by suppressing and stifling our affection, we may in time probably entirely extinguish it; but this was far from being my case, for I could not rise higher than a counterfeit tranquillity.

The birth of my eldest son Hadi somewhat abated my uneasiness, and that of Haroun gave me some transient glooms of joy; but these were quickly darkened by the Calif's informing me, that the province of Yemen had revolted, and that Zeid was at the head of the rebels. This unexpected event renewed my grief, being assured that love and despair were the motives that instigated him to such a fatal enterprize; and I had the mortification of daily seeing the preparations that were making against him, but had not the power to be of service to him by mitigating the Calif's resentment.

The personal bravery of my lover supported him a long time against the great superiority of his enemies; but being at last overpowered, he was taken prisoner by my father. I now exerted my utmost efforts for his preservation; I wrote to Mansor in the most pathetic terms, and had the good fortune to prevail with him to petition the Calif in favour of this unhappy Prince; and by seconding his request with the most persuasive eloquence love could dictate, I saved the life of my dear Zeid, but could not prevent his being imprisoned for life.

As I was before anxious for the fate of my lover, I now became much more so, knowing him doomed to endless misery; but even all this is nothing to those afflictions fate still kept in store for me.

Zeid

Zeid by ſome means or other eſcaped from priſon, and returning to Yemen raiſed a ſecond rebellion; this ſo incenſed Mahadi, that he went himſelf to ſuppreſs it, which he found a more difficult taſk than he expected. This ſecond war was of much longer duration than the former; and which ſide ſoever ſhould prove victorious, would be equally fatal to me. If the Calif ſhould loſe his life, it would ruin my project as to the ſucceſſion of my children; for the people would have given their brother Ibrahim, who was of age and capacity to govern, the preference to boys, who were not able to take care of themſelves: and if my dear Zeid ſhould fall, I ſhould become irretrievably miſerable. Harrowed with this cruel alternative, I again applied to Manſor, and begged he would permit me to write to Zeid, and would himſelf take the charge of my letter. His regard to the public tranquillity and the Calif's ſafety prevailed with him to grant my requeſt.

Every minute circumſtance relative to my unhappy paſſion and misfortunes is ſtrongly imprinted on my mind; and I ought not to omit any thing in my narration which may tend to palliate my conduct: the letter I wrote was as follows.

" You have ſufficiently revenged, dear Zeid, my perfidy; the inceſſant anxiety and affliction I have laboured under, have amply atoned for that breach of fidelity I was conſtrained to commit. Will you never ceaſe to torment a perſon whoſe only crime is a conſtant love for you? And though offended heaven juſtly pours its vengeance on my guilty head, ought you to be the inſtrument of its wrath? Put an end to this unjuſt war; for though the Calif deprived you of your miſtreſs, he did it ignorantly; but when he gave you your life, he knew you to be a dangerous enterpriſing rebel. I interceded for you, and return not my ſucceſsful en-

endeavours in your favour by such barbarous ungrateful treatment; comply with my request, or expect to hear that I am no more."

As I soon after learned that the rebels had laid down their arms, I was convinced of Zeid's compliance with my request; and this instance of his affection gave me no small satisfaction; for the concession was the more generous, as Mahadi had been unsuccessful in every attempt during the whole war. But I was very uneasy at not hearing from Zeid; for I expected an answer, which I should have accepted as the last token of our mutual affection. I was also solicitous for his safety, as the Calif made all imaginable search after him.—At last I suspected that Mansor had suppressed the so-much-wished-for letter, and calmed my disquietudes, by flattering myself that Zeid enjoyed in some happier clime, that tranquillity of mind I should for ever be a stranger to: for as the mind, when it is buoyed up with the expectation of pleasure, brooks no suspence or delay, and endeavours to calm its agitations by procuring the object it wishes; so also, when it is weighed down with grief and affliction, it naturally reclines itself on hope.

I now applied myself wholly to the education of my two boys, and prevailed with Mahadi to disinherit his eldest son Ibrahim. In this step I did not think myself liable to the charge of influencing him to commit an unjust action; for I knew that the descendants of Ali had alone an undoubted claim to the succession.

The affection of Mahadi, the nobleness of my birth, the sanctity of my father, and my own outward piety, gave me an authority and dignity, which I turned to the best advantage; and my power was shortly enlarged by an accident that happened to the Calif. As he was enjoying the chace, he received such a violent fall as greatly endangered his life; and

and though he ſurvived it, yet he never after enjoyed his health. Being now rendered inſenſible to the pleaſures of love, his heart was no longer divided among a number of rival beauties, and I had the good fortune to retain the ſole poſſeſſion of his affections, and thought myſelf happy in finding in his breaſt, inſtead of a tranſient paſſion, a real and ſolid friendſhip, confidence, and eſteem.

It was twelve years ſince my ill-fortune had united me to Mahadi, when the famous impoſtor Hakem made his firſt appearance at Merou, and encouraged by the credulity of the vulgar, he proceeded from thence to Keraſſan, and afterwards to Bagdad. This Falſe Prophet took up his reſidence in an old ruinated caſtle, which his enthuſiaſtic followers preferred to the moſt ſplendid palace; for bigotry has had as rigid votaries as religion, and vanity and ſuperſtition are often concealed under the maſk of faith and piety: happy is he who can diſtinguiſh the hypocrite from the truly religious! This was not the caſe of the Calif, for being prevailed upon to go and hear Hakem, his fallacious reaſoning made him believe the reality of his miſſion. This impoſtor ſtyled himſelf the Meſſenger of the Moſt High, and pretended to work miracles, which were only chemical and phyſical operations, that ſurpriſed the ignorant and indolent. I readily gave credit to the wonders related by Mahadi of this new teacher; and, as nothing but a miracle could make me happy, I was willing to believe that ſuch ſupernatural operations ſtill exiſted; for in every occurrence of life our deſires blind our judgment; and as the utmoſt of my wiſhes was to enjoy that ſteady compoſure of mind, which would protect my virtue, I flattered myſelf that propitious heaven would reſtore my tranquillity.

I, and two more of the Calif's wives, obtained leave to go and hear Hakem. This Falſe Prophet ordered

ordered our attendants to remain without the castle, while we, under no small confusion, were conducted into a private room, which he called his sanctuary. Here he entertained us with a very instructive oration on morality, to which we listened with attention; this being finished, he conducted us into separate apartments, where he left us, having previously admonished us seriously to weigh and consider what we had heard, and then to inform him in writing what favours we had to ask of the Supreme, whose Minister he was; assuring us, that, upon paying him a second visit, our requests would be granted. The great outward sanctity, and mysterious behaviour of Hakem, made me at first timorous and suspicious; but, on being left alone, I recovered my spirits. I seriously reflected on what I had heard, and ardently intreated the Almighty to grant my request. I was preparing to convey in writing my petitions to Hakem, when, influenced by an involuntary emotion of soul, which real lovers frequently experience, I said, Can I cease to love Zeid? Can I solicit the extinction of a flame so closely interwoven with my nature? Is not the anxiety and affliction I at present labour under, preferable to an insipid insensibility, with which heaven may but too soon inflict me? My dear Zeid probably exists only in my breast, and shall I, by expelling him thence, give him a second death? But, alas! my duty requires this severity; I have long been a slave to my passions, and it is fit I return into the paths of virtue! Just as I finished these words, a man seized me in his arms; I endeavoured to disengage myself from his ardent embraces, but was not able. How great was my astonishment on perceiving this bold intruder to be the individual Zeid! It is impossible to describe the agitations of a mind in love when thus circumstanced! What did I now feel from the influence of a violent, unhappy and ungovernable passion!

paſſion! An inundation of joy and love overpowered my faculties, and I fainted! Upon my recovery I found myſelf compleatly ruined; for Zeid took the advantage of the ſituation I was in, to gratify his deſires; and though his ardent embraces recalled my ſenſes, they entirely ſilenced my reaſon: who can reſiſt the united efforts of love and pleaſure! In ſhort, I yielded, and Zeid compleated his own wiſhes, and my guilt. Our raptures were not momentary, for being founded on real affection, they were not extinguiſhed by the gratification of ſenſe; and though the ſoul may ſhare in the pleaſures of the body, yet it enjoys others peculiar to itſelf.

I aſked Zeid a thouſand queſtions, to which he only replied by repeated careſſes: but our tranſports were interrupted by a confuſed noiſe; and fancying I heard my father's voice, I obliged Zeid inſtantly to leave me. After having in vain endeavoured to diſcover what it was that interrupted our felicity, I went in the greateſt confuſion to my companions, and we all three returned to Bagdad.

This ſtrange accident greatly perplexed me; I was ſatisfied that the pleaſure I had enjoyed was no illuſion; but whether the noiſe that interrupted it was a contrivance of Hakem's, whether it was imaginary or real, I could not determine.

Whilſt I was engaged in theſe reflections, Mahadi came into my apartment with a ſorrowful dejected countenance: every thing alarms a guilty breaſt; and though pleaſure may for a moment ſilence the voice of conſcience, yet fear ſoon rouſes that faithful monitor. The Calif, upon ſeeing me in ſuch confuſion, ſaid, You have heard, I ſuppoſe, that our father Manſor lies at the point of death: he was found in a fit upon the road to Bagdad, and they brought him to my palace, where he now remains in ſuch a ſituation as gives no hopes of his recovery, eſpecially as he poſitively rejects all aſſiſtance.

Come,

Come, my dear Osmaide, and try whether you can prevail with him to endeavour the preservation of his life, which at present he seems to detest.

This information quickly dispelled my doubts, and I was instantly seized with the most shocking apprehensions. I attended the Calif with trembling steps, and with difficulty reached my father's bed. My guilt was so strongly impressed on my countenance, that, to avoid his piercing looks, I fell down at his feet, and endeavoured to conceal my blushes. This discovery sunk me into the deepest abyss of despair.

Mansor remained for some time in sullen silence: at last he said to the Calif, Sir, they impose upon your goodness, this Hakem is a cheat; you know I suspected it; I have now had sufficient proofs, and am a victim to my curiosity! Good heavens! why do you suffer innocence to fall a sacrifice to hypocrisy! Order the castle to be immediately invested, and seize the wretched followers of that impostor; you will discover a scene of villainy that merits the most exemplary punishment; as for me, I am not able to survive the shock of having been a witness of such unparalleled wickedness.

Mahadi, astonished at this information, gave orders that my father's advice should be instantly put in execution. The uneasiness I could not help shewing on this occasion, increased Mansor's melancholy and resentment; he would not even look at me, or listen to my intreaties, and rejected with scorn my most affectionate assiduities, which behaviour greatly affected the compassionate heart of Mahadi.

The night was far advanced, when they brought to the Calif a female slave that belonged to Hakem; she threw herself at his feet, and said, Your officers, Sir, promised to spare my life, if I would open the gates of the castle; and I know your justice and

equity

equity too well to dread being punifhed for the crimes of others. I come to inform you of a fecret no perfon knows but myfelf. Your troops, upon finding none but me in the caftle, fuppofed that Hakem and his followers had miraculoufly vanifhed; but their not being to be found was owing to a moft fhocking barbarity, which I am going to relate. I was fo frighted at the indignation Hakem expreffed on finding himfelf detected, that I concealed myfelf in the moft private place in the caftle. I foon after heard him order his flaves and followers to ftand to the pofts he affigned them, and after haranguing them on the merits of obedience, he obliged them to fwear that they would punctually obferve his commands. After this, he filled a large veffel with a certain liquor, and affaffinating all thofe unhappy wretches he had feduced, threw them one by one into it, where they inftantly difappeared ; and laft of all he himfelf underwent the fame fate. But he previoufly committed to writing what he judged neceffary to perfuade mankind, that the Supreme, whofe minifter he was, had, in order to extirpate the Dervifes, and reform their religion, refcued him and his followers from the defigns of his enemies. As foon as my fears were fomewhat abated, I iffued from the place of my concealment, and went upon the battlements of the caftle, informing your troops that I would open the gates, on condition they would conduct me fafely to you. If you are defirous to punifh the fmall remains of this impoftor's followers that are in the neighbourhood, you will find them affembled in the foreft that lies on the eaft of your metropolis.

The Calif inftantly fet out in purfuit of thefe wretches, intending to extort from them the intelligence I dreaded. I was left alone with Manfor; and though, when he addreffed himfelf to the Calif, I was in the utmoft confternation left he fhould dif-

cover

cover my intrigue, I was now much more affected by the fatal intelligence I ſhortly expected; for love, being an original ingredient in the ſoul, is ſuperior to all the other paſſions, which, only accidentally, get poſſeſſion of that perfect image of our great Author. Manſor perceived the cauſe of my anxiety, and in a ſtern, reſentful accent, ſaid, Be gone, baſe wretch! thou canſt affectionately lament the fate of a gallant, but can'ſt unconcernedly plunge a dagger into a parent's breaſt; can'ſt unconcernedly ruin thy own reputation, and what is more, thy eternal ſalvation! No, thy baſe ſoul can never be deſcended from Ali! and, ſpeaking to his attendants, he ſaid, Take her away, and let not the preſence of ſuch a ſhocking monſter diſturb my laſt moments! Theſe violent exclamations made ſo ſtrong an impreſſion upon me, that I was deprived of every faculty both of body and mind; and happy would it have been for me, if I had never recovered them! A violent fever and delirium, which laſted for eight days, prevented my knowing the freſh calamities that had befallen me, which, upon my recovery, I found to be as follows.

The Calif, inſtigated by his indignation, cloſely purſued, during two whole days, the unhappy adherents of Hakem: this imprudent ardour ſo affected his ſhattered conſtitution, that he fell into a diſorder which ſhortly put a period to his life. In his laſt moments he appointed my ſon Hadi to be his ſucceſſor, and after him, in default of iſſue, Haroun: and in order to prevent any of his other wives ſetting up a claimant hereafter, he declared that he had been incapable of having converſation with women for a long time. I was alſo informed, that Manſor ordered himſelf to be carried to Mahadi in his laſt hours, and ſurvived him only two days.

As it was impoſſible to augment my woe, theſe ſhocking events did not much affect me; a ſeries of diſtreſs

diſtreſs makes a perſon at length proof againſt affliction: this was my caſe; and I not only ſeriouſly wiſhed for death, but reſolved to haſten its approach with my own hands. Upon this account my two ſons never quitted me; but all their tears and intreaties could not alter my reſolution. At laſt, Jahia, who was prime Viſir, and had, conſequently, the ſole government of the empire, found means to ſoften my deſpair.——Madam, ſaid he, I have too great a regard for you, to endeavour to influence your reſolutions by diſagreeable motives; but though truth is often a nauſeous draught, yet it is always ſalutary; juſtice, in the preſent caſe, calls for it, and I will offer it with the utmoſt frankneſs. Permit me, therefore, to repreſent to you the ſhocking interpretation that has been put upon your too exceſſive grief. It is thought to be very natural to mourn for the loſs of both a father and a huſband; but again, it is thought that you ought to endeavour to preſerve your life, for the ſake of your ſons, who are the darlings of the people. Deſpair, it is judged, ought to give way to maternal affection, which nothing can ſuppreſs but a guilty conſcience, that crueleſt tormentor of a mind naturally well diſpoſed. The very ſingular declaration Mahadi made on his death-bed, has already raiſed ſuſpicions upon thoſe of his wives, who went to viſit the impoſtor Hakem. Have you a mind that theſe ſurmiſes ſhould be fixed ſolely upon yourſelf? Reflect, that our ſhame exiſts when we are gone; and our children may bluſh for our follies when we are no more.

Theſe hints had the deſired effect, and, which is a remarkable inſtance of the influence of ſelf-love, I promiſed to ſpare my life, and not only patiently to bear, but even to overcome my anxiety; and the polite and friendly behaviour of Jahia confirmed me in this reſolution. I retired to the old ſeraglio, reaſſumed my devotion, and my undaunted deportment

ment greatly added to my fame. But, alas! It was no easy task to put on a feigned composure of mind, when I was sensible that the shameful consequences of my crime would betray me! And that same self-love which before prevailed with me to support life, at present excited me to destroy it, and I resolved to take a slow poison, and conceal both my shame and despair.

A few days before the execution of this sentence, which my honour had obliged me to pronounce upon my life, a Jewess, who traded in jewels, brought me a letter from Zeid. A blind man cannot, upon the recovery of his sight, have that excess of joy I felt on this occasion. When I was informed that Zeid still lived and loved, I instantly forgot all my former misery, and indulged myself in the enjoyment of this unexpected felicity; but again reflecting on the situation I was in, I reassumed my former resolution, and wrote to him as follows.

" Accept this, my dear but fatal admirer, as the " final adieu of an unhappy wretch who adores " you. I cannot reproach you for the misery I at " present labour under, for I still love the crime, " notwithstanding its consequences. The poison " which will shortly freeze my blood, will not cool " that ardour you have kindled in my breast; not " all my woes, nor even death itself, can tear your " image from my heart; I shall carry it with me " into the other world, and it will, in some measure, " alleviate those torments to which an offended " God consigns the guilty. But, my dear, what " am I going to sacrifice! Even the fruit of our " love, which I would gladly, if possible, preserve; " I would willingly submit to any thing but shame, " and might, possibly, if I had a faithful friend to " consult with, find means to conceal myself. But, " in my present situation, my conduct is diligently " scanned by the prying eyes of envy and jealousy;

" and

" and I am furrounded by a parcel of bafe wretches,
" who cringe and flatter in profperity; but, in
" adverfity, are the foremoft to betray and ruin.
" May you, my dear Zeid, be happier than I!
" May you fpend the remainder of your days in
" tranquillity and innocence! And may heaven ac-
" cept the facrifice I am going to offer as an atone-
" ment for your fins! I command you by the love
" you profefs for me, to anfwer this, and to pro-
" mife to preferve your life as long as fate will
" permit. This affurance will greatly leffen the
" horror of thofe moments, which, at the beft,
" are a dreadful, but neceffary relief of the un-
" happy."

I delivered this letter to the Jewefs, who, in a few days, brought me the following anfwer. " What information do you fend me? and what commands do you lay upon me? Your fhocking refolution, and affecting adieu, almoft deprived me of life, and it is impoffible for me to furvive the fatal facrifice you threaten. No, my dear, but unhappy Ofmaide, our fouls are too clofely united to exift feparately! I will attend you, whether it be to eternal mifery or blifs. Alas! a gracious Supreme will certainly be indulgent to the gratification of a paffion he has interwoven with our nature! But let us not trouble ourfelves about a dark and uncertain futurity, and truft your life and happinefs to my care! That love which occafioned your calamities ought to redrefs them; and as I left nothing unattempted to gratify a paffion I ought to have facrificed to your honour and repofe, it is my duty to exert my utmoft endeavours in defence of your reputation and tranquillity. Zeid would be the bafeft of mortals, if he was refolute only in a bad caufe. You may, my dear Ofmaide, be affured of the utmoft of your wifhes from the united efforts of my love and intrepidity; thefe will render my invention fertile in expedients for your safety; grant your guilty admirer two months for the execution of his projects, which a secret whisper assures me will be successful; but suppose they should not, the favour of so short a delay cannot be productive of such fatal consequences, as that I violently seized in the castle of Hakem."

Though I could not imagine how it was possible for Zeid to be of any service to me, yet I granted all he desired. But I became uneasy that I heard no more of him; the Jewess came not as usual to the seraglio, and the time appointed was nearly expired.

Notwithstanding my seeming composure of mind, my sons clearly perceiving that grief still preyed upon my spirits. Upon this account Hadi gave orders, that they should try every method to amuse and divert me. Accordingly, Mesrour waited upon me one day, and informed me, that the Calif had sent me an eunuch, who had surprising skill in musick, and who boasted by harmonious sounds to disperse the most confirmed melancholy, and therefore desired that I would be pleased to hear him. As I did not chuse to deny my son's request, I ordered the eunuch to be introduced, who threw himself at my feet, and in a very genteel manner presented me with a letter, which I instantly perceived to be wrote by Zeid, and found the contents to be as follow. "Order your attendants to retire, the eunuch Assad waits upon "you from Zeid." I instantly commanded my slaves to quit my presence. Assad still remained in his humble posture; and as I had a great regard to a messenger from my lover, I offered him my hand, desiring he would rise, and acquaint me with the commands of his master. But, without giving me any answer, he seized my hand and kissed it with the utmost rapture. This bold behaviour excited

cited my ſurpriſe and indignation: but his ſighs and ſubmiſſive deportment calling my attention, I traced the features of my adorable Zeid in this deformed miſerable eunuch. How expreſſive and eloquent was the firſt glance! I was unable to ſupport ſuch a torrent of joy. I threw myſelf into the arms of my lover; and ſighs, which proceeded from a mixture of joy, grief, and gratitude, were the only language I could for ſome time utter: at laſt I recovered myſelf and ſaid, O my dear Zeid, what have you done! to what condition has my fatal paſſion reduced you! I cannot ſurvive the thoughts of it!—What do you ſay, Oſmaide, interrupted he? Do you talk of dying when we are met to part no more? do you deſpiſe me, becauſe I can only preſent you with a pure ſpiritual affection? Alas, ſaid I, judge not ſo ſeverely! you are not ſuch a ſtranger to my diſpoſition, as to think my love will be diminiſhed, when you have hazarded your life for me. No, my gratitude will enliven my affection.—Our being, replied Zeid, conſiſts in ſoul, which is not the leaſt affected by the loſs of ſenſual pleaſures, as it takes delight only in thoſe that are peculiar to its own nature. I aſſure you, my dear Oſmaide, I ſhall enjoy more real ſatisfaction, when I ſhall ſee you enraptured with Platonic ſenſations, than I ever did in the pleaſures of ſenſe. But, ſuppoſing the joys we have loſt ſhould deſerve our real concern, we muſt reflect, that we were eternally excluded from them. You would have put an end to your life, and I ſhould have ſoon followed you; whereas by the ſtep I have taken, behold we are inſeparably united; and the pain I ſuffered to acquire this felicity, was not comparable to the torments of abſence.—Theſe obſervations of my lover made a deep impreſſion on my mind, and the ſtruggling paſſions of love, gratitude, and ſorrow, almoſt rent my heart; but, perceiving the force and truth of Zeid's discourse, my emotions gradually ebbed, and my breast was entirely calmed by his endearing caresses, which were as ardent as when we cherished an innocent, youthful flame, and were the sweeter, as in our present circumstances they were not sullied by any apprehensions.—At last I said, I begin, my dear Zeid, to perceive that propitious heaven will once more permit us to be happy; but I wish, alas, that our felicity had been procured at my expence! for when I see that you alone have voluntarily expiated our mutual crime, I cannot help being greatly affected by so generous a sacrifice. Since you desire me to imitate your resolution, and obliterate those pleasures which I had been a stranger to but for you, and the loss of which I only regretted on your account; I will commit my every wish, desire, and inclination, to your direction; you shall be my friend, my brother, and lover; my sole happiness shall consist in your company, and I will exist no longer than I shall be able to promote your felicity; the dear pledge of our love will increase our mutual satisfaction, and its education shall be the employment of our future lives. This was the utmost extent of my wishes, for the accomplishment of which you have generously made so great a sacrifice.

Mahadi's father had concealed immense treasures in a subterraneous cavern, which my husband was so fortunate as to discover, at a time when the people groaned under the heavy imposts, that were raised in order to prosecute the war against the Greeks. This fortunate discovery was a secret to every one but myself; the Calif being desirous that his generosity might be justly esteemed, and regain him the affections of his subjects, and the succession of profusion to a necessary oeconomy, would not have been duly valued, if the

the occaſion had been known. For vulgar minds always depreciate good actions, and deſpiſe virtue, to bring themſelves more upon a level with their ſuperiors. Mahadi did not diſcover this upon his death-bed; for as he had ſquandered the treaſure he found, the ſecret could be of no ſervice to his ſucceſſor. This cavern is in the gardens of the ſeraglio, and will be a very convenient aſylum in my approaching diſtreſs: we can here conveniently conceal the dear pledge of our love, a treaſure more valuable than ever it contained before. My authority ſhall ſoon make you ſuper-intendant of theſe departments, and then we can ſafely plan and execute thoſe meaſures that may be neceſſary for the preſervation of my honour: this, my dear Zeid, is my ſole hope and dependance. —I now expect you ſhould inform me by what enchantment you came into Hakem's caſtle, and by what means you avoided the ſhocking fate of the reſt of his followers, and the diligent ſearch of Mahadi. Give me a faithful account of your adventures ſince our fatal ſeparation; for though my affection and gratitude will admit of no addition, yet a recapitulation of the various incidents that have befallen our unhappy paſſion, will, in our preſent ſituation, give me a very ſenſible ſatisfaction. We may remain in private as long as we pleaſe without any apprehenſion, for your wretched condition ſufficiently guarantees our reputations. After ſome mutual careſſes, which were not in the leaſt chilled by our preſent or paſt misfortunes, Zeid began the recital of his adventures, or rather the anecdotes of his generous paſſion, in the following terms.

It is unneceſſary, my dear Oſmaide, to inform you with what reluctance I parted from you at Zabith; and though my buſineſs did not require a long abſence, yet my love abridged it as much as possible. Upon my return, I flew on the wings of love to that forest which had been the scene of our mutual passion: but how was I astonished on not perceiving those beautiful tents with which you before embellished that solitary place! And though this was a trifling circumstance, in which I might possibly be mistaken, yet it was sufficient to raise apprehensions in a mind so deeply pierced by love. I went trembling to that tree, under whose umbrage we had often indulged a sweet and innocent passion; but as the desire of seeing you, and the fear that some mischance had robbed me of that pleasure, engrossed all my faculties, I did not at first observe your affectionate inscription; which, alas, but too soon confirmed my suspicions! Good heavens, said I, am I then deprived of the sole object of my wishes! and, perhaps, for ever! O dear, cruel tree, what fatal information dost thou give me! Osmaide, in making thee the messenger of our woes, was but too well assured that our flattering hopes were entirely blasted! But why do I grieve, when the uneasy situation of her mind is but too evident from the distrust she expresses of my fidelity? I may possibly be alarmed by my own whimsical suspicions; Osmaide may probably be returned to Zabith, and not considering that love easily surmounts all obstacles, may suspect that I am prevented from seeing her; I will go and unravel this mysterious affair. I instantly repaired to the metropolis, where I was informed that you were gone to Bagdad, and pursuing you thither I arrived at the instant my cruel fate was determined.

As soon as I entered the city, I found the populace rioting in joy, the streets strewed with flowers, and a confused noise of music and acclamations. Every place was crouded; and though I eagerly enquired the cause of this excessive rejoicing, and

and desired every one I met to shew m
lace of Mansor, I could procure no in
I at last prevailed with an old man to h
request, who said, If you enquire, young m..
the residence of the friend of the Supreme, y
must go to the Calif's seraglio, for Mahadi and Mansor are this day united by a natural tie, as they were before by friendship; they will presently come out of the mosque, and pass this way, and you will have the pleasure of seeing the charming Osmaide, whose joy and modesty add a lustre to her beauty: she alone was worthy the affection of her sovereign, the brilliancy of her charms shone even through her veil. How happy shall we be, when the blood of Ali is re-established on the throne of the faithful!—The old man was proceeding with his narrative, without perceiving how it had affected me, for his intelligence deprived me of all my faculties, and I sunk down at his feet. This greatly surprised him; and being of a compassionate disposition, he ordered me to be carried to his house. My recovery served only to confirm my misery; rage, madness, sorrow and despair, alternately took possession of my breast. Base, perfidious Osmaide, said I, was it to triumph in my affliction, that you hinted to me, "there were calamities more tormenting than absence?" was it for fear I should not be sufficiently sensible of your perfidy, that you have set it forth in the most glaring colours? Fool that I am, I mistook the most barbarous insult for a compliment to my passion! But I will revenge this treatment, and appease my rejected love with blood and carnage; she, whom I adored when faithful, shall fall a sacrifice to her own baseness.

These fits of frensy succeeded each other almost every moment; and my host, being persuaded by one of my slaves, that I had for some time been

 disor-

n my mind, was more diligent in taking .e; for all true Musulmen have a sort of ion for lunatics, which was but too truly case; I frequently desired to see you, and to wait upon Mansor, and even Mahadi: I would gladly have got an opportunity to put an end to my miserable being under the walls of the seraglio; and when I at last recovered my reason, it was only to execute my revenge. I returned to Yemen, and raised a rebellion, which was easily done, as the inhabitants have a great veneration for the descendants of their monarchs; but though they thought they were fighting to gratify my ambition, they were only the tools of my resentment. If I had contended only for a crown, I could have easily conquered the Calif; the attachment and steadiness of my troops, together with my own personal courage, insured me victory. But vengeance was my sole motive, which, though it is always productive of resolution, yet it generally so blinds the understanding, that its votaries fall into fatal errors; and I had sufficient leisure to reflect on those it led me into, when imprisoned for life by the Calif's orders.

As I despised my life, I did not accept it as a favour; but, on the contrary, looked upon it as a scheme to lengthen my tortures, and resolved to employ my last moments in revenge. I accordingly gained to my interest those who had the care of me; and I need not inform you how successful I was in this second attempt, not by the advantages I gained, but in receiving your kind letter, and in having the pleasure of shewing you how much I still loved. I can, said I to myself, recover the dominions of my ancestors; but, if I disoblige my dear Osmaide, that acquisition will not make me happy; even the most solitary desert will be preferable, when joined to the pleasure of of obeying her commands. My heart is proof against very passion but love, the excess of which excited revenge; but as Osmaide has vouchsafed to clear her conduct, it is my duty to endeavour, by compliance and contrition, to atone for my suspicions, and the anxiety I have occasioned her. I wrote to you, while under the influence of these tender sentiments; and as soon as I had sent my letter to Mansor, disbanded my troops, quitted Yemen, and became a fugitive and vagabond, carrying my tormentor always in my breast.—The beauties of nature, and charms of society, became disagreeable to me: your dear image was the only company I could endure, and though it sometimes gave me great uneasiness, yet I always reflected on it with pleasure, and carefully preserved it.

As I was one day travelling on the frontiers of Khorassan, my spirits being exhausted by excess of grief and fatigue, I was obliged to repose myself in the open field. I lay enfolded in the arms of sleep until the night was far advanced, and upon waking, found myself greatly refreshed. I looked round me, and perceived a faint light on the top of a mountain at some distance; and Nature's importunity for nourishment supporting my resolution, I reached, with difficulty, the place where the light was. But what a spectacle presented itself to my view! I saw by the glimmering rays of a lamp a woman of exquisite beauty, naked, and chained to a tree; and near her laid a dead body, mangled in the most shocking manner.—As soon as she perceived me approaching, she increased her moans, and I made all possible haste to release her. But how was I astonished, when she, whose life I had saved, made an attempt upon my own! for she snatched my sword, and endeavoured to plunge it into my breast: however,

I at laſt, though with ſome difficulty, wrenched it from her, and perceiving her miſtake, ſhe ſaid: Good heaven! what have I done! intending to wreak my vengeance on a barbarous villain, I have probably attempted the life of my deliverer! Who art thou, continued ſhe, with a wildneſs of aſpect, which did not, however, eclipſe her charms? Is it to thy compaſſion I owe my life? or am I to be delivered to that villain Hakem? But whatever may be thy motive, I ſhall gladly truſt myſelf to thy protection, if thou wilt revenge the baſe treatment I have received from Hakem. Behold my unhappy brother! who has juſt fallen a victim to that monſter's barbarity, and he undoubtedly deſtined me to the crueleſt of tortures, which, however, I ſhould have greatly preferred to the horror of once more beholding that ſcandal to human nature!

I implicitly believed theſe allegations of Zemroude (for that, ſhe informed me, was her name) and promiſed to protect her from the inſults of Hakem. Follow me then, ſaid ſhe, for if we ſtay here he will probably ſoon be with us.

The dawn began to appear as I conducted Zemroude down the mountain, and I could not help admiring ſuch a profuſion of charms; for nature had been ſo laviſh of her favours, that ſhe ſeemed even to have outdone herſelf. Her full black eyes floated in pleaſure, and her raven-locks with wavy ringlets ſhaded near half of her body, which might, in whiteneſs, vie with the faireſt alabaſter, and which would have kindled an inextinguiſhable flame in any breaſt but that which was entirely devoted to Oſmaide; and even I myſelf durſt ſcarce truſt my eyes to rove among ſuch an infinitude of charms. The impreſſion, however, was not deep, and my heart remained untouched.

Zemroude, perceiving me ſtruck with her beauty, endeavoured, notwithſtanding the miſerable ſituation ſhe was in, to make the impreſſion deeper: her looks and ſighs informed me of her deſign, which was ſo far from ſucceeding, that her behaviour even effaced thoſe ſlight traces her beauty had made, for her aſſurance was ſhocking, when compared to that delicate, timorous, and chaſte paſſion, which I experienced in you during our happy retirement in Yemen.—Alas, my dear Zeid! interrupted I; why do you mention ſuch a mortifying circumſtance? why do you boaſt of a triumph, for which I have ſo ſeverely ſuffered? I am, by fatal experience, but too ſenſible of my paſſion; and that my honour remained unſullied, was entirely owing to your modeſt, reſpectful behaviour; for if virtue had been really ingrafted in my heart, it would have been impoſſible for me to have eradicated that faireſt of plants, at a time it was moſt neceſſary to my felicity.—Cenſure not yourſelf, replied Zeid, for an unavoidable ſlip: every human power and faculty is limited, even our patience, reſolution, and courage, have their appointed bounds.—How artful a rhetorician, ſaid I, is love? and how well can it defend a bad cauſe? But proceed with your narrative, and let me hear whether your conduct was throughout irreproachable.—I aſſure you it was, continued he; and conſtancy could never be more requiſite, or more amply recompenſed.—We arrived at length at a hut, part of which was hollowed out of the mountain, and the remainder ſo ſhaded with trees, that it could not be eaſily diſcovered. Here, ſaid Zemroude, we ſhall be ſecure, as Hakem is unacquainted with this beautiful retreat; refreſh your drooping ſpirits with this fruit and ſherbet, for it is my duty to take all poſſible care of a perſon, to whom I am indebted for my deliverance. I accord-

accordingly ſat down by Zemroude on the verdant turf; and having ſatisfied the cravings of nature, I deſired her to inform me what accident or barbarous treatment had placed her in that miſerable ſituation in which I found her? and who was that Hakem whom ſhe ſo dreaded and deſpiſed?—You are extremely judicious in timing your queſtion, replied ſhe, with a ſarcaſtic ſneer; I will, however, gratify your requeſt.—Hakem is a Perſian, who, doubtleſs for ſome villainy, is expelled his country, and fate, to my ſorrow, brought him to Merou. As favour and eſteem are always mercenary, his great affluence and unbounded liberality ſoon procured him univerſal reſpect. My brother being the chief of the Derviſes, Hakem was deſirous of his acquaintance, which he eaſily obtained: by this means he firſt ſaw me, and being ſo unfortunate as to engage his affections, my brother obliged me to marry him.—It was impoſſible we ſhould be happy, as I had the greateſt abhorrence to the alliance. His affection increaſed my averſion, and I experienced that nothing is ſo tormenting as the careſſes of a perſon we deſpiſe.—The converſation of my brother, whom I had an opportunity of frequently viſiting, was the only comfort I enjoyed; but this I was ſoon deprived of by Hakem's ridiculous jealouſy, who was ſo fooliſh as to entertain ſuſpicions of an intimacy ſufficiently guarded againſt by nature.—We always live in conſtant apprehenſions of loſing thoſe enjoyments which we are ſenſible exceed our merits; and ſelf-love, by magnifying our deſerts, makes us very punctilious in our claims.—Hakem, finding me to-day with my brother, and actuated ſolely by his jealouſy, inſtantly ſacrificed him to that blind ungovernable paſſion; but he prolonged my fate in order to increaſe its horror. Your approach checked his barbarous hand, he fled,

fled, and I owe my preſervation entirely to you! How ſhall I expreſs my acknowledgments for ſuch an extraordinary favour? The immenſe treaſures my brother concealed in this private cottage will not be a ſufficient recompence: a preſent of my perſon and affection can alone cancel my obligation, and of theſe, which you have ſo juſtly merited, I beg your acceptance.—Zemroude enforced this offer with the warmeſt careſſes; and her charms, which were ſtill expoſed to my view, received an additional luſtre from the warmth of her paſſion.—The remembrance of the lovely and adorable miſtreſs of my affections was the ſole conſideration that made me proof againſt theſe allurements; and I ſaid to Zemroude, I will not, Madam, take any advantage of your grateful diſpoſition; for as what I have done was only a common act of humanity, your offers greatly exceed my deſerts. Having thus ſaid, I endeavoured to free myſelf from her embraces.—No, replied ſhe, redoubling her careſſes, no, you ſhall by no means decline the gratification I offer, as that alone can ſecure you to me. That humanity you mention, is a weak, trifling conſideration, pleaſure alone is the univerſal motive of mankind. As I ſtand in need of your aſſiſtance, I inſiſt on your accepting in return, the full enjoyment of my charms; and as reaſon informs me this is equitable, I ſhall with the greateſt pleaſure comply with it.—While Zemroude expreſſed herſelf in this manner, ſhe embraced me with the warmeſt tranſports, and by a ſtrange mixture of contrarieties, I was at the ſame time enraged and enraptured. I admired her beauty and ſprightlineſs, but was offended at her indelicacy aud aſſurance: I was amazed how ſhe could ſo ſoon forget her misfortunes, and pay ſo little regard to her own character; in ſhort, I at the ſame time admired and deſpiſed her.—As I was ruminating on this ſtrange mixture

mixture of senſations, a perſon ruſhed furiouſly upon us, whom as ſoon as Zemroude perceived, ſhe cried, Good heavens! here is Hakem! Her huſband inſtantly plunging a dagger into her boſom, prevented her ſaying more. It was impoſſible for me to ward off the fatal blow, as Hakem had ſeized my ſabre which Zemroude had perſuaded me to put off; and as it was not now in my power to be of any ſervice to this unhappy wretch, I reſolved to revenge her death; and accordingly endeavoured to wrench my ſword from Hakem, who, ſtarting back, ſaid, Ah, my Lord, oblige me not to mingle your innocent blood with that of the vileſt of women! Can Prince Zeid, who has always acted with honour, and ſhewn himſelf proof againſt the allurements of pleaſure, become the patron of baſeneſs and perfidy. You, perhaps, do not credit what I ſay, continued he, as Zemroude may have given you impreſſions not much in my favour; but I conjure you, by the name of Oſmaide, to hear what I have to offer in my defence.—Being ſurpriſed at this requeſt, I interrupted him, and ſaid, with ſome eagerneſs, How came you acquainted with my paſſion for Oſmaide? and by what means do you know who I am? I will ſoon, replied Hakem, ſatisfy you as to theſe points; but let us, my Lord, retire from this object of horror, and let us leave both the ſhame and body of the wretched Zemroude buried in this retired place. Pleaſe to accept your ſword, for my ſincerity and innocence aſſure me you will not employ it to my prejudice.

I was greatly affected with Hakem's behaviour, which almoſt effaced the impreſſions Zemroude had given me of him; and following his ſteps, we retired to a private place, where ſitting down he began as follows.

I am a native of Gireſt: my mother was a diſciple

ciple of Ali, but my father was a follower of that fect who pay their adoration to fire, and was very zealous for that religion which was the firft of human invention; and as he difcovered that my mother privately inftructed me in the religion of Mahomet, he took me from her, and committed my education to a celebrated fage.—I looked upon that religion in which I was firft inftructed as the only true one; and the prejudices of education made me regard every other perfuafion as abfurd; but reafon and reflection at laft enlarged my ideas, and brought me to a more juft method of reafoning.—I confidered that thofe principles muft be moft eligible, that tended to the advancement of virtue, and the good of fociety, and the fole difficulty was to difcover what thefe were. As I had an infatiable thirft for knowledge, I thought experience and obfervation would, in time fettle my notions, and confequently refolved difpaffionately to examine all opinions, and in the interim to be directed by the dictates of nature.—With this view I left Tartary, and fpent near half my life in travelling in fearch of knowledge; but I could never come to any determination, as I found every where religion to be little more than a confufed mixture of good and bad principles, and eftablifhed by the craft of artful defigning men.—I judged every fpecies of worfhip abfurd in fpeculation, yet beneficial to the community; and I was as yet a ftranger to the profound and unfathomable fchemes of hypocrify.—If expence or danger are the fole characterifticks of generofity, the hypocrite muft be always looked upon as mean and pitiful; for he hazards nothing, the weaknefs and credulity of others being the fole inftruments he ufes, and bafely converts to his own vile purpofes thofe motives, which have the greateft influence on the human breaft.—I thus philofophically reafoned in my own

own mind, without being attached to any particular persuasion ; and was fully of opinion, that a hypocrite is capable of any thing, and that neither a regard to his character, or any other motive, will check his vicious pursuits.—The behaviour of the Dervises has but too much confirmed me in this opinion. Their sequestration from the rest of mankind, which they always involuntarily, or at least thoughtlessly enter into, makes them look upon themselves as detached from society, which they detest, and use every method in their power for its destruction. They scruple not to sacrifice the most important interests of the community to their own private advantage, and the sole employment of their retirement, is to invent methods of obstructing the pleasures and felicity of the rest of mankind. Instigated by envy, they are always watching an opportunity to execute their black designs, which they carefully conceal under a mask of religion.

I would have willingly disbelieved these base proceedings ; but being satisfied of their reality, I thoroughly detested their authors, and became determined to employ against the Dervises that indignation they have excited. By this means I shall satisfy my just revenge, and at the same time root out one error from the breasts of men, by which truth will flourish the stronger, whenever she shall deign to appear without disguise.—But it is necessary, in order to undeceive those who have been bred up in error, to continue the mask for some time, and artfully obstruct those rays of truth, which if permitted to burst upon them at once would dazzle their intellects.——The surprising secrets of every art and science, which I have acquired in the course of my travels, together with a perfect knowledge in the wonderful powers of nature, will make me be looked upon as a prophet, or even, if necessary, as a God ; for it is an easy matter to deceive

deceive those who court deception. And I am determined to extirpate those base Dervises, and the superstition that supports them. You will by and by perceive the reason of my forming such a design, and the occasion of that resentment which at present boils in my breast.——I have made mankind my study, without having any particular connections with them. I was at Bagdad when the Calif Mahadi married Osmaide, and lodged with the same old man who was so humane as to take care of you during your sickness. And as I was naturally inquisitive, I found your slave, like the rest of the fraternity, very communicative, and soon became acquainted with your love and misfortunes. I strongly interested myself in your destiny, and had recourse to every secret of Esculapius to preserve your life; I watchfully superintended your safety, dreading some bad consequences from the imprudence of your slave, whom, however, I prevailed with not to acquaint you with my assiduity in your service. I tried every method to recover your understanding, and knowing that employment is the best restorative to calm a disturbed mind, I excited you to revenge your cause, in order to prevent your melancholy reflections; I saw you set out for Yemen with this intent, and sent up my prayers for your success, which were not so fortunate as to be heard. As for myself, I soon after quitted Bagdad, and traversing many provinces arrived at last at Merou.—The inhabitants of that city are humane and hospitable, and my complaisance and generosity soon procured me many friends. It is an easy matter to gain the esteem of the good-natured and sensible part of mankind; and as I was possessed of large treasures, I thought I could not expend them better than in the purchase of favour and respect.—The Principal of the College of Dervises, being desirous to share in my liberality, courted my acquaintance; and disreregarding his motive, I ſoon entered into a ſtrict friendſhip with him. Cacem (for that was his name) beſides that turn for intrigue, which is common to all the fraternity, was poſſeſſed of extenſive knowledge, and great eloquence; but the receſſes of his heart were an inextricable labyrinth.—As he was very ſenſible of the extraordinary charms of his ſiſter Zemroude, he introduced me to her, in order to make ſure of me; and as I was before a ſtranger to love, I experienced with what violence that paſſion makes its firſt aſſault. He, however, ſoon put an end to my anxiety, and preſented me with the hand of the fair Zemroude, but reſerved her heart for himſelf.——I was too late ſenſible of my unhappy fate; I ſincerely wiſhed to be blind, for the light became odious to me, by making me a witneſs of Zemroude's ſhocking behaviour. I begged her to conceal her conduct from me, ſaying, diſſimulation is often a virtue in a woman, as it gives an air of modeſty, and may ſometimes even be a means of implanting that greateſt ornament of the fair ſex: it is, however, the only conſolation of an unhappy deſpiſed huſband, who, though too weak to baniſh his affection, may reſt ſatisfied under the perſuaſion of his wife's modeſty.—I enforced theſe reaſons by every method of behaviour I judged moſt likely to gain the heart of Zemroude; but her mind was too depraved to admit any ſuch impreſſions.—I experienced that grief and anxiety are ſo far from healing the wounds of love, that they make them the deeper. I had but at preſent an imperfect knowledge of my diſgrace, and was not as yet acquainted with the heinouſneſs of it. An impudent woman ſcorns to conceal her paſſions and inclinations; and whereas openneſs of temper in a virtuous diſpoſition is the parent of conſtancy and reſolution, in a vicious one, it is productive of ſhameful effrontery. I was abſolutely certain of Zemroude's inceſtuous paſſion; but

but how could I imagine that Cacem returned it! If, indeed, I credited my own ſurmiſes, he was as criminal as his ſiſter; but if I conſidered his great gravity and ſanctified converſation, it did not ſeem probable that he entertained ſuch a ſhocking thought.——I at laſt determined to inveſtigate this fatal truth; and with this view I put on a feigned compoſure of mind, and pretended that I was under an indiſpenſible obligation of taking a long journey. I diſguiſed myſelf by blacking my face and hands, and by this means I got eaſy admiſſion into the college of the Derviſes, by mixing with their ſlaves. —Here I ſoon became an unhappy evidence of my own ſhame and their wickedneſs. Good heavens! it was impoſſible for me to have conceived their ſhocking vileneſs. The abandoned Zemroude did not only gratify her brother's horrid luſt, but by turns that of all the reſt of the vile fraternity. I cannot expreſs the violent reſentment this conviction excited in my breaſt; I would have inſtantly put Zemroude and her paramours to the ſevereſt torture, if my power had been equal to my paſſion. But, upon recollection, I judged it beſt to ſuppreſs my rage at preſent, that I might more amply revenge my diſgrace.—I left the fatal college, planning a thouſand ſchemes to ſatiate my vengeance, and my mind being thus occupied, prevented my falling into deſpair. I compoſed a ſlow imperceptible poiſon, and gave it thoſe baſe wretches, in whoſe veins it now operates, and they will all of them die within two days. I was returning to Merou to compleat my revenge; but diſcovering Zemroude in the arms of her brother, my fury was rekindled to ſuch a degree, that I was unable to ſuppreſs it. I haſtened the laſt moments of the infamous Cacem, upon which Zemroude fled, and purſuing her I was upon the point of plunging a dagger into her breaſt, when a remaining ſpark of love checked my uplifted

uplifted arm. I blushed at my weakness, and dreaded the consequence of my unbridled passion; and thereupon I tied her to a tree, and on your approach retired. When you had released her, I followed at a distance, and was a witness of your virtue and constancy; I heard Zemroude's solicitations, and was ashamed that I had suffered such a monster of lust to exist: I have now freed society from a member that was a scandal to human nature; and her death has not cost me one sigh, for my affection is entirely extinguished by her unparallelled infamy.—If you will venture, Sir, continued Hakem, to trust yourself with me, I will, as soon as I have compleated my revenge on the Dervises, exert my utmost efforts in favour of your passion. I look upon myself as adequate to any enterprize, and the sincere friendship and esteem I have for you will easily surmount every obstacle.——This agreeable proposal made me look upon some circumstances in the foregoing narration with a more favourable eye; for we are always indulgent to those who have it in their power to be serviceable to us.——I judged by what Hakem had said, that he was of a frank, open disposition; and I knew from experience, that persons of a violent temper are generally most sincere. I was moreover under great obligations to him for his former kindnesses, and therefore readily accepted his proposal. We repaired to Merou, where Hakem had already acquired great credit and esteem; he assembled the inhabitants, and informed them of the hypocrisy and vile practices of the Dervises, and foretold their sudden deaths, as a punishment for their impostures. His prophecy was verified by the fact; and he soon acquired such an esteem for sanctity, that he was held in the highest veneration by a great part of the inhabitants of Asia.—I must own, that I had some remorse for having any connection with a person of Hakem's disposition; but a violent passion

paſſion often warps our integrity ; and
heart may at firſt recoil, it generally in .
ſubmits. Love, of all the paſſions, ſooneſt ſtiile
remorſe ; for being founded on opinion, which has the greateſt influence on the ſoul, it eaſily hoodwinks the underſtanding.—I am now come to that period when I was to reap the fruits of my criminal union with Hakem. I ſaw you, and though before I ſhould have looked upon it as the ſummit of felicity to be permitted to proſtrate myſelf at your feet, and breathe my ſighs at the ſhrine of your beauty, yet when I obtained this happineſs, my tranſports hurried me to an enjoyment I had not before entertained the leaſt thought of. It is unneceſſary for me to deſcribe to you my extaſy, as I flatter myſelf love has engraved it on your heart, and that the image of the enamoured Zeid in the caſtle of Hakem will always apologize in your breaſt for the wretched Aſſad. You may remember we lay intoxicated in the arms of pleaſure, when a ſhocking noiſe obliged us to part. I haſtened to Hakem, and informed him of my ſuſpicions, which were ſoon confirmed by one of my ſlaves, who ſaid, that he had ſeen Manſor go out of the tower in diſguiſe. Hakem immediately ordered the gates to be ſhut, and by promiſing them aſſiſtance from heaven, and certain victory, he eaſily prevailed with his ſlaves and diſciples to undertake the defence of the place. At laſt, having animated them by every conſideration our diſtreſſed circumſtances ſuggeſted, he took me aſide, and ſaid,—Moſt noble Prince, all is over, I am diſappointed of the glory of freeing mankind from error; I have, however, the honour of attempting it, and the pleaſure of having revenged the treatment I received, together with the ſatisfaction of having been inſtrumental to your happineſs, though it was but momentary! All that remains, is to make a noble exit, for it is not fitting that Hakem ſhould expoſe himſelf

ignominious treatment of his enemies! resolved that even my death shall be fatal to them, as it will confirm my followers, which are numerous all over Asia, in that abhorrence I have given them for superstition, and for those who make that a pretence to oppress them!—But the illustrious Prince Zeid shall not be buried under my ruins: depart before the tower is invested, for one person may easily escape the observation of the enemy, who are as yet at some distance, and being unknown and in disguise, you may easily avoid the resentment of Mahadi.—I rejected Hakem's proposal, thinking it base to abandon him in the distress he had incurred on my account.—By no means, my dear Prince, said he, for I do not look upon your offering to die with me, as a token of your affection. I can composedly meet that moment which is the unavoidable lot of mortality; but if you are a joint sufferer, I shall dread that fate which I otherwise should despise. If, therefore, you have any regard for me, weaken not my resolution; but preserve your life, that you may spread my fame when I am gone, and pretend to admire my miraculous death.—These arguments not being sufficient to divert me from my purpose, he added, Well, my Lord, your excessive generosity increases my affection, and to oblige you, I will not shorten my days, though my glory being vanished, and my expectations frustrated, life will soon be a burthen to me. It is, however, solely in your power to prevent the execution of my intention; as it would be ridiculous to stand a siege in this defenceless place, do you go into the neighbouring forest, where you will find a great number of my followers assembled, by a private order I have sent them; inform them of the danger I am in, and bring them to my assistance. We may probably conquer Mahadi, whose troops will be intimidated with the apprehension of fighting against a Prophet, and mine will be animated

animated by the glory of preſerving their legiſlator. And if it ſhould ſo happen, that we fall in this attempt, we ſhall die upon the bed of honour, and in our own defence.—This plan ſeemed to me very plauſible; for as Hakem had repaired the tower, he might eaſily defend himſelf there until the arrival of the ſuccours I went in ſearch of. Accordingly I left him, and traverſed every part of the foreſt, without being able to find the perſons I was in queſt of. I was at length informed of the laſt efforts of his barbarous magnanimity, and reflected with horror on the juſtice of heaven in detecting ſuch an artful impoſture.

I was, however, greatly affected by the loſs of Hakem, for I had an eſteem for him, and palliated all his crimes. He was naturally of a virtuous diſpoſition, and his becoming vicious was ſolely to puniſh vice, and he wore the maſk of religion only to promote the intereſt of virtue.—Some legiſlators and reformers have, in like manner, been neceſſitated to commit unwarrantable actions; but have they not always preferred the public to private utility? And can either this maxim, or their proceedings, be called in queſtion? The death of Mahadi and Manſor, and the dangerous ſituation I underſtood you were in, renewed my grief and anxiety.—I was at this time in the houſe of a Jeweſs, who had been one of my ſlaves when I lived in Yemen; and as I had given her her liberty, I could depend on her making the moſt grateful returns in her power. This was the perſon that conveyed my letter to you, and returned with your anſwer, which inſtantly overpowered all my faculties. The ſhame and deſpair of having plunged you into ſuch an abyſs of miſery, recovered me from this lethargy, and ſuggeſted the only way it was in my power to be of ſervice to you. The method appeared indeed at firſt ſight ſhocking; but my love, repreſenting it as

ab-

abſolutely neceſſary, greatly mitigated the horror of the attempt. Oſmaide is probably the only woman in the world that would have ſet a juſt value on ſuch a ſacrifice, for a cold acknowledgement would have been all the return I ſhould have met with from any other.——Zeid having finiſhed his narration, continued Oſmaide, I readily promiſed to comply with the utmoſt of his deſires; but my looks and tranſports, which ſpoke the language of my ſoul, were ſtronger evidences of my affection than words.—Zeid, being ſo fortunate as to reſtore the tranquillity of my mind, procured the advancement of Aſſad; for he ſucceeded Meſrour, whom Haroun, who at this time mounted the throne, appointed chief of the eunuchs in his new ſeraglio. —I gave birth to Zelia whom Zeid committed to the care of Repiſma, the Jeweſs he had formerly ſent to me; at the ſame time ſtrictly charging her, not to give her ward the leaſt hint relating to herſelf, or the Supreme, for he juſtly dreaded the blind zeal of a perſon prejudiced in favour of a falſe religion; and I had now reſtored Zeid to that pious way of judging and acting, which his acquaintance with Hakem had in ſome meaſure warped.—We ſpent our time in devotion, and thought that heaven, in return for our piety, gave a poignancy to our pleaſures we could not have expected in our preſent wretched ſituation.——But I was deprived of the pleaſure I had flattered myſelf with enjoying in frequently viſiting my dear Zelia, for I had too many eyes upon me to venture myſelf often in that obſcure retirement; and I was moreover, as ſhe advanced in years, diſtruſtful of her diſcretion. We by no means intended to keep her always immured in that dark receſs, which we judged the propereſt place for her, during her infancy, and from whence we could not prudently remove her, after we had entruſted her to the care of Repiſma. We afterwards com-

committed the care of her education to Fatima, being thoroughly ſatisfied of the prudence and virtue of that good woman; and as ſoon as Zelia became capable of that happineſs we intended for her, we were reſolved to put her in poſſeſſion of it with all convenient diſpatch. With this view, I was to procure Aſſad a permiſſion to viſit his native country, and we had agreed that he ſhould take Zelia and Fatima along with him, and that his father ſhould go in queſt of Giafar, and make him an offer of Zelia as his own daughter. We could not have fixed on a more worthy and amiable perſon for her huſband; and by this means we might have enjoyed the pleaſure of ending our days with the object of our mutual affection. We intended alſo to have given Fatima her liberty, and rewarded her ſuitable to her merits; for as ſhe was a ſtranger to our ſecret, we had nothing to fear from her; and though ſhe had been privy to the affair, we had a greater opinion of her honour than to dread her betraying us. But an angry unappeaſed God has baffled all our deſigns.—Upon your diſcovering Zelia, Zeid gave himſelf wholly to deſpair; as his honour would not permit him to divulge the ſecret, and as he clearly foreſaw the torments he muſt ſuffer from a rational curioſity, ſupported by abſolute power, he preferred death to diſgrace. And I ſhould have followed his example, if my affection for Zelia, and a regard to her happineſs, had not prevailed upon me to preſerve my wretched life.

Your blind criminal paſſion, continued Oſmaide, addreſſing her ſon, ſoon made me repent this ſtep, as every method I employed to oppoſe it proved ineffectual. All my hopes depended on the return of Giafar, to whom I intended communicating the ſecret, and leaving it to his prudent management. With this view I wrote to him that your tranquillity and honour were in imminent danger, being aſſured

 he

he would inſtantly fly to your aſſiſtance; and moreover, as an end was now put to the war with the Greeks, I thought he would make all poſſible haſte home, in obedience to your orders. I alſo begged a reſpite of Zelia, which proved too ſhort for my deſigns, and you have neceſſitated me to divulge my misfortunes and crimes; and that ſuſpicion which I have obſerved in you as to my honour and ſincerity, has obliged me not to omit the leaſt circumſtance in this narrative.——This is probably the laſt advice I ſhall have the opportunity of giving my dear Zelia, and I flatter myſelf that more ſalutary inſtructions could not have been conveyed by any other method. For, from my example, and that of Zeid and Hakem, ſhe may obſerve the dreadful conſequences of guilt, and learn to ſhun the allurements of pleaſure, and the fatal effects of unbridled paſſion.—As for you, my ſon, I beg you will pardon the ſhame and anxiety I have occaſioned you! I perceive by thoſe trickling tears you are deeply affected with my melancholy tale! Compaſſionate the ſufferings of an unhappy parent, and plunge me not again into deſpair! Examine your own breaſt, and if you find virtue predominant, enjoy as much of Zelia's company as you pleaſe, and treat her with the affection of a brother! but if the leaſt ſpark of a criminal paſſion is ſmothered in your heart, ſedulouſly avoid the object that may rekindle its fury, fly the converſation of Zelia, and permit her to retire for ever from your preſence; in ſhort, I humbly intreat you not to perpetuate the ſhame and guilt of your unhappy mother.——I can by no means, replied the Calif with great rapture, part with Zelia; I ſhall not be able to ſupport life without her agreeable company! for though I have now entirely eradicated my criminal affection, yet I am aſſured the abſence of Zelia would rekindle the flame. Reaſon and virtue cannot influence a mind where paſſion is predominant,

dominant, and absence would tear open the wound which is at present closed, and render it more dangerous than ever.—Osmaide was very sorry to hear such proofs of indifference, as carried the most evident marks of a violent love: she pretended, however, to believe them; for to express a diffidence in a person is the greatest of discouragements; and the surest method to confirm men in their affection and duty, is seldom to distrust but that they really are such as they ought and pretend to be, for suspicion always implies a possibility of their being otherwise!

Osmaide's recital of her adventures, gave Zelia such an insight into human nature as greatly astonished her. I thought, said she to Fatima, that your instructions had carried my ideas as high as it was possible for them to go, and that the knowledge of such things as are not the objects of sense admitted of no improvement; but my mother's narrative has convinced me of the contrary. It has had the same effect on my mind, as the light of the sun had on my senses; and example has given me a more thorough knowledge of the passions than the most abstruse reasonings could possibly have done. Is my knowledge limited? Or by what means may I prosecute my researches into human nature?—By examining your own breast, replied Fatima; Osmaide's narration has enlarged your understanding by touching your passions; this is an effect peculiar to history, and which vague abstracted reasonings have no pretence to. On this account, those who record the motives and actions of mankind, are judged worthy of the highest esteem, as their labours are of the utmost service to society. The most profound philosophy will leave no lasting impressions on the mind if it does not touch the heart. And even the flowery wilds of fable, when it tends to inculcate some useful moral, is preferable to insipid truth.—

He

He is not to be looked upon as the wisest man, who has the most intimate acquaintance with nature, for all our researches can make no addition to her operations: this title only belongs to him who best understands the human heart, and the surest method of inducing mankind to virtue, and in order thereto is master of such language as will rouse their passions. It has been the maxim of the greatest geniuses in all ages, that this is the best method of instruction; they have accordingly proceeded on this plan, and their fame is proportionable to the great advantages mankind have reaped from their labours, while the dry abstruse systems of philosophy procure but little honour to their authors, and are of no service to mankind.—You may still attain to larger degrees of knowledge. History affords us very useful instructions, but not equal to those we acquire by experience. If you should one time or other feel those passions which Osmaide has so strongly described, your notions then will be as different from what they are now, as a real from a painted object! but heaven shield you from such lessons!—Be not under any apprehensions, interrupted Zelia; every thing at present seems to insure my tranquillity. My brother's passion is the only thing that can at present disturb my peace of mind; but this cannot be attended with that pleasing anxiety and agreeable distress which Osmaide has just described in so lively a manner. Shall I confess the real truth? A compassionate concern was not the only emotion of my heart during her narration, an opposite sensation sometimes arose in my breast. I even envied Osmaide's misfortunes, as they seemed to be greatly overbalanced by the pleasures that attended them; and this sensation would have been predominant, if it had not been checked by her using the term *criminal.* But may not a person be innocently happy? If Osmaide had felt that warm, sincere affection for

for Mahadi which ſhe had for Zeid, ſhe would undoubtedly have enjoyed the moſt compleat felicity, without caſting any blemiſh on her virtue; and if my mother's deſign had took place, if I had been married to Giafar, and if I had loved him, how conſummately happy ſhould I have been? If you are ſufficiently acquainted with Giafar, my dear Fatima, to be able to gratify my curioſity, pray inform me whether the diſappointment merits my concern?—Giafar is the ſon of the Vizir Jahia, replied Fatima, whom you heard Oſmaide mention; he is deſcended from the ancient family of the Bermicides, who have always been as renowned for their virtue as their illuſtrious origin; and he has embelliſhed a fine majeſtic perſon with the moſt rare and valuable accompliſhments of the mind. As your brother and he were bred up together in the moſt affectionate friendſhip, the Calif honours him with an unlimited confidence, and his power is almoſt abſolute; but he uſes it in ſuch a manner as to ſilence the malevolence of envy. The afflicted and miſerable come from every quarter to implore his aſſiſtance; and diſtreſs, which has often the contrary effect, is the ſureſt recommendation to his patronage. By a judicious diſtribution of praiſe and premiums, he every where excites a noble emulation. You ſee him ſometimes employed in replacing a virtuous prince upon his throne, which had been unjuſtly uſurped; ſometimes inſtructing the ſages, though he pretends to conſult them.—Giafar has, by his valour, obliged all his maſter's enemies to ſubmit, and by rendering them happy, has inſured their allegiance.——I perceive, continued Fatima, that you ſigh, my dear Zelia; you probably imagine that you would have been moſt compleatly happy if you had been married to Giafar. Be not anxious on that account, as ſuch a ſtep would have rendered you the moſt miſerable of mortals.——As I had a great intimacy, and the most cordial friendship with his brother Mahomed, I by that means became acquainted with Giafar's disposition. He is an entire stranger to the pleasing pangs of love, and the most striking beauty has never made the least impression on his heart. Tenderness of heart, that necessary harbinger of love, is not the ruling quality in his mind, whose excellency arises solely from a good natural disposition, which he has carefully improved by virtue.——But is not gratitude a virtue, replied Zelia? and would not this have induced Giafar to make a suitable return to that affection I should undoubtedly have expressed for him? Nothing, interrupted Fatima, will pass currency in return for love, but love; this is one of those truths which you can alone learn from experience.—I clearly perceive your meaning, Fatima, replied Zelia. Our disquisitions on this subject are now useless; I must content myself with the enjoyment of your friendship, and endeavour to reinstate my brother's understanding, and replace in his breast that grandeur and dignity of sentiment which till now have rendered him a miracle of human nature; I must, in short, dedicate myself wholly to these, and my duty to a tender affectionate parent, whose misfortunes, and even failings, have rendered her more dear to me.

While Zelia and Fatima spent their time in such-like conversation, the Calif's breast became a prey to contending passions, and he was but too fully convinced that one conquest over love by no means insures our future tranquillity.—Giafar, far from suspecting such a fatal proof of Irene's hypothesis on love, indulged himself in a continual round of pleasure, which that Princess had the art to administer without satiety, and to make herself every day appear more charming. He flattered himself that the Calif also enjoyed all that luxury of pleasure which

which a warm conſtitution, and an agreeable miſtreſs, are capable of affording; and that he alſo experienced that delightful paſſion, which, though inferior to love, as to the degree of felicity, is probably the more pleaſing of the two.

After he had concluded a treaty greatly to the honour and advantage of his maſter, he gave the reins to his paſſions, and in gratitude to the Empreſs, whoſe charms he every day more admired, made a ſuitable return to her addreſſes. Theſe connections, which have always great influence on a generous and paſſionate breaſt, detained him at Conſtantinople, when he was informed that his preſence was abſolutely neceſſary at Bagdad.—He was alarmed by Oſmaide's letter; and could not conceive what it was endangered the glory of a Prince, who, ſo long as he followed the dictates of his own heart, could never act unbecoming his character, or be guilty of any ſtep derogatory to his honour. And his anxiety was increaſed by Haroun's preſſing ſollicitations for the return of his companion and boſom-friend.—Though Irene was unacquainted with the motives, yet ſhe ſhared in the uneaſineſs of Giafar, whom ſhe was not able to detain longer than was requiſite for a ſhort but affectionate adieu, which their mutual paſſion would not diſpenſe with, and promiſed her to return as ſoon as he could poſſibly leave Bagdad.

Oſmaide, by reflecting on her paſt misfortunes, and dreading that fatal event which ſhe but too clearly foreſaw, became every day more and more melancholy. One while ſhe lamented the loſs of Zeid, another, ſhe was anxious on account of her ſon's affection for Zelia; for ſhe was but too ſenſible that the flame, notwithſtanding his endeavours to extinguiſh it, was only ſmothered: and how deeply was ſhe affected, when ſhe conſidered, that ſhe had been the occaſion of endangering the virtue of a

 ſon,

fon, who had hitherto been the fole comfort and honour of her life, and who, by his renown for virtue, and an abfolute command over himfelf, had exalted her to the higheft pinnacle of glory !—She at firft wifhed to conceal Zelia's parentage from the public ; but, upon fecond thoughts, fhe judged it would be more prudent to facrifice her own reputation for the fecurity of her fon's virtue, reflecting, that as the fear of cenfure is often the ftrongeft barrier of duty, the making this affair public might be a means of extinguifhing his criminal paffion. She therefore entreated the Calif publickly to acknowledge Zelia his fifter, with which he readily complied, confidering it only as a ftep to enhance the dignity of this adorable Princefs.—The hiftory and fate of Affad was kept a fecret ; and when the Calif acknowledged Zelia for his fifter, he alfo proclaimed her the daughter of Mahadi.—This furprifing affair called to people's minds the laft words of that Prince, and was the foundation of various conjectures, which it was not fafe to divulge. But as habit and fear have a ftrong influence on the mind, that was foon looked upon as fact, which the people were at firft obliged to acknowledge as fuch. —Zelia took the title of Abbaffah, which is appropriated to the fifter of the Calif, and dreffed in black, which is the characteriftic of the Abbaffides. This colour gave a new brilliancy to her charms, and was a great improvement to her complexion and perfon. ——Though this new ftep increafed Zelia's graces, and confequently the Calif's paffion, yet it laid that unhappy Prince under the greater reftraint of concealing his love. Haroun, neverthelefs, fometimes forgot the unfurmountable obftacle of his felicity ; but Abbaffah always reminded him that fhe was his fifter, which obliged him to behave as a brother. It is a difficult tafk to keep the paffion of love under proper reftraint, and the Calif's extraordinary civility

and

and complaisance soon informed the whole court of a passion which it was equally his desire and duty to conceal.—A person of simplicity and integrity seldom distrusts the virtue of others; and notwithstanding the encomiums Giafar had given Irene of Zobeide, the real character of that Princess was quite the reverse. She was false and perfidious; malice and artifice supplied the place of wisdom and understanding; she had hitherto been always so successful in her schemes, that her hypocrisy and dissimulation had never been detected. Moreover, we generally disregard the vices of others, unless we dread some immediate danger from them, or have formerly been sufferers by them; and those countries are most exempt from these inconveniencies that are strangers to the pleasures of society; though in these the people are generally the most abandoned, because their actions are less liable to inspection.——Zobeide expressed a great desire to see Abbassah, with which the Calif was much pleased, and gave her leave to spend a few days in the old seraglio. Osmaide also greatly approved of this visit, as she thought her presence would be a check upon Haroun. Zobeide instantly affected the warmest friendship for Abbassah, though envy was the predominant passion in her breast: but she did not, however, suffer her presence to be any restraint upon the Calif, and always retired when he came to visit his sister.—This behaviour could not give the least suspicion of jealousy, as it had not any resemblance of that which is founded on love: but this passion had been long a stranger to Zobeide's breast; the jealousy she at present laboured under was that which arises from self-love, which is generally fertile in black designs, and can patiently wait for an opportunity to execute them. As Zobeide had diligently studied Haroun's temper and disposition, she knew that any obstacle to his pleasure, which was not the result of his own re-

reflection, tended only to inflame his passions, and hurry him into those extravagances he otherwise would have avoided. She thought, that his conquering his passion for Zeinib at the instant she promised to gratify the utmost of his wishes, arose from this turn of mind; for it is impossible to make a just estimate of a generous action, if our own breast is a stranger to that most excellent of social virtues.—Zobeide, however, rationally concluded, that as Haroun was naturally of a virtuous disposition, which he had improved by practice, he could not easily dispense with his duty; and that the struggles of virtue might turn the scale, or at least ballance the violence of his passion. She reflected that a person will not plead guilty that is conscious of his own innocence. Thus relying upon the Calif's principles for the recovery of his affection, she determined to seduce him into the commission of a crime which would give her ample revenge upon Abbassah for the triumph of her beauty.—— This shocking scheme, which could only be hatched in the most abandoned breast, she artfully executed. She prevailed with Abbassah to accompany her to her own apartment, where she induced her to bathe, and contrived that she should come out of the bath a little before the arrival of the Calif, whose company she had sent to request; and at the same time gave her a strong opiate mixed in some sherbet.— When the Calif arrived, Abbassah was fallen into a profound sleep; and Zobeide running to meet him, said, As the Princess has done me the honour of this visit, I was determined you should share in my pleasure; but her spirits being overcome with the heat, she is fallen asleep, and I beg we may not disturb her repose.—Upon this she drew the curtains of the bed where Abbassah was lying, and whose charms were only covered with a loose garment of crimson-gawse. The Calif, dazzled by such a blaze

of

of beauty, did not, for ſome time, obſerve that Zobeide had quitted the room.—How charming! ſaid he, attentively ſurveying her beauty. But, O heavens! ſhe is my ſiſter, and this cruel circumſtance renders me for ever miſerable! Alas, Oſmaide! why were you not more innocent, or more reſolute when guilty? Your crime and your virtue are equally my tormentors! why did you give birth to Zelia, or why did you divulge the fatal ſecret?——But checking himſelf, he continued, What am I ſaying? Can Haroun entertain a wiſh ſo derogatory to his honour! What! have I not already extinguiſhed a lawful and honourable flame! and ſhall I now fall the victim of a paſſion equally interdicted by religion and nature? But, alas! love is not to be conquered by braving his power; I refrained ſeeing Zeinib after my determination, it is therefore my duty to avoid the preſence of Abbaſſah.—This ſo laudable and neceſſary a reſolution was checked by Abbaſſah's moving, and giving him a more full and irreſiſtible ſurvey of her charms. The Calif, dreading her indignation if ſhe awoke, and conſcious of his guilt, ſtept back: but dragged as it were by an invincible, though inviſible force, he again approached the bed, and found that ſhe was ſtill faſt aſleep, and in a more tempting poſition than before.—It was now impoſſible for him to reſiſt the tranſports of his paſſion: Love fluttered the wings of triumph, and Reaſon and Virtue, as they had often done before, again acknowledged his ſovereignty. Hâroun had claſped his ſiſter in his arms, and imprinted a thouſand extatic kiſſes on her lips, and his enraptured eyes now ſhewed no mark of guilt, when the entrance of Oſmaide checked the progreſs of his pleaſure.—Zobeide had in vain attempted to prevent this Princeſs from interrupting her plot: ſhe ruſhed precipitately into the room; but how was ſhe ſhocked at ſuch an unexpected ſight! She threw herſelf upon her

her daughter, and inftantly became equally infenfible; her agonies were fo violent, that her life feemed to be in danger! The Calif, over-whelmed with confufion, endeavoured to conceal his fhame; his blufhes were redoubled when he was informed of Giafar's arrival, which had been the occafion of Ofmaide's waiting upon him, for a guilty confcience dreads a rigid and upright friend.

Haroun would have fled, if his love for Zelia, and affection for Ofmaide, had not detained him, and as it were nailed him to that fatal fpot which he had made a fcene of woe. It was impoffible to leave in fuch a fituation what was moft dear to him in life, and the diftrefs he had occafioned greatly enforced his refolution not to quit the room; but his fear, his compaffion, and every circumftance, tended to the increafe of his love.—While all prefent were bufily employed in affifting Ofmaide, Abbaffah opened her languifhing eyes, and perceived, by a glimmering ray that pierced the thick vapour which clouded them, her mother expiring, the Calif funk in grief and confufion, and Fatima, who had accompanied Ofmaide, bathed in tears! This affemblage of mifery at laft made an impreffion upon her, and difpelled that lethargy that clogged her fenfes. Alas, my mother, faid fhe! what is the meaning of thefe agonies? why do you fo much indulge your grief, as to keep me in perpetual alarms for your life? Will you forfake your Zelia, when you have promifed to live folely for her? O heavens! what is the meaning of thofe forbidding glances? Do you reject with fcorn my affection and affiduity? Am I become odious to you? Acquaint me with the caufe of this fevereft of my afflictions!—O my dear fifter! cried the Calif, what queftion do you afk? Thy fifter, interrupted Ofmaide! How can'ft thou pronounce that facred name which thou haft bafely

violated,

violated, and made the unhappy Zelia the victim of thy horrid passion!—Hold, replied the Calif, I acknowledge myself greatly culpable, but I did not enjoy that felicity you seem to hint at. What an expression! replied Osmaide, in a transport of rage. What! can he, whose heart was the residence of virtue, can he call the most violent outrage against God and nature a felicity? As the heat of passion is now subsided, what can palliate such language? Has vice got the absolute ascendancy over his mind? Has love destroyed his former good dispositions? Haroun, from henceforward, instead of rendering himself renowned for his virtue in the annals of mankind, will become a scandal to human nature by his unbridled passions! I, alas! am principally to blame: all this wickedness ought to be placed to my account, and I pray heaven may speedily chastise my complicated crimes.

Having thus spoke Osmaide again fainted, and upon coming to herself was seized with a violent fever.—The horror of Abbassah was inexpressible; she stood in solemn silence, and with a wild disordered countenance, cast such resentful glances on the Calif, as that prince, more miserable than herself, was not able to bear.—Neither of them for two days quitted Osmaide, who, during that time, was in such a violent delirium, as to be ignorant even of her own existence. The fermentation of the blood being at last abated by that languor which generally precedes dissolution, Osmaide came to herself and perceived that her last moments were approaching.—I am going, said she, in a faultering accent, I am going, my dear children, and may my death appease the offended Supreme, secure the innocence of Zelia, and re-establish the virtue of Haroun! O my son, continued she, addressing the Calif, lament not the arrival of my last moments!

It

It is in your power to make them happy. Come no more into the presence of that dangerous fatal object; marry Abbassah suiting her rank, and by that means secure her happiness and your virtue: if I could but hope this, I should die in peace! —Be assured of it, Madam, said the Calif, and live. I swear by the Almighty, Zelia shall be married! I command you, daughter, resumed Osmaide, to hasten the execution of this oath, and ever to bear in mind the sad, but instructive lesson of my woes. I am at last, my dear Zeid, continued she, coming to join you! and whatever may be our lot, whether that courage and those afflictions which shortened our days, be adjudged culpable or commendable, we shall in both cases be inseparably united.

Osmaide having thus spoke, expired in the arms of her daughter—Fatima forced Zelia reluctantly to leave the dear, but affecting remains, and diligently attended her unhappy friend. Friendship, by sharing our woes, lessens the burden; and Fatima mitigated the grief of Abbassah, while Giafar checked the despair of Haroun.—Filial affection, the rage of disappointed love, the shame of a criminal passion, the remorse of a virtuous disposition, what a brood of racking thoughts to take possession of one breast! The Calif was consequently seized with a violent delirium, and raving was the only token of his existence! One while he solicited Giafar and Mesrour, who constantly attended him, to put an end to his life; at another, he fell into a most violent passion, because they had not executed his orders. Giafar could not, from his rambling incoherent discourse, collect the cause of his despair; and though Mesrour was acquainted with the secret, he durst not inform him.—The passions of the mind resemble the disorders of the body, they are entirely similar in their

their increaſe and decline; their violence weakens their force, and hence we frequently miſtake the moments of inſenſibility and ſullen melancholy for intervals of eaſe and tranquillity.—Giafar having catched one of theſe favourable opportunities, threw himſelf at the Calif's feet, and ſaid, Do you give yourſelf up to deſpair, Sir, without informing me of the cauſe? Am I deprived of your eſteem and confidence? Alas! reinſtate in theſe valuable poſſeſſions a faithful ſubject, who never miſapplied your friendſhip, an active and honeſt miniſter, who never baſely concealed the truth! Put an end to that gloomy ſilence, or my life, which will be a burden, if not employed in your ſervice, and odious, if you diſtruſt my affection and integrity.—I entertain no ſuch doubts, my dear Giafar, replied the Calif, and a thorough knowledge of your virtuous diſpoſition is what determines me to bury this horrid ſecret in eternal oblivion. Alas! you alone of all I loved, have ſtill an affectionate regard for me! But what do I ſay? I will haſten my final deſpair: liſten to, and fly from an unhappy man, guilty of the blackeſt crimes. Can he, whom you ſtile maſter and friend, deſerve your compaſſion after committing inceſt and parricide? I conjure you inſtantly to abandon a wretch who abhors himſelf!—I abandon you, Sir, replied Giafar, closely embracing the Calif's knees in order to conceal his aſtoniſhment; I leave you! Can my heart, though I were not your ſlave, condemn you? Can a friend, though ever ſo guilty, become odious? It is impoſſible; for friendſhip was never the miniſter of juſtice, as it always palliates thoſe crimes which it cannot prevent. And in my opinion, Sir, if you are guilty of thoſe vices you charge yourſelf with, it was not in your power to avoid them, and repentance will ſoon re-eſtabliſh your virtue.—Repentance! Heavens! what an uncertain,

certain, hazardous remedy is that? The gulf ſeems perpetually to yawn under my feet; and ſuch is my ſituation, that it is impoſſible to avoid falling into it. Liſten, and I will inform you what confuſion wild extravagant paſſions have occaſioned in that breaſt, which you may remember the ſeat of virtue.

Haroun then gave Giafar a detail of his paſſion for Abbaſſah, and the various misfortunes and calamities he had ſuffered during his abſence.—Giafar was greatly affected by this ſurpriſing narrative, which however greatly diminiſhed his anxiety and concern for his friend; for he had literally underſtood what the Calif had before ſaid; whereas this full narration ſet things in a different light, and that which before he judged the moſt horrid crime, appeared now only a human frailty, which though dangerous was yet pardonable.—Can you, Sir, ſaid he to Haroun, can you deſpair of re-eſtabliſhing the throne of virtue in your breaſt, where ſhe is ſtill the predominant principle? Would you now hear her voice if ſhe had entirely deſerted you? By no means; for contrition was never the language of an abandoned diſpoſition? Doubt not obtaining a compleat victory over your preſent temptations, as every circumſtance ſeems to aſſure it. Give not yourſelf to deſpair, which always ruins the faireſt projects; reſtore the reins to reaſon, and ſhake off that lethargy which at preſent ſhackles your mind, whoſe tone, as it is an active principle, is relaxed, and is entirely deſtroyed by ſupineneſs and indolence. Dry up your tears, you have ſufficiently lamented the death of Oſmaide, and the moſt rational concern, if extended beyond due bounds, becomes criminal.—But Abbaſſah! ſaid the Calif in a mournful accent.—You muſt avoid ſeeing her, interrupted Giafar, and for that reaſon leave her in the old ſeraglio.

ſeraglio. You ſhall again enjoy the pleaſure of her company, when you ſhall be able to look upon her as an amiable ſiſter, and not as a moſt dangerous enemy.—O Abbaſſah, ſaid the Calif, muſt we for ever, ever part? Having ſo ſaid, he got up, and with a diſturbed anxious countenance, and haſty ſteps, quitted the room. Giafar notwithſtanding followed him, and having prevailed on him to ſtop, after gazing ſome time in ſullen ſilence, he broke into the following unconnected exclamation.

O Oſmaide! O unhappy cruel parent! I muſt then obey your commands.—I muſt punctually fulfil my oath, for I ſhould ſeverely puniſh ſuch an omiſſion in another!—Alas! why cannot I enjoy the company of Abbaſſah, after having voluntarily reſtored Zeinib to her lover, even when ſhe conſented to make me happy!—But there is one method of fulfilling my obligation without falling a ſacrifice to my cruel fate!—He has ſufficiently merited my confidence and eſteem, to be entruſted with this important affair!—But, good heavens! can I be guilty of ſuch barbarity! Such a ſtep will probably make him for ever miſerable! —No, friendſhip deſpiſes danger!—O my dear and faithful friend, continued Haroun, embracing Giafar, my peace of mind, honour, virtue, and life, are ſolely in your power! But, good God! upon what conſideration! The reinſtating me in theſe bleſſings will probably be a means of depriving you of all of them!—Be more explicit, Sir, ſaid Giafar, I ſhall judge nothing impracticable that will promote your happineſs, even my life.

What I ſhall requeſt, interrupted Haroun, is of higher importance than life! You muſt marry my ſiſter, you muſt live conſtantly with her, be daily expoſed, not only to her beauty, but heavens! to her endearing careſſes; and you muſt nevertheleſs reſiſt

resist these allurements; behave to her as your own sister, without discovering the cause of this strange indifference. What do you say, continued he, can you oblige me in this? Diligently examine your friendship, your courage, and virtue, and if you think, after due deliberation, that you are equal to such an arduous task, assure me by the most sacred oath that you will punctually observe these conditions.—Ah, Sir, replied Giafar, this is but a trifle; I could with pleasure, for your happiness, comply with much severer terms! I possibly may never experience that violence of affection which by many is judged invincible; but if I should, I swear by the Almighty, the author of my being; I swear by your sacred name, that I will never consider nor behave to Abbassah otherwise than a sister! May I, if I violate this oath, feel the weight of your resentment, and, which is the more shocking consideration, may I be deprived of your friendship and esteem.

If only my life and crown, replied Haroun, had been at stake, your word would have been sufficient; but in this more important affair, I judged a stronger security necessary. Observe what comfort your promise, like a healing balsam, has diffused in my breast. I can now make Abbassah easy, and have the pleasure of contemplating her beauty without alarming her virtue! I can now fulfil the dying request of Osmaide, without the mortification of seeing those charms I could not enjoy, in the possession of another. Come and live in my seraglio with as much freedom as if you were at home: as we shall soon be more nearly connected, I shall not be censured for this step, as departing from the usage of my predecessors. I shall now be compleatly happy by the united charms of friendship and love! for as that passion, under the direction of innocence and vir-

tue

tue, is never criminal, there is no occaſion to expel it my breaſt.—Thus Haroun's reaſon led him into an error, inſtead of preſerving him ſteady to truth and virtue. That faculty often cenſures the paſſions through prejudice, tho' it is afterwards obliged to acknowledge their ſuperior power; but in order to conceal its defeat, it endeavours by falſe colours to palliate its weakneſs, and by endeavouring to blind others, becomes really ſo itſelf. When paſſion ſubſides, it re-aſcends the throne, and ſwaggers with great authority until depoſed by another temptation.

Such is that lamp of the human breaſt which is by many ſo injudiciouſly both extolled and cenſured. It is never totally extinct, though ſometimes its glimmering rays, like an *ignis fatuus*, ſerve only to miſlead us; and then we ſeldom recover the right path till we have been embaraſſed in the bogs of vice and miſery.—Haroun ordered Abbaſſah to be informed that ſhe muſt quit the old ſeraglio the day following, and retire into that which is appropriated for the women and ſiſters of the reigning Calif, which was fixed for the reſidence of her and her intended ſpouſe. The name of Giafar was not mentioned, for Haroun envied that ſatisfaction Abbaſſah would enjoy on the proſpect of having ſuch an agreeable huſband. He was alſo unwilling to haſten the diſagreeable moment; for whatever conceſſions love may make in appearance, it is always ſelfiſh at the bottom.—Abbaſſah, not knowing who was deſtined for her ſpouſe, lamented her hard fate; ſhe communicated her anxiety to Fatima, tenderly bemoaned the loſs of Oſmaide, and reflected with horror on Haroun, whoſe baſe conduct had made a deep impreſſion on her mind. Fatima tried every method to dry up thoſe tears which greatly affected her, and for which there was but too much occaſion. Haroun's ſilence increaſed their alarms; but upon Meſrour's arrival

to

to communicate to them the commands of that unfortunate lover, their anxiety was inftantly turned into joy, which however foon funk into fufpenfe. In vain they interrogated Mefrour, for he could not give them the leaft intelligence of the perfon appointed to marry Abbaffah. This myftery renewed their uneafinefs, Zelia however defired Mefrour to inform the Calif, that fhe fhould with pleafure obey his commands. As foon as he was gone, fhe faid to Fatima, Alas, my dear, what is your opinion of my approaching deftiny? The profound fecrecy that is obferved in this affair, in my opinion, ftrongly indicates that my fate will be partially determined by a chagrined lover.—Jealoufy, replied Fatima, is undoubtedly the motive, for that is the reigning paffion of a difappointed admirer; and though the Calif has furmounted his paffion, yet this vile tormentor has taken its place; it is this that directs him in the choice of your hufband, and by judicioufly concealing the perfon, he prevents your making any remonftrance, whatever occafion there may be for it. --I affure you, Fatima, replied Abbaffah, I fhould not have expreffed the leaft repugnance, for the dangerous fituation I am in leaves no room for objections. My affections for the future fhall be wholly placed in that image of virtue which you have fo ftrongly impreffed on my mind: that calm tranquillity it will always diffufe through my breaft, will overballance the lofs of fenfual pleafures. And though I fhould be deprived of the gratification of an innocent affection, I fhall be lefs liable to fall a prey to a fhocking and criminal paffion.—Thus Abbaffah endeavoured to fortify her mind againft an imaginary evil, little thinking that greater calamities than thofe fhe now dreaded were referved for her in the bofom of fate. It is an eafier tafk patiently to bear an incurable evil, than calmly

calmly to forego a gratification which is in our power.—The whole night preceding the fatal day, Abbaſſah was haraſſed with the moſt ſhocking preſages. Either grief or joy in exceſs are naturally productive of a languor, and may ſometimes be relieved by repoſe, a happineſs incompatible with an uneaſy anxious mind.—As ſoon as Abbaſſah perceived the leaſt glimpſe of dawn ſhe aroſe: and having awoke Fatima, begun converſing on that fatal moment which reaſon made her dread, and virtue wiſh for, and which the muſic and acclamations in the ſtreets informed her to be approaching. —The Calif's palace was already illuminated with a thouſand tapers, whoſe rays were inveloped in the exhalations of the moſt delicious perfumes. Giafar had already repaired thither, and received that homage which was due to the high ſtation to which the Calif now raiſed him. Ambition, and the love of fame, are innate in a great and noble ſoul; Giafar conſequently was charmed with the honours that were paid him, his mind was quite ſerene, and he reflected with pleaſure on that integrity and fidelity with which he ſhould acquit himſelf in thoſe obligations he had laid himſelf under.— The Calif after ſome time came to wait upon his ſiſter, who was deeply affected on obſerving his melancholy countenance, dejected air, and faultering ſteps: ſhe threw herſelf at his feet, and endeavoured to kiſs the trembling hand he offered to her. Haroun raiſing her up, embraced her, which inſtantly rekindled his paſſion, and diſpelled the melancholy of his mind; but jealouſy ſoon eclipſed this tranſient gleam of pleaſure.—As you, my dear Zelia, are of a tender compaſſionate diſpoſition, love will eaſily make an impreſſion on your breaſt, eſpecially as Giafar—What of Giafar, Sir! interrupted Abbaſſah eagerly. I ſometimes, replied he coolly, am guided by reaſon and duty;

duty; Osmaide fixed upon him for your husband, and I think her judicious choice will greatly redound both to your honour and mine. This indeed was settled at a time when our consanguinity was not intended to be revealed; for the sisters of the Calif never marry below the dignity of a scepter. But Giafar's great accomplishments and many virtues render him preferable to a diadem, and I would have constituted him the sovereign of the greatest part of my dominions, but that I find his company and friendship essential to my happiness. As it would not however be proper that you should live in a private manner, I have appointed a palace for your residence: follow me, Zelia, the son of Jahia waits for you; and may I, in presenting you to him, re-instate my virtue and tranquillity! I desire, continued he, you would not by any affecting acknowledgments render my expectations precarious.—Abbassah gladly complied with the Calif's request; this wished-for, though unexpected event, gave a new spirit to her motions and actions, and greatly improved her charms; but as these were concealed by a thick veil, Giafar's fatal sentence was for the present postponed.—As Abbassah was already prepossessed in favour of Giafar, she no sooner saw him than her heart glowed with the warmest love; and she fondly indulged the flattering expectation of enjoying the most consummate felicity.—Her unhappy spouse soon fell a sacrifice to the same passion, and became, when too late, sensible of the rash obligation he had entered into, and the misery he had entailed on his future life.—The Calif was present at their first interview; but as fear generally weakens our discernment, he had not observed those very consequences he most dreaded. —After having conducted Zelia and her spouse to the palace destined for their residence, which was adorned with every elegance both of nature and art,

art, he desired Giafar to attend him to his own seraglio. He equally wished and dreaded to discover his real sentiments; for though before this event he had always entertained the most cordial affection for him, he now began to look upon him in the odious light of a rival. But being at last ashamed of such a mean ill-grounded opinion, he said, You are quite silent, my dear Giafar as to Zelia; do not her charms merit your approbation? I wish I could ascribe your seeming indifference to your insensibility! but I dread, alas! that a prudent dissimulation is the real cause—Abbassah, replied Giafar, is so beautiful, and you, Sir, so deeply enamoured, that I look upon myself to be in a most dangerous situation! not that I distrust my own resolution, for it is not in the power of love to make me violate my oath. I wish I could find it as easy a task to disperse your suspicions and calm your anxiety! Alas, Sir, what hellish spright, envious of my tranquillity, suggested to a you scheme which will prove my ruin! for notwithstanding my most inviolable fidelity and most zealous attachment, you will always distrust my honour. Jealousy looks upon those strange phantoms which are constantly floating before its eyes as realities; give me leave therefore to retire from this impending danger, suffer me to leave Abbassah sole mistress of my seraglio; she will be happy, as the loss of an untasted pleasure will not be productive of any great anxiety.—Alas, Giafar, said the Calif with great warmth, is the happiness I expected already interrupted by a mean repentance! What I demanded, and you promised, was, to look with indifference on my sister's charms, and not to fly from them! But growing more cool, he added in a milder accent, would you again plunge me in that despair from which you have just delivered me? No, I have a better opinion of your

your affection and humanity: I judged you worthy to be intrusted with the life of your friend and prince; I repent not this step, and will not for the future suffer any consideration to lessen the confidence I have placed in you. Go to Zelia, suffer her not to entertain a mean opinion of me, by supposing me the occasion of your cold behaviour; guard your heart, and be assured of my utmost acknowledgments. — While Haroun and Giafar were thus tormented by love, Zelia was happy in the indulgence of the same passion; for the pleasing anxiety of a rising flame, the first budding of hope and desire, are generally productive of more real felicity, than a full and free indulgence in pleasure. A too violent and extatic gratification cannot be called a real happiness; for true pleasure consists more properly in a tranquil mind, and calm passions, than in violent gusts of rapture, which are generally productive of bad consequences.

Fatima observed with concern Zelia's growing flame, but durst not at present acquaint her with the danger she was running into; for when passion is predominant, reason is silent; and if we would insensibly draw a person in this situation from pleasure to discretion, we must address ourselves to the reigning faculty.—Now, my dear Fatima, said Abbassah, my happiness is insured! what consummate felicity will arise from the union of two hearts, the one as tender and constant as Osmaide, the other as passionate and noble as Zeid. I may, I ought, nay I do love the man so deserving my affection. But what is the matter, Fatima? have I forfeited your friendship, that you seem not to share in my felicity?—Fatal experience, replied Fatima after some pause, has taught me, not to place any confidence in such momentary transports! Human nature is surrounded with such a number of of calamities, that it is impoſſible to enjoy unſullied happineſs in this mortal ſtate! and thoſe who endeavour, by indulging flattering expectations and idle pleaſures, to diſcredit this truth, become generally moſt ſenſible by fatal experience of its certainty. Thoſe philoſophers lay down the ſureſt rule for happineſs, who forbid our being anxious with reſpect either to the paſt or future; but as we are endowed with reaſon and ſenſation, this precept is almoſt impracticable. Let us exert our reſolution, and turn theſe fatal accompliſhments to our advantage; let us weigh our expectations in the balance of experience; by this means we ſhall be enabled more eaſily to bear thoſe calamities which neceſſarily attend our preſent ſituation, and acquire a habit preferable to the rules of philoſophy.—What am I then to expect, ſaid Zelia, in a mournful tone?—The moſt perfect happineſs, replied Fatima, if my prayers are heard; but if Giafar ſhould not entertain a paſſion equal to that you have conceived, nay, if he ſhould not have the leaſt regard for you, how will you ſupport an indifference, which you at preſent ſeem to judge impoſſible? You are beautiful, Zelia, you have every accompliſhment both of body and mind; but in order to excite love, we muſt pleaſe, which even a perſon with all theſe qualifications ſometimes finds impracticable.—The antient Greeks repreſented the various paſſions of the mind by different divinities, and aſcribed them attributes correſpondent to thoſe errors and follies into which they lead us. Love was a blind whimſical deity, whom they pretended laughed at the ſchemes and contrivances of men; it was he that induced them to form an ideal being, which they called Beauty, and after having adjuſted its properties and celebrated its influence, he makes them fall in love with the very reverſe of that wonderful aſſemblage of perfection, which they had conſtituted the idol of their heart. This fable is an exact delineation of the various ſenſations and caprice of the human mind.

Here Zelia interrupted her with ſome warmth, and ſaid, I perceive, Fatima, you have an intention to alarm me; but I aſſure you, your deſign will not ſucceed; for Giafar's looks ſufficiently countenance my warmeſt expectations; and to ſhew you how much I think beauty ought to be valued and eſteemed, I will endeavour to improve my own. Theſe jewels rather load than adorn me; and as art is only the tool of vanity, it can be of no ſervice to love. The only dreſs I intend to wear, is that robe which we have embelliſhed with the foliage of the needle, and the garlands we have wove; for the productions of nature are the propereſt ornaments of thoſe charms ſhe has been pleaſed to favour us with.—Fatima ſmiled at Zelia's ſentiments: ſhe however prepared her new dreſs, and as ſhe had a real friendſhip for her fair pupil, her attendance in theſe affairs was not accompanied with that falſhood and flattery ſo much practiſed by the generality of women in ſuch employments. She ſaid, however, as you are an enemy to art, Zelia, how will you comply with that deceit ſo much practiſed in this country?—After a woman has freely acknowledged her paſſion, and though ſhe be even ſcorched with deſire, yet, in compliance with cuſtom, ſhe muſt for a long time defer thoſe very pleaſures ſhe ſighs for, ſhe muſt fly from the arms of her lover, nay, of her ſpouſe, though ſhe at the ſame time wiſhes to be for ever encircled in them. And in ſome countries it is the cuſtom to keep even their ſentiments a long time concealed.—But why, interrupted Zelia in ſurpriſe, ſhould we protract the wiſhed-for moment, which we ought rationally to haſten by every means in our

our power?—That we may the more ſtrongly enflame the heart of our admirer, replied Fatima.—A winning, obliging complaiſance, returned Zelia, would, in my opinion, better anſwer that purpoſe. —True, continued Fatima, but you are ignorant of the misfortunes attending our ſex. The men have abuſed our good nature and compliance, which they have made the foundation of certain fooliſh imperfect inſtitutions, that are an inſufferable oppreſſion upon the whole ſex. Our natural vivacity is entirely ſuppreſſed by theſe rigid rules which are founded on prejudice, ſuperſtition and ignorance; the improvement of our faculties is prevented, by our being always engaged in mean, trifling employments; and our ſincerity and integrity give place to that diſſimulation and hypocriſy theſe tyrants oblige us to practiſe. The men haughtily avow the moſt violent paſſions; but the women muſt not even diſcover the ſlighteſt inclinations. They expect, that an ardent love, and a rapid purſuit of pleaſure, ſhould be looked upon as a merit in them, but a blemiſh in us. What miſerable wretches would they be, if this ridiculous contraſt was real!—The Calif's ſiſter ought not to countenance theſe unnatural prejudices; her elevated mind, and ſound judgment, need not be aſhamed to own her real ſentiments. There is nothing vicious or criminal in the paſſions, if they be neither miſapplied nor indulged in exceſs. We are excited to the noble actions by ambition and a thirſt for fame; and the love of pleaſure is implanted in our nature to ſmooth the rugged paths of life; therefore our principal care ſhould be, to regulate, and not to conceal our paſſions. Let not your ardour anticipate the tranſports of Giafar, neither defer your happineſs by a childiſh unbecoming reſiſtance.—How eaſy, cried Zelia, is it to obſerve the laſt part of your inſtruction! but how ridiculous is it to ſuppreſs our own raptures, in order to augment thoſe of another? None but perſons of mean ſouls and contracted ideas can, in my opinion, ſubmit to ſuch prejudices. But it is impoſſible that Giafar, as you have repreſented him, can entertain ſuch mean abject notions; his heart will inform him, that to love, is the ſureſt method to render ourſelves beloved; my own ſenſations I am ſure convince me of this truth.—Fatima was going to reply when Giafar entered, which obliged her to withdraw. Abbaſſah in a ſhort time ordered her to be recalled, which ſummons ſhe obeyed. She dreaded the conſequences of this viſit, and her ſuſpicions were confirmed when ſhe ſaw her dear Zelia bathed in tears; for Fatima's experience and penetration eaſily diſcerned that they flowed from the fountain of grief. —Abbaſſah, obſerving that her friend had diſcovered the cauſe of her uneaſineſs, ſaid, Yes, my dear Fatima, Giafar is inſenſible to love, and I enraptured and miſerable! Alas! I am too late convinced of the truth of your conjectures as to my approaching miſery!—As ſoon as you left the room, he placed himſelf by me; I looked upon that confuſion and embaraſſment he in vain ſtrove to conceal, as the effect of his love! he at length looked upon me with aſtoniſhment, and of a ſudden ſighed and turned his eyes to the ground. I experienced the ſame agitations, and attributed our ſimilar ſituation to the ſame cauſe. I did not in the leaſt wiſh to break a ſilence which I looked upon as the enchantment of love; but I was, alas! too ſoon rouſed from this pleaſing delirium! Giafar recovered himſelf, and began to appear more calm, and his compoſure and indifference made a ſhocking contraſt to thoſe flattering agitations he had before expreſſed. At laſt, inſtead of thoſe tranſports, I expected, and which I felt in my my own breaſt, I received only cold inſipid aſſurances of ſubmiſſive deference and profound reſpect. —Being unable patiently to hear ſuch an unexpected addreſs, I interrupted him, and ſaid, Ceaſe, Sir, ceaſe, I beſeech you, theſe diſagreeable offers, you are a ſtranger to the heart of Abbaſſah, if you think her capable of ſuch ridiculous arrogance; my breaſt is filled with ſentiments productive of happineſs, and it is impoſſible for me to behave otherwiſe than the wife of Giafar, though I am the Calif's ſiſter. —I ſee with pleaſure that my brother's choice has flattered your ambition, and I ſincerely wiſh that you may poſſeſs in me every thing requiſite to your happineſs. You ſay, you will treat me with all deference and reſpect; as for myſelf, it will be the ſole employment of my life to expreſs my affection for you, and to merit the return of your's; my heart, when I firſt ſaw you, taught me the one, and I hope you will be pleaſed to inform me how I may obtain the other.—He replied with ſome precipitation, Ah! what do you demand, Abbaſſah? Do you diſtruſt the power of your charms? Muſt I augment your triumph? But, continued he with an air of indifference, ſince you are deſirous to know my pleaſure, if you will deign to conform to it.— Entertain no ſcruple on that head, replied I with ſome warmth; will the moſt diligent aſſiduity, the moſt tender affection, the moſt lively paſſion, ſatisfy your demands? No, anſwered Giafar with a ſigh, no, Madam; overpower me not with your favours, for I muſt not enjoy them, and they greatly exceed my merits. All I requeſt of you is, to treat me with that reſpect and friendſhip as if I was your brother. I ſincerely wiſh you all felicity; but endeavour not to render me miſerable by deſtroying the tranquillity of my mind, the only happineſs I enjoy!—Having ſo ſaid, he aroſe without waiting for my anſwer; and, though he ſaw me plunged in

 grief

grief and bathed in tears, instantly quitted the room. I remained for some time in a state of insensibility, and nothing but the hopes of your assistance and consolation could have recalled my lost senses!—Pity my case, my dear Fatima, and by your compassion extinguish that raging flame that consumes my heart. I simply thought, that a lawful passion must certainly be productive of happiness; but since innocence is no protection against misery, help me by your advice to recover my reason, which has been led astray by passion.—Resentment, replied Fatima, can alone effect what you desire, and if that should fail, my endeavours will answer no purpose.—I will, replied Abbassah, follow the dictates of my just indignation, for they are most deserving of base treatment who take it patiently. But what must I do to avoid such mortifying behaviour for the future? For as Giafar is my husband, I must be obliged sometimes to be in his company. Alas! I shall think it a sufficient self-denial, if I do not even solicit his visits; for as I have exhaled that delicious air impregnated by his infectious breath, the disease of love is too much diffused through my whole frame.—Conceal your passion, replied Fatima, under a mask of indifference; practise in your defence a lawful dissimulation, or even that base hypocrisy I taught you to disdain; for the best precepts must sometimes give way to necessity.——We have entertained a better opinion of Giafar than he now appears to deserve: we thought he would be sensibly affected with an open, sincere passion, and like the rest of his sex be offended by dissimulation and chicanery; let us now punish him for leading us into this error. Counterfeit a mortifying insensibility; and, if there is opportunity, pretend a most violent antipathy to his caresses. These are the only means in your power, unless you can entirely conquer your passion. Alas! I wish I had

I had obſerved this advice, and my fatal experience ought to induce you the more readily to follow my directions.—Your friendſhip alone, anſwered Zelia, ſufficiently claims my unlimited confidence, eſpecially when my miſerable afflicted ſituation ſtands in ſo great need of your aſſiſtance; but I have not the leaſt hope that our endeavours will prove ſucceſsful.——Encourage not, replied Fatima, ſuch gloomy thoughts; for as we ought not to be too elate and confident in a ſeries of happineſs and proſperity, ſo neither ſhould we fall a prey to deſpair and melancholy, when attacked by adverſity, and diſappointed in our moſt ſanguine expectations.—Giafar, notwithſtanding he was the cauſe of ſo much anxiety, was more to be pitied than Zelia, as he could not relieve his uneaſineſs by complaining. Being conſtrained to obſerve a tormenting ſilence, and ſecretly brood over his own thoughts, he was racked both by his own miſery, and that which he occaſioned others. He was deeply affected by the paſſion Abbaſſah had expreſſed for him, enraptured with her piercing looks, and inchanted with her ſweet voice! He had nevertheleſs affected a cruel inſenſibility; but this firſt ſtruggle, though he came off victorious, was far from inſuring his future tranquillity. He was prevented avoiding any future attacks of her charms by retiring, which is the only reſource againſt love; honour was his ſole ally, and gave him ſuch encouragement, that he flattered himſelf he ſhould be able to ſubdue this unconquered tyrant of the human breaſt. But his raſhneſs ſoon received a check, for as Abbaſſah's frank acknowledgment of her paſſion had at firſt made him uneaſy that he could not make a proper return, he was now greatly more affected by that coldneſs and indifference he obſerved in her behaviour. He reproached himſelf for the rude requeſt he had made to her; and as he now in his turn experienced the cruelty of it, he wondered how he became guilty of ſuch a baſe propoſal.—The approach of night, which is generally propitious to perſons in their ſituation, increaſed their uneaſineſs. Giafar and Abbaſſah, formed for love, and united by a reciprocal paſſion, in vain ſighed for that happineſs which their charms and mutual affection ſo highly deſerved. The day following, inſtead of that tranquillity, and calm compoſure of mind, which is always the effect of lawful gratifications, their countenances ſhewed the ſtrongeſt marks of grief and anxiety.—Haroun ſpent ſome part of this day in Abbaſſah's apartment, which was the firſt time his company was agreeable to her, ſince it inſured her that of Giafar. The Calif diligently examined the behaviour of this unhappy couple; but could not diſcover the leaſt ſign of that calm ſerenity which always attends the indulgence of an innocent paſſion; and the ſettled melancholy in Zelia's countenance gave him a ſecret ſatisfaction. Alas! that love ſhould be productive of ſuch cruelty! How could a breaſt ſo renowned for candour and equity become ſuſceptible of ſuch baſe ſentiments? But thoſe ſhining virtues for which he had long been ſo renowned, were now buried under the rubbiſh of paſſion, and he was become entirely inſenſible of their influence, except by that remorſe their ſtruggles ſometimes occaſioned.

All parties continued for many days the ſport of turbulent paſſions. Giafar was ſometimes almoſt prevailed upon to indulge his love, and voluntarily expoſed himſelf to the enchanting charms of Zelia; but inſtantly reflecting on his obligations, he fled from her preſence with horror. As he became every day more enamoured, he became every day more miſerable, and the fatal oath he had taken was the bane of his repoſe. What he had experienced in the affair of Irene, occaſioned his forming a wrong

judg-

judgment of his heart, as his affection had not on that occasion made the least opposition to the demands of friendship and duty. But he was now, when too late, convinced, that there was a wide difference between a transient liking, and real passion; he became sensible that every agreeable woman, especially when seconded by our own vanity, may excite the first; but that she who is blessed with every charm and accomplishment both in mind and person, will excite a passion of a different nature, and much more violent. The grief and anxiety he laboured under from this fatal error entirely put a stop to Abbassah's designs of revenge, for we easily pardon the object of our affections upon discovering the least contrition.

End of the FIRST VOLUME.

ORIENTAL

ANECDOTES:

OR,

THE HISTORY OF

HAROUN ALRACHID.

In TWO VOLUMES.

VOL. II.

DUBLIN:

Printed for PETER WILSON, JAMES POTTS, ALEX. M'CULLOH, and JAM. WILLIAMS.

M,DCC,LXIV.

HISTORY
OF THE REIGN OF
HAROUN ALRACHID.

PART III.

GIAFAR every morning quitted his uneaſy down before Aurora gilded the portals of the eaſt, and diſregarding the beautiful walks that ſurrounded the palace of Abbaſſah, retired into the ſhady groves in the gardens of the ſeraglio. The gloom of night, when increaſed by the moſt profound ſilence and ſolitude, is always agreeable to perſons in diſtreſs, as it gives them a more lively ſenſe of their woes; and we naturally ſeek to improve every ſenſation of the human breaſt, whether ariſing from joy or grief.—Abbaſſah being one night more uneaſy and reſtleſs than uſual, aroſe and went in great confuſion to the place where Giafar was walking. He was ſo wrapt up in his own reflections, that he did not obſerve her approach until it was too late to avoid her preſence; and being inſtantly ſeized with the moſt violent agitations from the contending paſſions of pleaſure, love and fear, he ſunk down upon a verdant bank.—Abbaſſah came up to her huſband, and preſſing his hands in the moſt affectionate manner, endeavoured, but in vain, to ſpeak, for ſhe could utter nothing but ſighs, and he for ſome time could only reply in the ſame language.

language. But at last recollecting himself, and reflecting on his duty, he with an affected sternness and indifference exclaimed,—Is it the princess Abbassah that stands before me! what malicious spright has dragged you from the down of sleep into this awful solitude, which the law forbids you to approach!—How can you, cruel man, replied Abbassah, ask such a question! do not my anxious looks give you sufficient information? Can love neither open your eyes nor touch your heart? But this is not the case, insensibility is not the cause of your behaviour, you despise me. I despise you! interrupted Giafar: ah, my dear Zelia, how can you entertain such a thought! but seek not to discover the secrets of a heart that labours under the most severe stroke of fortune.—Impart the cause of your grief, replied Zelia, to a mistress, nay to a wife, that adores you; this I beg, not, alas! for the love you bear me, but for the cordial friendship that subsists between you and my brother!——Giafar, greatly affected at this request, replied, O cruel reflexion!—cursed place!—fatal day!—Leave me, leave mē, Zelia, oblige me not to augment your woes! kill me not by your enquiries!—I have no such intention, replied Abbassah, reluctantly endeavouring to retire; I perceive but too plainly the cause of your grief, and whatever may be the consequence to myself, I will pay a proper regard to your tranquillity!—Giafar, distracted between love and duty, was going to prevent Abbassah's retiring, when his chief eunuch Nair brought him an order from the Calif to repair instantly to a certain place where his presence was absolutely necessary.—He therefore left Abbassah with Nair and Fatima, who, uneasy at the absence of her dear Zelia, had just joined the rest of the company. These two friends directed their steps toward their apartment,

and

and Fatima easily perceived by the countenance of Abbassah the distraction of her heart.

This unhappy princess, under the most violent agitations, walked in a slow tottering pace, and every instant looked back upon that fatal spot which had been witness of Giafar's cruel return to her most tender and affectionate behaviour. The presence of the beloved object has always a great influence on a mind in love: this the happy lover experiences with the most sensible pleasure, but the unhappy by the severest torture.—Abbassah chanced to cast her eye upon a letter that was lying on the spot Giafar had just quitted, and, turning hastily, she ran and snatched it up; but what was her surprize when she found it addressed to her husband in the following terms!—" Either forbear to inform me of your repeated kindnesses, or come and receive the reward of your fidelity, which is the more meritorious as it is now become an antiquated virtue. My heart is too much in the possession of love to admit of the inferior influence of gratitude, and I would in return for your favours instantly fly to your arms, if the consideration of that honourable connection which the Calif has presented you with, did not suppress my ardour. Abbassah would but too plainly read in our eyes the cause of your cold behaviour, and would soon deprive you of her brother's friendship. Alas! rather return her love than expose yourself to her resentment, for I had rather see you faithless than miserable. But can you find no excuse to leave Bagdad? If nothing else will do, rekindle the war, and come and subdue the Greeks a second time; I am not in the least ashamed at this request, for I look upon any step as lawful that promises me the sight of the person I adore!"—Though this letter had no name affixed, and Abbassah was consequently ignorant who her rival was, yet she was but too fully

fully convinced that this person was the cause of all her misery. Her eyes instantly became dim, and she sunk motionless into the arms of Nair and Fatima, who conveyed her to her apartments, and by their diligence recovered her. Upon coming to herself she exclaimed, I am utterly undone! I could have supported the indifference of Giafar, and it was some consolation to me that he took no particular notice of any of his beautiful slaves, and I was still in hopes of gaining his affections: but now all is over; a fatal unknown has deprived me of him; and without hope, which was the sole balm of my cares, it is impossible for me to support life! O Fatima, give me that cruel sentence of my fate, let me re-peruse it and die!—A disappointed lover is always very imprudent! Abbassah uttered the above expressions in the presence of Nair; and when Fatima ordered the eunuch to withdraw, she detained him, desiring him to go and inform her brother what situation she was in, but not to acquaint him with the cause; and to tell him that the preservation of her life was solely in his power, and without his immediate attendance she should expire. She charged him not even to mention the ungrateful Giafar, and told him that his dispatch and discretion should not go unrewarded.—Nair, after receiving repeated orders from Abbassah, departed, though Fatima endeavoured, but in vain, to prevent this message. What are you going to do, Zelia, said she? Consider that repentance always closely pursues revenge; but more particularly when it falls on the person we love, we soon become sorry for the evils we have occasioned, we detest ourselves for such meanness, and our love is encreased by our compassion and remorse. Defer accusing Giafar to the Calif until reason and resentment have restored the balance of your mind. We can no more safely ly retaliate the injuries received from an ungrateful wretch when our affection for him is extinguished.—Flatter me not, replied Abbassah faintly, with a tranquillity it is impossible for me ever to enjoy, nor terrify me by representing to me those horrors I should have already experienced, if I had been capable of entertaining a thought to the prejudice of Giafar! I will not even mention this letter to Haroun, which confirms what I have long dreaded, for it would raise his indignation too much; I will therefore return it to my faithless spouse. But may not I earnestly intreat my brother to remove me from this disagreeable situation? May not I acquaint him with the intolerable torments I suffer, without censuring the cold behaviour of Giafar? I will beg the favour of him to permit me to spend the remainder of my miserable life in the old seraglio, and I think he has too much affection for me to refuse such a request. If you will accompany me thither, Fatima, I will desire you to close these eyes, for grief will soon put a period to my wretched existence. I shall soon follow my mother, than whom I am greatly more miserable, for her anxiety had the pleasing alloy of the most extatic raptures; but I have nothing to reflect on but a series of ingratitude and contempt. Fatima was going to oppose this strange resolution, but was prevented by the entrance of Haroun. Come, Sir, said Abbassah, as soon as she saw him, come, and if you have any affection for your unhappy sister, deliver her from this abyss of misery! —How cruel is it, replied the Calif affectionately, to entertain such a doubt! Did I ever cease a moment to love, nay, even adore my Zelia?—True, Sir, replied Abbassah sighing; and if, by a strange fatality which cannot be ascribed to me, you have experienced the anxiety of a hopeless passion, I in my turn share the same fate! Giafar

looks

looks upon my most tender affection with a cold indifference! an involuntary aversion keeps him from my embraces! I conjure you in the name of Osmaide to put an end to our mutual distress, and suffer me to return into the old seraglio!—Are you in love then, Zelia, replied the Calif after a gloomy pause! and is your passion so violent! This confession pierces my very vitals!—Yet it is only a suitable return to my unparalleled barbarity!—You, Sir, barbarous, interrupted Abbassah! I will not trouble you with solicitations if you refuse my first request!—You rack me replied Haroun; even a prince must, is a slave to the law. Giafar solely can grant the separation you desire, for it is not in my power to procure it: I will, however, employ my utmost interest to gratify your request. But demean not yourself too much, Zelia: complaints, however justly founded, by humiliating the sufferer, aggrandize the aggressor.—But what am I saying? you should ascribe all your afflictions to your unhappy brother, for I am the sole occasion of them! If it had not been for me, your life would have run in an even smooth channel, unruffled by boisterous passions. Revenge yourself upon me! pierce my heart with the recital of your woes! for no one ought to share in them but myself. Alas! if you were but sensible of what I suffer! if the least spark of that flame which devours my heart, could but fall upon your breast, it would dissipate your disquietudes, and we should both be happy! Mistake me not, I mean only an innocent, not a criminal affection.—Hold, Sir, interrupted Abbassah, astonished at such violent transports; hold, you transgress the bounds of brotherly affection and compassion. I but too plainly perceive that a calm retreat will never be the happy lot of the unfortunate Zelia: but the choice between an unhappy and criminal flame admits

of

of no doubt. I will continue here with my husband; I have gone too far, by supposing that your reason had conquered your passion: excuse the anxiety this mistake may occasion you, I will henceforward bear my unparalleled misfortunes without complaining.—Haroun, struck dumb by this just reprimand, and greatly affected by the resolution his sister had taken, which he ascribed to a return of her passion for Giafar, and the fear of being separated from him, retired without making any reply. This monarch was undoubtedly the most miserable of mortals; for though that spirit of liberty, or rather licentiousness, which is connate with human nature, may render a prohibited pleasure more poignant and attracting, yet this is only when our endeavours are successful; for disappointment is a servitude which increases every other calamity by weakening the faculties of the mind; it even deprives virtue of the power it otherwise would have to induce the passions to give up an improper pursuit, and complaining is the only effort of a mind labouring under misfortunes.

As soon as Haroun recovered the free use of his reason, he looked upon his sister's passion for Giafar as a happy circumstance, that would gradually extinguish his love, and induce him to restore to a person, for whom he entertained the sincerest regard, that felicity he at present so unjustly deprived him of. But this triumph proved only imaginary; for self-love quickly induced him to look upon the Vizir's indifference as a more favourable step towards the accomplishment of his wishes than he could have expected; he went to visit him in his own palace, and presented him with the highest dignities, the most immense riches, and the warmest acknowledgments; but at the same time put him to the severest torture, by relating with the highest

higheſt tranſports the converſation that had paſſed between him and Zelia.

Notwithſtanding Fatima's advice, Abbaſſah gave herſelf wholly to deſpair; for when a perſon labouring under affliction has ſeized the ſmalleſt twig of hope, and that fails, he becomes incapable of further efforts, and ſinks under that preſſure of woe he before thought to ſurmount. Zelia had depended on her brother's aſſiſtance; ſhe had flattered herſelf that he would procure her a ſeparation, or rather her huſband's affection; for love is generally inconſiſtent in its plans, and depends on a gleam of hope reaſon would deſpiſe.—I think, ſaid Abbaſſah to Fatima, that Giafar's baſe behaviour ought to have excited the Calif's reſentment; but will love liſten to a laudable indignation, at a time when it even ſilences the voice of honour? A brother, who ought to have been my ſupport, plans my deſtruction! I have kindled a flame in his breaſt which makes me ſhrink with horror: but I cannot make the leaſt impreſſion on the obdurate heart of my ſpouſe! How greatly was I miſtaken, when I dreaded ruining Giafar, by acquainting Haroun with this affair! for can the Calif be concerned for the honour of a ſiſter whom he endeavours to ſubject to the greateſt infamy, and render as criminal as ſhe is unhappy! O Zeid! my unfortunate father, I could by following your example put a period to my woes: you, however, enjoyed ſome felicity in life, of which I have no farther idea than what ſerves to increaſe my affliction.—The diſtreſs of her friend ſo ſtrongly affected Fatima, and recalled in ſo lively a manner her own ſufferings that ſhe was not able to make any reply. For as ſhe had experienced the various diſquietudes and calamities attendant on love, Zelia's afflictions made the ſtronger impreſſion on her mind. At laſt ſhe ſaid with a ſigh, Ah! my dear

Zelia,

Zelia, reserve those irresistible tears for the reception of an obdurate husband, whom they may probably mollify; for I am informed that Giafar is arrived, and intends shortly to wait upon you; beauty in distress generally proves triumphant.— No, Fatima, replied Zelia, I am but too sensible of its inefficacy; I will retire and avoid such an afflicting interview. Give Giafar the letter he dropped; but censure not his conduct, as my silent grief will at least give him some compunction. Having given these orders, she shut herself up in her closet.—Abbassah's retiring, the great anxiety that appeared in Fatima's countenance, and the letter she presented him, threw Giafar into the utmost consternation! He read it over and over, and could scarce believe his own eyes! His uneasiness was soon relieved by a torrent of indignation, which he thought there was a sufficient foundation for; and if Fatima, who had just retired, had seen the Vizir's emotions, Haroun's grand secret had been disclosed.—O base! perfidious friend, said he, you increase your barbarity by the blackest calumny! Was it not sufficient to rob me of a pleasure you yourself were unable to enjoy; but must you also render me the most wretched of mortals! To oblige you, I give up that highest of pleasures, the rendering the person I adore happy, by acknowledging a mutual flame; must I also to gratify your unreasonable demands, render myself the object of her hatred! You are the only person, induced by the anxiety I suffer on your account, who could have joined the most odious of falshoods to cruel truths! But this letter, in which every circumstance shews the perfidiousness of its author, shall not produce the intended effect. I wish to heaven I might be the sole victim of this mean artifice! But, alas! will the tender heart of the adorable but unhappy Zelia be able to support such a

shock?

ſhock? Good God! can ſhe believe that I have ſacrificed her to a rival, who is repreſented capable of ſuch mean, deſpicable ſentiments, when even Irene herſelf has not been able to diſpute with her the empire of my breaſt! though I am always ready to ſacrifice my honour and life for that lady. Can ſhe believe that I behave to another woman with that cruel indifference which daily coſt me ſo many tears, the unfeigned tribute of my afflicted ſoul! When I am diſtracted with ſuch complicated diſtreſs, how can you, ungrateful Haroun, rely on that fidelity and ſecrecy which I have ſo imprudently ſworn to obſerve! Reflect, I have not promiſed what is not in the power of human nature in thoſe unforeſeen circumſtances under which you have laid me! Alas! though your diſtracting tranſports had chilled my ſoul, I nevertheleſs came to comfort Abbaſſah, and to ſacrifice my love to that fidelity of which you are ſo little deſerving! But if you practiſe deceit, I will do the ſame, and will inform Zelia of your abſurd deſigns, and my own raſh vows; I will bury in her arms my imprudent oath —Dreadful oath— Heavens! what have I promiſed?—Honour check me: this I muſt not do; one crime can never juſtify another, nor ought Giafar to be perjured, becauſe Haroun is baſe! Let me rather avoid a conflict of the fatal conſequences, of which I am but too well aſſured. If when abſent I entertain ſuch mean deſigns, how ſhall I, when preſent, ſupport my integrity againſt the looks, the tears, the enchanting careſſes of my dear Abbaſſah. To ſeek excuſes for my conduct would be my ruin; and of the two it is preferable to treſpaſs upon love rather than honour. I will therefore conceal my anxiety, that not even Haroun himſelf may perceive it, except by its conſequences: and, as it is inconſiſtent with real friendſhip, I will not put him to the bluſh; for what can the

the foregoing ſuch a gratification coſt him who has foregone his all.

Such were the reflections of Giafar as he retired from Abbaſſah's apartment; his error and reſentment were both very excuſable, and his cruel ſituation deſerved the moſt tender compaſſion. He never in the leaſt ſuſpected Zobeide to be the author of a malicious deſign, which he aſcribed to a prince incapable of entertaining ſuch a thought. A violent paſſion may hurry a noble mind into follies, or even crimes; but can never make it guilty of meanneſs or treachery.—Perſons of bad principles are ſeldom diſcouraged by diſappointment; their ſtrong attachments to vice gives them ſteadineſs and reſolution to plan and execute new projects; and though theſe two powers of the mind ought always to be the handmaids of virtue, yet they are but too often the ſlaves of vice, and the moſt renowned exploits have generally been the effect of extravagant and ungovernable paſſions, and motives contradictory to honour and virtue.—The death of Oſmaide made Zobeide ſome amends for her unſucceſsful attempt to ruin Abbaſſah; for ſhe now reflected, that ſhe, whom ſhe deſired to ſacrifice to her jealouſy, and ambition of reigning the ſole miſtreſs of Haroun's affection, would be no longer under the protection of a tender and affectionate parent. And the Calif, far from ſuſpecting the baſe deſign which had ſo endangered his virtue, looked upon her vile artifice as the dictates of a friendly compaſſion, though the danger he had eſcaped might have taught him better.—Thoſe who ſooth and compliment our follies, have it always in their power to betray us, and inſtead of having their ſincerity ſuſpected, are ſure of the moſt unlimited confidence.—Zobeide quickly took this method with Haroun, for ſhe had been greatly aſtoniſhed at the reſolution he had taken to marry his ſiſter to Giafar, and could not believe

that

that he had gained ſuch a compleat victory over his paſſion ; and the Calif, deceived by the counterfeit concern Zobeide expreſſed for his uneaſineſs, acquainted her with the whole affair. To place too much confidence in thoſe we have a good opinion of, is a weakneſs common to moſt men ; but in a lover is an act of neceſſity, for he is unable to conceal the fluctuations of his mind, which is haraſſed with perpetual deſires, though frequently aſhamed of them.—As ſoon as Zobeide was informed of the oath Haroun had exacted of Giafar, ſhe was in the higheſt tranſports of joy : ſhe fully perceived the violence of his love from the blindneſs of his hope; and as ſhe was of opinion, that duty, when oppoſed by love, muſt always yield, ſhe judged it impoſſible for Giafar to fulfil his engagements. She, however, endeavoured to raiſe the Calif's expectations, that his diſappointment might be the ſeverer. The violent reſentment he had expreſſed when he judged Zeinib guilty of perjury, gave her an opportunity of judging of the implacable rage the ſame offence in a rival would throw him into ; his indignation would be enflamed by the other's happineſs, and, ſince he would not pardon the perſon he adored, he would undoubtedly inflict upon Giafar the ſevereſt of puniſhments.——To accompliſh this villainous ſcheme, Zobeide bribed Nair, who was the chief of Giafar's eunuchs, and learned from him the mutual affection and anxiety of this unhappy couple, which it was impoſſible to conceal from a ſlave whoſe curioſity was inſtigated by ſelf-intereſt.—When a diſpute between too ſincere lovers comes to be adjuſted, reaſon always quits the chair to love. Upon this principle Zobeide, to gratify her implacable reſentment, contrived, by the aſſiſtance of Nair, that Zelia ſhould find the forged letter above-mentioned, obſerving to her baſe confidant, that not all the humility, nor even the reſolution of Abbaſſah, would

would be proof againſt the torments of jealouſy; and that the fear of rekindling a paſſion ſhe abhors, or of being the ruin of Giafar, will prevent her complaining to the Calif; and that her huſband, chagrined by a ſcandalous reflection which he could attribute to no perſon but Haroun, would give himſelf up to the dictates of love. Your circumſpection, continued ſhe, will detect his perjury, of which I will inform the Calif, who will take exemplary revenge, and I ſhall enjoy the utmoſt of my wiſhes. ——It is ſurpriſing that baſe perfidious wretches ſhould depend upon the fidelity and aſſiſtance of others! Is it not more rational for them to judge of others by themſelves? Nair, who betrayed his maſter, did the ſame by Zobeide, in hopes of a larger gratuity; and as he had been a witneſs of Abbaſſah's paſſion, he looked upon that mark of confidence as moſt worthy his purſuit. He being intruſted with the ſecrets of the Calif's ſiſter, gave him ſuch expectations of advancement, as eaſily induced him to give up Zobeide's promiſes, with whom he inſtantly dropped all communication; but he took care, to conceal from Zelia his former perfidy, as that might have deprived him of the eſteem and confidence he was in hopes of acquiring.

Giafar continued to be haraſſed by the contending paſſions of love and friendſhip; he thought himſelf hated by a wife he adored, and baſely treated by a friend for whom he had the warmeſt regard, and by his cruel ſituation was prevented from coming to an explanation with either. The anxiety of his mind at length occaſioned a violent inflammation in his blood, and he ſunk under the preſſure of the complicated diſeaſes of mind and body.—The Calif, greatly alarmed at the dangerous ſituation of his Vizir, conſtantly attended him: but his utmoſt care, affection and ſolicitude had no effect upon Giafar! for the mind is leaſt able at a time when the body is enfeebled by ſickneſs, to lay aſide its prejudices, and judge impartially; but the powers of ſenſe are not ſo eaſily blunted, and the ſight of Abbaſſah gave ſome relief and ſatisfaction to Giafar.

This princeſs, laying aſide her reſentment, conſtantly attended her ſpouſe; and what an affecting ſight was it for Haroun, that not even his preſence could reſtrain her expreſſions of grief and affection! Friendſhip for a while ſuppreſſed the eruption of jealouſy, and an odd accident at laſt entirely freed him from that tormenting paſſion; for going one day abruptly into Giafar's cloſet, he perceived a pocket-book lying on the table, and opening it, he found the letter which Zobeide had forged.—This treacherous project, which had coſt Abbaſſah ſo many tears, quickly calmed the diſquietudes of Haroun. After reading this he was only ſolicitous for the recovery of his friend, who was become more dear to him by this proof of his not interfering with his own paſſion. His attendance and affection produced a different effect than he expected, for the longer Giafar was obliged to ſuppreſs his uneaſineſs, the more his malady increaſed.

The Calif, thinking he knew the ſource of his diſorder, and not being able to find an opportunity of ſpeaking to him in the abſence of Zelia, ſaid to him at laſt in her preſence,—Will you then, my dear Giafar, by rejecting my affectionate ſolicitude, throw me into deſpair! Alas, are you determined to die! I am ſorry you have not thought me worthy of your confidence! Prolong your life, that you may be the honour and ſupport of me and my crown! I will ſend you again into Greece; and ſince that will make you happy, I ſhall more eaſily diſpenſe with your abſence! Haroun imagined that Giafar only would underſtand what he meant; but Abbaſſah inſtantly fell into a violent agony, which

Giafar

Giafar perceiving, he looked upon what the Calif had said as the highest insult and most consummate villainy; and scarce was he gone out of the room when the two unhappy lovers giving vent, to their mutual anxiety, exclaimed at the same instant; Am I then, cruel husband, the cause of your unhappiness?—Can you, my dear Zelia, believe me insensible to your charms?—Your life and death I find depend solely upon another!—No; you, my dear, are the only person I adore, for you only I live!—These tender expressions occasioned such an inundation of joy in the affectionate heart of Abbassah, that she could not help clasping her husband in her arms; and pressing his pale lips with her's, they mingled their mutual sighs and tears! At last she said, am I not mistaken? Does my dear Giafar really assure me of an affection I judged him incapable of entertaining? Or is it an illusion produced by my wishes? O happy object of his love!—Hold, Zelia, interrupted Giafar, hold! how can you credit so base a calumny? That letter which has given you so much uneasiness!—O your brother!—Alas, my honour!——Speak out, Sir, replied Abbassah with more vivacity than usual, speak out, and increase not my woe by keeping me in doubt. Will my death, or, which is worse than death, our separation, make you happy? Delay not acquainting me with your wishes, which shall be instantly complied with! Giafar, in a languishing voice, occasioned by the final struggle between love and duty, replied, I will, my dear Zelia, I must acquaint you with the whole affair! I am on the point of quitting this world, and I had rather die guilty of such a crime than despised by Abbassah: listen then to my woeful tale!—A most shocking oath obliged me to practise a feigned indifference, for which I have dearly paid by the inexpressible tortures I have undergone! Your brother, before ever I had the pleasure of

H 2 seeing

ſeeing you, obliged me to enter into this obligation, and I have been juſtly puniſhed for my imprudent temerity. And ſince our union, the Calif, diſtruſtful of my fidelity, has undoubtedly attempted, by that forged letter which he found means to convey to you, to excite your jealouſy, and ſeparate us for ever, that he might more eaſily execute his baſe deſigns. His artifice and ſuſpicions have occaſioned my deſpair, and the malady I at preſent labour under, and nothing but my regard for you enables me to bear them with patience. The remembrance of my ingratitude would have made you look upon me when I was gone as the moſt odious of mortals; whereas you will now conſider me as the moſt affectionate of huſbands, who, not being able to enjoy your charms, and render you happy without becoming the baſeſt of wretches, preferred death to treachery, or a ſeries of miſery.

It is impoſſible to deſcribe the emotions of Abbaſſah during the above narration: at laſt, after a moſt expreſſive ſilence, ſhe ſaid, Do not, my dear, encourage theſe gloomy thoughts; if you love me, live for ever, and let love be the happy conſtellation by which we may ſteer through the ſtorms of life; imbitter not your moments through the fear of a lapſe, from which I will inſure you! I am very ſenſible of the influence of honour on a ſoul like your's, and ſhall chearfully ſubmit to the reſtrictions it preſcribes; for as you have entruſted me with the ſecret, it is incumbent upon me to ſecure the obligation you have entered into. I ſhould undoubtedly with pleaſure have complied with the happy laws of our union, which my obligations and duty exacted; but as the caſe now ſtands, I will chearfully comply with thoſe reſtraints your cruel oath has laid us under. The noble and generous paſſion of Zeid ſhall revive in his daughter: you are no ſtranger to the ſacrifice he voluntarily underwent, than which

ours

ours will be more glorious, as it will be more frequently repeated. Our reſtraint will not probably be ſo mortifying as we may imagine, for I believe there are pleaſures more ſolid and durable than thoſe which you have renounced. Yes, my dear Zelia, replied Giafar; the ſenſations which you at preſent excite in my breaſt, convince me of the exquiſiteneſs of thoſe pleaſures you ſpeak of. Happineſs depends not on the gratification of ſenſe, and ours ſhall be uninterrupted, if you tempt me not to tranſgreſs my obligations. Acquaint Fatima with our ſecret, and order her to attend us conſtantly, for her preſence will help us to maintain our ſteadineſs: let us conceal our mutual affection in the preſence of the Calif; but let us deceive him, by adhering more ſtrictly to our obligations than he imagines.—Notwithſtanding mankind are born to ſervitude, their pride makes them look upon themſelves as free; every little reſtraint is judged inſupportable, and to break through it gives them the moſt exquiſite pleaſure. Have legiſlators been ignorant of this bias of the human breaſt? Or have they contributed to our happineſs by their numerous prohibitions?

Giafar was now delivered from his tormenting reſtraint; and though he had in part violated his oath, yet the hopes of obſerving it in the moſt eſſential article, freed him from any uneaſy reflections. Having it now in his power to expreſs his own paſſion, and receive a return of Abbaſſah's, his health was quickly re-eſtabliſhed.—The Calif attributed this ſudden and unexpected change, to the hopes he had given him of returning to Greece; but he was ſo doatingly fond of his company, that he was in no haſte to fulfil his promiſe.——Fatima was at preſent the only unhappy perſon in this company; the violent tranſports and great freedoms that paſſed between Giafar and Abbaſſah made her very uneaſy ; and as a moment might prove their ruin, and every circumſtance ſeemed to haſten that fatal inſtant, ſhe was very anxious for their ſafety. When ſhe perceived that her preſence was often diſagreeable to this fond couple, and that they expreſſed in their countenances the higheſt ſatisfaction whenever ſhe was obliged, though only for a moment, to quit the room, ſhe could not help preſaging the moſt fatal conſequences.—At laſt ſhe ſaid, You will, perhaps, my dear Zelia, deſpiſe me for what I am going to ſay ; but I ſhould be guilty of the greateſt cruelty, if I did not endeavour to ſtop you when on the brink of the moſt frightful precipice ; for love, which has brought you into this danger, will not bring you off ſafe ; truſt your fate therefore to my friendſhip, which, though it may appear rigid, will undoubtedly preſerve the life of Giafar. This ſeraglio is crouded with venal wretches, who poſſibly only wait for an opportunity to betray you : a powerful prince ſees with the eyes of all his ſubjects ; reflect on the fate of Giafar !——Zelia interrupting her ſaid, How can you entertain ſuch a thought ! can the mild, the juſt, the generous Haroun be capable of ſuch barbarity !—Rely not on virtues, replied Fatima, which have not been tried and found proof againſt the paſſions. A prince is often a ſtranger to his own diſpoſition, and much more to his ſubjects ; and an abſolute monarch can eaſily obtain the reputation of juſtice, clemency, goodneſs and generoſity, ſince a cheap purchaſe of fame is the principal prerogative of ſovereignty. But the more powerful any prince is, the more is he piqued and prejudiced by oppoſition ; and he only, who is abſolute maſter of his own paſſions, deſerves the encomiums you mention, and not he, whoſe clemency and goodneſs are the effect of a weak mind.—You are ignorant, then, replied Abbaſſah, that the Calif has already merited the character I give

give him. He was formerly passionately in love with the princess of Circassia, and though on the point of marrying her, he readily sacrificed his own gratifications, and presented Zeinib to the prince of Carismia, between whom there had long subsisted a mutual flame, notwithstanding she even offered to resign her lover in gratitude to my brother. This noble action, which I learned from Giafar, greatly abates my fears.—This circumstance, replied Fatima, is not sufficient to depend upon in such a dangerous case. Alas! my dear Zelia, you distinguish not between a public action, of which vanity and the hopes of praise is generally the motive, and a private one, to which no such incense will be offered. Moreover, in punishing Giafar's perjury, Haroun may think himself actuated by a laudable zeal, though love and jealousy are in reality his motives. This consideration shews but too plainly how little you can depend on his virtues, which probably may be only nominal. Alas! his passion for you, and indeed every circumstance, seems to threaten the most fatal consequences; for he that is base enough to make both his friend and his mistress miserable, will not shew much clemency if they gave him an opportunity to exercise his resentment.—You shock me, Fatima, replied Abbassah with a sigh! Alas! that very passion you seem to dread is our greatest security, and you may also depend on the inflexibility of Giafar's honour, which I am certain is proof against the most enticing allurements of love!—— Malice made Zobeide as uneasy as friendship did Fatima; she had enjoyed a barbarous satisfaction from the Calif's jealousy, which he was often unable to suppress, and was very sensibly concerned for having put an end to it by the letter she had forged. She likewise greatly dreaded an explanation between the Calif and Giafar, which would convict her of such a base artifice as no one but herself could be guilty of. My Lord, said she to him, you have, I think, sufficiently discharged the duty of a friend by the promise you made Giafar of sending him into Greece; and it is his duty to solicit its accomplishment, since that will deprive you of the pleasure you now enjoy in a frequent intercourse with Abbassah while her husband is with her. The Vizir ought to return your favours by an unreserved confidence; but can we expect such a confidence from a friend who is sensible it would be disagreeable to both parties? Giafar, assured that if you were acquainted with the real merit of his self-denial, it would appear but a very small compliment, chuses rather that you should judge of it by what you feel in your own breast; though to depreciate a laudable action discourages the author from repeating it. Thus Zobeide, though ignorant of the effect her scandalous letter had on Giafar and Zelia, endeavoured to secure the consequences she so much wished for. It is strange that so many artifices should be requisite to entangle in the toils of pleasure two hearts so deeply enamoured, two lovers, whom opportunity, and the importunity of their passions, were every moment seducing!—-Giafar was never easy but when with his dear Zelia; Zelia lived solely for him, and unacquainted with the snares of love, was lavish of the most endearing caresses. Many days were spent in these amorous transports, which were increased by that restraint the presence of Fatima laid them under; and these efforts of passion were succeeded by a languor, as a tender flower, which the rising sun embellishes with the highest lustre, fades under its meridian rays.—It was their mutual desire, though they dreaded its consequences, to enjoy each other's company in private, unmolested by the impertinent eyes of curiosity; and wished-for opportunities, however fatal they may prove, are never long wanting to those who have

them

them in their own power.——Giafar and Abbaſſah chanced to meet one morning in the ſame ſhady walk, which had been the firſt witneſs of their mutual anxiety. They were at firſt greatly ſurpriſed; they approached each other with trembling ſteps, and in great confuſion! their meeting eyes communicated the mutual ardour of their breaſts! Both of them, actuated by the moſt violent paſſion, extended their arms to the object of their wiſhes, which they encircled in thoſe ſoft bonds! Sighs were the only language they uttered! Thus enfolded in each others arms, they ſunk down under the violence of their tranſports, and Nature's carpet, whoſe beautiful verdure was enamelled with a thouſand flowers, ſupplied the place of the nuptial bed, and Aurora was the Hymeneal torch! Giafar compleated his perjury before he recollected his oath!—Abbaſſah, recovering firſt from her extaſy, ſaid with a ſigh, Alas! what have we done! you will now deſpiſe me! your deſires being gratified, you will not be able to ſupport that remorſe the violation of your oath gives but too juſt occaſion for, which obligation the violence of paſſion made you forget.——I will then, replied Giafar, for ever blot it out of my memory. The ſame ardour unchilled by enjoyment, ſhall always reign in my breaſt. But how can you give way to ſuch alarming thoughts? Can a breaſt enraptured with love, can Zelia in the arms of a huſband that adores her, entertain ſuch fears and ſuſpicions?—The fear of loſing my charming ſpouſe, replied Zelia, occaſions this anxiety; the more happy I am, the more am I ſhocked at the proſpect of my approaching miſery; and what felicity is proof againſt ſuch apprehenſions?—Though revenge and jealouſy, my dear Zelia, replied Giafar, ſhould puniſh our raptures with the moſt ſhocking death, yet even that could not diſunite us! Let us not haſten our woes, let us rather become every moment the more criminal. I, for my part, ſhall never in the leaſt ſcruple it.—The ardour of your paſſion, replied Zelia, diſtracts me; it greatly increaſes the flame in my own boſom, and I am at preſent infinitely more happy than when I firſt enjoyed the light of the ſun after ſo many years of confinement. The moment that bleſſes an enraptured heart with the object of its wiſhes, is ſunſhine to the ſoul, and without love, life is a dark, dreary deſert!—Giafar and Abbaſſah did not think of parting, until their prudence was awaked by a noiſe in the ſeraglio. Abbaſſah inſtantly repaired to her apartment in great fear and confuſion, though ſhe much more dreaded the diſcernment and friendſhip of Fatima, than the many dangerous ſpies which ſurrounded her. A ſweet ſlumber ſoon calmed all her fears; and as ſoon as ſhe awoke, her felicity was renewed by the embraces of Giafar, who, unwilling to diſturb her repoſe, waited under the ſtrongeſt emotions of love for the dawn of her bright eyes! Though Fatima had frequently ſeen them laviſh of the moſt tender careſſes, yet, from the matter of expreſſing their affection at preſent, ſhe clearly diſcerned what had paſſed between the two lovers; and by taking particular notice of Abbaſſah, her ſuſpicions were quickly confirmed; ſhe, however, concealed this diſcovery, for uſeleſs reproaches ſerve only to expoſe a mean ſplenetic diſpoſition.—Abbaſſah had ſpent many enraptured nights in the arms of her huſband, when ſhe ſaid one day to Fatima, You have undoubtedly experienced the utmoſt ardour of love, ſince you are ſo well acquainted with the nature of that paſſion, and the many errors it leads us into, making us ſometimes tranſgreſs even the ſacred laws of friendſhip. I have, my dear Zelia, interrupted Fatima, and upon that account excuſe your conduct. The pleaſure you have enjoyed gave me great uneaſineſs, but

but I did not think proper to moleſt you; and the dread you had of my admonitions, by increaſing your watchfulneſs, has prevented a diſcovery of the affair. When the mind is enraptured with the enjoyment of its wiſhes, it is happy in itſelf; it then diſregards friendſhip, whoſe aſſiſtance it only wants when in miſery and diſtreſs; and I did not wiſh to be again honoured with your confidence on theſe conditions.—Alas! replied Zelia, you ſhock me by attributing to ſuch motives my confeſſion, which was the only circumſtance wanting to compleat my happineſs, and which nothing but the fear of alarming you could have ſo long ſuppreſſed: but ſince you are ſo intimately acquainted with my breaſt, it is unneceſſary to inform you what I ſuffer. —What! replied Fatima, has your brother detected Giaſar's perjury? Has Nair betrayed you?—— No, returned Abbaſſah, Nair has been the faithful guardian of our pleaſures; it is the unhappy Zelia that will accuſe her ſpouſe. Alas! what will become of me, ſince I ſhall ſhortly be an undeniable proof of Giafar's perjury! I ſhall not be able to deceive the watchful eyes of Haroun, who ſo frequently viſits me! How can I avoid his prying curioſity in my preſent dangerous ſituation! how can I conceal myſelf from him in a place where he is abſolute! Giafar will fall a victim to his brutal jealouſy; but as I alone am culpable, I will ſuffer firſt! Pity me not, Fatima! your ſuſpicions are juſtified by my unpardonable imprudence!—I ſhall not reproach you, replied Fatima with a ſigh, but on the contrary uſe the beſt means in my power to protect you, if poſſible, at leaſt to comfort you; for your caſe really deſerves pity rather than cenſure, and the impracticableneſs of an injunction renders the breach of it very excuſable. But that ſame love, which hurried you into this imprudence, ought to ſupport your ſpirits under the preſent

diffi-

difficulties; for a too violent remorſe and inconſiderate dread, by weakening the faculties of the mind, increaſe our danger. Let therefore the remembrance of your paſt happineſs ſupply you with ſufficient reſolution to defend yourſelf in your preſent dangerous ſituation.—This advice of Fatima ſomewhat abated the fears of Abbaſſah, which were quickly after entirely diſpelled by the arrival of Giafar. Dry up your tears, my dear Zelia, ſaid he with an air of ſecurity, for love has ſuggeſted to me a ſcheme that will undoubtedly preſerve us both. Counterfeit, when in the preſence of your brother, the moſt confirmed melancholy, repreſent to him in the moſt affecting terms my coldneſs and indifference, and at laſt inform him, that, in hopes of freeing yourſelf from an hopeleſs paſſion, you have vowed to our holy prophet to make a pilgrimage to Mecca. Haroun will make no objection to your deſign, as he will be but too much intereſted in its ſucceſs; and to make this journey the more agreeable, Nair and Fatima ſhall attend you.—How can you, cruel man, interrupted Abbaſſah, imagine, that I ſhall be able to ſupport life, even for a moment, under the torments of abſence. It would to be ſure, replied Giafar with ſome warmth, be very proper to excuſe you this anxiety; but ſhall not I myſelf be an equal ſufferer? If you approve not what I propoſe, let the Calif pierce this perjured breaſt in your arms; your innocence I ſuppoſe will protect you, and you will have the pleaſure of receiving my laſt breath! The affection I ſhall then expreſs in my countenance will inform Haroun better than his own ſenſations, at what price I ſold my life!—What a ſhocking image, replied Abbaſſah, is this you repreſent to me? Do you thus ſeverely puniſh the blind and excuſable ſuggeſtions of an unhappy paſſion? Well, I will endeavour to get the better of my weakneſs; I approve of your

projeƈt,

project, and will bear without repining the pangs of separation, if such a case can be supposed to happen to two lovers whose hearts are eternally united! —Fatima had for once the pleasure of seeing love follow the dictates of reason. Haroun would not have been easily induced to part with Zelia, but that in depriving himself of the pleasure of her company, he at the same time removed her from a rival whom she adored; and in such circumstances we can readily part with the object of our affection.

The Calif, ignorant of the tender adieu that privately passed between Giafar and Abbassah, saw only a cold indifference in the countenance and behaviour of the former, which gave him no small satisfaction; and this seeming composure, together with the departure of Zelia, entirely dispersed all his fears. Zobeide indeed plainly perceived that they ought to have produced a contrary effect; but she durst not communicate her suspicions, for fear she should lose the Calif's esteem, by not being able to justify them: she therefore waited for a more favourable opportunity to gratify those black passions which preyed upon her soul. She in vain offered Haroun an eunuch to attend, or more properly to watch Abbassah, in whom she could confide, for he would trust her with no one but Mesrour, who was by no means a proper person for Zobeide's design.

Mesrour, if he had been so disposed, might have easily shared the Calif's confidence with Giafar; but being very well satisfied with the second place in his favour, and incapable of envy, his behaviour to the Vizir was guided by sincerity and truth, and not by a jealous ambition. Having more of the philosopher than courtier in his disposition, he was so far from considering the confidence his master placed in him as a blessing, that

he

he looked upon it as a ſnare that would involve him, either in thoſe misfortunes which are generally attendant on a ſtrict attachment to truth and ſincerity, or in that torturing remorſe which always follows a perfidious policy. Having been a witneſs of the firſt irruption of the Calif's paſſion for Abbaſſah, he even then foreſaw its fatal conſequences; and though Haroun had never ſince dropped the leaſt hint to him about this unhappy affair, yet he plainly ſaw the progreſs of his affection, and the ſchemes he was planning to gratify it. He was ſincerely concerned for Giafar's unhappy ſituation, and, ſuſpecting ſome ſecret reaſon for Abbaſſah's journey, he with greater earneſtneſs undertook the charge of conducting her, for he thought he could not ſerve his maſter better, than by protecting innocence, and ſeemingly countenancing his ridiculous ſcheme.—Abbaſſah, who was very well acquainted with Meſrour's diſpoſition, knew that virtue and humanity had a ſtronger influence on a mind like his, than the moſt unlimited confidence; ſhe therefore ſhewed him that diſtant reſpect, which, by not appearing to have any ſuch deſign, more eaſily gains a perſon to our intereſt than coaxing and flattery.

Nair ſet out upon his journey ſometime before Abbaſſah; and as he had been for a long time a ſlave to the Iman of Mecca, he very well knew the high eſteem he entertained for the family of Ali, and did not in the leaſt doubt intereſting him in the favour of a princeſs who was deſcended from the ſame illuſtrious origin as himſelf.—Not all the care and aſſiduity of Meſrour and Fatima, nor thoſe high honours and ſplendid entertainments, which were in every place preſented to Abbaſſah, could for a moment baniſh from her breaſt her anxious concern for the ſafety of Giafar, whoſe fate her imagination always preſented to her in the moſt

ſhocking

ſhocking colours. For that prudence, and thoſe well-grounded apprehenſions, which we frequently ſacrifice to our pleaſures, amply revenge themſelves upon us, for not following their direction, in the gloomy hours of remorſe. The various diſtreſſes of Oſmaide, which Zelia had never ſo much as thought on in her happy hours, were now ſtrongly recalled to her mind, and filled her breaſt with the moſt dire omens! Fatima in vain endeavoured to call her thoughts and attention to the beauties and curioſities of the different countries through which they travelled. No, my dear Fatima, ſaid ſhe, the united wonders of nature and art make not the leaſt impreſſion on my breaſt; a violent paſſion has taken poſſeſſion of every faculty of my ſoul, and excludes all other objects. In the hour of my eaſe and tranquillity, every thing ſurpriſed and charmed me. But now the moſt agreeable amuſements are inſipid, nay even give me diſguſt! You may remember, Fatima, I then ſaid to you, can I ever ceaſe to admire the wonderful variety of nature? alas, I now experience it! But is not this the caſe with all the world? who is not in love? and who is not on that account unhappy? Tell me, Fatima, is not mine and Oſmaide's fate the common lot of mankind? But why have not you acquainted me with thoſe misfortunes your anxiety convinces me you yourſelf have undergone? Ought ſuch an intereſting detail to be concealed from a ſincere and affectionate friend?—Cenſure me not unjuſtly, anſwered Fatima: when you enjoyed an eaſy tranquil mind, I was very careful not to raiſe any commotions in your breaſt, by the leaſt hint concerning a paſſion, the very deſcription of which is dangerous; and during your reſiſtance, and the tumultous agitations of your own heart, my narration would have been very improper, as it would have probably haſtened that unhappy moment, but

but not however have delayed it; for love is a dangerous infectious paſſion. A recital of my woes will at preſent be very proper, as it will take off your attention from your own ſufferings; and that anxiety you will of neceſſity expreſs for me, will in ſome meaſure diminiſh your own. Liſten then, my dear Zelia, and judge if I am not juſtified in giving you a ſhocking portrait of that paſſion which has been the bane of my happineſs.

I was born in Sarmakande, which is dependant on the Califs, in the reign of Uſbec Kan, or more properly in that of his wife Rezia. This city, which has always been renowned for its magnificence, and for its ſurpriſing and delightful ſituation, was at that time the ſeat of gaiety and pleaſure. Rezia had expelled all diſagreeable reſtraint, and unſociable moroſeneſs, which were ſucceeded by taſte, ſpirit and politeneſs. The women were not here ſuch ſlaves as they are in the other provinces of Aſia, for Rezia had enacted laws, which gave them an equal authority with the men; and the very high accompliſhments both of mind and perſon, which this princeſs was poſſeſſed of, gave her an abſolute ſway over her huſband. As her authority was ſuperior to his in all the Leſſer Tartary, ſhe preſcribed every thing that was contradictory to the ſweets of ſociety. And though this liberty was ſometimes abuſed, yet particular caſes were no reaſon for altering thoſe inſtitutions which conſtituted the happineſs of the community. In ſhort, ſhe made no diſtinction between entertainment and utility, pleaſure and happineſs. The deſire of rendering themſelves agreeable and pleaſing was become the univerſal motive of both ſexes; and this change was eaſily effected, as the natives of Sarmakande have been always remarkable for having naturally more vivacity than other people in Aſia; and they were now convinced that real

real felicity muſt be founded in the heart, and has no connection with the wild extravagant reveries of the imagination.—Their ancient form of government had naturally brought them to a good diſpoſition and gentleneſs of manners, qualities which Rezia enjoyed from nature, who had alſo endowed her with abilities ſurpaſſing all her own ſex, and even the other, which arrogantly takes the liberty of excluding us from the more profound parts of ſcience, to which this princeſs had applied herſelf with great diligence and ſucceſs.

Sarmakande was founded by one of the kings of Yemen, of that illuſtrious family of the Hemiarites, from which you, my dear Zelia, are deſcended; and from this prince they received thoſe wiſe inſtitutions which the tyranny of the Caliſs had not entirely effaced when Rezia again reſtored them.—If education has the power of giving us prejudices which are really contrary to our nature and diſpoſition, how great muſt be its force when it joins the bent of our own inclinations? Hormoz, for that was the name of my father, educated me in the principles of Rezia; he was connected by conſanguinity with Uſbec Khan, and was particularly intimate with his wife from their great ſimilarity of taſte and diſpoſition; this ſecond ſpecies of connection, though not ſo warm as love, nor ſo reſtraining as friendſhip, is probably the moſt agreeable of all unions; for in this caſe, complaiſance coſts nothing, or more properly loſes its name and becomes inſtinct, when two perſons are united by ſuch an exact uniformity of thought.—Hormoz, being deſirous that I ſhould attain thoſe accompliſhments of ſcience, which he ſo much admired in Rezia; and that, like her, I ſhould join a love of virtue to the enjoyment of all innocent amuſements, and be able to diſtinguiſh between reaſon and prejudice, entruſted the care of my education

to

to the philoſopher Mondir.—Mondir was a very agreeable man, though a very extraordinary character; his country and family were entirely unknown. He uſed frequently to expreſs himſelf to his friends in the following manner: I have too great a regard for ſociety not to pay a proper reſpect to its obligations. I can neither attempt to eradicate prejudices that are univerſally received, nor ſuffer myſelf to be enſlaved by them; thoſe we generally retain for our friends, and our native country are, in my opinion, fooliſh and trifling; and as I am entirely ignorant of the place of my nativity, I am free from that foible which otherwiſe I might have thought my duty. Every man of honour and honeſty is my friend and relation; and the place I like beſt is my country.—Mondir joined to the moſt extenſive knowledge, the moſt fertile and brilliant imagination, and to the moſt perſuaſive eloquence, the happieſt elocution and the juſteſt ſtile; and the goodneſs of his heart, the ſweetneſs and freedom of his manners, added a luſtre to the accompliſhments of his mind. He was grown old in the purſuit of knowledge; and, which was his only defect, was too much inclined to ſcepticiſm, a misfortune often attendant on a rigid enquiry after truth. He aſcribed too much to chance; and tho' endowed with the moſt conſummate prudence, he diſregarded this uſeful qualification, from an attachment to his ſyſtem. He uſed to ſay, that of all the faculties of the ſoul, foreſight was the moſt uſeleſs to mankind, for ſince they are the ſport of chance and accident, of what ſervice can this be to them?—Mondir had quitted Greece to reſide at Sarmakande; and upon coming there, he waited upon Hormoz, and ſaid to him, Sir, my name is Mondir, and the ignorance or prejudice of the world has diſtinguiſhed me by the title of Philoſopher. My years have been divided

vided between dignity and honour, misery and poverty ; but a thirst for truth, a love of study, and a warmth of temper, have rendered me insensible of the calamities of life. Moreover, I was not desirous of accumulating riches, being sensible that such a step would be attended with the loss of my liberty, a blessing I esteem above every consideration ; and what chains can be so galling as those acknowledgments men of spirit are sometimes obliged to pay a mean, pitiful benefactor?—I know you very well, Hormoz, continued Mondir ; I have been sufficiently informed of the greatness of your soul, and fear not being treated by you with contempt, a thing I have always sedulously avoided. The comforts of life are all I require, for I am past the pleasures of it. I am come to end my days with you in ease and tranquillity, and hope also to enjoy the pleasures of society and the sweets of friendship.—The noble assurance and frankness of Mondir gave Hormoz great satisfaction ; he has ever since lived with my father, and they are now united by the most indissoluble friendship.

Hormoz was of opinion that Mondir should proceed with all haste to form my judgment and morals ; Mondir, on the contrary, thought that it was too early to undertake that task. Let us wait a little, said he, and let us, if we can, discover the bent of Fatima's disposition. A blind man frequently quits the smooth even track, and falls down the very precipice he dreaded. Whilst we are endeavouring to secure Fatima against one passion, we shall strengthen its opposite, which may possibly be the most prevailing and dangerous ingredient in her constitution.—I by no means approve of your system, replied Hormoz. It is much easier for reason to repel than to eradicate the passions. Let us be as expeditious as we can to guard Fatima against the snares that may be laid

laid for her virtue. Cannot you, while I am looking out for a proper match, and endeavouring to make her happy in a lawful paſſion, check the ardor of youth, and prevent any ill conſequences from her free and unconfined manner of living, by engaging her thoughts, and by that means confine her more ſtrongly than we could by ſeverity? Cannot we fully employ her mind, without deſtroying its tranquillity?—Undoubtedly, replied Mondir; the neceſſity of loving, and the deſire of knowledge, are innate principles in our ſouls, and ſuch is their violence that they very ſeldom ſubſiſt in the ſame breaſt. But how can we determine in this caſe? for both theſe principles have their good and their ill conſequences. Though ſcience informs and directs us, yet, by exciting ſelf-love, it hurries us into ſuch extravagances as render us inſupportable to others, and often even to ourſelves. And love, though it ſoftens our manner, and conſtitutes the pleaſure of ſociety, yet it often tranſgreſſes its limits, and renders us equally criminal and miſerable. I muſt confeſs, however, that to inſpire women with a becoming pride, is the leaſt hazardous of the two; for it is a check upon their virtue, and their natural weakneſs and ſoftneſs of diſpoſition will prevent their being hurried by this vice into thoſe extravagances the men too frequently are guilty of. I promiſe you therefore, continued Mondir, to follow the plan you propoſe in the education of your daughter.—It was neceſſary, Abbaſſah, to bring you acquainted with Mondir; it is to him you are obliged for thoſe uſeful and inſtructive leſſons I have given you; you have reaped the fruit of his admonitions to me. You will ſee by the detail of my errors and follies, that I did not inſtil into your breaſt thoſe ſentiments which proved my own ruin; but thoſe which ought to have regulated my conduct, and which have at

laſt

laſt reſtored me to a juſt way of thinking and acting—Mondir delivered all his admonitions with ſo much politeneſs and good humour, as made them very engaging, and I willingly poſtponed every amuſement and pleaſure to liſten to his inſtructions. —Let us, ſaid he, ſurvey with admiration the wonders of nature; let us examine her productions, and endeavour to diſcover the ſupreme director of this ſpacious univerſe, a very ſmall part of which is ſubjected to our inſpection. We ſhall not, indeed, attain the end of our enquiries, but we ſhall reap this advantage, we ſhall free ourſelves from thoſe groveling vulgar notions, ſo unworthy of the great author of nature.—Mondir then acquainted me with the imperfection of human nature in the eyes of the ſupreme, and the neceſſity of public worſhip to implore his pardon and protection. He then inſtructed me in the Greek and Roman mythology, and in the myſteries of the ſeveral religions that have ſucceeded them. He explained to me the reaſons why legiſlators have differed in their moral inſtitutions, and proved to me, that the various diſpoſitions and paſſions occaſioned by the variety of climates neceſſarily produced a difference in morality.—Though the inſtructions of Mondir had the effect Hormoz expected, yet they were alſo productive of that which Mondir dreaded. Elate with the extenſive ſcience I had acquired, I did not perceive the leaſt vacancy in my breaſt; my enlarged ideas made me look on the infirmity of love, and the ſtrength of the paſſions, with a ridiculous ſcorn and contempt. I deſpiſed all my admirers who appeared to have a deſign upon my liberty, and looked upon their propoſals as the higheſt inſult. My ſpirit and vivacity gained me the admiration of all the gentlemen of the court; but I quickly found that the women looked upon me with all the eyes of hatred and jealouſy; they had

had excused my great superiority of beauty, but could not bear my boasted proficiency in science. The accomplishments of person are not so liable to excite envy as those of the mind; the former are not in our power, and we may even flatter ourselves that we are possessed of them when we are not; but we cannot help perceiving with the most sensible concern our deficiency in the latter.—I had for a long time vainly placed my whole felicity in my boasted superiority, when a fatal moment overturned my whole system.—Usbec Khan had assisted Zeid in the rebellion he raised against Mahadi; but the articles of his alliance with that prince were a profound secret until some years after, when, upon banishing his Prime Vizir, this private contract was revealed to the Calif, who immediately sent an army against the monarch of the Lesser Tartary. Usbec Khan was slain in the first rencounter; and Rezia, reduced to a private station, was obliged to quit her palace to the governor Mahadi appointed over Sarmakande. Hormoz received her into his own palace, and, disregarding the Calif's resentment, shewed her the same respect as he did when she sat upon the throne.

The Tartars had always entertained a great affection and veneration for Rezia; and since, when in power, she had used her authority with great moderation, they were at present so far from triumphing in her fall, that every one exerted his utmost to alleviate her misfortunes. She had even at present more power in Sarmakande than the Calif himself. having the entire possession of every person's affection.—After her first transports of grief, which arose from the loss of Usbec Khan, and not of her own dignity, were abated, she rendered the palace of Hormoz the seat of wit and pleasure, and the residence of the graces. Every agreeable

agreeable person of both sexes in Sarmakande met there every day, and their assembly was solely directed by the sincerest and purest love. The Calif's deputy at first censured this freedom, as he had never before seen any such usage; but, as soon as he was acquainted with its innocence, he took it as a particular favour to be admitted one of that society which he had before intended to suppress.—Rezia never failed to procure the affection of every one that had the happiness of her company, in which I spent the greatest part of my time. I found her one day more thoughtful and melancholy than usual, and her natural evenness of temper made me suspect that there was some very serious motive for her anxiety; I therefore most affectionately intreated her to acquaint me with the cause of it, and she answered as follows.

I need not inform you, Fatima, that at the time Usbec Khan fell a victim to a base traitor, the prince Mirza my son was at the court of Mahadi, and educated along with the two young princes Hadi and Haroun. I was at that time very solicitous lest he should be involved in his father's misfortune; but the friendship Haroun had conceived for him protected him for the present, and the death of Mahadi, which happened soon after, entirely calmed my disquietudes on that subject.—During the whole reign of Hadi, and ever since the commencement of that of Haroun, I have tried every method to procure the return of my son, but to no purpose. He could not be branded with the odious appellation of rebel, since he did not appear in arms against the usurper, and the province of Little Tartary was upon the point of recovering the liberty of Mirza by force. Your father approved of my plan, and supported my endeavours to secure to my interest the principal personages of the province; my gratitude for these services, and my affection

affection for you, induced me to promise him that you should be married to my son.—Our project has not been betrayed; but whether they dreaded our influence, or suspected our design, they have removed all those persons that were able to execute our plan, by ordering them to repair to the Calif's court. This step gave me great concern; and though the dispatches I have just received from the Calif have dispelled my anxiety on this head, yet they have thrown me into fresh perplexities. He is at last pleased to restore me my son, and to place him on the throne of his father; but he commands him to marry a princess of the family of Abbas. Mahomed will shortly attend him and his spouse, in order to present them with the scepter of Sarmakande.—Judge, my dear Fatima, what anxiety I at present labour under!—I must not only be united to a family which the unhappy fate of Usbec Khan has rendered odious to me, but I must also resign my hopes of having you for my daughter, for whom I have as strong an affection as if you had been my own child. I have moreover given my solemn promise to Hormoz, and sooner than violate that, I will refuse my consent to the match they have obliged Mirza to accept.

I am not insensible that Mirza might both marry the Calif's relation and fulfil my engagement; but your rival might prove an imperious mistress, and your merits, my dear Fatima, claim a better treatment. I thought that you were the only woman in the world that could make my son so compleatly happy! Alas! my plausible project is blasted. But I perceive Hormoz is coming, I will communicate the affair to him, and we will consider of proper methods to prevent this step, and calm my anxiety.

Hormoz, greatly affected by the noble disinterestedness of Rezia, did not yield to her in point of generosity.

generofity. He begged her not to pay any regard to their former engagements: he chearfully refign-ed the promife fhe had made him, and folemnly de-clared, that he would not upon any confideration be an obftacle to Mirza's felicity. Thefe deter-minations gave me the higheft fatisfaction, for fuch was my ridiculous vanity, that I did not think the man was yet born who could merit the facrifice of my liberty. Such was my error, for which I have fince atoned by the moft excruciating torments.—The Tartars were enraptured at the fight of their prince, and Sarmakande rioted in joy upon his arrival. The ladies exerted their utmoft art to captivate his af-fections, in which every one hoped to fucceed. It is impoffible to defcribe the grandeur of Rezia's court on this joyful occafion; the magnificent ap-pearance of the men, and the richnefs and elegance of the dreffes of the ladies, gave an additional luftre to the genteelnefs of the one, and the beauty of the other. I was too haughty to comply with that affiduity and forwardnefs which I looked upon as a meannefs in the reft of my fex; I even neglected the proper refpect I owed to Rezia to gratify my vanity, and I did not go to court till fome time af-ter the reft of the company; where, though with-out the advantage of drefs, I attracted the notice of Mirza.—Rezia had given me fuch high enco-miums in her letters to her fon, that he was pre-judiced in my favour, and the firft glance I had of Mirza made an impreffion on my heart, which all the ardour and affiduity of my other admirers had never been able to effect. I inftantly thought him the moft agreeable of his fex, and quickly per-ceived that he was poffeffed of every foible and every grace neceffary to captivate a female heart.—Mir-za is perfectly well-made, his air is noble, and his whole figure is conformable to the niceft pro-portions of beauty; but it is difficult to examine theſe perfections, ſince you always meet in his countenance either a commanding air that intimidates, or ſuch a languiſhing paſſionate expreſſion as neceſſarily repells your eyes.—Being born with good natural parts, and educated in the moſt ſprightly and polite court of Aſia, Mirza can render himſelf engaging whenever he pleaſes. But he frequently, through a caprice which he himſelf is not ſenſible of, alters his behaviour from the moſt entertaining to the moſt diſagreeable. The juſteſt and moſt elegant compliments offend his modeſty, and his ſelf-love is too well regulated to permit his declaiming on his own excellencies. He gives an air of ſimplicity to every thing he ſays and does, nay even to that extraordinary pomp and pageantry with which he is ſurrounded. One cannot diſcover in him the leaſt ſpark of ſelf-love, except by that contempt which he ſometimes caſually ſhews to others. He frequently makes the quickeſt tranſitions from the higheſt aſſurance to the moſt cringing timidity, and from the greateſt eagerneſs to the moſt cold indifference, but without forfeiting his ſincerity, for his diſpoſition is not falſe and perfidious, only haſty and paſſionate. He is violently attached to pleaſure, but incapable of refined ſenſations. He pretends to diſregard the ladies, though he is at the ſame time their moſt aſſiduous adorer. His impetuoſity and impatience, which are his diſtinguiſhing characteriſticks, muſt be aſcribed to the violence of his paſſions. In ſhort, he is naturally brave and generous, but thoughtleſs, and incapable of reflexion. From this portrait, my dear Zelia, continued Fatima, you will eaſily foreſee the calamities in which I was involved! I did not chuſe that you ſhould draw his character from the ſequel of my narrative, but give you it before, that you may the more eaſily comprehend and compaſſionate my melancholy tale.—Notwithſtanding the great

great gallantry and politeneſs that reigned at Sarmakande, there was ſomething in the air and manner of Mirza that greatly affected me. A noble freedom gave a grace to every thing he ſaid, I liſtened to him with pleaſure, and could not look upon him without a ſecret irreſiſtible emotion; which Mirza perceiving, he increaſed my embaraſſment, by taking more particular notice of me, and was himſelf in his turn equally perplexed.—The flattering ſarcaſms of Rezia, on perceiving my ſituation, threw me into the greateſt confuſion; for notwithſtanding all my efforts to the contrary, the prince of the Tartars engroſſed all my thoughts. I was very deſirous of diſcovering his real ſentiments, but dreaded finding the ſame fickleneſs in his breaſt which I obſerved in his countenance and behaviour. The manner in which Mirza treated thoſe who courted his favour and affection, gave me an anxiety I could not account for; and thoſe ladies of the court, whoſe beauty I before looked upon with contempt, now appeared poſſeſſed of the moſt enchanting charms, and notwithſtanding my vanity, I almoſt repented my not following their example, in embelliſhing my perſon with the higheſt decorations of art—Theſe notions and diſquietudes deprived me of that ſteady, ſerious reflection which could alone reſiſt the paſſion that at preſent poſſeſſed my heart. Mondir, perceiving my ſituation, ſaid to me, lay it down, my dear Fatima, as an infallible maxim, that love always renders thoſe the meaneſt of his vaſſals, who boaſt the higheſt diſregard of his power.—This pertinent obſervation awakened by reflection; and interrupting him with ſome warmth, I ſaid, Is it poſſible, Mondir, that you can diſcover in my breaſt a ſingle ſpark of that flame which I have always treated with the higheſt contempt, though it probably ought to be conſidered in a more ſerious light than I have yet looked upon it?—Alas! my dear Fatima, replied Mondir, love has undoubtedly taken poffeffion of your heart, fince you begin to dread its influence; but be affured that the perfon, upon whom you at prefent place your affection, will only render you the flave of a hopelefs, tormenting paffion.—I was juft going to cenfure Mondir for this difcouraging prediction, when Mirza, cloyed with the repeated attempts to gain his affection, came to attack a breaft that would have gladly had it in its power to have refifted his folicitations. Mirza had partly heard the laft words of Mondir; and faid, I am not in the leaft furprifed, Madam, to find that your charms have made an impreffion even upon the philofophic difpofition of Mondir; but it gives me the higheft fatisfaction, that you permit your fuppliants to complain. This addrefs, or rather the gay unconcerned manner of delivering it, greatly offended me, and I only replied by a difdainful fmile.—Mirza, perceiving that a light foppifh behaviour would not anfwer his purpofe, quickly became more ferious; he expreffed in his countenance the greateft ardour of paffion, or more properly the refemblance of it, whilft I myfelf was folely agitated by a real flame. My refentment was, however, foon calmed by Mirza's changing the manner of his addrefs; and he has fince told me, that my looks infured him that forgivenefs which he folicited by his own.—Thefe forts of reconciliations, and that rapture, which is occafioned by an expreffive glance, are the moft tempting fnares of love, the origin, power and effects of which I was at prefent an entire ftranger to. Mirza now became my conftant companion, which occafioned Hormoz and Rezia no fmall anxiety; but as I did not in the leaft fufpect from what had paffed that my behaviour would difoblige them, I did not alter my conduct; and as their converfation ſation would in my preſent ſituation have been very taſteleſs and inſipid, I avoided their company as much as I could; for what I moſt wiſhed for at preſent was ſolitude, that I might have leiſure to examine thoſe new ſenſations which at preſent had the ſole poſſeſſion of my heart.—That regard, which the deſire of rendering myſelf ſuperior to the reſt of my ſex, had induced me to expreſs for their foibles, quickly diſcovered to me my own weakneſs, and I was aſhamed of entertaining ſuch a mean ſentiment. But can the bias of inclination be checked by reaſon? My judgment endeavoured to vindicate what it durſt not condemn, and was the more dangerous caſuiſt, the more it had been improved by inſtruction.—I thus reaſoned with myſelf. The virtue of moderation exiſts ſolely in narrow minds, whoſe contracted views fetter their abilities; for no perſon commits himſelf to the guidance of his paſſions without being maſter of ſufficient art to juſtify his extravagances. May not a noble ſoul follow the dictates of love, without being aſhamed of a chain which nature has formed, and pleaſure rendered light and eaſy; and which reaſon or reſentment can eaſily throw off whenever we pleaſe?—Sleep was ſo far from interrupting my agitations and errors, that it increaſed them by the moſt enchanting illuſions. One morning when I awoke, a ſlave preſented me with a baſket of flowers ſent by Mirza, and whilſt I was enjoying the odoriferous perfume, I perceived a paper faſtened to the ſtalk of a moſt beautiful carnation.—The celeſtial art of poetry, which is juſtly eſteemed the higheſt effort of human abilities, undoubtedly took its origin from the warm and fertile imaginations of the inhabitants of the eaſt; and Mirza being a maſter of this ſcience, made uſe of it to acquaint me with his paſſion; and his verſes, which would

 have

have even done honour to that prince of bards Aboukakemi, were a pattern of the higheſt juſtneſs and ſtrength of expreſſion, together with the moſt conſummate taſte and elegance.—When the judgment is only caſually miſled by inclination, a lucid interval may be of the higheſt importance; but when it is become totally the ſlave of paſſion, our ruin is inevitable. I ſhould not have anſwered Mirza's billet, if it had not excited my vanity, and love readily dictated a proper reply, without my knowing the real motive of my wit. I ſoon reflected that this ſtep might too much countenance Mirza's pretenſions; and to confirm my conjecture, the firſt time I met him in Rezia's apartment, he behaved with all the rapture and aſſurance of a ſucceſsful lover. To check his warmth, I ſaid with a ſternneſs which I with difficulty aſſumed, Do you not know, Sir, that the intended union betwixt you and me is entirely diſſolved? Has not Rezia and Hermoz informed you of this affair?—I cannot at preſent, Madam, replied he, recollect what they may have ſaid on this ſubject, for your preſence effaces every conſideration; on you alone depends my fate, and from you alone I will receive my doom. You ought, replied I, to be ſatisfied with that felicity which the Calif has allotted you, and which, from my friendſhip for Rezia, and duty to you my ſovereign, I will exert every method in my power to promote.—While I thus expreſſed myſelf, Mirza gazed on me with ſuch an enchanting look as entirely deſtroyed my pretended auſterity, and I could not help expreſſing myſelf in an accent more tender and paſſionate than I firſt intended. He permitted me to proceed ſome time without interruption; but at laſt he exclaimed, Can my dear Fatima entertain a ſentiment ſo contradictory to the high opinion I had conceived of her underſtanding! I might even appeal to yourſelf with reſpect to a prejudice ſo incon-

inconſiſtent with your diſcernment! I might prove to you that our inclination and diſpoſition ought to be the ſole rule of our actions! but ſince you will not conſent to make me happy without the approbation of Hormoz, I muſt enquire who has informed you that I would diſpenſe with the promiſe he has given me on this point. As to Rezia's conſent, that is of no importance, for it is not in her power without my compliance to deprive me of ſuch an ineſtimable bleſſing.—Would you have me then, Sir, replied I, to become a ſlave to my rival? Your rival, my dear Fatima, replied he with great ardour! Heavens! what a raviſhing expreſſion! You have, I aſſure yon, no reaſon to dread a caſe which is impoſſible to happen; and I will reject Haroun's intended favour, if I cannot otherwiſe calm your anxiety. But I can eaſily make a difference betwixt you and the Calif's niece that will ſatisfy all your ſcruples; for if ſhe, to whom you vouchſafe the appellation of rival, ſhould expreſs the leaſt diſapprobation of my conduct, I can eaſily, being both her huſband and ſovereign, ſuppreſs her complaints.—You will by that means, ſaid I with a ſigh, incur the Calif's reſentment. I ſhall, replied he with great warmth, readily deſpiſe that, rather than become the ſlave of a woman; for, continued he in a milder accent, I cannot ſubmit to the dictates of any but her whom I adore!—I was going to reply to Mirza, and even perhaps to avow thoſe ſentiments which his ardour and generoſity had excited in my breaſt, when we were interrupted by Mondir, who came to wait upon me by the command of Hormoz.—It was impoſſible for me to conceal from Mondir the agitations of a heart, with which he was ſo intimately acquainted: and as ſoon as Mirza was gone, he ſaid to me, I have, my dear Fatima, thoroughly examined your diſpoſition, and finding pride and vanity your predominant

dominant paſſions, was in hopes they would have protected you from the influence of love; but ſince this laſt has got poſſeſſion of your breaſt, the others will be ſo far from reſcuing you from it, that they will render its effects more violent and fatal. Mirza is fickle and inconſtant, and will pique your vanity by placing his affection on ſome other perſon; but you will notwithſtanding be unable to recover your loſt liberty, for pride and reſentment have often a contrary effect to what might be expected; they will, in your caſe, become the allies of love, and render his chains the more galling.—Alas, Mondir, replied I with great concern! how is it poſſible for you to have formed already any true judgment of Mirza's diſpoſition? how can you prognoſticate ſuch fatal events from mere ſurmiſe? —Do not you perceive, Fatima, ſaid he, how love has already hoodwinked your underſtanding? You can even diſpute my friendſhip, and the ſincerity of my intentions, rather than ſuſpect Mirza, whoſe diſpoſition you are not the leaſt acquainted with, and whoſe intereſt and ambition render it impoſſible for him to be your's. Being educated in thoſe prejudices againſt your ſex, which Rezia has ſo lately expelled from this province, he will undoubtedly re-eſtabliſh them, and you will be the firſt victim of this reformation.—That inconſtancy, in which he has been educated from his infancy, is of too contagious a nature not to have infected his heart, and his fickleneſs will increaſe with his power; for when he ſhall have rendered himſelf the abſolute ſovereign of the ladies, he will treat them as a maſter, and not as a lover. Nothing can unalterably fix the affections of man, but the fear of loſing the object of his paſſion, and love quickly vaniſhes when we have it in our power to gratify it at pleaſure. You will experience theſe truths with the more pungent concern, by not having reflected on them before-hand, and you will plunge yourself into eternal misery for the enjoyment of a few momentary raptures!—Hormoz, continued Mondir, requested me to check you on the brink of this dangerous precipice, for he is not so anxious for your exalted situation in life as for your happiness, which, he thinks, the high honours Mirza offers you will be very far from effecting. But as he judged your own discretion, supported by my advice, would be sufficient for this purpose, he did not chuse to interpose his paternal authority. —I have literally repeated, continued Fatima, Mondir's admonitions, because I am uncertain whether they will palliate or enhance my crimes, or whether they more strongly evince the weakness of my resolution, or the violence of my passion.—As Mirza had looked upon my sighs and agitations as a full confession of a mutual flame, he was greatly surprised the next time he waited upon me, to find in my behaviour a coldness and indifference he had so little reason to expect; he, however, soon altered my conduct. The whole artillery of love is placed in the eyes of the beloved object, and Mirza was but too well acquainted with this maxim. But, alas! if he had been totally incapable of this tender passion, how could he discover the least symptoms of it in another? Therefore it only increases my affliction when he declares himself naturally perfidious; his crime was only inconstancy, for I am satisfied, by the most endearing proofs of affection, that he once loved me, and——But excuse, my dear Zelia, continued Fatima, interrupting her own narration, excuse my unavoidable agitations! You are able, from what I have already said, to form a judgment of my future misery, and suffer me for a moment to bewail an error, the consequences of which can never be erased from my breast!—After

ter a few ſighs, which Zelia affectionately return-ed, Fatima was going to proceed with her narra-tion, when ſhe was interrupted by the arrival of Meſrour, who, under great confuſion and anxiety, addreſſed himſelf to Abbaſſah as follows. I come, Madam, to inform you, that you are even at pre-ſent ſurrounded by the baſe deſigns of the meaneſt treachery; I wiſh I may be always equally ſucceſ-ful in detecting them; but be careful of what you ſay or do, if you would avoid the ſnares of your enemies.—Am I ſtill, alas! replied Abbaſſah with great ſurpriſe, purſued by my brother's love and jealouſy? You, my faithful Meſrour, muſt be beſt acquainted with the motives of theſe proceedings.—I ought, anſwered Meſrour, to be ignorant of thoſe ſecrets which my maſter has not thought pro-per to communicate to me; but I can aſſure you it is not love, but the more dangerous paſſion of ha-tred, which at preſent plans your ruin. A favou-rite ſlave of Zobeide's, whom I have diſcovered amongſt your own, and whom I will immediate-ly ſend to you, will inform you of the ſuſpicions and deſigns of that perfidious princeſs. I have promiſed her her life, on condition that her in-formation is full and ſincere; do you yourſelf ex-amine her, and afterwards determine her fate: as for me, my zeal and friendſhip will ever render me watchful over your ſafety.—Meſrour having thus expreſſed himſelf, departed, leaving Abbaſſah ſtruck dumb with fear; ſhe could not help ima-gining herſelf ſurrounded with unavoidable difficul-ties, but Giafar's ſafety was the principal object of her anxiety. Fatima comforted her by every con-ſideration ſhe could ſuggeſt, for ſhe was more ſo-licitous for Zelia's happineſs than for her own; and as ſhe had been accuſtomed to diſtreſs, her re-ſolution was not ſo eaſily baffled. Misfortunes are naturally productive of courage, which is a [illegible]

proviſion

provision of nature to prevent our sinking under the unavoidable weight of disappointments.

Zobeide's slave came, trembling, and, prostrating herself at Abbassah's feet, said, I wholly rely, Madam, on the known goodness and generosity of your disposition; I acknowledge that I intended to betray you, but punish me not for a design which I was compelled to undertake. Having been bred up in Zobeide's service, I looked upon it as my duty to pay an implicit obedience to her commands; but I hope my sincere confession and repentance will atone for this error.—You may be assured, said Abbassah, of a full pardon; rise and inform me of the motives of a resentment which greatly astonishes me.—Zobeide, replied the slave, is naturally intrepid and designing; and though frequently the sport of the most violent passions, can at pleasure put on the mask of the greatest coolness and moderation. Her birth, beauty and fortune, procured her many admirers, whom she scornfully rejected; and being sole mistress of herself at an age when independance generally proves fatal, she affected the most rigid severity of manners, and publickly declared that she would not entrust her heart or her liberty with any man. I censured this ill judged determination, and endeavoured to excite in her a love of pleasure, and a just regard to her own happiness; but I soon afterwards discovered that her indifference and self-denial were the effect of her ambition, for her vanity suggested to her, that the Calif only was worthy of her affection, and she flattered herself that the fame of her beauty and virtue would attract his regard.—This pursuit employed Zobeide's utmost solicitude, till love occasioned a revolution in her breast; she casually saw Giafar, for whom she conceived so violent a passion as entirely erased every other object. She every day feigned some

business

bufinefs or other to wait upon the Vizir, who always received her with the higheft politenefs, and by flattering her vanity, increafed her paffion. Her haughtinefs would not permit her to acknowledge her flame, nor her impetuofity to wait the event of her endeavours; and fhe contrived to folicit Jahia to marry her to his fon; but Giafar not only difregarded her immenfe riches, and the dignity of her family, but even depreciated her beauty.

Upon this Zobeide's affection was inftantly turned into the moft violent refentment; but fhe found it equally difficult to gratify this new paffion, as Giafar, protected by the friendfhip of Haroun, was impenetrable to all her attempts. Difficulties however have never obliged her entirely to quit her defigns, and fhe renewed her attempts on the Calif's affections. With this view fhe again became a recluse, and very feldom appeared abroad but at the mofques, and in fuch places where her charity and devotion gave an additional luftre to her charms. By this means fhe became the idol of Bagdad; and Haroun, attracted rather by her virtue than her beauty, at length prefented her with his hand.

Giafar, who always fhewed a proper regard to his mafter's inclinations, paid the moft fincere homage to Zobeide, little imagining the rancour that feftered in her heart, as he was fully perfuaded that fhe was unacquainted with his refufal.—Zobeide however employed a thoufand artifices to ruin Giafar, whom Haroun's fincere friendfhip rendered impregnable; and the affection fhe in a fhort time conceived for this amiable monarch, fufpended for a while the efforts of her refentment. But her breaft being a den of turbulent paffions, it was impoffible fhe fhould long enjoy peace of mind; and accordingly fhe quickly fell a prey to jealoufy. Zeinib would have been the victim of this paffion, if if Zobeide could have safely executed her designs, and the self-denial she was in this case obliged to practise greatly abated her affection for the Calif. The succeeding tyrant of her heart was ambition, which for a while comforted her for every disappointment, and gratified her utmost wishes; but this soothing passion was dethroned, and Zobeide driven into despair, by the affection which the Calif conceived for you.

When a woman is not under the influence of love, but only through vanity thinks she ought to be the unrivalled mistress of the person she fixes on, her pride in this case is much more dangerous than a disappointed passion. Accordingly Zobeide determined to render you odious in the eyes of your brother, by exposing you to his criminal desires.—Good God! interrupted Abbassah, what do I hear! was the danger Osmaide so opportunely rescued me from a plot of Zobeide's—It was, Madam, replied the slave; and when this horrid plot had miscarried, Zobeide artfully concealed her resentment, to prevent her being suspected the author; and as the Calif soon after informed her of the oath he had extracted from Giafar, this intelligence gave her the highest satisfaction, and in some degree balanced her late disappointment.—The two objects of her resentment being now so closely united, and so circumstanced, that nothing but a miracle could protect them, she looked upon them as the certain victims of her hatred. But Giafar's steady adherence to his engagement baffled her designs, and, in order to weaken his integrity, she contrived, by what means I know not, to convey to you that letter which gave you so much anxiety. Since that time she has been fully satisfied in her own mind, that Giafar has violated his oath; but as she could not prove her suspicions, she durst not communicate them to the Calif. She still diligently watches all your motions

and

and in order to procure intelligence, ſhe ſold me to the maſter of your eunuchs, intending to purchaſe me again at your return from Mecca ; but my fate is now ſolely in your power, and I humbly implore your clemency.—Abbaſſah and Fatima were greatly ſhocked at this intelligence, and could ſcarcely credit the poſſibility of a perfidy ſo repugnant to their own diſpoſitions ; they, however, ordered the ſlave back to Meſrour, without aſking any further queſtions.

As ſoon as he was gone, Abbaſſah ſaid to Fatima, you may now plainly perceive that I ſhall be the deſtruction of my dear Giafar : for, if he had not been ſeduced by my fatal paſſion, he would have religiouſly obſerved his engagements to Haroun, and the barbarous Zobeide would have been deprived of the pleaſure of glutting her revenge ! But now, alas ! I have provided her a dagger, with which ſhe will aſſaſſinate my huſband ! What dreadful images does this conſideration preſent to my view ! I even imagine that I ſee him expiring under the wounds which my own hand has given him !—Baniſh theſe gloomy thoughts, replied Fatima ; Meſrour's care and circumſpection will protect you from ſuch fatal events ; he will acquaint Giafar with this diſcovery, and will be watchful over your ſecurity ; moreover, the ſureſt method of preventing your impending misfortunes, is to preſerve a ſteady compoſure of mind. The advice I give you was the rule of my conduct when in the like ſituation. Continue then, replied Zelia, continue to ſupport my reſolution by your advice, and the recital of your own misfortunes !——This requeſt drew a ſigh from Fatima ; and though ſhe promiſed Zelia an exact account of her woes, ſhe could not help being deeply affected by the anxiety this narration would give her : but to complain, and to recite our misfortunes to a perſon that will ſhare in them, is the ſole gratification an

afflicted

afflicted heart is capable of enjoying! ſhe therefore recommenced her hiſtory as follows.——As ſoon a Mirza had perſuaded me of the ſincerity of his own paſſion, he demanded a ſimilar acknowledgment from me, which he no ſooner obtained, than he increaſed his demands. He fancied himſelf to have the ſole poſſeſſion of my affections, even before I was acquainted with my own ſentiments, and he ſeemed to doubt my ſincerity when I acknowledged a mutual paſſion. He inſiſted upon ſuch proofs of my affection as were impoſſible for me to comply with; and to prevent his ſolicitations, I urged the inſtructions I had received in my infancy, and the admonitions which Mondir had given me in my riper years; but theſe objections he treated with a childiſh and ſupercilious contempt, and his behaviour was at the ſame time very rude and unbecoming.—If I had been then as thoroughly acquainted with the wiles and artifices of men as I am at preſent, the ſucceſs of my paſſion, which induced me to comply with his requeſt, would have rendered my reſiſtance inſurmountable.—How ridiculous is it, for the men to ſuppoſe, that our minds, which they judge to be much weaker than their own, ſhould reſiſt, both their allurements, and the efforts of a paſſion to which they themſelves ſo frequently ſubmit! How inconſiſtent is their conduct! They try every method to inflame our paſſions, and intoxicate our hearts with love in order to facilitate their deſigns, and afterwards puniſh us for our compliance! But it is too late to reaſon upon their abſurd behaviour, when we have fallen the victims of their treacherous contrivances.—Mirza tried every method to bring Hormoz and Rezia to countenance his paſſion; but Rezia aſſured him, that it was impoſſible for that union to take place until he had fulfilled his engagements with the Calif, and married the lady he had alotted him: this delay gave him no no ſmall uneaſineſs, and the polite, though undeciſive anſwer he received from Hormoz, made him ſuſpect him alſo averſe to his propoſals, which greatly increaſed his anxiety. He for ſome time hoped to ſurmount all theſe obſtacles by the aſſiſtance of my paſſion; but found his expectations diſappointed by my refuſing to ſee him, except when my mother was preſent. Finding himſelf under this reſtriction, he frequently wrote to me, and his letters were penned with that elegance, ſentiment, and ardour of paſſion, that they became like ſo many flaming darts which reached the moſt ſecret receſſes of my heart. I even to this moment feel the effects of thoſe dear but deceitful pledges of his love; and Mirza's letters are the ſole remains of my unhappy flame, and ſupply the place of hope and felicity; nay, they even ſometimes throw me into ſuch a delirium as renders me for a moment compleatly happy.—— Mirza replied to my reproaches on the impetuoſity of his paſſion with ſo much eloquence and love, that he even baffled my reſolution, and made me diſpute the validity of the beſt-grounded arguments. If I was your ſlave, Sir, ſaid I, my reſiſtance, inſtead of being a virtue, would be criminal; for it is our duty to pay all obedience to thoſe who have the ſupreme command over us; but you, Sir, are not as yet even appointed my ſovereign, and I ſolely owe allegiance to Hormoz's paternal authority. I cannot therefore become the property of another without his permiſſion; and though the hopes of being your's might tempt me to elude his vigilance, yet how ſhall I be able to bear the remorſe neceſſarily conſequent on ſuch behaviour; not even all your tenderneſs will be able to ſupport me under the anxiety ſuch a ſtep would occaſion.—The ſole reaſon, replied Mirza, for my endeavouring to bring you to a ſettled determination, is to diſpel your doubts, and to convince you of of your ill-grounded apprehensions, and the sincerity of my passion. Your fluctuating disposition gives me great concern; for I had much rather find you cruel than inconstant, since to live with you and for you is the sole object of my most ardent wishes! Could you, my dear Zelia, imagine that a person of a fickle, roving disposition, was capable of such tender and delicate sentiments!—Mondir supported my faultering resolution by increasing my doubts, and by the prudent instructions he gave me; for he plainly perceived the occasion I had of his assistance, notwithstanding the reserve my vanity made me practise towards him.—During these transactions, Mahomed arrived at Sarmakande; but did not bring along with him the princess who had been destined for Mirza's bride. For the Calif, being greatly surprised at the intimations he had received of Hormoz's and Rezia's designs, was resolved to defer conferring his intended favours on Mirza, until he had married in his presence the lady he had allotted him.—Your affection for Giafar does not, I hope, my dear Zelia, render you insensible to the merit of others; and I assure you, that the highest accomplishments and most exalted virtues are the settled characteristicks of all the family of the Bermicides, which Mahomed's behaviour was very far from disgracing. He had private orders to examine the conduct of Hormoz and Rezia; but not being able to make any discovery to their prejudice, it gave him great pleasure to be able to assure the Calif of their innocence. This circumstance afforded him the more sensible satisfaction as he had conceived a violent passion for me.—I received the addresses of Mahomed with an indifference which he was far from ascribing to my affection for Mirza. For the great reserve I constantly practised, and the situation of Mirza, which rendered it impossible for him to offer me that

dignity

dignity of which Mahomed judged me highly deserving, and the great liberty enjoyed by the ladies of Sarmakande, which made them disdain sharing the affections of a husband with a rival, would not permit him to entertain a thought so repugnant to my haughty spirit, and he accordingly demanded me of my father.—Hormoz, being afraid of incurring either the resentment of Mirza or Haroun, replied to Mahomed's request, that he did not chuse to lay his commands upon me in this case, and that the aversion I had always expressed to a connection which would deprive me of my liberty, had obliged all my admirers to drop their solicitations.——Mahomed was too polite and generous to oppose my father's determination; he resolved to efface the impression I had made on his heart, and for this purpose to quit Sarmakande with all possible expedition: he accordingly informed Mirza, that he had orders to conduct him back to Bagdad.——The thoughts of this separation chilled the very blood in my veins! and though Rezia had for some time dreaded this event, which destroyed her ambitious views, yet she received the intelligence with a seeming satisfaction, and endeavoured to persuade Mirza to look upon it in the same light; but love was the sole director of his sentiments.—He very warmly solicited me, in order to suspend our impending fate, to practise a deceit which my present circumstances made me judge very justifiable; the apprehension of my lover's absence, and the fear of losing him for ever, if I should refuse this specimen of my affection, induced me to comply with his request. My enticing glances retarded the departure of Mahomed, and he feigned excuses for his remaining where he was until he could insure to himself that felicity which my enchanting looks seemed to promise him. Mirza has since reproached me for practising this deceit, by making me the subject of

his

his artifice, whereas Mahomed has generoufly forgiven me: ingratitude always fhields itfelf under fome reproachful furmifes; for the bafe wretch could not but be fenfible, that he was the fole object of my affection. But this unjuft treatment was not the only ill confequence of my foolifh compliance with his requeft; it led me into fuch a feries of errors, as at length made me fully fenfible of the heinoufnefs of that crime, which the ominous conftellation of my nativity doomed me to be guilty of in order to compleat my misfortunes.—The more reftraint I laid myfelf under, by the refpect I fhewed to Mahomed, the lefs I thought myfelf liable of being fufpected of entertaining a real affection for him; a furmife which would have given me the moft fenfible concern. I did not even expect the leaft fuccefs from the artifice Mirza prevailed with me to practife, unlefs love, by blinding my admirer, fhould favour the defign. I at laft difcovered that Mahomed had acquainted the Calif with the neceffity of deferring his departure, and Mirza was employing all his friends in the court of Bagdad to procure a difpenfation for his return thither.——Though I had never verbally given Mahomed any deceitful promifes, I now began to repent of the approbation I had frequently expreffed in my countenance, and I refolved for the future not to be guilty of an artifice which my confcience obliged me to difapprove; but I was too late in forming this refolution.——Being one day at Rezia's court when there was a very numerous and brilliant appearance, Hormoz and Mirza, at whofe abfence I had been furprifed, entered the drawing-room together, and it appeared by their countenances that they were engaged in fome weighty and important affair. Mirza went up haftily to Rezia, and whifpered to her with an air of great fatisfaction: Hormoz in the mean time came to me, and after

taking

taking me afide, faid, I have at laft, my dear Fatima, determined to poftpone my own fcruples to your felicity, even Rezia has advifed me to lay afide my doubts, and I come to inform you that I confent to your marriage with the perfon you adore; the Cadis has finifhed the neceffary inftruments for this purpofe ; but it is requifite that the affair, for reafons I need not acquaint you with, be kept a profound fecret. Retire to your apartment, where your fpoufe will quickly wait upon you, and your felicity will, if poffible, be increafed by the fatisfaction it will give me.——I was ftruck dumb by this fudden inundation of joy, but even my filence fufficiently expreffed the fenfations of my heart : I made all poffible hafte to obey Hormoz's commands, that I might conceal my embarafſment and blufhes from the obfervation of the company.—Safia, faid I, as foon as I got into my own apartment along with my favourite flave, my dear Safia, what excefs of happinefs fhall I now enjoy! Mirza is my hufband! his generous paffion has induced him to hazard his all to haften this joyful hour, and unalterably to fix my felicity ! I fhall no more be alarmed by my rival at Bagdad, over whom I fhall now undoubtedly triumph ; and though fhe fhould even recover her place in Mirza's affections, yet the confideration of my being for ever united to the dear object of my wifhes, will make every accident in life fit light and eafy ! Though an excefs of paffion may frequently be productive of jealoufy, yet it fometimes very unaccountably has the contrary effect, and the enjoyment of the beloved object fuperfedes every other fenfation. But, interrupting myfelf, I continued, what do I fay ? Why fhould I fuppofe the remote hours of my life to be clouded with misfortunes, when I at prefent enjoy the moft ferene profpect that a fuccefsful paffion can give ?—Safia had been always a well-wifher to Mirza, and fincerely congratulated

gratulated my ſucceſs. During our converſation one of my eunuchs called her out of the room, and ſhe quickly returned attended by Mirza. I inſtantly aroſe, and went eagerly to meet him; he received me with open arms, and placing me on a Sopha, and preſſing me cloſe to his boſom, ſaid, Fatima, my dear Fatima, you have at laſt then conſented to make me happy! I comply with pleaſure, replied I, ſince my father approves; and it gives me the higheſt ſatisfaction to be able to ſhew you that I wanted nothing but his conſent to grant you that felicity which you have ſo earneſtly ſolicited! Mirza ſcarce permitted me to utter theſe words, his ardent careſſes inſtantly prevented my ſpeech, I could only receive the vital air from him, or more properly, his eager embraces ſupplied its place; I thought I ſhould have expired under ſuch extatic raptures; and how happy ſhould I have been, if that delicious moment had proved the period of my life! for that which ſucceeded was the date of my woes!—I return thee, O ſupreme deity of love, ſaid Mirza, my ſincere acknowledgments for the ſucceſs of an artifice which has given me ſuch infinite pleaſure! Though I did not underſtand this ejaculation, yet it gave me great uneaſineſs, and I was going to aſk its meaning, when Safia, in great confuſion, came to inform us, that Hormoz and Mahomed were coming to my apartment. Mirza inſtantly retired with the greateſt precipitation, and preſſing my hand, he had but juſt time to ſay, Ah! my dear Fatima, I hope love will plead my excuſe! forget not that you are mine! Safia conducted him with all expedition to a cloſet, and ſecured the door.

I did not know what to think of the ſurpriſe, precautions, haſty retreat, and unconnected diſcourſe of Mirza; and Mahomed's very unſeaſonable viſit equally aſtoniſhed me! But the firſt words of Hormoz

Hormoz were to me as a thunderſtroke, which cleared my doubts, and ſtruck me ſpeechleſs with ſurpriſe! My father, addreſſing himſelf to Mahomed, and preſenting him with my hand, ſaid, Receive, Sir, your ſpouſe, who I hope will merit, by her affection, ſubmiſſion and fidelity, the good opinion you have conceived of her, and will confirm you in the reſolution you have taken, not to treat her as the generality of the ſex are, who bear the whole weight of the yoke of matrimony, which ought to be an equal reſtraint upon both. I aſſure you, Sir, I ſincerely hope that my dear Fatima will always be the ſole miſtreſs of your affections, and that ſhe will find in you a tender lover, rather than an auſtere maſter, and that ſhe will be always able to congratulate herſelf on the prudent choice ſhe has made. I will leave you, my dear children, continued he (aſcribing my confuſion to modeſty) and may your hearts be always influenced by the ſame ſentiments which at preſent inflame them, and which I hope will render the evening of my life ſerene and chearful!—I had not power to interrupt Hormoz, much leſs to prevent his retiring.

As ſoon as he was gone, I threw myſelf upon the ſame ſopha which had ſo lately been a witneſs of my tranſports, but was now, alas! my ſupport under the greateſt affliction that could poſſibly befall me! In order to conceal my tears I covered my face with my veil; but my ſighs diſcovered my anxiety! Mahomed approved himſelf a better judge of my ſituation than Hormoz: he quickly became as uneaſy as myſelf, and with great concern ſolicited to know the occaſion of my violent agitation. I returned no anſwer, for what could I ſay! You may judge, my dear Zelia, the horrors I was under, and the torments I at that time indured! What could I, or what ought I to have done? To acquaint Mahomed with Mirza's treachery, would have raiſed a

fatal

fatal enmity betwixt them, which would have terminated in the ruin of my lover, for whom I still entertain the most affectionate regard ; what do I say ? He was even become more dear to me than ever, since I judged of the violence of his passion by what had so lately passed ! I was therefore very averse to punish him for a crime, which, notwithstanding the dictates of my own reason, and my abhorrence for so base a treachery, I could not help reflecting on with pleasure ! I could not persuade myself to expose him to the resentment of the Calif, and the indignation of Hormoz and Mahomed, whose noble and generous sentiments would render them the more rigid judges of his conduct. And to comply with Mahomed's request; when I was no longer in my own power, to put such a scandalous trick upon him, to ratify a contract which I had already violated ; to accept him for my husband when my heart was engaged in favour of another ; in short, to throw myself into the arms of Mahomed when the impression of Mirza's embraces was so strong upon my mind ! Was it possible for me even to entertain a thought so repugnant to honour, honesty, and love ! Having so many circumstances to weigh, and the agitations of my breast to calm, it was some time before I could give an answer to Mahomed's affectionate interrogatories. At length my regard for him, and the necessity I was under of coming to an explanation, gave me sufficient resolution for that purpose. I attempted prostrating myself at his feet, which he prevented. Sir, said I, that humble posture is most suiting a person who is going to request a favour on which her life depends ! Such humiliation, replied he, is by no means necessary ; I shall look upon the request of Fatima as sacred ! Speak, Madam, demand whatever you please, I am ready to grant every thing, except parting

parting with you.——To be for ever rejected and despised by you, Sir, replied I, is most suiting my conduct; revenge yourself, Mahomed, on Fatima, by leaving her to her own froward fate! I am very well acquainted with, and revere your signal virtues, and am satisfied they will render the person compleatly happy whom you shall honour with your choice. I have a real regard for you; but——but you love Mirza, interrupted Mahomed with some warmth. I acknowledge it, replied I, with confusion! Alas, said he, my heart always foreboded this unhappy circumstance! but your civility and consenting looks made me disregard my suspicions; and why did you make me the subject of such a cruel artifice? I am sufficiently punished, replied I, with a sigh, and hope you will on that account pardon me. You were on the point of leaving Sarmakande, and Mirza being obliged to accompany you, I was desirous of detaining you that I might not lose him! I am sufficiently sensible of the heinousness of my crime; but since you yourself are no stranger to the influence of love, I hope you will the more readily pardon me; love alone can palliate the deceit I have put upon you and my father, and mitigate the horrors I at present labour under!—The blindness generally attendant on that passion, replied Mahomed, has been the occasion of my deception rather than your artifice; make yourself easy therefore, my dear Fatima, for my own sensations plead your excuse! But why should I forego the happiness of possessing your charms. Why may not I hope to eraze the impression of the too happy Mirza? You will soon find the difference between being the sole idol of my affection, and sharing Mirza's with a rival; it is unnecessary to inform you, that the prince of the Tartars is under such engagements with the princess Abbasside, that it is

impossible

impoſſible for him to offer you more than the ſecond place of dignity, whereas your high accompliſhments merit the firſt rank in the univerſe!——How partially you judge of me, replied I! If you did but know all .... If you could but diſcover the ſecrets of this breaſt, you might perceive that I would .... nay, that I ought to be, rather the ſlave of Mirza than the wife of Mahomed. Let me therefore for ever forfeit a title I am ſo undeſerving of; go and find Hormoz, inform him of my treachery, and break a connection which would be greatly to your diſcredit! If you refuſe me this requeſt, my immediate death ſhall free you from a reflection which love prevents your being informed of at preſent, and with which the blood of the Bermicides ought not to be ſtained!——The emphaſis with which I pronounced theſe laſt words greatly alarmed Mahomed, and threw him into a profound reverie. At laſt, he ſaid, I will, Madam, comply with your requeſt; I will wait upon Hormoz, and will endeavour rather to excite his compaſſion for, than reſentment againſt you. I will not even haſten the departure of Mirza, upon account of the anxiety it will give you. I ſincerely wiſh you may be as happy in the poſſeſſion of my rival, as I flattered myſelf to make you! But a ſecret impulſe aſſures me that this will never be the caſe. Ah, my dear Fatima, if either reflection or reſentment ſhould ever free you from your engagements, with Mirza, reſerve your heart for a lover who has formed the trueſt eſtimate of its value! Every thing you have urged gives me the higheſt proof of your good diſpoſition, and it is your extreme delicacy which makes you more concerned for your thoughts and inclinations than another perſon would be for putting them in execution.—The only reply I made to Mahomed's compliments was a ſigh, which, if he had underſtood the real motive, would have enabled him to have formed a better judgment of my conduct. My mind was for sometime totally occupied by various sensations, which the peculiarity of my situation necessarily occasioned. At last the great generosity and politeness of Mahomed kindled my resentment against Mirza, and the genteel behaviour of the one made me the more sensible of the perfidiousness of the other. My heart in that instant seemed to incline to my disappointed admirer, and detested the base wretch that had hitherto possessed the first place in my affection. But these sentiments immediately vanished on Mirza's coming from the place of his concealment, and the first glance of his bewitching eyes instantly procured his pardon.——I have, my dear Fatima, said he, heard all that has passed, and beg you to accept my warmest acknowledgments. I wish you would permit me to return your kindness with the most ardent caresses! By no means, replied I, endeavouring to free myself from his too powerful embraces, by no means! I cannot possibly consent to such a base proposal! Is this a proper return to my affection? Postpone the gratification of your passion until you have made an honourable amends for the violence you have offered me, and endeavour not by your solicitations to render me still more culpable!—Mirza paid no regard to my remonstrance; and my resistance, if the efforts we make against our own inclinations deserves that appellation, proved ineffectual. At last, I said, leave me, cruel man, leave me!—How could you be so base as to use violence to a woman whom you had before betrayed, and whose greatest misfortune is her regard for you? Was not my passion a sufficient assurance for the success of your own? You might have depended on all possible assistance from such an ally, whereas your impetuosity has now deprived you of such a charming conquest.—I am at present, replied Mirza, as happy as it is possible for mortal to be; the being long detained from an expected felicity

felicity weakens our desires, whereas I have gratified mine when in their meridian, and the dictates of an ardent passion are greatly superior to the gentle whispers of reason! You must acknowledge, Fatima, that that ardour which you censure in me, will make a stronger impression on a female breast, than the cold indifference of Mahomed. That which you call in him generosity, ought only to proceed from his being acquainted with the happiness I have enjoyed, and as you did not give him the least hint on that subject, his behaviour was certainly very absurd; but, in my opinion, this artful lover only puts on a pretended indifference to prevent his forfeiting my friendship and esteem.

These observations, and the attitude and accent in which they were pronounced, pierced my very soul! A flood of tears sufficiently expressed my anxiety, which was the more severe, as at this instant every circumstance, even the raptures I had so lately enjoyed, combined to make it the more pungent.—Mirza seemed to be alarmed at my situation, and asked with an affectionate concern the cause of my tears. Ungrateful man, replied I, instead of silencing my too-well-grounded suspicions, you renew, nay even justify them. Can you even in my arms disclaim a mutual passion! Can you calmly avow your indifference and inconstancy, and at the same time enquire the cause of my uneasiness! —What ridiculous caprice is this! replied Mirza; does that, Fatima, which ought to give you the highest satisfaction, render you uneasy? Alas! what a strange notion have you formed of love! Ardour and impetuosity always precede the gratification of passion, which is followed by a calm satisfaction, and the enchanting toyings of love; these rekindle that flame which a pensive languor would utterly extinguish.—How can you, replied I, even in that very

 moment,

moment, that fatal moment, when you have exposed me to shame, remorse, and the resentment of my father, launch into such extravagant notions, which would have been scarce pardonable if you had even been innocent! Is this all the comfort you give me? Ah, Mirza! I too fully perceive your intentions, but this base treatment comes too late! What have I done that merits such treachery? And what have I done that calls for so speedy an explanation? Was it requisite to confirm my misery by adding perfidy to violence!—Why do you dream of such a thing as misery, replied Mirza? Will not my affection, and the power I shall shortly have in this province, dispel such gloomy presages? I solemnly promise that your felicity shall be without alloy, if it is in the power of your prince and your husband! Let not your happiness depend on a squeamish delicacy. Come, and bury in my arms all your anxiety, which I would call folly, if I did not dread the exciting your resentment a second time. My embraces will more expeditiously dispel your uneasiness than my arguments, and I will behave to Hormoz in whatever manner you shall please to dictate. Keep your distance, replied I, or I will instantly myself inform Hormoz of the injury you have done him. I will publish my own shame and your baseness! Begone, I am not as yet either your slave or your wife; and my resentment will free me from those woes which such connections would necessarily entail upon me. Your behaviour has been the most villainous, and I beg you would quit my presence, that I may indulge that resentment which such treatment necessarily excites. ——I expressed the above reproofs with so much warmth, that Mirza was obliged to quit my apartment without making any reply.

As it is impossible, my dear Zelia, to describe my situation at this juncture, I shall not attempt it.

You

You may easily guess what I suffered by the account I have given you of my disposition, and the situation of my heart. Love may in some degree alter, but cannot totally change our natural temper. You have already seen the frailty of Osmaide, notwithstanding her rigid virtue, and the remorse consequent on her lapse; and you now perceive me humbled, notwithstanding my haughtiness, but without any hopes of recovering my former independance!—I but too plainly foresaw all my woes, and was but too sensible that it was in my power to avoid them. I in vain summoned pride to my assistance, for love easily repulsed all its efforts. I sincerely wished never more to see the face of Mirza, nay, even to break off all commerce with mankind; and these so requisite, but impracticable determinations alternately harassed my breast.

All nature, nay, even the ungrateful Mirza, lay folded in the arms of sleep, when Mondir, at the request of Hormoz, came and interrupted, not my calm repose, but the most violent agitations of a distracted mind. Mahomed could not avoid acquainting my father with his motives for refusing my hand; and though he had employed every argument to appease his indignation, yet he had not in the least softened his resentment. Mondir very severely reproached my conduct and treatment of Mahomed; but when (having previously replaced myself in his affection, and prepared him for the secret I intended to communicate) I informed him of the mistake occasioned by my father's orders to me when last at Rezia's, and Mirza's treachery consequent thereon, he shared my woes, and expressed the most sincere compassion for my situation.—It would be barbarous, said he, to censure your behaviour any more, since you are sufficiently punished for concealing your sentiments from me, and for your base treatment of Mahomed; only reflect on the difficulties into which your pride has led you, and take care that you do not again ſplit upon the ſame rock. It is by no means proper for you at preſent, to retaliate the injury you have received by a blind reſentment, ſince common prudence will inform you, that it is better to overlook than fall a victim to such an artifice. Your honour renders it requiſite for you to be married to Mirza, and to diſpenſe with his abſence is a duty you owe yourſelf. I will conceal his baſeneſs from Hormoz, and I beg you would not on any account retard his departure, ſince that is the only method of haſtening the reparation he in juſtice ought to make you. I will mitigate the reſentment of Hormoz, and induce him to proſecute thoſe ambitious views which your preſent ſituation call for; the beſt formed plans muſt always be directed and governed by circumſtances.

Mondir's advice was too ſuitable to my inclinations not to be eagerly embraced. I was, however, deſirous to have Mirza's behaviour previouſly vindicated, and the melancholy ſituation he at preſent appeared to be in ſeemed ſo natural, that I could not help cenſuring myſelf for being ſo warm in my reſentment. I aſcribed my improper behaviour to a vicious ſelf-love, and in the preſent ſituation of affairs readily took all the blame to myſelf. Mirza ſoon after informed me of the very particular incident which occaſioned his practiſing ſuch a deceit upon me. Having been informed by Hormoz, that I was to be that day married to Mahomed, and having in vain made his application to Rezia, he inſtantly came to ſolicit me to refuſe my conſent to the match; and Safia, to whom he applied for informing him of the joy my miſtaken ſituation gave me, it came into his head to turn this intelligence to his advantage; and he prevailed with her not to undeceive me. He moreover ſaid, that his motive

was

was not to betray my virtue, but to render my refusal of the intended marriage absolutely necessary; and he also put a favourable construction on those observations of his which had given me so much uneasiness. How shall I proceed! The curb which my resentment had put upon my love only increased its violence; I laid aside my too-well-grounded suspicions, and buried my indignation in oblivion. The faint glimmerings of reason I had left became extinct, and illusion took the sole possession of my breast. I even imagined Mirza to be actuated with the same sentiments as myself, the ardour of whose passion occasioned this mistake, and greatly facilitated his base designs. The first freedoms a woman permits her lover to take, and the first pardon she grants him, are equally dangerous; the one gives him a right to take improper liberties, and the other assures him of forgiveness. Mirza quickly threw off all restraint; he even boasted of his inconstancy: and such was the infatuation of my love, that I was charmed with the elegant apologies he made for a behaviour which proved my ruin. I often flattered myself that his heart-piercing harangues were only intended to display his wit; and the warmth of his passion confirmed this mistake. I wish that this agreeable delusion had never vanished!——Mondir had already brought Hormoz to embrace his sentiments, who, at his solicitation, had granted me a full pardon; but it was requisite to conceal from him the private intercourse between me and Mirza, which his circumspection greatly interrupted, and by that means helped me to discover my real situation. I at present never saw Mirza but at those places of assignation which he contrived to indulge his passion, the ardour of which I mistook for real affection, till a fatal incident opened my eyes, and made me for ever miserable!—As I was one day sitting with Rezia, a slave of her's brought me a letter from

 Mirza,

Mirza, in which he requested me to meet him in the evening, in a grove in my father's garden. At the time appointed, I flew on the wings of love without being observed; but how was I thunder-struck on my arrival at the place of assignation! I heard Mirza conversing with great earnestness, and listening, found him exerting the same oratory with which he had seduced me, to procure the affection of Dilnouze, than whom I could not have met with a more mortifying rival!—Dilnouze was not only undeserving of a real passion, but even of a transient connection; and both her personal and mental qualifications being of the lowest stamp, she had only been concerned in some scandalous intrigues; but notwithstanding this she was at present thought worthy of being my rival. Let not my affection for Fatima, said he, in the least alarm you; I must indeed acknowledge her to be a lady of very extraordinary accomplishments, but her too scrupulous delicacy has cast such a damp upon my passion that it is almost extinct. Ambition points out two ladies to my choice; but if they should both prove of the same disposition, and become slaves to the racking passion of jealousy, I shall not take so much pleasure in their company as in that of women of your stamp, with whom I will have my seraglio well furnished. This mortifying discourse obliged me to give an involuntary shriek, which prevented the acknowledgments of Dilnouze and Mirza's felicity. Upon discovering me they instantly fled; I endeavoured to pursue, but my violent surprise prevented me, and I sunk down, void of all sensation, at the foot of a tree! Mondir, whose watchful circumspection observed my every motion, having followed me, came to my assistance. As soon as I had recovered my faculties, he said to me, You give yourself, my dear Fatima, too much concern. Alas, Mondir, replied I, pardon my infirmities, and spare your censure

censure and advice, which in my present situation are entirely useless! I have seen Mirza in the arms of——I am ashamed to say whom——he treats her with the same affection he ought to do Fatima! The same enticing language! the same transports ——I have heard all that passed, replied Mondir, I have seen Dilnouze, and am very sensible what agitations you must at present labour under. But you are ignorant, replied I, of the manner in which Mirza has betrayed me! I have lost all that is dear to me in this world! I am become odious to the person I adore! Such is my wretched condition at present! I might have supported life in company with Mirza inconstant as he is, but it is impossible for me to exist without him! Why do you, replied Mondir, entertain such a thought? The same fickleness, which has deprived you of him at present, will again restore him to your arms, and then you will have an opportunity to reproach his infidelity. That, replied I, with a sigh, would not give him the least concern! He intended even to make me an eye-witness of his perfidy, and by that means oblige me to free him from an obligation which honour at present lays him under, and which he would undoubtedly pay no regard to, if my passion for him should prove the sole director of my actions, and induce me to expose myself to all those miseries consequent on an union, which, alas, it is become my interest to avoid!—Mondir could not persuade himself that he was guilty of such an atrocious villainy, and he proved indeed to be in the right. Mirza was not capable of such baseness, and this strange accident happened by his slave's delivering me a letter intended for Dilnouze, whom he casually met at the place he had appointed before he discovered the mistake. Notwithstanding the many anxieties he has occasioned me, I will do him justice; a duty we must never omit, even to our very enemies, and which we always with pleaſure diſcharge to our lover, when it either gratifies or excuſes our paſſion. There was a great deal of good-nature and integrity in Mirza's diſpoſition, and it was an eaſy matter to excite ſentiments of affection and gratitude in his breaſt before prejudice had taken poſſeſſion of it, an evil which is with difficulty ever eradicated. Theſe circumſtances have occaſioned me ever ſince to labour under the galling chain of love and miſery; how unhappy was it for me to find in the ſame perſon, the virtues which excite affection, and the vices that puniſh it!—Mondir, having conducted me home, conſtantly attended me; he ſhared in all my woes, gave an attentive ear to all my projects, and afterwards pointed out their dangerous conſequences: in ſhort, the friendſhip and familiarity with which he treated me, was the ſole happineſs I at preſent enjoyed; for it is a very flattering circumſtance, to find thoſe perſons making allowances for human infirmities, whoſe profound wiſdom ſeems to place them in a higher ſcale of Beings.—Mondir ſo artfully rekindled the ſmall remains I had of pride and vanity, that I thought I had conceived a fixed averſion to love, and Mirza; for he very prudently judged, that the appearance, at leaſt, of ſuch ſentiments was abſolutely neceſſary to recall an ungrateful lover, whoſe ſilence and cold behaviour merited a real diſdain: but pique and reſentment bear too near a reſemblance to this paſſion; their effects are the ſame, and they are both equally attendants on love.

I wrote to Mirza with all the indignation an injured heart could ſuggeſt, but he had too much ſpirit to be offended at the tranſports of my rage; and though it was undoubtedly his duty to have given me ſome little conſolation, yet he thought proper to chaſtiſe, in order to correct, my behaviour. But in what had I treſpaſſed? In nothing, alas, but entertaining

tertaining a too ſincere affection for him !—Mondir tried his utmoſt efforts to excite my ſelf-love, in order to leſſen my grief; he frequently propoſed to me at Rezia's ſome very ſingular queſtions, but ſuch as his former inſtructions had rendered very obvious to me ; yet this method did not in the leaſt recall my vanity, which was at preſent extinguiſhed, or rather ſmothered under the reigning paſſion of love. All I could boaſt of at preſent was Mirza's high accompliſhments, and ſo far was I from diſputing the prize with him, that I enjoyed the higheſt ſatisfaction when his ſuperior knowledge, taſte, and eloquence, were univerſally acknowledged. How ſuperlatively happy ſhould I have been if he had proved as eminent for his conſtancy ! But hold ! Mirza's affection and conſtancy could not have augmented a paſſion which was already at the higheſt pitch. Mondir ſaw with concern that the ardour of my love did not in the leaſt abate, and therefore he made it the ſole aim of his future care to induce me to conceal it.——Mirza having one day excited the admiration of the whole court, Mondir reprimanded me for the joy that ſparkled in my countenance on that occaſion. Your cenſure, replied I, is unjuſt, for the pleaſures ariſing from noble ideas, elegantly expreſſed, is the only ſatiſfaction I can at preſent reliſh ; do you hear me commend the owner of theſe abilities ?——Can there be a higher or more ſincere encomium than love, replied Mondir ? The countenance with which we behold the perſons we love, is a ſtronger mark of our eſteem than the moſt exaggerated commendations : and the perſon with whoſe company and converſation we are never ſatiated, and who conſtitutes the ſum of all our wiſhes, poſſeſſes in our opinion beauty, wit, and whatever accompliſhments fancy repreſents as agreeable and entertaining !—Well then, replied I eagerly, I can aſſure you, Mondir, that I am not in that

that ſituation; I deſpiſe Mirza, his conduct calls for it, and it is impoſſible I ſhould ever entertain a favourable ſentiment of him!—Mondir ſmiled at theſe warm expreſſions of my reſentment, which Mirza unfortunately overheard; not that this circumſtance determined his future conduct, for his vanity would not permit him to ſuffer my reaſon to triumph over my paſſion; and as he always interpreted the impetuoſity of his deſires for love, he now made it his ſole buſineſs to endeavour to convince me of the return of his affection, and of the ſincerity of his contrition for his former conduct.—Mirza had not viſited me ſince the fatal diſcovery of his perfidy, and I had not ſufficient reſolution to prevent his ever approaching my apartment again; for want of this precaution, I found him proſtrate at my feet before I was aware of his approach. Recovering from my ſurpriſe, I withdrew from him, and ſaid, Surely, Sir, this exceſs of affection ariſes from ſome miſtake! Did you come here to look for Dilnouze?—No, madam, replied he, taking care at the ſame time to prevent my retreat, no, I ſeek not Dilnouze, but a generous pardon from my dear Fatima! You are too late in your application, replied I; I formerly loved you, and with the utmoſt affection!—But inſtead of paying a proper regard to my paſſion, you have treated me with the higheſt indignity! You have barbarouſly diſcarded a heart whoſe very exiſtence depended on you! A juſt indignation for ſuch treatment has for ever deprived you of my eſteem; reaſon has diſpelled the miſts of paſſion, and your behaviour has cauſed in my breaſt an unſurmountable antipathy. As you have deſpiſed the offer of my affection, you ſhall dread the conſequences of my reſentment!——I dread nothing, replied Mirza, at the ſame time warmly embracing me, notwithſtanding my reſiſtance. What! does Fatima aſſure me of her reſentment in the moſt tender accents of love! I find you ſtill love me, and am the happieſt of mortals! Such indeed Mirza might have been, if he could have preferred the pleaſures of a ſincere mutual affection to thoſe which are but a faint reſemblance of them! I inſtantly forgave all, forgot all, and began as it were again to exiſt. Mirza aſſured me that the profeſſions I had heard him make to Dilnouze were far from being the real ſentiments of his heart, and even promiſed me never to ſee her more: this indeed was no ſelf-denial in him, whoſe higheſt ſatisfaction conſiſted in inconſtancy.—Mondir congratulated me on this happy revolution; and though he looked upon it only as a deluſion, yet he judged it prudent to hazard my tranquillity, ſince my union with Mirza was become abſolutely requiſite to preſerve my honour. Mahomed having obſerved Mirza's indifference, was chagrined at our reconciliation. It deſtroyed all his hopes, but the promiſe he had made me prevented his haſtening their departure, though he greatly wiſhed for it, and the ſilence of Haroun gave him greater liberty in this affair. The governor of Sarmakande had informed the Calif not only of the change in Mirza's affections with reſpect to the princeſs Abbaſſide, but even of his minuteſt words and actions; and the application which the prince of the Tartars had made to himſelf to diſpenſe with his return to Bagdad confirmed this intelligence. A love of independance, and an unſurmountable antipathy to ſervitude, were the ſecret motives that occaſioned Mirza's diſlike to the court of Haroun, and he proceeded ſo far on theſe principles as to be for ever excluded from it. He was ſupported by Hormoz and Rezia, not indeed in that extravagant behaviour which was his greateſt error, but in his deſire of being independant on the Calif [illegible] Rezia at length perceiving, from Haroun[illegible] behaviour,

haviour, that he greatly suspected their late conduct, she reflected, that it was dangerous to appear guilty of but a trifling crime in the eyes of an all-powerful monarch; and that when subjects have once intimated that their yoke is galling, it is their interest to endeavour to shake it off as soon as possible. The great affection my father had for me, and his eager desire of seeing me placed on the throne of Little Tartary, made him eagerly enter into Rezia's projects, which brought upon me the heaviest afflictions, and terminated in the loss of both my friends, and my lover.

Mirza was already weary of deceiving both me and himself, and relapsed into those errors which had before cost me so many tears. Neither my reason nor my pride, which I had formerly sacrificed in compliment to him, were now able to give me any relief; his conduct greatly affected me, but did not in the least excite my resentment. Love was the only passion I was at present susceptible of! and love was my sole comfort and dependance! I flattered myself that my constancy would at last recover Mirza's affection, and I was encouraged in this opinion by the concern he expressed for my anxiety; but such compassion for a heart so deeply affected deserves rather the appellation of barbarity!—I acknowledge, my dear Fatima, said Mirza, that I am highly culpable; I ought to have considered the sincerity and violence of your passion, and ought consequently to have dreaded its effects; yet notwithstanding I imprudently rekindle the flame when it is probably almost extinct, I shall prove the bane of your life, though I would gladly free you from the least of your woes, even at the expence of my blood. It is in vain for me to flatter either you or myself, that I shall for the future prove constant, since, if I had been capable of that virtue, your behaviour

and

and accomplishments would have rendered this apology unnecessary. I am very sensible what concern my expressing myself thusmust give you; but I should be still more cruel if I continued to deceive you. We do not form our own dispositions, neither is the choice of our passions in our own power; all I can offer you is friendship, and nothing less than love will satisfy your demands! You look upon the former as too minute to gratify your noble and enlarged soul, and I look upon the latter as a phantom that eludes my grasp. Pity me for not being able to adore you alone of all the sex, but do not let me incur your resentment.—I sincerely compassionate your case, replied I, and assure you, that even these tears I shed on your account, are, in my judgment, preferable to any gratifications that are not founded on love; a sensation of which you are not capable, soothes my woes; and since you acknowledge the ebb of your desires, your situation demands my pity. But are not you one of those evil geniuses who labour under the displeasure of the Supreme, who, being exiled from heaven, wander upon the earth, and endeavour to make us the companions of their misery? They, like you, have the faculty of thinking, but are not capable of tender sentiments; they have the power to please, but are not susceptible of love. I sometimes thus reasoned with Mirza; at others I represented ingratitude to him in the blackest colours. You may judge, said I, of the heinousness of this vice, by the origin one of the most learned and polite nations have given it.

Discord, say the Greeks, returning to the infernal regions from the marriage of Thetis, and reflecting on the pleasure her intelligence would occasion in those dominions she entered Charon's barge in the highest raptures. As all the wicked crew reposed themselves on the bosom of Sin, Discord

cord alſo fell aſleep, and the boat foundering, the Goddeſs tumbled into the river. Lethe inſtantly ſeized the prize, and raviſhed her, in conſequence of which ſhe became pregnant with a daughter. But the drowſy deity ſoon forgetting his miſtreſs, ſhe in revenge gave his hateful offspring the name of Ingratitude. This new divinity being refuſed a place in the infernal domains, was obliged to take refuge on earth, where men ſoon erected altars to her honour.

In this manner I converſed with Mirza; for the deſire of convincing him, and the pleaſure of entertaining him, reſtored to me ſometimes the uſe of my faculties; and this kind of converſation was much more agreeable to him, than that which is dictated by the tender paſſions. The pleaſure he took in hearing me rekindled his affection, and gave me great hopes of reclaiming him; but I unknowingly thwarted my own intereſt in exciting a paſſion of which I was not to be the ſubject.

Dahy, one of the Calif's chief eunuchs, being conducting ſome ſlaves to Bagdad which he had purchaſed for that prince, came to Sarmakande; for being indebted to Mirza for his high poſt, he was deſirous of paying him his acknowledgements in perſon. Amongſt the ſlaves purchaſed for the Calif, there happened to be one that had a moſt enchanting voice, and was alſo miſtreſs of the higheſt taſte and art, that could make it appear to the beſt advantage. Dahy, imagining that the Calif would reſerve wholly for himſelf the enjoyment of this excellent accompliſhment of Balkis (for this was the name of that fatal ſlave) made his friend the compliment of hearing her, as he knew it would highly entertain him. Mirza accepted the offer, he heard Balkis, and was inſtantly ſeized with the moſt violent paſſion for her. The united charms of perſon, wit, and ſenſe, could never make

make an impreſſion on Mirza's heart equal to that occaſioned by the enchanting airs of Balkis. Of what trifling conſideration, alas! are the moſt excellent accompliſhments, when the preference is given to talents of ſo greatly inferior a nature!—The firſt digreſſions from virtue are generally productive of a total depravity; and Dahy, having already ſwerved from his fidelity to his maſter, did not heſitate to be guilty of treaſon, and ſold Balkis to Mirza. I was an entire ſtranger to this imprudent ſtep; but going caſually to viſit Hormoz at his country-ſeat, which was in the neighbourhood of Sarmakande, I was overtaken by a terrible ſtorm on the road, and happened to fly for ſhelter to the very houſe which Mirza had made the private retreat of his pleaſures. The ſlave who kept it ſeemed greatly embaraſſed on ſeeing me; but I went in without taking any notice of this circumſtance. How great was my ſurpriſe, when a woman entirely unknown to me threw herſelf at my feet! Balkis, for it was ſhe that thus proſtrated herſelf before me, moſt paſſionately entreated me to reſcue her from the arms of Mirza, and reſtore her to the Calif! This requeſt, which I did not at firſt fully comprehend, threw me into ſuch confuſion, that I did not conſider the ſituation of Balkis; but at laſt recovering myſelf, I raiſed her up, and ſhe informed me of Mirza's baſeneſs; and gave me to underſtand, that ſhe greatly preferred the honour of amuſing the Calif, to the ſole enjoyment of the affection of the prince of the Tartars. Upon this I could not help exclaiming, Does Mirza then love without meeting with a ſuitable return! The offended Deity is at length taking his revenge on him!—Balkis, perceiving that ſhe had been addreſſing herſelf to a rival, changed the ſtile and manner of her diſcourſe, which ſhe thus purſued. Being deſirous, madam, of intereſting you in my favour,

favour, I thought it neceſſary to conceal my weakneſs; but ſince I find that we are both ſo nearly concerned in the ſame affair, I will freely confeſs to you that my heart enjoyed a ſecret pleaſure in . . . . ſhe was going to proceed, but was interrupted by the entrance of Mirza. It is impoſſible to deſcribe his confuſion and ſurpriſe! His countenance was a mixture of rage, reſentment, and fear; but my falling into a flood of tears gave him time to recover himſelf.—Having ordered Balkis to withdraw, he came up to me, and addreſſed himſelf as follows: You are undoubtedly acquainted with my baſe behaviour, which, though it gives me the moſt ſincere contrition, yet my bluſhes and confuſion can by no means merit your compaſſion. Judge of my caſe, Fatima, by your own; I ought to love you, and you ought to deſpiſe me! . . . . I am captivated with the charms of Balkis, but ſhe diſregards my addreſſes; thus love revenges your cauſe. If this does not ſatisfy you, inflict whatever puniſhment you think proper upon me; but I muſt inform you that it is impoſſible for me to exiſt without Balkis!—What ſuſpicions, replied I, though almoſt ſuffocated with grief, have entered into your head? Do you imagine Fatima will betray you, and deliver you to the Calif's reſentment! No, I ſcorn ſuch baſe revenge! The remorſe my quitting a life that is become unſupportable may occaſion you, will be the ſole puniſhment I ſhall inflict; and this you have no occaſion to dread, as it will make no deep impreſſion on your gay diſpoſition!—If you ſtill retain any affection for me, replied Mirza, with great tenderneſs, drop this melancholy ſubject; I greatly more dread the effects of your love and deſpair, than thoſe of your reſentment. Ceaſe to increaſe my woes by the too-affecting relation of your own, of which I am the ſole cauſe, for I aſſure you,

Fatima,

Fatima, that I am greatly more unhappy than yourſelf!—Mirza's affliction made ſo deep an impreſſion upon me, that I inſtantly poſtponed every conſideration to adminiſter comfort to him, for a heart deeply ſmitten is always more prone to compaſſion than reſentment. What were my ſenſations when he, having conducted me back to Sarmakande, inſtantly quitted me, and returned to Balkis! But as the agony of the heart greatly exceeds the power of expreſſion, we cannot attain an adequate idea of it from deſcription. His firſt treachery ought to have made me proof againſt any future accident of that kind; and his contrition and return ought to have left ſome flattering ſparks of hope remaining in my breaſt. But there are certain ſituations and circumſtances, in which experience and reflexion can neither inſtruct nor conſole us, and, entirely diſabled by the weight of our woes, we only exiſt to ſuffer.—Notwithſtanding I was in this ſituation, I could not help being greatly concerned for Mirza's ſafety, and my fears for him gave me more uneaſineſs than what I felt on my own account. As Balkis had appeared to me not to entertain the leaſt affection for him, I ſuſpected ſhe might take the firſt favourable opportunity to betray him. The confidence ſhe was going to repoſe in me when he came and interrupted us, gave riſe to a thouſand ſuſpicions which I durſt not communicate to him, becauſe he would have aſcribed them to jealouſy; I therefore patiently waited until I could get better information. I had a ſecond opportunity of converſing with Balkis, who, inſtead of that freedom ſhe before ſeemed to uſe, behaved with the utmoſt reſerve; and though I very earneſtly requeſted her freely to open her mind to me, I could procure nothing but a falſe and evaſive reply. She pretended that her anxiety would not permit her to to converſe with freedom; whereas her real motive was, that ſhe did not chuſe to have any intimacy with me; for it is a general error of women to begin with an imprudent confidence, and then endeavour to correct their miſtake by falſhood.—I now imagined that Balkis had a real affection for Mirza; but my knowledge of his diſpoſition prevented my being anxious on that account, for I did not in the leaſt doubt, but that as ſoon as Mirza had obtained his wiſhes he would ceaſe to love; but his continued aſſiduity and anxiety obliged me to change my opinion. How wonderful are the effects of love in a breaſt deeply ſmitten! The ſacrifice of our pride, reſentment, and jealouſy, are but trifling conſiderations; for we attempt every thing, pardon every thing, and ſubmit to every thing; and this may be laid down as a maxim, that thoſe who have the leaſt ſpark of ſelf-love remaining, are not the ſubjects of this all-powerful paſſion.

Being deſirous of making my company agreeable to Mirza, I even made Balkis the ſubject of my converſation; this threw him into ſuch raptures, that he was incapable of obſerving what I ſuffered on the occaſion. But I reſtrained my tears, and ſuppreſſed every expreſſion of grief, which, though they might probably have excited his compaſſion, would have made him inſtantly quit my company, and his preſence greatly over-balanced, in my judgment, the ſevereſt tortures. The only pleaſure I indulged myſelf in when he was with me, was expreſſing my warmeſt wiſhes for his felicity. Why is not the happy Balkis, ſaid I, poſſeſſed of my eyes and my heart!—Why do not I, interrupted he, entertain thoſe ſentiments for you of which you alone are worthy! You, alas! Fatima, have inſtructed me in the nature of love, that ſurpriſing paſſion which conſtitutes both the joy and bane of our

our lives, and I quote your own ſentiments againſt yourſelf. Can you excuſe ſuch treatment, and ſtill retain an affection for me? All the anſwer I returned was an expreſſive look, which greatly affected him, and I was unable to prevent his flying to my arms in order to ſooth his anxiety. At the touch of his lips all my woes were inſtantly converted into raptures! So much affection and conſtancy ought to have enſured me the ſole poſſeſſion of Mirza; but they were productive of the contrary effect, an effect too fatal to my unhappy paſſion. Deſpairing of being able to excite the ſame ſentiments in the breaſt of Balkis which he found in mine, he ſoon again forſook me, my company became inſupportable to him, and even compaſſion had no longer any influence on his obdurate heart!—The ſight of you, ſaid he, by ſetting before my eyes an example of the partiality of love, renders my ſufferings greatly more poignant. Either ſuppreſs thoſe marks of your affection which I am entirely unworthy of, or permit me for ever to fly your company, which ſerves only to inſpire me with ſentiments very unworthy the affectionate regard you entertain for me. This reſolution of Mirza's filled up the meaſure of my woes. The current of my life was now entirely imbittered, and I meaſured the moments with my tears. My ſufferings alſo were not a little increaſed by my being obliged to ſuppreſs them on his account, who was the ſole author of my miſery, and whoſe duty it was to have made me happy. Mahomed, notwithſtanding my counterfeit ſerenity, diſcerned the agitations of my heart: but he was too polite to make an improper uſe of this diſcovery; he warmly repreſented to me the ſincerity of his paſſion, but did not take the leaſt notice of the cruel treatment I had met with. He found that he had not the leaſt glimpſe of hope, and that my paſſion

was

was proof againſt the ſevereſt trials; he might indeed have freed me from the daily repetition of my ſufferings by removing of Mirza, but the Calif's orders obliged him to remain ſome time longer at Sarmakande.

Mirza now reſided almoſt entirely in his country villa with Balkis, and ſcarce ever viſited the palace of Hormoz. His abſence, by throwing me into deſpair, made a total change in my diſpoſition, and the firſt opportunity I had of ſeeing him, I employed entreaties, tears, and even menaces, to bring him back to my arms, but could not even obtain a few moments of his company, which I would willingly have ſpent in condoling his own ſufferings. Upon this, his preſence, which uſed always to inſpire me with love and tenderneſs, was productive of nothing but jars and invectives, and he ſhewed his cruelty to be ſuperior to my folly, by reproaching me for the violence of a reſentment which my long and conſtant affection, and the cruel treatment I had met with, ſufficiently apologized for. Notwithſtanding this, I exerted the utmoſt circumſpection for his ſafety, which was the only thing I was capable of attending to; and having bribed a ſlave in whom Balkis placed great confidence, I by that means got intelligence of all her deſigns.—This ſlave one day brought me information that Balkis had introduced into Mirza's houſe a lover, of whom ſhe was paſſionately fond, and who was to have reſcued her from the eunuch Dahy, if Mirza's purchaſe had not ruined their plan. She added, that Balkis and her lover had formed a ſcheme for the deſtruction of Mirza, the particulars of which ſhe was unacquainted with. It was abſolutely neceſſary for me to inform him of the danger he was in, and my alarms made me think every moment of delay might prove fatal. But as I ſuſpected his prejudice might prevent his

paying

paying a proper regard to my information, I contrived that he ſhould privately receive this fatal intelligence.—I had a little recovered from that hurry of ſpirits occaſioned by this event, when Mondir, who had for a long time encouraged the indulgence of my paſſion, came to ſee me, and with a dejected air, addreſſed himſelf as follows: I am come, Fatima, to try whether you have profited by my inſtructions, and whether you are miſtreſs of that reſolution which they ought to have inſpired. Mirza has not only been a traitor to you, but alſo to his prince; he has raviſhed one of the Calif's ſlaves, having previouſly ſtabbed her lover; in conſequence of which ſhe has informed againſt him; and as the governor of Sarmakande, who bears him an implacable reſentment, has already ſeized him, his friends have reaſon to dread the moſt fatal conſequences. But . . . . He was going to proceed, when he perceived that what he had already ſaid had deprived me of my faculties, and almoſt brought me to the verge of life. The violence of my paſſion was more inſtrumental in recovering me, than all the other methods that were tried. I inſtantly flew to the priſon that contained my dear Mirza, and endeavoured to gain admittance, by ſtyling myſelf his miſtreſs and his wife. But what influence can ſuch tender appellations have on the flinty breaſts of thoſe who preſide in ſuch places? And when men have once bid adieu to all humanity and compaſſion, they ſoon grow callous to every tender ſentiment. Upon this I applied to Mahomed, whom his brother's influence with the Calif rendered of great weight with the governor of Sarmakande; and he, deeply affected with my diſtreſsful ſituation, inſtantly conducted me to Mirza's new and horrid manſion, without paying any regard to his own paſſion or jealouſy.—O, Zelia, how ſhocking is it even to reflect on this interview!

Mirza's

Mirza's deep dejection, together with the darkness of the prison, prevented his observing my approach. Upon my bathing his hands with my tears, and uttering the strongest expressions of grief, he perceived who I was, but for some time only replied to my sighs and groans in the same language. At last, he said, was it possible, Fatima, for me to be a moment doubtful who you were? Your generous passion has brought you to these dismal abodes, to visit a wretch who merits severer punishment from you than from the Calif. But why do I go about to augment my despair, the consequences of which have been already suspected, and therefore these shackles prevent my procuring that relief from my woes which I can only hope to obtain from you? And this I demand either from that affection you are still so kind as to entertain for me, or from that resentment which I have given you but too just occasion for. The one ought to make you desirous of freeing me from my haughty foe, and the other ought to gratify its utmost wishes. Revenge yourself therefore on a faithless wretch who has loved, nay, who still loves Balkis!—Cruel man, replied I! do you wish to see me expire at your feet! . . . . You certainly do not speak your real sentiments; you must be too great an enemy to perfidy, than still to entertain a passion for the base creature that has betrayed you! Love, interrupted he, palliates her behaviour; I in a mad fit of jealousy stabbed her lover in her arms, for passion makes us view the most barbarous actions in a favourable light. But what do I say? Balkis, probably more innocent than I suspect, has only taken a just revenge? Instigated by a piece of fatal intelligence, I have, probably murdered her brother or her husband. Perdition fall upon the author of that information which occasioned my taking such a rash step!

You

You may very well perceive, Abbassah, continued Fatima, that it was by no means proper for me at present to acknowledge myself the author of the above affair, since such was the partial and passionate disposition of Mirza, that he would have severely punished my well-meant assiduity. I came moreover to soothe, not to augment, the agitations of his mind, and in his present situation he undoubtedly stood in great need of my assistance. --Haroun, being at last fully assured of the secret designs of Rezia and Hormoz, ordered them to be arrested; but they getting intelligence of it by their private emissaries, avoided their destined fate by a precipitate flight. Hormoz in departing entrusted me to the care and protection of Mondir and Rezia, recommended her son to me in the most pathetic terms, for she was sensible that his life solely depended on my affection for him, and Mahomed's love for me. Such a cruel parting as this would have deeply affected me, if I had not at the same time laboured under so many other calamities; and a mind totally engaged by a favourite passion is insensible to every other object.—I never quitted Mirza's company, and by my affectionate sedulity rekindled in his breast the sentiments of gratitude and affection; but his fatal passion still maintained its influence, and gave him much uneasiness, and our mutual anxiety occasioned us frequently to intermingle our tears!—In the mean time Mahomed had wrote to Bagdad in favour of the prince of the Tartars, and received in answer from Giafar, that Haroun was inflexible, and instead of pardoning Mirza would shortly fix his doom. He came, and with great anxiety informed me of this fatal intelligence, which more deeply affected me than any accident I had either before or since experienced. Though the person we love may be base and ungrateful, yet we may have still some connections that make life desirable; but to be for-ever separated from the object we adore, makes existence a burden! A person in this situation is like a solitary animal in the midst of a dreary desert, and the very air he breathes becomes offensive! The violence of my passion hurried me into concessions I ought to have dreaded, and threw me into a situation it is impossible for me to describe! —Alas, Sir, said I, to Mahomed, prostrating myself at his feet, you are benevolent, and have been so kind as to express a passion for me; I wish your affection or generosity would prevail with you to preserve Mirza. And if that self-complacency, which always accompanies a great and good action, is not a sufficient recompence, and if the unhappy Fatima still possesses a place in your breast, receive her as your slave. You may depend on her gratitude and affection; for we can easily comply with any terms to secure our favourite passion. Mahomed, after a considerable pause, and expressing an uneasiness at my proposals, which greatly enlivened my hopes, thus replied; In what a cruel dilemma am I situated! How can you, Fatima, lay such snares for my integrity! Are not your entreaties and tears sufficient to induce me to postpone my duty to my prince to oblige you, but must you also offer me such terms as I cannot, and yet ought to refuse? I could have easily stifled my jealousy, and hazarded my all, even my life to oblige you; but to forego the terms you offer me, and the gratification of my passion, is absolutely impracticable! . . . . But what do I say! what ridiculous folly am I fallen into? Could I even be happy with Fatima in my arms, since she would censure my weakness, and reproach me for not imitating her in a noble disinterested passion! Go, Madam, continued he, go and wait upon Mirza, inform him that I will conduct him to the place

you

you ſhall appoint; prepare him for his flight, and permit me, by the ſame method, to ſecure my virtue.—This generous behaviour drew from me the moſt unfeigned tears of gratitude; but what gave me the greateſt uneaſineſs in my preſent ſituation, was the thoughts of parting from my good friend Mondir, who was ignorant of the cauſe of my anxiety, and my reſolution of following the fortune of Mirza; the concern this ſtep would give him greatly allayed my joy, and it was neceſſary to conceal my intentions, leſt he ſhould exerciſe the authority Hormoz had given him, and ruin my deſign. But the thoughts of enjoying the company of my dear Mirza amply compenſated all my cares.—The Calif having ſubdued all Aſia, Greece was the neareſt aſylum to which we could direct our flight. I was not in the leaſt intimidated by the danger and length of the journey, and we quitted Sarmakande as ſoon as the cloſe of the evening favoured our deſign. I never in my life found a night ſo ſhort as this, which, in my judgment, was greatly preferable to the fineſt day I had ever ſeen. Mirza, at firſt, made ſome ſlight objections to my accompanying him, but being deeply affected with the ardour and conſtancy of my paſſion, he ſoon became enraptured with my company. We ſoftened the fatigue of the journey by the moſt tender endearments and affectionate expreſſions of love. But while we were totally intent on theſe enchanting enjoyments, our guide miſtook his way, which obliged us to ſtop at a little cottage we accidentally met with. Mirza was deſirous of taking a refreſhing nap on ſuch a bed as the place afforded, which I myſelf prepared with my own hands, and he enjoyed in my arms thoſe ſweet ſlumbers in which I did not chuſe to ſhare, as it would have been an interruption to thoſe raviſhing reflexions on my felicity, which at preſent totally

 occupied

occupied my breast. After so long a series of calamities and disappointments, after having lost all hope, how consummate must be my happiness in the arms of the man I adored! I assure you, Zelia, that the sole remembrance of this delicious night has frequently put a cheque to my despair, and the only consideration that prevented my putting a period to my being, was the consummate felicity I had experienced it capable of enjoying. But the approaching day was doomed to be the period of my happiness, and to fill up the measures of my woes.

As we could not prudently continue our rout before the close of the evening, Mirza strongly pressed me to take a little repose, with which I at last complied. But, as it was not possible for me to be long absent from him, I was preparing to rejoin him, when he, coming into the apartment in such a manner, that the remembrance of it greatly affects me to this moment, said, Hold, Fatima, do not flatter yourself, that I will join my fate to that of a woman who is capable of the blackest treachery. What value can I put on your affection for me, when I find myself the victim of your resentment! Your generosity, I perceive, was solely the effect of artifice, or a transient contrition, and I was going, in gratitude, to make you a present of a heart, of which I find you are entirely undeserving! But, thanks to my stars, I am now better informed; I find . . . I listened in the utmost amazement to this fatal declaration, the last words of which rouzed my faculties, and eagerly seizing him, I exclaimed, Good heavens! will my dear Mirza forsake me! I was not for some moments able to utter another word: recovering myself at last, I proceeded, No, this can only be an illusion occasioned by my fears! You can never, dear ungrateful man, treat my affec-

tion

tion with ſuch barbarity ! . . . You cannot imagine what horrors you have thrown me into ! How is it poſſible for you to ſuſpect Fatima guilty of perfidy ? What have I done ? I have loved you with the moſt ſincere and ardent affection ; I have ſacrificed every conſideration to ſerve you ; theſe are my only crimes : do they merit the ſevere puniſhment you threaten ? . . . . But is it the faithful intelligence I gave you that has incenſed you againſt me ? I confeſs that I was ſolicitous to preſerve you from the reſentment of Balkis, but to avoid incurring your diſpleaſure I contrived . . . I was going to proceed, when Mirza, ruſhing from my arms, ſaid, This confeſſion is ſufficient, you acknowledge half the crime I ſuſpected you guilty of, and I take the reſt for granted : you have not only expoſed Balkis to my reſentment, but alſo excited the Calif's indignation againſt me, by making him ſuſpect me guilty of treaſon. Make what haſte you can to Sarmakande, and give them directions to purſue me, for I ſhall prefer the ſevereſt of deaths to ſpending the remainder of my life with ſuch a wretch as you.

After theſe ſevere and unjuſt reproaches, to which I had ſcarce the power of attending, Mirza departed, leaving me totally deprived of my faculties, and almoſt of life. I remained for ſome time in this happy ſtate of inſenſibility, when an old woman, the miſtreſs of the houſe where I was, made me fully ſenſible of my wretched ſituation, by recalling my faculties. How can you, Madam, ſaid ſhe, be ſo much concerned for the loſs of ſo perfidious a wretch ? Deſpiſe the diſregard he has ſhewn to your beauty, for he is ſufficiently puniſhed by the wretched choice he has made ; your rival . . . What rival, cried I ? had Mirza any company with him whilſt he was here ? You are unacquainted then, I find, replied Cadige (for that was

 the

the name of this compaſſionate old woman) that your lover has quitted you for the ſake of a woman called Dilnouze, with whom, after a warm conference, he went off, at the ſame time recommending you to my care.—You may judge, my dear Zelia, what were my ſenſations at that juncture, by the emotions this recital occaſions in my breaſt; and indeed I ought here to put a period to my affecting ſtory, as the ſequel of it greatly exceeds all the powers of deſcription.—Fatima, interrupted by her ſighs, gave Abbaſſah an opportunity of wiping up her tears; and the former, encouraged by the latter's ſympathiſing with her, continued her narration as follows.—Cadige requeſted to know who I was, and offered to conduct me to Sarmakande; but the ſole object of my thoughts, at preſent, was to be freed from an exiſtence become inſupportable; and tho' I was totally abandoned to deſpair, I had the cruel ſatisfaction of being concealed from all the world. Every freſh emotion in my breaſt was productive of a new reſolution. One while I determined to go and confute the ſcandalous imputations which I imagined Dilnouze had thrown upon me, and, by vindicating my conduct, endeavour the recovery of Mirza's affections: another, I reſolved to put an end to my woes, by expiring at the feet of that ungrateful wretch; for whom, notwithſtanding his villainous behaviour, I could not help entertaining a paſſion.—But theſe deſigns proved only fleeting phantoms, and fate ſtill reſerved for me freſh calamities.

You might now, Zelia, reaſonably imagine, that I was ſunk in the loweſt abyſs of miſery; but I was doomed to ſuffer an additional trial, which made all the wounds of my former woes bleed afreſh, and rouzed me from that lethargy into which they had thrown me.—I had now lain two days in a languiſhing condition, without receiving any nouriſhment, which greatly alarmed the good Cadige, who came to me with great eagerneſs, and ſaid, You have, Madam, your revenge! the all-juſt Supreme has not long delayed the puniſhment of your perfidious lover, he has been ſeized by the troops ſent in purſuit of him, for I juſt now met him loaded with chains, and ſurrounded by his conductors.

As the ſtorm obliged them to take ſhelter in a neighbouring cottage, I endeavoured to get an opportunity of ſpeaking to him, but was not permitted: all I could learn was, that this hateful monſter would ſoon receive the reward of his villainies; and what ought to be an addition to this good news is, that your rival was the perſon that betrayed him.—Cadige ſoon perceived how much ſhe had miſtaken my diſpoſition. This information raiſed my drooping ſpirits, and I eagerly replied, What fatal intelligence is this you bring me? Having thus ſaid, the violence of my agitations interrupted for ſome time the uſe of my faculties; recovering at laſt, I threw myſelf at the old woman's feet, and embracing her knees, added, I beg you, my dear good Cadige, to compaſſionate my diſtreſs. Let us, if poſſible, ſave the prince of the Tartars, for it is he, it is my huſband, that you ſaw in chains! Let us reſcue him from his cruel executioners. But, interrupted ſhe, how is it practicable? There is no difficulty, replied I, provided you will give your aſſiſtance, and you ſurely cannot refuſe me this favour, when you conſider that Mirza is your prince, and that you will be inſtrumental in preſerving my life, which, alas, ſolely depends upon his! I conjure you in the name of the Supreme whom you adore, and who at preſent directs my thoughts and actions, to comply with my requeſt, which if you refuſe I ſhall expire at your feet. Reflect, continued I, that mercenary dispositions are not proof against bribery; return therefore to the troops that guard Mirza, and, offering them a much larger reward for his liberty than they could expect, beg them to wait a few moments for the completion of your promise. In that interval you shall conduct me to the nearest market, and sell me to a slave-merchant; the money you will receive on that account, together with a few jewels that I have, will be sufficient to warp the fidelity of his conductors, and procure the freedom of Mirza! Fear nothing, my good mother, continued I, for heaven is always the protector of virtuous actions.—What, exclaimed Cadige, in astonishment, will you voluntarily submit to such a cruel fate, to serve a man, who, though he is your husband, has treated you in such a barbarous manner? Yes, I will, replied I, and I look upon it as my duty, for the misbehaviour of others can never justify our own. My life, my liberty, my all, are his property to whom I have given my hand, and ought not I freely to part with them to procure the same blessings for him? Moreover, Mirza is not so blameable as you imagine, for an infamous aspersion was the occasion of his treating me in such a manner. But, continued I, let us lose no time, and I once more repeat to you, that if you refuse me your assistance I shall expire at your feet. O most generous of women, replied Cadige, at the same time embracing me, and bedewing my face with her tears, I will punctually obey all your commands, and will instantly endeavour to execute your instructions. Do you, in the mean time, recruit your drooping spirits, that you may be the better able to finish the sacrifice you are determined to make. I readily complied with her advice, I even set about rectifying my dishabille, in order to set off my beauty to the best advantage. This

employ-

employment, however inconſiſtent it might be with my preſent ſituation, was undoubtedly of too great importance to my lover to be neglected. Ah! Mirza, ſaid I to myſelf, theſe charms, which your ungenerous treatment had even rendered odious to me, are again become the object of my attention, ſince it is in my power to dedicate them to your ſervice! Though they have not been able to make an impreſſion on your heart, yet they ſhall be inſtrumental in the preſervation of your life, and the felicity they give me on this account, will induce me to pardon, nay even to bury in oblivion, the many calamities they have brought upon me. Theſe reflexions ſupported my reſolution, and ſoftened the rigour of that ſentence which I had condemned myſelf to undergo. In ſhort, my dear Zelia, the efforts we make to gain the man we love, are the only ſupport we have againſt his cruel and ungenerous treatment.—This train of thoughts was followed by an anxious concern for the ſucceſs of Cadige, which her arrival ſoon diſſipated. My daughter, ſaid ſhe, your plan has ſucceeded, and Mirza's guards only wait for the completion of my promiſes. But ſince, alas! your own liberty is to be the price of his, do not you repent ſuch an unmerited act of generoſity? Does not your heart even cenſure itſelf for ſuggeſting ſuch a deſign? By no means, my good mother, replied I, and let us haſten the execution of a plan for which I would gladly ſacrifice a thouſand lives.—Having ſo ſaid, I hurried away Cadige, and aſſiſted her in walking faſter than her uſual pace; the exerciſe, together with the emotions of my breaſt, by throwing a ſtronger bloom on my countenance, greatly added to my beauty, and facilitated our deſign, Cadige inſtantly receiving the price ſhe aſked for me. May our holy prophet, ſaid ſhe going to leave me, amply reward your virtue; and may Mirza ever lament his blind prejudice, which your generous treatment will render greatly more poignant. Alas, my good mother, said I, detaining Cadige, by no means acquaint Mirza, that I have reduced myself to the miserable condition of a slave for his preservation: he may possibly come and hazard his own life for my liberty, and such a step would be the destruction of us both! You shall therefore swear to me, that you will not acquaint him with my situation, only inform him that the person, who has been so solicitous for his safety, begs he would instantly quit the Calif's dominions, and after you have delivered this message, come and see me once more. Cadige promised faithfully to execute what I requested; but, alas! the fear of Mirza's endangering his own safety on my account was not the occasion of these orders, for I had but too much reason to believe, that a fatal prejudice had eradicated every sentiment of benevolence and gratitude. All I intended by the above request, was to prevent any addition to his sufferings by the remorse my present situation might occasion him. I had not as yet reflected on the horror of my own fate; but as soon as my anxiety for Mirza abated, this presented itself to my thought. But I did not repent of the sacrifice I had made him, though the consideration of being the property of any other person than him I loved, greatly tarnished the pleasure I had in preserving his life. When I reflected in what manner I should behave to the master into whose hands I might fall, I could not help wishing, that it was in my power to exchange my beauty for deformity, and would have gladly engaged in the meanest offices and hardest labour, rather than be guilty of a breach of fidelity to him, whom, of all mankind, I solely adored. I considered also, that, if times should take a more favourable

vourable turn, I might even recover my liberty, and that either Hormoz or Rezia would pay any price for my ransom; but at present, I had no friend but Mondir, and I could not induce myself to molest his grey hairs, and break in upon that comfortable subsistence, which Hormoz had given him when he quitted Sarmakande. I was even concerned for having mentioned the name of that ancient sage before Cadige, whom I never had the pleasure of seeing again, being sold the same day to some eunuchs employed by Assad; but the good opinion I had conceived of her, has always induced me to believe that she faithfully observed all I requested.

Assad had purchased me for the Calif; but he afterwards changed my destination, and placed me in a much more agreeable situation, since, my dear Abbassah, he has dedicated the remainder of my days to your service. That gloomy retreat in which I found you, was very suitable to my disposition, but it made me greatly anxious for your fate. I thought, that the instructions which Assad ordered me to give you, might prove of fatal consequence, and could not approve of giving you any idea of the dangerous passion of love. For I reflected, that to have no other sense of our existence but by the miseries of life, is greatly inferior to total ignorance; and I sincerely wish that you may never experience this fatal truth!—Ah, Fatima, exclaimed Zelia, how can you bestow encomiums upon Mirza, which are so repugnant to his behaviour? Censure me not on that account, replied Fatima, for my pencil has not in the least flattered him. Those infirmities, of which every mortal has but too large a share, frequently destroy the best dispositions. Prejudice can see nothing in its proper colours, but takes every *ignis fatuus* for its direction; and passion destroys all the most amiable qualities

qualities of the mind. These two vices have been the occasion of my cruel fate ; and in my character of Mirza I have represented him as totally under their influence. But as he has been for a long time left to his own reflections, he has probably ere this amply suffered for the cruel treatment I have received at his hands.

Abbassah was astonished at the power of a passion, which not only enables a person that is under its influence, cheerfully to support the various calamities of which it is frequently productive, but which induces us to excuse, nay, even vindicate the author of our sufferings. She, indeed, was not doomed to the same cruel fate which Fatima had experienced, though to be the innocent cause of the ruin of the person we adore, and who entertains a mutual affection for us, bears some proportion to that of being obliged to sacrifice one's-self, to preserve the life of an ungrateful and ungenerous man whom we love.

P A R T IV.

THE reflections which Abbassah made on Fatima's narrative, were succeeded by those which her own situation administered, but too just occasion for, and her apprehensions were increased, as the critical moment which was to be the period of her anxiety approached. At length, after a tedious journey and various agitations of mind, she arrived at Mecca, where the Iman engaged in her interest, by the assistance of Nair, received her with all those demonstrations of joy and respect that were due to the Calif's sister. This princess, being lineally descended from the great Ali, and as conspicuous for her beauty as her misfortunes, excited in his breast the warmest religious

gious zeal, and the most tender sentiments of compassion; he provided an apartment for her in the Temple, where, in a short time, receiving in his arms the son of Giafar, he vowed that he would be to him as a father, and offering the most ardent petitions in his favour, he dedicated him to God and his Prophet; and Abbassah, not reflecting that the decrees of heaven are unfathomable, flattered herself, that the prayers of so devout and good a man in favour of innocence would prove effectual for its protection.

During these transactions the benevolent Mesrour used the utmost circumspection to prevent the discovery of this important secret, which, at the same time, he seemed to be utterly unacquainted with. This good natured and generous behaviour greatly affected Abbassah and Fatima, who, notwithstanding, only expressed their acknowledgments in an obliging smile, which silent, though expressive approbation, was sufficient for the nice and delicate Mesrour. The violence of Abbassah's passion was now, in some degree, mitigated by maternal affection; but nothing could cool Haroun's ardent love, nor could any consideration in the least soften Giafar's remorse and anxiety; and the absence of Abbassah, by exciting the one, greatly increased the other. Haroun never conversed with him on any other subject than his dear Zelia; he described his passion to him in the strong tints of a constant, but unfortunate admirer; he even sometimes gave him remote hints of a jealousy which greatly alarmed him: but what most affected the unhappy Vizir was, when the Calif condescended to converse with him in the utmost freedom and intimacy, and gave him the strongest marks of a most sincere and cordial friendship. And how were all his sufferings augmented, when he was informed by the faithful Mesrour of

Zobeide's

Zobeide's treachery, and when he perceived, by the Calif's discourse, that he himself was deceived by that scandalous letter of which he had suspected him the author? Every thing that Haroun had said to him at the time when he laboured under that conflict between love and duty, and which had greatly contributed, though improperly, to the victory his passion then gained over his reason; nay, even that very assiduity and compassion, which he had before looked upon as the basest insult, now appeared to him as undoubted marks of the most sincere esteem; and it was the constant torment of his life that he had behaved unworthy of this friendship, and violated the engagements he had entered into. The poignancy of our remorse is generally in proportion to our crimes and fears, and so violent was Giafar's contrition when he reflected on his perjury and ingratitude, that he was almost induced to undeceive Haroun, and make an open confession of his baseness, if the interest and safety of Abbassah had not restrained him. The Calif, indeed, might have easily perceived the real state of the case from his great anxiety and embarassed countenance; but this prince, being under the influence of prejudice, ascribed these circumstances to that passion for Irene which he imagined his friend laboured under. Haroun, at last, determined to sacrifice his own happiness to that of his favourite, whose absence he knew would occasion him many anxious moments; he therefore seized a very convenient and honourable opportunity to oblige him with that absence, which he imagined was the object of his wishes.

Giafar very clearly perceived Haroun's sentiments; but it was not in his power to undeceive him, as his error was so requisite to his own safety: he considered moreover, that by this means he should be obliged to quit that place which hourly recalled to his mind, what he now looked upon as the most

heinous

heinous of crimes, and thoſe ſweet retirements which would ſoon again be the witneſſes of his perfidy, ſince Abbaſſah's return began to draw near; but it was not without a very ſevere conflict, that his virtue, which before had been obliged to yield, gained this aſcendancy over his love!—Haroun, if we except that unhappy paſſion, which was equally the bane of his felicity and glory, was undoubtedly a prince as diſtinguiſhed for his virtues and greatneſs of ſoul, as for his power and magnificence; his heart was formed for the acquiſition of true glory, to which he always paid a proper reſpect, in whoſe poſſeſſion ſoever he found it; and he accordingly expreſſed a great regard for thoſe illuſtrious perſonages that were his cotemporaries, and ſeemed deſirous of equalling, or even excelling his extenſive fame. It is from a meanneſs of ſoul that we envy thoſe whoſe merits we cannot but eſteem, and whom a noble and generous diſpoſition would make us love. That regard which he paid to the virtues of others, was the occaſion of his entering into a ſtrict alliance with Charlemain, and their reſpective ambaſſadors were charged with the warmeſt aſſurances of a reciprocal eſteem.

Upon this occaſion Giafar ſet out for the court of that Emperor, carrying along with him very curious and magnificent preſents; and the Calif commanded him to make ſome ſtay at Conſtantinople when he returned, thinking this order the greater compliment, the leſs appearance it had of being intended as ſuch. The grief which the Vizir, notwithſtanding his ſpirited reſolutions, laboured under in quitting that place where he ſoon again expected to ſee his dear Abbaſſah, could be equalled by nothing but the ſenſations of that princeſs on her arrival at Bagdad. How many tears had ſhe ſhed in parting with her ſon! How often had ſhe made the Iman and Nair, to whoſe care ſhe committed this dear pledge of her love,

love, repeat their aſſurances of ſecrecy and fidelity! Her love for Giafar was her ſole ſupport at this juncture; how great therefore muſt be her ſurprize, when, inſtead of finding herſelf in the arms of her dear huſband, ſhe perceived herſelf in thoſe of a brother, whom ſhe dreaded! It was impoſſible for her to conceal her agitations, and ſhe could not help exclaiming, Ah, Sir, where is Giafar! what am I to ſuſpect! . . . . I can no longer, replied the Calif, inſtigated by jealouſy and reſentment, conceal from you his ingratitude; you have a rival that enjoys the greateſt ſhare of his affections, he is gone to viſit her, little regarding the uneaſineſs this ſtep would occaſion you, and is therefore undeſerving your ſolicitude.

Abbaſſah looked upon theſe inſinuations, as the baſeſt calumny, and a continuation of Zobeide's treachery, with whom ſhe imagined the Calif joined in ſupporting this ſcandalous aſperſion; and the antipathy this ſuſpicion gave her to Haroun, was not in the leaſt diminiſhed, when ſhe was informed of the real cauſe of Giafar's abſence; for ſhe aſcribed that to the Calif's wicked deſigns, which was in reality the effect of his nice ſenſibility of ſoul. The paſſions not only blind the underſtanding, but deſtroy our charity, and yet they are the higheſt ornaments of virtue when engaged in its favour. Abbaſſah indulged her reſentment by ſcrupulouſly rejecting the moſt innocent aſſiduities of her brother; but ſhe at the ſame time concealed her affection for Giafar, and aſſured the Calif, that God, at the interceſſion of Mahomed, had re-eſtabliſhed the tranquillity of her breaſt. Neceſſity, the author, and probably the juſtifier of every invention, obliged her to practiſe this deceit.—Haroun, deceived by the ſeeming tranquillity of his ſiſter, determined to follow her example, and endeavour to procure in the prophet's temple, that compoſure of mind which he had in vain

vain tried by other methods; but he resolved to wait for the return of Giafar, in order to carry along with him a friend, who was equally dear and formidable to him; for it would have been too severe a mortification, to have permitted him to enjoy the company of his dear Zelia in his absence. The Calif's sufferings, by weakening his faculties, increased his devotion, which, instead of conquering his passion, greatly added to his anxiety.

Zobeide, who was always ready to second any proposal that suited her interest, greatly approved of this journey, the inutility of which she was thoroughly satisfied of in her own mind, and also that its length and expensiveness would be prejudicial to the state. She always imagined that some mystery was concealed under Abbassah's pilgrimage to Mecca; and having heard nothing of her slave or Nair since they set out on that expedition, her suspicions were greatly increased; she therefore, in hopes of procuring some insight into this dark affair, prevailed on Haroun to permit her to accompany him. Persons of vile dispositions are always prying into the failings or misfortunes of others; and the reason is, that they suspect every one to be as wicked as themselves, and take a pleasure in the calamities of their neighbours. Instigated by these principles, Zobeide at last unravelled this secret.—Whilst Abbassah was lamenting to Fatima a separation, which the places that had been the witnesses of her raptures rendered both more poignant, and also in some degree mitigated, Giafar received at the court of Charlemain, not only those honours which were due to his character, but also the strongest marks of personal esteem and affection. An ambassador is greatly deficient, and disgraces his royal master, that cannot command respect by his real merit and accomplishments, exclusive of his public character; it is therefore the duty of those that are appointed to this high dignity,

to

to render themſelves deſerving of that homage which they expect to receive as the repreſentatives of a prince, which is not to be effected merely by idle pomp and empty pageantry. Giafar's great abilities and extraordinary accompliſhments did not require theſe inſtructions, and he, in a ſhort time, experienced the effects of his conſpicuous endowments.

France never could in any other age boaſt ſuch a number of heroes as at preſent. Courage and true greatneſs of ſoul, of which every nation has afforded ſome ſtriking examples, ſeemed now the ordinary and natural accompliſhments of the whole nation, and they had almoſt even eradicated thoſe conſtitutional imperfections peculiar to the climate: theſe, indeed, are not ſo conſpicuous when the attention is engaged by more important conſiderations; but, to the reproach of the human breaſt, they make a deeper impreſſion on the mind than national virtues. Therefore that decline, which all ſtates have ſucceſſively experienced, is always aſcribed to their natural diſpoſition; envy and malice perpetuate the miſtake, and poſterity are ſo far from contradicting their miſrepreſentations, that they even treat as fables thoſe encomiums which truth has beſtowed on men of renown; and fiction, endeavouring to embelliſh grand exploits by an addition of the marvellous, has been inſtrumental in the propagation of this error.

Thus, without ever examining the true ſtate of the caſe, it is generally believed that the French under Charles the VIIth, being the dupes of their own folly, and totally intent on their inteſtine broils, to which every trifling occaſion furniſhed a pretence, cowardly gave up a part of their dominions to an enterprizing nation, who was too powerful ever to live on good terms with them; and from the ſame motives it is looked upon as fabulous, that they de-

defended their territories under Charlemain, by the moſt ſurprizing acts of courage, againſt a moſt numerous and powerful enemy. The names of Orlando and Rinaldo, together with thoſe illuſtrious Engliſh heroes that were the ornaments of Arthur's reign, ſeem only to have ſtemmed the tide of oblivion to be buried under the extravagancy of fable; whilſt that of Alexander, which excites no national jealouſy, is preſerved with reſpect. But this error, which is greatly owing to the freedom of the poets, whom we readily excuſe, on account of the pleaſure we receive from their labours, is not to be followed by an hiſtorian. He is obliged to introduce upon the ſtage ſuch heroes or heroines as really exiſted, notwithſtanding their names may ſeem to carry an appearance of fable.

Giafar diſtinguiſhed himſelf in all the public entertainments that were then the taſte of Europe, and carried off the prize in many trials of courage, activity and courteſy. The great perſonages who were his antagoniſts in theſe combats, extolled without the leaſt mixture of envy his high accompliſhments, and Rinaldo and Orlando in particular gave him ſingular marks of their affection and eſteem. It was with difficulty that Charlemain ever parted with his company, being inſatiable in his enquiries about the fame of Haroun and the cuſtoms of the Aſiaticks; and he exerted every argument to prove, that tho' they abounded more in luxury and magnificence, yet their manners had not that freedom and ſweetneſs that diſtinguiſhed thoſe of the Europeans; the juſtneſs of which obſervation was candidly acknowledged by the Vizir. But notwithſtanding the general eſteem that was expreſſed for Giafar, none of the many renowned knights which then embelliſhed the court of France, ſhewed ſo cordial a regard for him as Ruggier; their mutual affection was increaſed by their being of the ſame religion,

religion, and, in a ſhort time, grew into the moſt ſincere friendſhip.

As theſe two were one day hunting in a foreſt, they were caſually ſeparated from their attendants and a cooling ſhade formed by the interwoven foliage of a thick grove, together with a purling ſtream, whoſe banks were embelliſhed with a beautiful verdure, invited them to repoſe. The ſimilarity of the ſituation inſtantly recalled to Giafar's mind, that fatal moment which was the date of both his felicity and perfidy ; but a ſigh from Ruggier recalled his wandering thoughts, and being ſurpriſed to ſee him in the ſame reverie with himſelf, he was going to enquire the occaſion, when the young hero ſaved him the trouble, by addreſſing him as follows :

I cannot, Sir, ſaid he, make a better apology for indulging that anxiety which your company ought to have reſtrained, than by acquainting you with the occaſion of it ; and the preſent ſituation of my mind ſtands too much in need of the advice and aſſiſtance of a faithful friend, to permit me to over-look this opportunity. Whatever may be the occaſion of your uneaſineſs, replied Giafar, you cannot find a heart more diſpoſed to ſhare either in your pleaſures or anxieties than mine. This place, replied Ruggier, recalls to my mind ſome circumſtances that have occaſioned me many ſtruggles, of the perplexity of which you ſhall be judge. I am entirely unacquainted with my origin, and can give you no account of my birth, except that an old man, who was the guardian of my youth, aſſured me that I was deſcended from illuſtrious anceſtors. He exhorted me upon his death-bed to continue a zealous Muſſelman, having educated me in that religion ; but I could not by any means extract from him the ſecret of my birth, ſince that diſcovery would, he aſſured me, prove fatal to my honour or life. Make for yourſelf, ſaid he, a name, the glory of which will be ſolely

solely of your own acquiring; endeavour to obtain a renown from which your ancestors can make no deductions; chuse your country and sovereign, whom you will on this account serve with greater fidelity, as that allegiance, which is often galling when the effect of necessity, is rendered less burdensome when it is our own option. I was very desirous of executing his commands whom I had always looked upon as a parent; and accordingly I resolved to place myself under a sovereign who acknowledged the great Mahomed: on this account I entered into the service of Marsilius, King of Spain, at a juncture when the Saracens were preparing to make an irruption into France. Having the good fortune to be successful in a few enterprizes during this expedition, the king bestowed upon me great rewards, and the highest marks of his esteem, which soon excited the envy of all the grandees of the court, who could not bear to see a stranger basking in the sunshine of royal favour, a situation each of them was ambitious of obtaining for himself. I severely punished all those who durst give any public marks of their envy and malevolence; but I found it impossible to guard against the insinuations and prejudices they instilled into the breast of my sovereign; for which reason I determined to retire until the war was over. That humanity and true greatness of soul, which several campaigns had given me frequent opportunities of observing in the French, made me desirous of being more intimately acquainted with enemies whom I was obliged to esteem; and I was in a short time united to them by connections which nothing but death can ever dissolve.

As I was casually one day crossing this forest, the beauty of this very spot attracted my attention, and I stopped to take a little repose as we have done at present. A sweet slumber was just going to lull my

faculties

faculties to reſt, when ten men, whoſe approach the thickneſs of the wood had prevented my obſerving, furiouſly attacked me, and I had but juſt time ſufficient to ſeize my arms, and put myſelf in a poſture of defence, but was obliged to leave my helmet upon the ground. Four out of the ten had already paid the forfeiture of their lives for this baſe and cowardly behaviour, and I was reſolved to ſell my blood at as dear a rate as poſſible to the remainder, when a generous ſtranger came to my aſſiſtance, whoſe courage ſoon determined the victory in our favour. The laſt blow my friend received had caſually ſtruck off her helmet, and I perceived, by the long flaxen treſſes that flowed upon her ſhoulders, and an enchanting ſweetneſs of countenance, that I was indebted to a lady for my life. This diſcovery greatly increaſed my gratitude, which almoſt inſtantly grew into a violent paſſion; and proſtrating myſelf at the feet of my kind protectreſs, I endeavoured to expreſs the warm ſuggeſtions of a moſt grateful and enraptured breaſt. But interrupting me, ſhe ſaid, in the ſweeteſt accents, Follow me, Sir, immediately, that proper application may be made to your wounds before you are too much weakened by ſo copious an effuſion of blood; the brave Ruggier cannot make a more acceptable return for my poor ſervices, than by endeavouring to preſerve a life in which I am greatly intereſted.

Theſe affectionate expreſſions gave me a very agreeable ſurpriſe; but my kind protectreſs would not permit me to make my acknowledgments, and I followed her with a pleaſing anxiety, the very recollection of which excites even now the higheſt raptures in my breaſt. We in a ſhort time came to a caſtle which belonged to the valiant Rinaldo, where I learned, that it was to his ſiſter, the renowned Bradamante, that I was indebted for the

pre-

preſervation of my life. The care and aſſiduity of my kind entertainers greatly forwarded the cure of my wounds; for which indeed, the balſamic looks of Bradamante would have been ſolely ſufficient; for our reciprocal glances were ſo much in uniſon, that I could not help entertaining the moſt flattering expectations, of which ſhe ſoon gave me the happy, or more properly fatal confirmation. Addreſſing herſelf to me one day, ſhe ſaid, I perceived, Sir, that you were greatly ſurpriſed at my knowing you before, and aſcribed my conduct ſolely to humanity, when the real motive was gratitude. Try if you cannot recollect your being challenged to a ſingle combat the laſt general engagement, and the generous treatment you ſhewed your adverſary by diſmounting and diſengaging him from his horſe which was fallen upon him.—I am aſtoniſhed, replied I; was my guilty arm raiſed againſt you! Why did not my heart, of which you were doomed to be the idol, by ſome ſecret impulſe check my uplifted hand! I might poſſibly have ſhed that blood, the leaſt drop of which I would gladly purchaſe at the expence of my life. Ah! pardon, Madam, pardon this preſumptuous declaration, which the warmth of my tranſports would not permit me to ſuppreſs! —What you have ſaid, replied Bradamante, does not give me the leaſt diſguſt, and I ſcorn to affect an auſterity ſo repugnant to the real ſentiments of my heart. I perceive, Ruggier, continued ſhe, that the frankneſs and ſingularity of my ſentiments greatly ſurpriſe you; I muſt therefore beg leave to inform you, that Bradamante looks upon diſſimulation and falſhood as the higheſt villainy. Thoſe reſtraints which the men have laid upon our ſex appeared to me always rather as inſults than a tender regard for any weakneſs in our nature, which is only a fiction of their ſuggeſting, in order to make us the tools of their power. But my parents and relations, en-

entertaining more juſt and exalted ſentiments of our ſex, have permitted me to follow the bent of my ſpirited diſpoſition, a privilege which but few women enjoy; I have ſerved my prince with ſome degree of reputation, and have always ſought the moſt hazardous enterpriſes in order to ſignalize my courage. Our troops had ſuffered too much by your tremendous arm, not to have the terror of your name ſtrongly imprinted in their breaſts; and I was engaged in the hotteſt part of the action, when I caſually heard ſome perſon mention your name, and at the ſame time ſaw you give ample proofs of your renowned prowefs. I inſtantly thought ſuch an adverſary worthy my courage, and accordingly attacked you; but when, in order to aſſiſt me, you lifted up the viſier of your helmet, I gladly accepted your generous offer, and inſtead of approving your propoſal of finiſhing our combat, I inſtantly retired with great precipitation, which I hope you aſcribed to the mortification conſequent to my defeat. The lineaments, notwithſtanding, of my conqueror, remained ſtrongly imprinted on my mind; but the anxiety they occaſioned me did not ſuppreſs my courage, and I ſhared with our moſt celebrated warriors the laurels of that glorious day. Thus, Sir, as I am experimentally aſſured, that a woman can defend her country, ſo I am alſo fully perſuaded that ſhe can protect her virtue, which, in my opinion, ſhe does not in the leaſt hazard, by acknowledging a natural and laudable inclination. She who can check the rudeneſs, or revenge the perfidy of a lover, runs no riſk in acknowledging a paſſion, the abuſe of which ſhe can eaſily puniſh. But though you do not find in me thoſe uſual obſtacles which men have invented in order to make us the more eaſy dupes to their caprice, yet there is one objection, ariſing from the difference of our religion, which may prevent our mutual felicity, and which
it

it is solely incumbent upon you to remove. To desert those evident and important truths which I have embraced, would be the highest reflexion on my character; whereas your mistaken principles will be easily dispelled by the piercing rays of the most evident conviction.—Ah! Madam, said I, with a sigh, what a fatal conclusion do you put to the most enchanting harangue! Ruggier adores you; and though he thinks it impossible for him to incur your displeasure, yet he could chearfully submit to whatever punishment you might think proper to inflict upon his inconstancy, or any other crime he might be guilty of; but to betray his honour, his conscience, and his God, would certainly render him much more unworthy your esteem than what you call his mistaken principles.—The happy moment of your conviction, replied Bradamante, is not yet arrived, and it is very far from my intention to insist upon an implicit compliance; all I intended, was to apprise you of an obstacle my friends and my own inclinations would make to our mutual felicity. I hope, however, continued she, that you will fix your residence among us; my brother has informed the Emperor of my good fortune in assisting you against the assassins, whom Marsilius had procured to intercept you, and those of them that escaped our fury have been punished suitable to their baseness. You will enjoy the same rank and favours in the court of Charlemain which you had in that of Marsilius; but with this additional advantage, that you will not be exposed to the mean artifices of jealousy, for with us the only effect of merit is emulation and esteem.

I accepted these proposals with the greatest joy, as they were so agreeable to my disposition, and also consistent with my principles, and I became in a short time more attached to the Emperor by inclination than gratitude. If I could credit the secret ſuggeſtions of my own heart, I am of French extraction, and a natural ſubject of Charlemain; and this notion, which I frequently reflect on with great pleaſure, has, by the aſſiſtance of my paſſion, often ſtaggered my original principles. Notwithſtanding this ſituation of affairs, I had the pleaſure of enjoying Bradamante's company every day, and Rinaldo and Orlando countenanced my paſſion. Their exalted ſentiments eaſily induced them to overlook the obſcurity of my birth, which might have been an objection to this alliance; but they would not diſpenſe with the difference of our religious principles, and inſiſted upon my removing that impediment.—I could not refuſe her, who was the ſole object of my wiſhes, the trying every method to procure that conviction in this affair which I ſhould have been very glad to have met with. But whether it was the apprehenſion of being influenced rather by my paſſion than truth, or whether thoſe arguments which were laid before me ſeemed equally to enforce both profeſſions, the methods that were tried proved ineffectual; for to change my principles when there was the leaſt doubt remaining upon my mind, appeared to be a very diſhonourable proceeding.

Bradamante, incenſed at my conduct, which ſhe ſtyles obſtinacy, without reflecting that I may with equal juſtice retort the ſame upon her, has refuſed to ſee me, and my apologies and anxiety have not as yet made any impreſſion on her obdurate heart. This cruel treatment has greatly increaſed my love, and of conſequence my doubts and agitations; and it is on you alone, my dear Giafar, that I depend for aſſiſtance and comfort under my preſent grief and perplexity, and I have the ſtrongeſt reaſon to believe that I ſhall not be diſappointed.

Giafar was going to reply, when the unexpected arrival of Bradamante put a ſtop to their converſation;

tion; and Ruggier was in great agitations on the so sudden appearance of a person, who was both the joy and torment of his heart. The pleasure this unexpected visit gave him, was greatly diminished by the dread of meeting in her countenance, that rigid austerity which had for some time given him great uneasiness; but when he saw in her face, those enchanting smiles which at first captivated his heart, his apprehensions instantly vanished.—Bradamante invited the too friends to go and refresh themselves in the same castle, whither she had formerly conducted Ruggier. They accepted the invitation; and having spent the day in various amusements, which were greatly improved by Bradamante's sprightliness and elegance, they were in the evening conducted to such apartments as Giafar, who had always been accustomed to taste and magnificence, could not but greatly admire. As for Ruggier, his thoughts were totally engaged by this sudden and unexpected change.—Giafar was preparing next morning to set out for the court of Charlemain, when a slave of Ruggier's came and informed him, that his master was gone the same road some hours before; and upon this account he instantly set out by himself. But when he came there, he was greatly disappointed in not meeting with his friend, who was become more dear to him by his having treated him with so much freedom and confidence. He had spent many days in fruitless enquiries; and the Emperor and the whole court begun to be as uneasy as himself; when the same slave who had brought him the above message in Bradamante's castle, delivered him a letter from Ruggier, in the following terms.——
"Come, my much honoured friend, come and rescue me from the greatest dangers that can possibly assault my virtue; come and deliver me from a prison which is equally enchanting and formidable. Bradamante, dreading the influence of your advice,

and desirous to secure the conquest her charms had made, confined me in the castle till you were gone. Since that time, her most engaging accomplishments have frequently staggered my firmest resolutions. It is impossible for me long to resist the piercing sweetness of her looks, and enchanting accents of her voice. Every glance, nay, every motion of her's, almost persuades me to think and act just as she would have me. That maxim of mine which denominates him the meanest of wretches who sacrifices to his passion, those principles which ought to be sacred and inviolable, has now but little influence upon me. I therefore beg you would be as expeditious as possible, in delivering me from my too happy confinement; for even this request may be the last effort I shall be able to exert in defence of my principles and honour. But in preserving my character, I desire you will have a particular regard to that of her, who is the most virtuous, as well as the most cruel of her sex."

This letter laid Giafar under inexpressible difficulties. He could not communicate the secret to Rinaldo or Orlando, as it probably might have occasioned their passing too rigid censures on Bradamante's conduct. He could indeed have rescued Ruggier by force; but he judged this method very improper, looking upon it as scandalous for a man to use violence, who is skreened by his public character from any punishment or retaliation. At last, he determined to apply to Charlemain himself, reflecting, that he would be particularly careful not to excite any jealousies amongst those renowned heroes who were the support of his power and dignity. This method fully answered his expectation; for the Emperor soon found a pretence for ordering Bradamante to come and wait upon him, and during her absence he set Ruggier at liberty.— That joy, and those acknowledgments which Ruggier

gier thought himſelf obliged to expreſs to his deliverer, were very inconſiſtent with his real anxiety; and Giaſar, eaſily perceiving that he lamented that recovery of his liberty, which both reaſon and honour had made him ſo much wiſh for, recalled to his mind his former reſolutions, and enforced them by ſuch arguments as his ſincerity and cordial friendſhip ſuggeſted. But nothing could calm the diſquietudes which Bradamante's treatment occaſioned him, for ſhe had very ſeverely reprimanded him for endangering her reputation with Charlemain, and affected to deſpiſe his behaviour, which made a deeper impreſſion upon him, than the moſt violent reſentment could have done; and in a few days he had an ample teſtimony of the warmth of her indignation. As he and Giaſar were caſually in the ſame foreſt which had before been ſo fatal to him, they were attacked by two cavaliers armed at all points. Ruggier was ſo far from ſuſpecting that he was defending himſelf againſt Bradamante, that he did not even examine her atchievement, which would have given him ſufficient information; for he did not imagine that her reſentment was ſo violent as to demand his blood. Upon theſe accounts he was reſolved to exert his utmoſt, and was juſt upon the point of giving her a fatal ſtroke, when Giaſar's ſhout of triumph, who had that moment diſarmed his adverſary, checked his uplifted arm; and Bradamante making a furious aſſault the ſame inſtant, laid him level with the ground. I ought, ſaid this enraged lady, to deprive you of a life which you have ſullied by thoſe blackeſt of crimes, perfidy and ingratitude; but I ſcorn to ſtain my ſword with the blood of ſuch a wretch, and permit you to exiſt, that your ſcandalous behaviour may be the never-ceaſing torment of your breaſt. Having thus ſaid, ſhe retired with great precipitation. As ſoon as Ruggier recovered from the ſurpriſe occaſioned by

M 3 his

his defeat, having in all his former combats proved victorious, he fell into the most violent agitations for having attempted the life of the person he adored, and resolved to follow Bradamante, and sacrifice at her feet that blood, which she had scorned to shed; but Giafar diverted him from this too precipitate determination. His fixed melancholy greatly retarded the cure of the wound he had received in this rencounter, which, however, was at last effected by the great care and assiduity of his friend.

During these transactions, the time appointed for Giafar's leaving France drew on; and as he had informed Charlemain of his intention to make some stay at Constantinople, that prince was too well acquainted with his interest in Irene, not to beg his assistance in a design which he had much at heart for many years. I have before remarked, that this prince being very desirous of reuniting the eastern and western empires, had tried every method to procure Irene's affection, and had ascribed his disappointment to the empress's dislike of a husband who had not the charms and vigour of youth. Upon this persuasion he had new-modeled his plan, and intended to propose his son to the empress; and thinking Giafar a very proper person to negociate this affair, he pressed him so strongly that he could not possibly refuse his request. The Vizir was too sagacious a politician, and too strongly attached to his master, to wish the success of this design, and it was to no purpose that Charlemain recommended the undertaking to him as beneficial to his own country, by making very advantageous offers to the Calif on condition that the negociation succeeded; for what induced him to attend to these proposals, was the unsurmountable obstacles he knew they would meet with from Irene. His sincerity indeed, would not suffer him to conceal from the Emperor the little hopes he had of success in this affair; but when vhen he ſaw that he could not be diverted from the projeƈt, he repreſented to him, that the tedious̄neſs of ſuch a negociation would not permit him to take it wholly upon himſelf, and therefore he demanded Ruggier as an aſſiſtant, to tranſaƈt this buſineſs after his departure for Bagdad; and Charlemain had too high an opinion of this young hero to refuſe him this mark of his eſteem.

Ruggier was greatly alarmed when he was informed of this prudent and friendly ſtep taken by Giafar; for though he at preſent never ſaw Bradamante, and had the greateſt reaſon to believe that ſhe deſpiſed him, yet he had the conſolation of breathing the ſame air, and living in the ſame country; and he flattered himſelf (for the ſmalleſt thread frequently ſupports a lover's hopes) that ſome fortunate incident might give him an opportunity of ſoftening her reſentment; whereas ſo remote a ſituation deprived him of all theſe comforts; and it was with difficulty that Giafar made him underſtand the neceſſity of this ſtep. At laſt theſe two friends departed, the one with the greateſt reluctance, and the other with the higheſt eſteem and veneration for a people whoſe treatment could not but make the deepeſt impreſſion on ſo noble and generous a diſpoſition.—Do not, my dear Ruggier, ſaid Giafar, indulge ſo unreaſonable and almoſt ſhameful a dejeƈtion; you are indeed going to be removed a great diſtance from the objeƈt of your affeƈtion: but ſince an invincible obſtacle prohibits your felicity, you ought to look upon this voyage as a fortunate circumſtance in your favour; for the haughtineſs and cruelty of your miſtreſs will have their proper effeƈt, and re-eſtabliſh the tranquillity of your breaſt, when you are removed to a ſituation where you will not be expoſed to the faſcination of her eyes, and you will then refleƈt with pleaſure, how prudently you have aƈted in ſacrificing your

 love

love rather than your principles, which would have imbittered every future moment of your life. Fatal experience, alas! has made me but too good a judge of your case! I am greatly more unhappy than yourself. I am going to see a person who amply returns my warmest love, and yet the idea of those raptures I shall enjoy in her arms, instead of pleasure, occasions me the most violent agitations, which will always be the case when our happiness and duty are repugnant to each other. I wish that confidence which you merit, and which I am going to place in you, may prove a useful and salutary lesson for yourself. Giafar then gave Ruggier a detail of his unhappy passion for Abbassah, and the various doubts and disquietudes that harassed his breast; but though by this method he for a while suspended the anxiety of his friend, yet he renewed his own, which their approach to Constantinople greatly increased. For a sincere affection is productive of a constancy greatly superior to that which only depends on caprice, and will not permit a person to transgress the dictates of love; and though by the Mahometan law the men are exempt from that fidelity with which Giafar treated Abbassah, yet his behaviour in this respect was as irreproachable as if the laws of his country had in that case limited his conduct. These being his sentiments, he was greatly embarassed on reflecting that he was going to spend some time with Irene, who would claim a share in his affection, as her vanity might flatter her that she had a place in his breast; and to be in any respect ungrateful, is very disagreeable to an ingenuous disposition. If he had reflected on the Empress's fickle and changeable temper, he might have spared himself this anxiety, for which he found by experience there was no real foundation.

The raptures of Irene, on being informed of Giafar's

Giafar's return, inſtantly ſubſided as ſoon as ſhe ſaw Ruggier; and the blooming youth and fine perſon of this renowned hero, made a deeper impreſſion on her breaſt than ſhe had ever before experienced. The anxiety ſhe manifeſtly laboured under, greatly increaſed Giafar's uneaſineſs, as he imagined himſelf to be the cauſe; but he was ſoon made ſenſible of his miſtake. The Empreſs retarded the private audience ſhe was obliged to give Giafar, with the ſame aſſiduity which ſhe would have exerted to haſten it, if the change in her diſpoſition had not made her dread this interview; and this behaviour made Giafar ſuſpect his apprehenſions to be groundleſs, which were entirely diſperſed as ſoon as he was admitted to her preſence. The moſt exaggerated and repeated encomiums on Ruggier, together with an eager curioſity to know the particulars of this young hero, quickly diſpelled Giafar's doubts, and diſcovered a paſſion which the Empreſs in vain endeavoured to conceal. At laſt, ſhe ſaid to the Vizir, I cannot cenſure your inconſtancy, for which the charms of Abbaſſah are a ſufficient apology. But as in a good diſpoſition the warmth of love ſubſides into a fixed and laſting eſteem, you may depend on finding in my breaſt the moſt cordial friendſhip, of which the confidence I am going to place in you will be a ſufficient aſſurance. I cannot perſuade myſelf that you heartily approve the alliance propoſed by Charlemain, ſince the union of the two empires would form too formidable a neighbour for the Calif: but I would not have you in the leaſt ſuſpect the ſucceſs of his negociation. The contemptible diſpoſition of the prince propoſed for my huſband, may make you quite eaſy in this reſpect; for I aſſure you it requires a perſon of greatly different qualifications to ſurmount my averſion for an indiſſoluble connection. Speak out, Madam, interrupted Giafar with a ſmile, and frankly acknowledge that nothing less than a Ruggier can induce you to change your condition. I will, replied Irene, treat you with the utmost freedom and confidence; for you are so intimately acquainted with the human breast, that it is impossible to conceal from you its most secret movements I have for a long time been a great admirer of Ruggier's renown, and his presence has been productive of a passion of a different nature. I greatly wish that the birth and origin of this amiable youth may prove favourable to my inclinations, for the difference of our religious principles will not be the least objection to me. But though both these impediments should prevent my paying him that compliment which his merit deserves, yet they shall not hinder my bestowing on him the greatest favours in my power, that gratitude may detain in my service a man who will be the honour and support of my crown. I shall be much obliged to you, if you will favour me with your opinion as to the success of these projects. The strict friendship, replied Giafar, that subsists between Ruggier and myself, not only makes me very zealous for his welfare, but also gives me that knowledge of his disposition, that I can inform you of the sole method in which you can execute your plan. His breast is not susceptible of meanness and artifice; and if you deprive him of the hopes of succeeding in the negociation he is come to execute, his attachment to his sovereign will induce him instantly to return to France, to acquaint him with the bad success of his design. I therefore advise you to defer giving an absolute refusal, which will instantly ruin your project; but keep him in suspence, until your charms have taken that effect which they cannot fail of producing; the more generous it is in me to give you these instructions, the more they merit your serious attention. I am, replied Irene, very sensible of the generosity and im-

importance of your directions. But what do you mean, Sir, by this intimation? Has that very uncommon example of sincerity I have just given you, in divesting myself of that disguise which is allowable in our sex, made no impression upon you, that you practise that reserve which I have laid aside out of the great regard I have for you? You would perhaps, make me believe, that you yourself sacrifice your love to friendship; but I would not have you flatter yourself with that expectation, for the great affection I entertained for you induced me to procure such intelligence as renders your dissimulation fruitless. But the only revenge I will take shall be to offer you an asylum in my dominions. Come, and bring Abbassah along with you, to Constantinople, and expose yourselves no longer to those jealousies and fears, which greatly imbitter that felicity of which your mutual affection would be productive. I will marry Ruggier, and we will endeavour to procure you, in a calm retreat, the uninterrupted pleasures of love and friendship. You will not be then every moment apprehensive of falling a victim to the Calif's resentment, whose weakness and caprice I always strongly suspected; and as you express a great regard for his glory, that, as well as the preservation of your own life, ought to be an inducement to accept the proposal I make.——Ah, Madam, replied Giafar with a sigh, Haroun's glory will not receive the least stain from the punishment of a perfidious subject. As you have been informed of my unhappy situation, you are undoubtedly no stranger to my crimes, which I should greatly enhance if I accepted the generous offer you are so kind as to make me; for I think it my duty, whatever may be the consequence, to endeavour by my future fidelity in some degree to efface the baseness of my perjury. This topic being too affecting for Giafar,

Giafar, Irene inſtantly turned the converſation to leſs intereſting ſubjects.

The Empreſs's very frank and ſincere behaviour effaced from Giafar's memory the many foibles which ſhe had undoubtedly been guilty of; and moreover, as the fortune, and probably, the tranquillity of his friend depended on the affection he had excited in her breaſt, he tried every poſſible method to induce him to make a ſuitable return. When he informed him of the Empreſs's ſentiments, he ſtudiouſly dropped every circumſtance that might be diſcouraging; and Ruggier, notwithſtanding his affection for Bradamante, was prevailed on by the perſuaſion of his friend, and by thoſe allurements with which perſons of his years are eaſily captivated, to pay ſome regard to his advice.——But he ſometimes, notwithſtanding, would ſay to Giafar, I would not have you imagine, that my attachment to Irene is to be compared to the affection I entertain for her, who alone is deſerving of the ſole poſſeſſion of my heart. Not all the charms of that princeſs, nor the ſplendor of a crown, can expoſe me to thoſe dangerous conflicts between love and duty, in which the accompliſhments and virtue of Bradamante have ſometimes almoſt overthrown my firmeſt reſolutions. I endeavour by thoſe addreſſes I pay another miſtreſs, and which are far from having any real foundation in my breaſt, to ſtrengthen and ſupport my too feeble reſolves; and that certainly can never be termed inconſtancy, which is rather an effort of reaſon than a ſuggeſtion of paſſion. The hopes alſo of ſerving my prince is a further inducement to this method of proceeding; but as ſoon as I ſhall be aſſured that my endeavours in his favour are fruitleſs, I ſhall inſtantly fly to that dear but fatal country, and again expoſe myſelf to thoſe torments which have for ſo long a time haraſſed my breaſt, and

ſhall

ſhall think myſelf happy if I have acquired more ſtrength to ſupport my ſufferings. Giafar tried every method to perſuade Ruggier to continue with Irene, but they were equally fruitleſs, with the advice Ruggier gave him for the preſervation of his life and tranquillity, or to prolong his ſtay at Conſtantinople. Neither love, duty, nor the cruel decrees of fate, would permit the unhappy Vizir to ſtay a moment longer than the time appointed by the Calif. But though he reſiſted both the ſolicitations of his friend, and the generous offers of the Empreſs; yet, on taking his leave of them, he was not able to refrain from tears, which a fatal preſage, that it was their final farewel, rendered greatly more affecting.

During theſe tranſactions, jealouſy began to infuſe its poiſon into the breaſt of Abbaſſah, occaſioned by Giafar's too long abſence, and his ſtay at Conſtantinople; and even thoſe inſinuations of Haroun, which ſhe had looked upon as falſe and ſcandalous, appeared now in a different light. But the return of him, whom ſhe accuſed of ingratitude, at leaſt, if not of infidelity, quickly diſpelled all her anxiety, and made her moſt conſummately happy. She clearly perceived by his countenance, that there was no foundation for her ſuſpicions, and inſtantly buried all her cares in his arms. Giafar, intoxicated with love, and enraptured with the careſſes of the moſt beautiful and paſſionate of women, was equally unmindful of the reſolutions he had lately made, as he had before been of his oath to the Calif, which indeed the impoſſibility of withſtanding ſuch irreſiſtible temptations eaſily apologized for. But their felicity, with which two hearts ſo deeply enamoured were never clogged, was ſoon interrupted by the diſquietudes of Haroun, who, hoping to re-eſtabliſh the peace of his mind by a pilgrimage to Mecca, gave Giafar orders to prepare to attend him. Both

Giafar

Giafar and Abbaſſah were greatly alarmed at this cruel ſeparation, and that reflection which had ſupported them in the like caſe before, had now loſt its influence. Thoſe ſecret apprehenſions, which we generally look upon as unmeaning agitations of the ſoul, are often fatal meſſengers of our future woes, and take their origin from the perfection of our nature: that particular account, moreover, which Abbaſſah had given Giafar of Zobeide's perfidy, made him reflect with horror on the ſentiments he had entertained, and the reſolutions he made on the firſt diſcovery of that affair. It was to no purpoſe that Abbaſſah endeavoured to perſuade him that Haroun was an accomplice in this villany; for his breaſt was incapable of entertaining ſuch a ſuſpicion, for which ſhe was excuſable, in having no other knowledge of the Calif, but from his crimes. Giafar's anxiety and deſpair were ſtrongly painted in his countenance; and there never was an adieu attended with leſs reſolution, or ſtronger expreſſions of grief and affection. After a very affecting ſilence, Abbaſſah thus expreſſed herſelf. The invariable tenor of my unhappy life makes me entertain a ſecret dread, which I cannot ſurmount: ſcarce had your return reſtored life and joy to my deſponding breaſt, when a ſecond parting plunges me again into the deepeſt deſpair! What ſecret, alas, is ſo impenetrable as to be proof againſt envious times and the prying eyes of love! If Haroun has ſuſpected the real motive of my journey, and goes only to ſatisfy his doubts, the intelligence he will receive, will ſo exaſperate his reſentful diſpoſition, that all the interceſſions I can make, inſtead of preventing, will only haſten your deſtruction! Ah, my dear Zelia, replied Giafar, expel from your amiable boſom ſuch ſhocking reflections, and let the whole load of our misfortunes lay wholly upon me, as I alone deſerve ſuch

ſevere

ſevere puniſhment! The guilty wretch ought always to conſider the ſword as ſuſpended over his head; but a lover ought to conceal his apprehenſions from the ſole miſtreſs of his affections. I hope that the powerful reaſons which may be alledged in excuſe of my perjury, will, in the eyes of the Supreme, in ſome meaſure palliate my infirmity: and I am well aſſured from the Calif's affectionate behaviour, that he does not in the leaſt ſuſpect my treachery; for being ſo intimately acquainted with his diſpoſition, I can eaſily perceive the moſt ſecret movements of his ſoul; but how often has a fatal infatuation made me diſregardleſs of this circumſtance, if I had preſerved my integrity . . . . But what am I going to ſay! I am attempting to vindicate my conduct, when your beauty and my own heart ſufficiently aſſure me, that it was impoſſible for me to obſerve my engagements; whereas to calm the diſquietudes of my dear Zelia, and give her ſome reviving hopes, ought to be at preſent the ſole object of my attention; for it is by no means proper that you ſhould ſhare in this firſt ſtage of my puniſhment . . . . The Iman and Nair are ſo zealouſly attached to our intereſt, that I am aſſured I ſhall return to your longing arms, and ſhall have the pleaſure of conveying to you thoſe ſweet and innocent embraces I ſhall receive from your ſon . . . . I moſt ſincerely wiſh, interrupted Abbaſſah, that your expectations may not be fruſtrated; but, alas! notwithſtanding your kind endeavours to ſupport my drooping ſpirits, I but too clearly perceive your own apprehenſions!—— An exceſs of grief, replied Giafar, rouſes every faculty of the ſoul, and makes us feel at the ſame inſtant every calamity which can aſſault the human breaſt. Mutually enfolding each other in their arms, they exclaimed at the ſame inſtant, how fatally do we at present experience the truth of this observation! Ah, Zelia!—Ah, Giafar! . . . . I wish I could expire in your arms!—Good heavens! we are the most miserable of mortals!—Fatima was present at this affecting adieu, and exerted her utmost endeavours to soften Abbassah's anxiety. She recalled to her mind her own sufferings, and endeavoured to persuade her to emulate her fortitude. Do not in the least doubt, said she, but that your affectionate husband will again return to your arms; he is as sensibly affected as yourself on being obliged to leave you; whereas the man I adore has cruelly condemned me to never ceasing woe: but though Mirza's barbarous and ungrateful treatment has occasioned me the most pungent grief, yet it has not effaced my passion, and I bear my sufferings with resignation. It is much more noble and heroic, to support ourselves under the cruel allotments of fortune, provided they are not attended with infamy, than to harass our minds with future events, which may probably bring upon us that greatest of evils, the loss of a good name.—Haroun's parting with Abbassah was not so affecting as the above, because he was obliged to suppress his sensations: but his situation was the most severe, as he had no partner to share those agitations which were doomed to be his destruction. May I, said he, affectionately embracing his sister, procure from propitious heaven the re-establishment of my virtue and reason! May I never see you again but to promote your happiness and tranquillity!—A monarch has less to dread from his subjects murmuring at his extravagant magnificence, than from their despising his meanness, and want of that princely dignity which excites their astonishment; for men oppose those they fear, and always obey those they admire.—During the Califf's whole journey there was the greatest profusion of of Aſiatic luxury; all the road from Bagdad to Mecca was ſpread with the richeſt carpets, and at every ſtage he was received with the higheſt eſteem, acclamations and magnificence. He repoſed himſelf during the heat of the day, and as ſoon as the cool breezes of the evening invited him to reſume his journey, the lamps and perfumes that were diſperſed in the trees, gave a light more agreeable than that of the ſun, and a fragrancy more exquiſite than the ſpring. — The Calif's journey had greatly alarmed the Iman, who had as an affectionate regard for Abbaſſah's ſon as if he had been his own. He therefore placed him and Nair in the moſt private part of the temple, to approach which was prohibited by Mahomed himſelf, thinking it the moſt proper and ſafe aſylum for innocence.

Whilſt Haroun was engaged in petitioning heaven to reſtore him by a miracle, that tranquillity for which he ſhould have ſolely depended on time and reflection, Giafar amuſed himſelf with embracing his ſon, and receiving the return of his tender careſſes: he expreſſed his warmeſt acknowledgments to the Iman, amply rewarded the fidelity of Nair, and was permitted every evening to viſit this dear pledge of his love, the exact copy of his charming Zelia.—Zobeide was ſolely employed in making ſecret enquiries relative to Abbaſſah's tranſactions during her ſtay at Mecca; but the watchful circumſpection of Meſrour, who was greatly ſolicitous for Giafar's and Abbaſſah's ſafety, rendered her inveſtigations fruitleſs; and it was to chance alone that ſhe was indebted for the ſucceſs of her baſe deſigns. Both ſhe and the Calif were, in regard to their dignity, accommodated within the temple, and the windows of her apartment happened to look into a garden which was reſerved for the ſole uſe of the Iman.

A male-

A malevolent difpofition is more tormenting to the poffeffor than to thofe whom it perfecutes, for it never permits either the body or mind to enjoy repofe. Zoheide, whofe fleep was interrupted by her malicious machinations, frequently arofe before the dawn of the morning, and inhaled thofe refrefhing breezes which heaven, if it were as circumfpect in preventing as in punifhing villany, would have deprived her of. How great was her furprife and joy, when fhe one morning cafually difcovered in the arms of Nair an infant, whofe beautiful features bore a great refemblance to thofe of Abbaffah; fhe thought that that myftery, which had been fo long the fubject of her enquiry, was now unravelled: fhe called Nair to her, and, by employing both menaces and promifes, eafily extracted from the breaft accuftomed to perfidy this fatal fecret. The hopes of being freed from his prefent confinement, which he looked upon as a prifon, fuppreffed the ftruggles of confcience, and moreover treafon itfelf is amiable in the eyes of its votaries. Both honour and property are frequently dependants on power. The Iman had always thought himfelf fupreme in the Muffulman profeffion, and a great part of the people had acknowledged his claim: but Haroun being of a different opinion, and fupporting his pretenfions by a numerous army, at prefent enjoyed the revenues of this dignity. The defcendant of Ali, being on this account eclipfed and degraded by the Calif's prefence, fcarce durft fhew himfelf even in thofe places which were fuperftitioufly confecrated to his fole ufe; even his retired garden was polluted by Zobeide's fixing upon it as a proper place to execute her black defigns. She was too great a proficient in wickednefs to take upon herfelf this odious impeachment, and therefore refolved that Haroun fhould himfelf difcover Giafar's perfidy. For as ſhe had thoroughly ſtudied the human heart, ſhe was very ſenſible that the ſame object will to-day excite our reſentment, and to-morrow our compaſſion, and that revenge is frequently ſucceeded by pity; in ſhort, ſhe was not ignorant, that, having deſtroyed the object we admire, we vent our reſentment on thoſe who have occaſioned us to commit ſuch a precipitate action. Upon theſe accounts Zobeide contrived to bring Haroun and Giaſar into the Iman's garden, where Nair was appointed to meet them with Abbaſſah's ſon in her arms. But what were Giafar's ſenſations on ſeeing him approach. The Calif indeed did not obſerve his agitations, neither did he know Nair, for his attention was ſolely engaged by this beautiful infant, whom he loaded with the moſt affectionate careſſes. Zobeide, who dreaded the event of theſe tender ſentiments, determined to ſuppreſs them by exciting his jealouſy. I am not at all ſurpriſed, Sir, ſaid ſhe, at your affection for this infant, ſince it has ſo ſtrong a reſemblance of the perſon you adore. This malicious inſinuation gave Haroun a dark, but fatal hint, who turning to Giaſar, and obſerving the grief and deſpair which were ſo ſtrongly expreſſed in his countenance, wanted no further information. At laſt, recollecting Nair, he ſaid to him in a furious and menacing accent, To whom belongs that child? Inſtantly confeſs the truth to your maſter, or the ſevereſt puniſhment . . . . There was indeed no occaſion for threats to induce Nair to make a premeditated confeſſion; he therefore inſtantly diſcovered to him the whole affair. —The violent fury of the Calif could be equalled by nothing but Giaſar's grief and deſpair; but the deplorable condition in which the unhappy Vizir was, did not make the leaſt impreſſion upon him. Baſe traitor, ſaid he, is this the return of my friendſhip and eſteem! You have concealed, I find, your

your ingratitude and perjury under a mafk of integrity and honour! Good heavens! What mean artifices muft you have employed to deceive me! I am furprifed that the Supreme would permit fuch a perjured traitor to exift! But fince the All-wife has committed your punifhment to me, fhame and death fhall be your doom, for to inflict the latter without the former, would be fhewing too great lenity. The ungrateful Zelia, who has acted fuitably to her fhameful origin, is as culpable as yourfelf; and as fhe has abufed my devotion and credulity, fhe fhall feel the weight of my refentment, and augment your punifhment. I will degrade her from the dignity of Abbaffides, and you fhall have the mortification to fee her in the arms of the meaneft of my flaves.—Ah, Sir, cried Giafar, throwing himfelf at the Calif's feet, be not fo cruel! invent what tortures you pleafe for me, but do not difgrace your mother and your fifter! It was I that feduced Zelia, and prevailed on her to deceive you, on me therefore only let your refentment fall. I alone am guilty of this treafon, and revenge in whatever manner you pleafe this infult upon your friendfhip; I fhall not endeavour to excite your compaffion, or awaken thofe fentiments of affection, which I fhould never have forfeited, if it had not been through the influence of a fatal paffion, the power of which you are no ftranger to; punifh the guilty, but fpare the innocent!—How canft thou, perfidious wretch, replied Haroun, pretend to folicit favours of me at this juncture? How canft thou intimate thy own virtue, and at the fame time cenfure my innocent paffion, which, though it was the occafion of a condefcenfion which thou haft abufed, did never excite the leaft criminal defire in my breaft! I would have thee know, that if thou hadft imitated me, thou hadft not been guilty of fuch bafenefs, and that treachery

is

is a crime of a blacker dye than inceſt! But to permit ſuch a monſter in human ſhape, who has converted my moſt friendly and affectionate ſentiments into the moſt horrid averſion, to appear before me, is what I cannot bear! Take him hence, continued he, and load him with fetters; on my return to Bagdad, he ſhall ſeverely ſuffer for betraying his friend, diſgracing his ſovereign, and diſregarding the dictates of honour and the laws of God! Let no perſon, in the mean time, on pain of my diſpleaſure, preſume to ſolicite a mitigation of his ſentence!—The Calif's orders were punctually obeyed, and Giafar was confined in a frightful dungeon until Haroun's departure. Every perſon lamented his rigid deſtiny, and grief diffuſed an univerſal melancholy over the whole city; but no one was ſo deeply affected as Meſrour. The unhappy fate of Giafar and Abbaſſah gave him the moſt pungent concern, and the ſtain the Calif was going to throw upon his renown made him almoſt diſtracted; for he had that noble and generous affection for his prince, which rendered him more anxious for his reputation and virtue than for his life. He was very ſenſible that the Calif deceived himſelf in thinking his reſentment founded on juſtice, for he did not look upon Giafar as guilty of any heinous miſdemeanor, but only of a trifling weakneſs, which was very excuſable; and he thought him greatly more blameable for entering into ſuch an imprudent engagement, than for the violation of an oath it was impoſſible to obſerve, and which his ſacred obligations to Abbaſſah totally cancelled. Upon theſe accounts he reſolved to try every method to re-eſtabliſh in Haroun's breaſt ſentiments of juſtice and humanity; and a tender compaſſion for the unhappy, but innocent cauſe of ſo many misfortunes, obliged him to pay his firſt attention to the ſon of Giafar; and taking advantage of the Calif's perplexity, he

ſeized

ſeized both him and Nair; the latter of whom he ſeverely puniſhed: and committing the other to the zeal and affection of the Iman, he aſſiſted them in making their eſcape. The next ſtep his generoſity prompted him to take, was to inform Abbaſſah of Giafar's unhappy ſituation, and the puniſhment to which ſhe herſelf was ſentenced. He accordingly diſpatched a friend on whom he could rely to Bagdad, with a letter to Abbaſſah, adviſing her to avoid by flight that infamy ſhe was doomed to ſuffer; and in order to ſecure her compliance with theſe directions, he enforced them by the commands of Giafar. He alſo repreſented to her the inutility and danger of making any application to the Calif in favour of her unhappy ſpouſe; and gave her reaſon to hope, that time and reflection would mitigate Haroun's reſentment, and make him entertain more juſt and equitable ſentiments; and in the concluſion, he informed her of the place where ſhe might find the Iman and her ſon.

During theſe tranſactions, Haroun laboured under thoſe boiſterous fluctuations of paſſion conſequent on ſo ſudden a change in his diſpoſition, and in being obliged ſeverely to puniſh thoſe who had hitherto held the firſt place in his eſteem and affection, for having deceived and inſulted him. One while he was tranſported with a furious rage, which he miſtook for a laudable zeal; another, he ſunk into deſpair; and being conſtantly the prey of contending paſſions, he was even weary of his exiſtence. Sullen, gloomy, and fierce, no perſon but Zobeide durſt approach him, who ſmothered the ſmall ſparks of virtue that ſtill remained in his breaſt, and made him proof againſt the ſuggeſtions of humanity: and ſuch was his blindneſs, that he miſtook this inſenſibility for a happy compoſure of mind. How can you, ſaid ſhe, diſpute the juſtice of a ſentiment that has the ſanction of the Su-

preme,

preme, for of all the passions, revenge alone is claimed by him as peculiar to himself; and therefore not to regard it as a virtue, would be the highest contempt of the divine attributes. To pardon an injury, is to become the patron of vice; but to resent it, is the surest sign of courage and steadiness; and a person of a noble disposition, neither can nor ought to overlook an affront, as it is a strong characteristic of pusillanimity. Such discourse and horrid advice, which, to the reproach of human nature, is apt to have too great influence, would at any other juncture have met with a severe reprimand from Haroun; but he was at present the dupe of prejudice, and readily embraced any errors that mitigated the tortures of his breast. —Abbassah, on receiving Mesrour's letter, was seized with such violent agitations, that Fatima was frequently apprehensive of the most fatal consequences. The dread of that infamy to which, as she was informed, she was to be exposed, sometimes rouzed her spirits, and made her reflect, that a moment's delay might render her flight impracticable, which, notwithstanding her numerous friends and absolute power in the Seraglio, would be extremely difficult; but a cloud of grief soon intervening, dissipated these lucid intervals. The assiduity of Fatima, and the desire of seeing her son, gave her at length sufficient resolution for this necessary step, and after a tedious journey she arrived at the place appointed for meeting him and the Iman.

How necessary was her presence to this dear pledge of her love; for the Iman bending under a load of years and disappointments, was approaching his last moments.—I restore to your arms, Madam, said he to Abbassah, that dear pledge which you committed to my care, but not, alas, till he has proved fatal both to you and himself! The

precious

precious remains of the blood of Ali, though deserving of a happier lot, is now buried in misery and oblivion! The traitor Nair has ruined us! How easily do persons of innocent and undesigning dispositions fall a prey to artifice and perfidy! This ought to be a lesson to us, not rashly and imprudently to place our confidence, or intrust our weighty concerns, but with persons of approved integrity! I implore the Supreme, continued he in a faultering accent, to mitigate your sufferings, and to accept of my death for an atonement! May those fatal presages which imbitter my last moments never be permitted to happen! Having thus expressed himself, the Iman expired, enfolding in his arms the son of Giafar, whose tears greatly added to this affecting scene!——Abbassah, unable to support herself under such a group of woe, fainted; but the cries of her son soon recalled her faculties: she seized him in her arms with the most eager affection; but instantly pushing him from her with horror, she said, Dear, but fatal pledge of an unhappy passion, how cruel is thy destiny! Thou, who art the monitor of my felicity, and the fruit of my crimes, destroyest the one and punishest the other! Ah, Fatima, what will become of this unhappy infant, when fell barbarity shall have destroyed his father, and despair his mother! How miserable will he be when he shall hereafter be informed, that he occasioned the death of his parents! But as Haroun's resentment may extend even to him, his attention may be solely engaged by his own sufferings; and the ignominy which the Calif throws on the memory of his mother, and his insensibility to the dictates of friendship and nature, gives me the most shocking apprehensions. Alas! if I thought he would sentence the son of Giafar to disgrace and slavery, I would deprive his malice of so sweet a morsel!

I would

I would instantly pierce his innocent bosom, and drawing out the reeking steel would plunge it into my own! Pity often excites rage, and justifies even cruelty!—Abbassah's agitations were as strongly expressed in her countenance as in her speech; and her fierce gloomy aspect made the little tender infant that occasioned it, shrink back with fear; but seeing no persons to protect it, he again, directed by instinct, clung to his mother's bosom, and seemed by his tears and tender caresses to solicit her protection as his only support. These emotions, which could not at his age be the result of reason and reflection, are implanted in us by nature for our preservation; and as they never fail to affect the most obdurate, what must their influence be on the tender heart of a mother! Abbassah wiped away the tears of her son, and gently fondled and encouraged him. She now listened to her faithful friend Fatima, who endeavoured to support her spirits by the hopes Mesrour expressed of bringing about a reconciliation.—Fear is always destitute of foresight, and consequently Abbassah and Fatima, under those perturbations in which they had quitted the Seraglio, had forgot to take money sufficient for their subsistence, and consequently their misfortunes received the additional load of poverty and distress. They had now fixed their abode in a little village on the banks of the Tigris, where some charitable fishermen supplied them with necessaries sufficient to support their wretched beings. But the necessity that obliged them to subsist on such poor fare, did not give Abbassah so much concern, as the not having it in her power to recompence her kind entertainers, and the miserable situation into which Fatima's friendship had brought her. Leave me, said she to her, for I cannot bear to see you spend a life

 which

which may have happier hours allotted in ſucceeding years, and which . . . . Say no more, Zelia, cried Fatima, what have I done to deſerve ſuch an affront? Neither hope, nor even a certain proſpect of happineſs, can diſſolve thoſe connections by which I am united to you, with whom I am firmly determined both to live and die.—Well then, my dear Fatima, replied Abbaſſah, let us return a little nearer to Bagdad, and conceal ourſelves in ſome private corner in that neighbourhood; for as Haroun will ſhortly return, we ſhall find ſome opportunity of informing Meſrour of the place of our concealment, and he will acquaint me with my huſband's deſtiny, whom, if poſſible, I will endeavour to ſave; if not, I am determined to die with him.

Fatima approved of this propoſal, and as they were not at a very great diſtance from Bagdad, they prevailed on one of the fiſhermen to conduct them to the foreſt, where, as ſoon as they were arrived, they diſcharged him. That tower where Hakem formerly practiſed his impoſtures was now demoliſhed, and its ruins concealed under the thick umbrage of the neighbouring trees. Abbaſſah and Fatima, who had carried the child by turns, and were fatigued with their journey, caſually ſat down to repoſe themſelves under one of the trees that ſhaded theſe ruins; and Abbaſſah, caſting her eye on an inſcription which informed her in what place they were, gave a ſudden ſhriek, and fainted. Fatima was ſo ſurpriſed at this ſudden and unaccountable incident, that ſhe was not able to aſſiſt her friend; and the gloom of night, which ſhortly after came on, greatly added to her perplexity: ſhe was alſo ready to ſink under the fatigue ſhe had undergone, and was afraid to leave the place where they were, in order to procure ſome aſſiſtance.—In this ſhocking ſituation her horrors were greatly augmented,

augmented, by hearing ſome perſons approaching; but her concern for Abbaſſah got the better of her apprehenſions, and even fear itſelf is often productive of reſolution. She aroſe, and went towards the perſon ſhe heard, whom the darkneſs prevented her ſeeing, and proſtrating herſelf at their feet, ſhe ſaid, Whoſoever you are, give your aſſiſtance to the moſt unhappy of women, whom, if you could but ſee the ſituation ſhe is in, I am ſure you would compaſſionate.—Scarce had ſhe uttered theſe words, when one of the two perſons to whom ſhe addreſſed herſelf, ſaid, Ah! my good father; it is Fatima!--it is ſhe! What, Mirza! ſaid Fatima in return; good heavens, I ſink with ſurpriſe! Mirza inſtantly ſeized his miſtreſs in his arms, who was almoſt fainting; but the conſideration of the condition in which ſhe had left Zelia, prevented this incident having that violent effect, which might have proved of fatal conſequences in the weak ſituation ſhe was at preſent in. Mirza, ſaid ſhe, as I know you to be of a humane and compaſſionate diſpoſition, I beg you would run to Zelia's aſſiſtance, whoſe groans will inform you of the place where ſhe is; your friend will aſſiſt me in following you; for though Abbaſſah is dying, yet my exhauſted ſpirits will not permit me to hurry to her aſſiſtance. That I will, replied the other, who had not yet ſpoke; and Mondir offers you an arm, which his concern for you has greatly more weakened than the weight of age. Such a croud of happy circumſtances in Fatima's favour, might have proved fatal to Abbaſſah, if Mirza, eager to obey the commands of his miſtreſs, had not run to her aſſiſtance. He inſtantly took her in his arms, and Mondir carrying the child, and conducting Fatima, they quickly arrived at a houſe, which was concealed by the ſurrounding trees and ruins, where with great care and difficulty they recovered Abbaſſah. Fatima

 did

did not at present want any assistance, for the enchanting looks of Mirza would have been almost sufficient to have raised her from the dead.—Where am I, said Zelia, on returning to herself! Am I still in Hakem's tower! Yes, Madam, replied Mondir. This then is my grave, returned she; that offended Supreme, who is terrible in his judgments, and who punishes the children for the crimes of their parents, has brought me hither, that I may finish my wretched life in the same place where I first received my criminal existence! —Mondir was no stranger to the unhappy fate of Giafar and Abbassah, and exerted the utmost efforts of his wisdom to dispel her gloomy thoughts, and prevent her falling into despair. And whilst he was engaged in this friendly office, Mirza threw himself at the feet of Fatima, who was in such raptures that she could scarce believe her own eyes. At last she said, Is it Mirza that I see! that Mirza whom I have so long loved with the most cordial and steady affection! Is it possible that his eyes, which always darted an ill-grounded resentment, should speak the soft language of love and contrition! . . . . But is not all this a pleasing delusion, which will probably soon vanish!—Mirza only replied by a dejected supplicating look, which was a more prevailing apology than the most eloquent harangue. At last he broke silence, and said, Does my Fatima still love me! and a consenting reply expressed by her countenance rather than her voice, threw Mirza into the highest raptures.—Abbassah's anxiety was in some degree softened by Fatima's felicity, whose happiness in return was alloyed by the distress of her friend. Mondir promised them to wait upon Mesrour as soon as he returned, and even upon Haroun himself if necessary; and in short, to exert his utmost for the service of Abbassah;

baſſah; and theſe friendly offers, in ſome degree, ſoftened the anxiety of this unhappy princeſs.

Mirza, however, notwithſtanding what had paſſed between him and Fatima, was deſirous of extenuating his guilt, and of making ſome apology for that reſentment and barbarity with which he had quitted her. Be ſilent, ſaid ſhe, on that ſubject, for my affection is a better apology than all you can ſay; I have the pleaſure of ſeeing you again, you aſſure me of an inviolable paſſion, and with this I am fully ſatisfied. But I am not, replied Mirza; for though a generous pardon is very captivating, yet when it is not merited, it ſometimes proves of fatal conſequences. A mere penitent contrition is not the only return I ought to make you, and I beg you would liſten to the dictates of my warmeſt gratitude in return for your undeſerved affection. But how can I recal to your mind, thoſe circumſtances which have imbittered my ſucceeding life, and given me the deepeſt ſhame and remorſe!

Dilnouze, continued he, proved the ſcourge of my infatuated breaſt; ſhe aſſured me that it was you that had accuſed Balkis, though you were convinced of her innocence. Fatima, ſaid ſhe to me, knew very well that Balkis was in the arms of her brother, and not of a lover; and ſhe inſtigated you to this unjuſt reſentment, in order to revenge herſelf of a perſon who poſſeſſed the firſt place in your affection, and to render you odious to her. She has carried her artifice ſtill further; ſhe has betrayed you, in order to procure, by ſaving you afterwards, that eſteem of which ſhe is ſo little deſerving. Nothing is ſo dangerous as a woman whoſe faculties are ſuperior to thoſe of the reſt of her ſex; and in order to free you from any future, and perhaps, more fatal difficulties in which ſhe may entangle you, I have purſued you hither, and if you will follow me, I will conduct you to an asylum unknown to your pursuers, and where you may safely remain till they are weary with searching. Dilnouze's advice was the fatal occasion of my sacrificing you, and I did not discover her perfidy until it was too late to correct my error. She and I had taken up our residence at a cottage in the middle of a thick wood, where, a few days after our arrival, I found myself surrounded by the Calif's troops. Dilnouze now threw off the mask, she came to me with the most resentful countenance, and said, I have now revenged your quitting me for your faithful Fatima; deceived by an unsuspected stratagem, you have treated her affectionate fidelity with the most shocking barbarity, and she is probably this very moment expiring with grief. That just punishment you will soon receive, the being rescued from which by your generous and affectionate mistress, I have sufficiently guarded against, prevents my entertaining any apprehensions of your resentment. Dilnouze, having thus expressed herself, left me, but first received of those who were loading me with chains the reward of her perfidy, which, and not revenge, was probably the real motive of her conduct. Dilnouze's shocking treachery did not so much affect me as her vindication of your conduct, the sole motive of which was to increase my tortures. Ah, Fatima, said I, adorable, virtuous Fatima! how could I suspect the sincerity of your heart! I am, alas, the cause of your death! . . . . Dilnouze, even the infamous Dilnouze, is better acquainted with your noble disposition than I, and knows you this moment to be expiring under my cruel treatment! . . . . I see your beautiful eyes wading in the midst of death, and yet even then sending up an imploring look to heaven for my safety! . . . . I wish some sudden judgment would free me from

these

thefe intolerable reflections, and revenge my ungrateful behaviour! In this ftate of diftraction I followed my conductors; but what were my emotions when we approached the place where I had left you; and when I faw Cadige at fome diftance, I would freely have given the laft drop of my blood to have had the liberty of defiring her to inform you, that I fhould die with the higheft fentiments of your virtue and goodnefs, and that I reflected with pleafure, that that moft inhuman of wretches, who had infulted and treated you in the moft cruel manner, would fhortly be no more.

Grief and contrition at laft rekindled in my breaft, all that warmth of paffion which I at firft entertained for you; Balkis was totally effaced from my memory, and this was my fituation of mind, when my guards came to take off my chains, and to inform me, that the perfon who had interefted himfelf in my fafety, begged that I would inftantly avoid by flight the Calif's refentment. I was not ignorant of the beneficent hand that raifed me thus a fecond time out of the gulph of defpair, and was fully perfuaded that your generofity had induced Mahomed to procure my enlargement. I inftantly went in queft of Cadige, but could not find her; and her houfe being fhut, deprived me of the confolation of bathing that fpot with my tears, which had been the fcene of your cruel fufferings. I refolved, however, to wait for her return, notwithftanding the dangers fuch a ftep might expofe me to; but being difappointed in my hopes of feeing her, I led a folitary roaming life, until I grew weary of my exiftence, and had determined to return to Sarmakande, in order to enquire after you of Mahomed, when I cafually met with Mondir; whom, inftead of avoiding, I frankly accofted, and ingenuoufly acknowledged my crimes. He at firft looked upon me with horror; but my violent agitations softening his resentment, he treated me with familiarity, and acquainted me with the sacrifice you made for my safety.—This incredible proof of an affection I so little merited, threw me into such violent agitations as it is not possible for me describe. To have procured your liberty, I would not only have embraced with joy the most galling chains of slavery, but even, if possible, have suffered a thousand deaths. Mondir checked my violent resolves, and informed me that Cadige, whom he had dispatched for that purpose, was returned; and not finding you with the slave-merchant, had learned that you had been sold to some eunuchs that came from Bagdad. He added, that, upon receiving this information, he ordered his slaves to get ready two camels, and load them with his most valuable effects, with which he intended immediately to set out in order to purchase your ransom. I begged of him to accept of my company; to which he consented, after advising me to disguise myself in the dress of a slave. We accordingly set out for Bagdad; and while we were one day beguiling the fatigue of our journey, by making you the topic of our conversation, we were attacked by some banditti, who deprived us of every thing but life, and by taking away our treasure ruined our whole plan. I now in my turn supported the drooping spirits of Mondir, and flattered myself, that I should still be able to procure your freedom on the same conditions you had done mine; but our most diligent enquiries for you at Bagdad proved unsuccessful.—We could not however prevail upon ourselves to quit a place where we hoped some fortunate incident might inform us of your abode; and as the Calif's resentment rendered it necessary for me to live in privacy and solitude, we fixed our habitation in this forest. How often, grown weary of my existence, would I have

fur-

ſurrendered myſelf, if Mondir had not prevented me, who, inſtead of reproaching me as the cauſe of your misfortunes, looked upon me as abſolutely requiſite to your felicity in whatever ſituation we might find you. The moſt prevailing arguments he uſed for my preſerving my life, were founded on a poſſibility of my being inſtrumental to your happineſs. And what pleaſure ſhall I receive from following his advice, if my poor endeavours will in the leaſt contribute to your felicity; if my contrition and affection will obliterate my paſt behaviour, and free you from any doubts as to my future conduct; if, in ſhort, you will condeſcend to unite your fortune to that of an unhappy wretch condemned to perpetual exile, and inſtead of a ſceptre with which he would gladly preſent you, will deign to ſhare in the pleaſures of a rural life, the only choice fortune at preſent allows us. Mondir indeed, prefers our ſituation to the falſe glitter which attends the great, and he never returned from Bagdad, where the hopes of finding you frequently induced him to go, without making very advantageous compariſons in favour of our manner of living, in oppoſition to that of the inhabitants of that ſuperb ſeat of empire; and I ſincerely wiſh, that love may have the ſame influence on your diſpoſition, as philoſophy has on that of Mondir.

That, my dear Mirza, you need not make the leaſt doubt of; but how can that ſtate of life be properly called exile, in which we enjoy not only the moſt pure and tranquil amuſements, but alſo every ſocial ſenſation, and the warmeſt raptures of heart? Receive a ſecond time my hand and my vows; I think myſelf this moment infinitely more happy than I ſhould have been, if I had ſhared with you the higheſt honours the Calif can beſtow; I deſpiſe not only his reſentment, but al-

 ſo

ſo the vulgar prejudices againſt a private obſcure ſituation, and even poverty itſelf. If I have but the pleaſure of enjoying your company and affection, I ſhall diſregard all the allurements of honour and fortune; for I look upon a heart that is ſolely influenced by vulgar notions and prejudices to be truly deſpicable. I wiſh it may be in my power to recompence your ſufferings, and to ſupply every deficiency in your breaſt! Your inconſtancy is the only thing I dread; but I ſhall ſtill be able to bear it without abating my affection, for a real paſſion is invariable, and riſes ſuperior to every obſtacle.

How completely happy would Fatima have been, if Zelia's fate, which every day wore a more gloomy aſpect, had undergone ſuch a happy revolution! But the malicious inſinuations of Zobeide were more prevalent than the interceſſions of Meſrour; and Haroun, on his leaving Mecca, would not permit Giafar, even for a moment, to appear in his preſence. The unhappy Vizir did not want to ſolicit his own pardon, but only that of his dear Zelia, an aſſurance of which would have mitigated his cruel fate.—That ſentence, ſaid he to Meſrour, which you look upon as barbarous, is no more than I deſerve; for a perſon that betrays his prince and his friend, ought to be condemned by him who bears thoſe ſacred titles to the ſevereſt tortures. And if, alas, I had not involved my dear Zelia in my ruin, I could have met my approaching fate with the utmoſt compoſure! I beg, Meſrour, you will continue your generous ſervices to that unhappy princeſs and my ſon: be a brother to the one, and a father to the other; for you are the only friend they have to depend upon!—Giafar had but too good a foundation for expreſſing himſelf in this manner; for the blind impetuous reſentment of the Calif had deprived Abbaſſah of the

the ſupport ſhe might have received from the family of the Barmecides, by ordering them all to be arreſted, and the priſons of Bagdad were at preſent filled with theſe illuſtrious victims: and he had even forbid any perſon to preſent any petitions, either in theirs or Abbaſſah's favour.—But though heady and boiſterous paſſions had expelled Haroun's breaſt every ſentiment of virtue and generoſity, yet theſe principles had their full influence with ſeveral other perſons, and Meſrour was not the only one that hazarded every thing for the defence of injured innocence.— The Calif made ſome ſtay at Mecca ſince the commencement of theſe barbarities. Zeineb, to whom he had ſent orders to arreſt Mahomed, who was then in Cariſmia, having learned the cauſe of the diſgrace of that illuſtrious hero, to whom ſhe was indebted for the life of her ſpouſe, inſtead of complying with ſuch unjuſt orders, adviſed him to retire to the court of Irene. But Mahomed would not pay the leaſt attention to his own ſafety, until Zeineb had promiſed him inſtantly to go herſelf, and exert her utmoſt for the preſervation of Giafar and Abbaſſah. —The queen of Circaſſia made all poſſible diſpatch to fulfil her engagement; and the more ſo, as the honour of her friend the Calif was ſo nearly concerned in the event; for ſhe retained the moſt inviolable attachment for him, which was founded on the higheſt eſteem and warmeſt gratitude. She flattered herſelf that her preſence, by recalling to his mind the influence virtue had formerly had on his determinations, would give him reſolution ſufficient to ſurmount paſſions of a greatly more criminal nature than thoſe he had formerly overcome. Encouraged by theſe hopes, ſhe went to meet the Calif, who was, by ſlow marches, returning to Bagdad. The war which the king of Caſhgar had declared againſt Ahmed, was a lucky

pretext

pretext for this journey, and she flattered herself that she would succeed the better in her real design, by appearing only to come to solicit succours for the war. But the Calif obstinately refused to see her; being sensible that such an interview would be productive of the most galling reflections on his own weakness: he therefore readily granted that part of her errand, which was of the least importance.—Zeineb and Mesrour lamented the unhappy infatuation which the Calif laboured under, and studied every method to prevent the execution of that unjust and cruel sentence, which they were sensible would be productive of the most piercing remorse, and leave an indelible stain upon his character. Mesrour imparted to Zeineb his anxiety for Abbassah, and prevailed with her to try her utmost to mitigate her sufferings; and for this purpose, he informed this generous princess of the place were Zelia and her son were concealed, which he had discovered from some hints in a letter from Mondir.

When Zeineb arrived at Hakem's tower, she found Abbassah, who was agitated by a thousand fears, and laboured under the most excruciating grief, in a languid, declining state; and such was the poverty of Mondir and Mirza, that they were not able to procure her necessary subsistence. As she had given up all hope, she was the more sensible of any friendly attempts in her favour; but her jaded spirits would not at first permit her to express her acknowledgments, otherwise than by an affecting silence. Though Zeineb's kindness might have excited her gratitude, without any mixture of those selfish murmurings, to which human nature is very subject when disappointed, yet a just reflection on the judgment of heaven made her exclaim, We ought, O Supreme, to adore thy impenetrable decrees! Who could

could have imagined, that the ſiſter of the monarch of Aſia ſhould ever be obliged to accept the charitable aſſiſtance of a ſtranger!—Ah, madam, continued ſhe, addreſſing herſelf to the queen of Circaſſia, May your conſpicuous virtues protect you from ſo cruel a fate! It is not for the indulgence of an innocent paſſion, which a raſh oath could never render criminal, that I am become an object of the divine indignation, and removed from the higheſt pinnacle of honour into the loweſt abyſs of miſery; but my ſufferings are the conſequence of my being guilty of the fooliſh ridiculous vice of pride. When I was acknowledged the Calif's ſiſter, and when I was free from the connections of an unhappy paſſion, I was proud of having a mother and a brother that ſtood in the foremoſt liſt of fame; and even deſpiſed the homage and adoration that were paid me; this is what has drawn upon me a torrent of divine vengeance. The crimes alſo of others, in which I had no ſhare, have contributed not only to my ſufferings, but alſo thoſe of a huſband, whoſe greateſt misfortune is, his being united to a perſon doomed to miſery. At preſent, inſtead of immenſe treaſures, inſtead of that magnificence which I deſpiſed as inferior to my dignity, inſtead of a croud of attendants, and the having the diſpoſal of ſceptres in my power, I am obliged to fly and conceal myſelf in this frightful place, in order to avoid that infamy with which I am threatened by enraged malice. I am now forſaken by my cringing flatterers, reduced to appear in the moſt pitiful, ragged condition; and if it had not been for your generoſity, my ſon would have ſhortly expired in my arms through the moſt ſhocking diſtreſs, and I ſhould have quickly ſhared the ſame fate, with the additional horror of bringing my generous friends into this miſerable ſituation. But ought I, alas, to accept of your kind endeavours in my favour! Ought

I not

I not rather to remind you of the Calif's injunction, and to beg you would not expose you self to his resentment!—But what do I say! you have nothing to dread on that account! Your eyes have the power of exciting virtuous sentiments in Haroun's breast, whilst mine only excite a criminal passion! O generous Zeineb, employ this happy influence in favour of Giafar! The success of such an undertaking must afford the highest raptures to a person of your disposition! Give me this glimpse of hope, which alone can enable me to support life, and hereafter acknowledge you my sole benefactor!—This speech of Abbassah's drew the deepest sighs from Fatima, and even tears from Mirza and Mondir: instead of being able to console them, Zeineb was obliged to join in the general concern, and her spirits were totally depressed by the cries of the infant, who was affrighted at such a gloomy assemblage of woe: she, therefore, addressing herself to Abbassah, said, I must beg leave, Madam, to retire from this too affecting scene, in order to preserve spirits sufficient to execute your commands: I will instantly go to Bagdad, and seize the first favourable opportunity of prostrating myself at Haroun's feet, in which position I will expire rather than not excite those sentiments of compassion which are so highly requisite to his honour, and of which the petitioners are so highly deserving.

The Calif was as yet ignorant of Zelia's flight; for the orders he had given, that no person should mention her name in his presence, and the dread of hastening the fate of Giafar, had occasioned a general silence on the subject; even Zobeide herself was unacquainted with it. Haroun had ordered his sister to be arrested, and he thought his commands had been executed.—When the mind is involved in any affliction which does not entirely suppress its faculties, it takes a pleasure in communicating its sufferings;

ſufferings; but when they exceed its powers, and bury them in gloom and melancholy, it becomes incapable of confidence and friendſhip.——Haroun, being grown even more inſupportable to himſelf than he was to others, could not enjoy a moment's tranquillity. He ſoon conceived an antipathy to Zobeide, whom he looked upon as the author of that fatal diſcovery which had proved the foundation of his miſery. How juſt a puniſhment for her baſe proceedings! and the envious and malevolent are always more miſerable than thoſe they oppreſs; the latter excite our compaſſion; but the former, that averſion and horror which they ſo juſtly deſerve!——As the Calif approached Bagdad, his torturing agitations were greatly augmented; but love, which was the cauſe of his ſufferings, gave him ſome more lucid intervals, and his mind was frequently balanced between revenge and compaſſion.—Am I going then, ſaid he, to ſhed the blood of thoſe I moſt eſteem! Shall thy firſt act of barbarity, Haroun, fall upon thy friend! canſt thou pronounce ſuch a cruel ſentence! canſt thou inflict ſuch infamy on his wife and thy own ſiſter! What have they done to merit ſuch treatment! They have broke an injunction which it was probably impoſſible for them to obſerve; and as my criminal paſſion was the occaſion of that reſtraint, I ought to expiate my cruelty, by pardoning the violation of it. .... But, reſumed he, pardon them! is it poſſible, when they have occaſioned me ſuch excruciating tortures! when my perfidious friend, whom I admitted into the inmoſt receſſes of my breaſt, has deceived and betrayed me! Ought not I moreover, as the repreſentative of the Supreme, to revenge this flagrant violation of his laws! Has not Giafar been guilty of perjury! and how ſhall I hereafter preſume to puniſh others for that moſt hateful of crimes, if I excuſe him who was thoroughly acquainted with its heinouſneſs, oufness, and who was very sensible that he would find in me an inexorable judge? Ought justice to be warped by the suggestions of friendship or affection! ——Add to these considerations, that fatal letter which the guilty Vizir had undoubtedly forged to prevent my suspicions! That sham devotion of Abbassah! . . . . They shall suffer! The shame and remorse they will occasion me, by forcing me to divulge my mother's infamy, and my own criminal passion, shall receive that additional anxiety, which their punishment will give. Even Zelia's tears shall not soften this just severity! Good heavens! Is it possible that her prayers should in the least alter my firm resolves! . . . . to dry up her tears, to sacrifice myself and the duty of a sovereign.

Such were Haroun's reflections, while Giafar was conducted behind him in chains; and what a prodigious change of circumstances was there between his setting out and his return! Joy, esteem, and affection, had before sparkled in every countenance, but now all was melancholy and horror. The Calif arriving at last at Bagdad, immediately ordered Abbassah to be brought before him; but into what transports did he fall on being informed that she was fled! The united influence of grief, rage, and despair, were never productive of more violent agitations; he roared, threw himself upon the ground, and committed every extravagance! At last, he said, all avenues to compassion are now shut! The perfidious Giafar shall die! His blood, and that of all the Barmecides, shall pay for the guilty Zelia's escape, which they have undoubtedly assisted her to accomplish! Having thus expressed himself, he for some moments lost the use of his faculties, and upon recovering them, he instantly passed sentence on Giafar and all his family. But whilst he was signing with a trembling hand that cruel warrant, which struck all his attendants with the

the deepest horror, Zeineb, breaking thro' all opposition, came into his presence, and checked his design. Hold, Sir, said she, in an undaunted accent, do not commit an act of cruelty and injustice, which will cast an indelible stain on your character, and will make you look upon yourself ever after with shame and horror. Ah, continued she, prostrating herself at his feet, and perceiving in his countenance some sparks of that compassion which she hoped to excite, ah, Sir, if your resentment cannot be appeased without a victim, plunge a dagger into my breast, for I shall think myself happy, if I can by any means prevent your committing those cruel extravagances which will render you a spectacle of horror to all the world! Whom shall we have for a pattern of virtue and magnanimity, if Haroun suffers his character to be sullied by wild extravagant passions? What! does Zeineb, said the Calif, with a little more temper, solicit me to pardon perjury, when she knows experimentally the inflexibility of my justice! If you did but know, alas, continued he with a sigh, how I have been betrayed, and how my credulity and friendship has been abused! .... But you intimate something of cruelty .... of injustice .... Let us examine the affair attentively .... He was going to proceed, and Giafar's pardon seemed certain, when Zobeide, precipitately entering the room, said, Is it possible, Sir, that you should hesitate any longer, since your irresolution is likely to be attended with the most fatal consequences, for a great number of strangers with Mahomed at their head are endeavouring to force open the prison, and raise an insurrection among the people, under pretence of restoring Giafar to Abbassah.

Zeineb's fair prospect of success was instantly blasted by this fatal intelligence. Haroun relapsed to his former fury, and went immediately to put himself

himself at the head of his guards. Giafar's friends were obliged to submit to superior numbers; but night coming on, they most of them by that means escaped, and carried off with them a person who seemed to be their chief, and who was very much wounded. Mahomed was found among the slain, happy in having gloriously sacrificed his life in defence of innocence, and in not being one of those unhappy victims whom the Calif ordered instantly to be executed.—Giafar received his sentence with the utmost composure, and did not drop the least hint of resentment even against Haroun, for his thoughts were at present solely engaged by his dear Zelia. Embracing Mesrour, he said to him, My dear friend, receive my last adieu, collect my departing sighs, and convey them to Abbassah, for she alone is the cause of them! Tell her, that if it had not been for the violation of my oath, I should have thought that I had purchased her favours too cheap even at the price of my blood! Tell her to die rather than be exposed to infamy, and not to entertain any horrors, with regard to a futurity, where she will again meet the most affectionate of husbands! But if she can by any means escape the Calif's resentment, I charge her, by our mutual love, to endeavour to prolong her life for the sake of my son! O my dear boy! . . . . O my Zelia! . . . . Having thus expressed himself, he presented his neck to the executioner; but, to his great surprise, he was reserved for a punishment more cruel than death itself.

They conducted him into the court of the palace, whither they had brought the whole family of the Barmecides, in order to avoid a tumult, and the first person he saw was his father Jahia. This venerable old man, who had grown grey in the laborious employment of minister of state which he had executed with the greatest ability and integrity, was the idol of the

the people ; but instead of seeing his death-bed surrounded by those he had rendered happy, and having the comfort of their affectionate condolence, a premature period was going to be put to a life which was almost expired, and which had been gloriously spent, by the same steel which is allotted to the vilest of malefactors. Those hands which had always been extended for the relief of the afflicted, were now loaded with chains which they were not able to support !——This shocking spectacle entirely destroyed Giafar's resolution ; he threw himself at Jahia's feet, and said, Alas, my father, am I the cause of your death ! am I doomed to see your blood, and that of the rest of these innocent victims, shed before I receive the fatal, but too tardy stroke ! Barbarous Haroun ! how canst thou be guilty of such cruelty ! am I obliged to die with sentiments of aversion and horror for him, whom I should to the very last moment of my existence have esteemed, if he had only punished me for a crime of which I only am guilty !—The emotion with which Giafar pronounced these words, drew tears from Jahia, whom all the apparatus of death had not in the least affected ; he bathed the face of his son with his final affectionate adieu, and said, Moderate thy grief, and adore the unsearchable decrees of thy Creator, whose judgments fall equally on the just and the unjust. It is of his appointment that we suffer this cruel fate, the secret reason of which is alone known to him, whom, notwithstanding we may have lived uprightly, and have the fairest prospect of a happy futurity, we ought always to fear. I have spent a long life in the study and practice of the law, and have for sixty years been an impartial distributer of justice, without the least respect of persons ; neither the widow nor orphan can impeach my integrity ! I have served my sovereigns with

with the utmoſt fidelity; I have always told them the truth, without the leaſt mixture of diſſimulation; and my determinations have always been free from any imputations of intereſt or fear; for theſe reaſons I can with the utmoſt compoſure and aſſurance, repoſe myſelf on the boſom of my gracious Creator. The only thing that diſturbs my laſt moments is my ſon's guilt; if the breach of a promiſe, which was made out of friendſhip, and which was ſuperſeded by a violent and lawful affection, deſerves that harſh appellation, O my Giafar! let that integrity, which gives me the moſt comfortable aſſurance, have the ſame influence upon you! O my friends, continued he, addreſſing himſelf to the Barmecides, you have deſerved a better fate! accept of my ſon's deep contrition as an atonement for his being the occaſion of your deaths! Extend your forgiveneſs, alſo even to Haroun, who will dearly purchaſe it by the moſt forturing reflexions, while we enjoy unalloyed felicity in the bliſsful realms of eternity!—Having thus expreſſed himſelf, Jahia, beholding the fatal ſteel with the utmoſt compoſure, preſented his neck to the executioner, who inſtantly ſtruck off his head and thoſe of the others, concluding with Giafar, whom this ſhocking ſcene had deprived of all ſenſation; and if it had not been for his uttering the name of Zelia on receiving the fatal blow, it would have been doubtful, whether or not there were any remains of life in him .... Meſrour, in the firſt eruptions of the Calif's fury, which he perceived was greatly increaſed by Abbaſſah's flight, had ſent a meſſenger to that unhappy princeſs, to deſire her to come and try her only remaining effort for Giafar's preſervation.

Abbaſſah, with death ſtrongly pictured on her quivering lips, entreated Fatima not to accompany her, but to remain and take care of the child:

attended

attended therefore only by Mondir, ſhe ſet out for Bagdad; but ſhe was weakened by a long ſeries of grief and affliction, that ſhe could walk but very ſlowly, and did not arrive at the palace till her misfortunes were compleated. Juſt as ſhe entered the court, the fatal blow was given, to have prevented which ſhe would have gladly ſacrificed a thouſand lives. But it was now too late, and Giafar was no more! She threw herſelf on the body of her huſband, and attempted again to fix in its place that head which was equally the object of her love and terror. She would have gladly heard from thoſe lips, to which ſhe preſſed her own, one tender accent more, one endearing ſigh! But in vain! nothing now remained for Abbaſſah but deſpair, which ſoon put a period to her woes; for ſeizing a dagger, ſhe plunged it into her breaſt, and inſtantly expired upon the body of her huſband!

This horrid ſcene had thrown Mondir into ſuch confuſion, that he was not able to prevent the fatal effects of Abbaſſah's deſpair; and though he was grown grey in the ſtudy of wiſdom, yet he could not at preſet refrain from the moſt violent expreſſions of grief. Zeineb and Meſrour, drawn to this frightful place by his cries, were equally affected with himſelf; but they at length reflected, that to ſtand and weep, was not performing the laſt offices of freindſhip; and they accordingly removed the bodies of this unhappy couple. Neither they, nor the reſt of the people who were ſolicitous to beſtow an honourable interment on the Barmecides, were in the leaſt interrupted in the execution of this pious office.—Haroun, during theſe tranſactions, was ſhut up in the moſt retired part of the palace, and was ignorant of what was paſſing without; he had only been informed in general, that his orders were executed, and this intelligence had thrown him into ſuch agitations, that they durſt not acquaint him with the

the death of his sister; for he could not have possibly supported the united reproaches of both love and friendship, for having shed so much innocent blood. He was for some time in a violent delirium; during which, he frequently called Giafar, by all the most sacred names of friendship; at other times, he expressed the most virulent invectives: one while he condemned himself as the most wicked of men; at another, he sought every argument to justify his proceedings. Zobeide did not fail, when he was in this last disposition, to represent the Barmecides as the vilest of rebels, who had formed a conspiracy against him. And in order to instigate his resentment by jealousy, she procured a repetition of those orders which she had already issued with respect to Abbassah.——Haroun could not bear to see any person except Zobeide; for being in that unhappy situation, in which the company of vile wretches affords some consolation, and that of the virtuous is irksome, her presence did not excite the least remorse for his late cruel proceedings. He dreaded the sight of Mesrour and the virtuous Zeineb; for though he was very dubious as to the nature of his crime, yet a secret impulse assured him that he was highly guilty; and though he had an aversion for Zobeide, he could not apply to any one else for a solution of his doubts. But she, instead of calming his passions, and softening his anxiety, made him commit still greater extravagances. He prohibited, under pain of death, that any one should presume to celebrate the Barmecides, or give them any other titles than those of traitors and rebels. He commanded their palaces to be erazed, and repeated his orders for the discovery of Zelia, and to prevent her escaping out of his dominions.—While he was engaged in giving these useless directions, the remains of that unhappy princess, and those of her husband, drew the warmest tears of condolence from their worthy friends.
Mondir,

Mondir, intending to convey the bodies to Hakem's tower, and there to inter them, begged Zeineb to go before and remove Fatima and the child from so affecting a scene; though Fatima's grief, on being informed of the death of Zelia, could not admit of any addition. She, at first, insisted on taking a final farewel of her dear departed friend; but at last resigned this poor consolation upon account of the child, whom, taking in her arms, and bathing with her tears, she retired into a private apartment, while Mondir, Mirza, and Zeineb, were performing the last sorrowful office for Giafar and Abbassah. The execution of this ceremony, which was retarded by grief, was interrupted by the arrival of a pale meagre person, who seemed almost in the very agonies of death; and who, after greatly surprising the company, threw himself on the body of Giafar, where he, for some time, remained in the most violent agitations. At last he said, in a feeble accent, ——O my dear and much esteemed friend, have I then the pleasure of giving you a final embrace before I die! Your soul, alas, is not sensible of the melancholy satisfaction this circumstance gives the unhappy Ruggier! Since my valour never submitted to any obstacle, but your cruel destiny! since it was not in my power to protect you, I will follow you! Grief will soon put a period to those small remains of life, which my utmost attempts in your service have left me!

Ruggier's entensive renown had rendered his name well known among the Arabs; upon which account Mondir instantly applied himself to mitigate the violent agitations of this hero, and at last induced him, by the charms of the most persuasive eloquence, to attend with a little more composure, though not less grief, the last office to his dear friend. He was afterwards conducted into their poor cottage, where this sage philosopher supplied him

him with every thing that was requiſite in his preſent ſituation, of both body and mind.—As ſoon as Ruggier was able to bear it, he was introduced to Fatima and the ſon of Giafar, which affecting interview re-kindled his former grief. Madam, ſaid he, addreſſing himſelf to Fatima, the ſage Mondir endeavours to prevail upon me to preſerve a life which I had dedicated to the defence of my friend, and which ſince the loſs of him is become irkſome. You have undoubtedly been informed of that moſt cordial friendſhip which ſubſiſted between me and Giafar; for as he always expreſſed the higheſt eſteem for you, I am aſſured that he treated you with the utmoſt confidence. Alas, a ſecret impulſe, for which there was but too much foundation, made me dread that we ſhould part never to meet agin! And how often, inſtigated rather by thoſe ſecret dictates of my breaſt which made me anxious for his ſafety, than a deſire of his company, did I oppoſe his leaving Conſtantinople. Being well acquainted with his dangerous ſituation at Bagdad, I endeavoured to perſuade him to leave his native country, which would ſooner or later prove fatal to him, and retire into France, where he would meet with a ſafe and an agreeable aſylum. Carry nothing along with you, ſaid I, but Abbaſſah, Fatima and your ſon, for we will ſupply you with every thing elſe to the utmoſt of your wiſhes. Inſtead of an unjuſt prince, a barbarous friend, and malicious ſpies, you will meet with nothing but true friends, who, from a real reſpect, will be eager to ſhew you that they are judges of true merit. But Giafar was unhappily too ſtrongly attached to Haroun, and what he thought to be his duty, to follow that advice which his ſituation but too clearly ſuggeſted; he could not bear even the ſlighteſt reflections on the Calif; and I was obliged to be ſilent on this ſubject, leſt my too frequent ſolicitations ſhould make him

repent

repent of the confidence he had placed in me.—I had not fully recovered my spirits after his departure, when Mahomed arrived at Constantinople, whom Irene received with all the distinction due to the brother of Giafar, and to whom I took the first opportunity of expressing the warmest sentiments of affection and esteem. But how was I alarmed, on being acquainted with the unhappy situation of my friend? No consideration, not even the generous intercession of the Queen of Circassia, and her great influence upon Haroun, could dispel my anxiety for his safety; and I endeavoured to persuade Irene to march some troops under my command to the assistance of Giafar. But Mahomed rejected this proposal with horror; and said, That he would rather see the destruction of his brother, and the whole family of the Barmecides, than that any one of that illustrious race should stain its dignity, by kindling the flames of war in his country, and rebelling against his sovereign. Ah, Sir, continued he, if Giafar should see us in arms against Haroun, he would himself either instantly oppose us, or put a period to that life which occasioned us to be guilty of such rash and unjustifiable proceedings.—Well then, replied I, let us contrive some method of saving him, which may not be repugnant to his rigid virtue and punctual fidility. We may, without communicating our design to Irene, set out this moment for Bagdad, where we shall arrive as soon as Haroun, and by forcing the prison, set Giafar at liberty.—Mahomed approved of this second proposal, in the execution of which we have been so unfortunate. But as I have survived this attempt in favour of my unhappy friend, I shall now dedicate my affection to his son; and I hope, Madam, that you will give me leave to supply to him the loss of his father. Not that I would deprive you of the pleasure of expressing your friendship and affection for him;

 but

but I would advife you to follow me into France. I am no ftranger to the connection between you and the prince of Sarmacande; and it muft, I think, give you no fmall uneafinefs to fee him expofed to perpetual alarms, and dragging on a wretched life in fuch miferable obfcurity; I therefore beg he would accept a fituation more becoming him, in a country not fo much expofed to fuch boifterous commotions, and I hope Mondir will be fo obliging as to make one of the company.—Zeineb, who was feldom abfent from thefe noble, but unfortunate inhabitants of Hakem's tower, was prefent when Ruggier expreffed himfelf as above, and did not omit fo favourable an opportunity of comforting a heart which was oppreffed with the fincereft grief, and which fhe found capable of the nobleft fentiments. The Queen of Circaffia, notwithftanding the blind prejudices and furious paffions of Haroun, ftill retained for him that inviolable attachment which was founded on allegiance and gratitude. She thought that he merited compaffion rather than cenfure; for fhe was affured that it was not fo much his own unhappy paffions, as the malicious influence of Zobeide, which hurried him into thefe extravagances, and that fhe practifed every artifice to keep him ignorant of the heinoufnefs of his proceedings. The fuccefs fhe was fatisfied fhe fhould have had in her application for Giafar, if fhe had not intervened, confirmed her in this opinion, and was the occafion of her entertaining a thought, which at prefent engroffed all her attention. She was affured that the Supreme would give him grace to repent, upon account of the many virtues that had fignalized the former part of his life; but the difficulty lay in bringing him into that difpofition, when he was ftill furrounded by thofe very fnares which had proved his ruin; while he was clofely attended by that vileft of women, who had been the caufe of his

errors,

errors, and while the ſtill ſmall voice of virtue was tuned by jarring paſſions.—Zeineb was very ſenſible that theſe ſentiments would make no impreſſion on the friends of Giafar, as they could not be ſuppoſed to intereſt themſelves in Haroun's unhappy ſituation, as ſhe did in their's. But Ruggier having made the above offer, ſhe thought proper not to omit ſo favourable an opportunity of communicating her thoughts.—Madam, ſaid ſhe to Fatima, you will not make the leaſt heſitation in accepting Ruggier's generous propoſal. But, alas! I am afraid you will find it very difficult to execute! The Calif is ſtill ignorant that deſpair has put a period to his ſiſter's life; and though his officers are well acquainted with this circumſtance, yet they implicitly execute the orders he has iſſued for preventing the eſcape of the unhappy Abbaſſah. Upon this account they ſeize all thoſe that attempt to go out of the kingdom without a paſſport; and you may be aſſured that yourſelf, Mirza, and the ſon of Giafar, are the principal objects of their watchfulneſs. What a dangerous riſque will you therefore run while Haroun continues in his preſent barbarous diſpoſition? If, alas! even the ſacrifice of my life would have reſtored him to his former way of thinking and acting, I would not have made the leaſt heſitation. How often have I attempted to throw myſelf at his feet, but was prevented by Zobeide, who dreads every circumſtance that may diſcover to him the infatuation he at preſent labours under! We are deprived of a very uſeful friend by the unhappy ſituation into which grief has thrown Meſrour; but I hope to extract from thoſe very extravagances which I lament, an expedient that may be of ſervice to us in our preſent ſituation. Every day affords inſtances of perſons, whoſe affection and gratitude ſurmounting their fears, diſregard the Calif's prohibition with reſpect to lamenting or praiſing the Barmecides, and are consequently sacrificed to their manes. I hope that some one of these, (taking advantage of the rule he has laid down for himself, namely, to see every person on whom he passed sentence, and which he has never yet violated, except in the late unhappy case) will represent to him his injustice and cruelty in such strong terms as may rekindle the small remaining sparks of virtue. But the misfortune is, these unhappy victims are not able to support the resentful countenance of their sovereign, which instantly quenches their zeal, and the prejudiced Haroun looks upon their silence as an acknowledgement of their guilt, and upon this account never fails to punish them. —His being under the influence of such a fatal error, replied Fatima, is a just punishment for his late conduct—But, interrupted Ruggier, who can molest us in our journey? I will collect my few remaining friends that assisted me in my attempt to rescue Giafar, and since we cannot possibly meet with any obstacles, except upon the frontiers of Haroun's dominions, we will desire the sage Mondir, whom no person will suspect, to go before us to the nearest towns under Irene's jurisdiction, from whence he will bring us assistance, if we should meet with any difficulties that our own personal valour cannot surmount.

Hatred and resentment had prevented both Fatima, Mirza, and Ruggier, from observing the drift of Zeineb's discourse. But tho' Mondir had as affectionate a regard for the memory of Giafar and Abbassah as any of the others; yet being, by experience and philosophy, freed from the influence of the passions, he could pardon their fatal effects on others, and even the Calif himself was not excepted from this equitable rule by which he judged of the actions of men. Accordingly his greatness of soul, and perfect knowledge of the human heart,

heart, induced him to approve of thoſe ſentiments which gratitude had ſuggeſted to Zeineb. He moreover greatly diſliked Ruggier's laſt propoſal, for he could not bear that beings, doomed to inevitable deſtruction, ſhould blindly haſten that very fate which they moſtly dreaded; and whatever might be the pretext for a war, he equally compaſſionated both the victors and vanquiſhed. He looked upon thoſe flattering titles which men beſtow upon valour, as artificial incitements to that rage and fury which are repugnant to the ſecret dictates of nature.—Theſe reflections were the occaſion of his forming a deſign which he quickly put in execution, without even communicating it to Zeineb, whom he accompanied to Conſtantinople. He went and ſtood upon the ruins of Jahia's palace, and loudly lamented the fate of the Barmecides, exalted their many great accompliſhments, and gave a detail of their noble exploits. The people inſtantly crouded round him, and every breaſt was deeply affected by his powerful eloquence, which had the greater influence, as it tallied with the private ſentiments of all his auditors.—This bold ſtep ſoon produced the effect he wiſhed for; he was ſurrounded by the guards, ſeized, and carried before the Calif, who, in a menacing accent, demanded of him, if he was not acquainted with thoſe orders he had lately iſſued?—I am, Sir, replied Mondir, looking at him with the utmoſt ſternneſs, but too well acquainted with your cruel injunctions; but as I look upon them as unjuſt, I did not think it incumbent upon me to obſerve them. Is it rational that I ſhould be obliged to bury in oblivion the virtues of the Barmecides, who have been the fathers of their country, becauſe Haroun chuſes at preſent to act the tyrant? Ought a prince, who, from being the idol of his ſubjects, become their ſhame and dread, to meet with

with none but abject ſlaves that compliment his extravagant paſſions, and humbly bend under the galling yoke of his cruelty? What have theſe noble perſonages done whom you have ſacrificed to a blind reſentment? Have they not always been ready to ſpend in your ſervice the laſt drop of that blood which you have thus barbarouſly ſhed? Have they not been conſtant examples to your ſubjects of thoſe virtues which conſtitute the ſupport and dignity of your crown? And yet becauſe Giafar has been guilty of a trifling weakneſs, which in your eyes only appears a crime, you have ſentenced theſe worthy ſubjects to an ignominious death; and not content with this, you endeavour to bury their memory in eternal diſgrace. What perſon that has the leaſt remains of generoſity and virtue can be an unmoved ſpectator of ſuch licentiouſneſs of tyranny! Alas, Sir, if the agitations of your own breaſt would but permit you to take a view of that univerſal grief and horror which you have diffuſed over all your dominions, you would be fully ſatisfied as to the cruelty of your proceedings; for the general voice of the people is the echo of the voice of God! When all mankind are unanimous in cenſuring an action which has but one perſon to defend it, this circumſtance is undoubtedly the ſtrongeſt demonſtration of his error. If ſubjects punctually obſerve the ſevere laws they have laid themſelves, not to inſult their ſovereign; a guilty prince ought, by parity of reaſon, to be influenced by that unerring impulſe of nature, which in every countenance condemns his proceedings. This ſpecies of cenſure, which no injunctions can reſtrain, ought to appear in his eyes greatly more ſhocking than that which his unlimited authority gives him the power of publickly proclaiming.

While

While Mondir thus expreſſed himſelf, Haroun was ſeized with the utmoſt confuſion and horror, and his embaraſſed countenance fully indicated the agitations of his breaſt. Cruel ſage, replied he after a conſiderable pauſe, what a ſhocking ſcene do I diſcover by the light of thoſe truths which thou haſt communicated? Is it poſſible that I can merit thoſe ſevere reproaches of which thou haſt been ſo laviſh? But how can I entertain the leaſt doubt, in a caſe which is but too evident, from that horror and deſpair which riot in my breaſt! Ah! fly from an unhappy wretch to whom thou haſt diſcovered the abyſs into which he has fallen, and from which he will never be able to emerge, for I cannot bear thy piercing looks . . . . Be not afraid of my puniſhing thy boldneſs; for upon whom can I now paſs ſentence, when I myſelf have been guilty of a crime which exceeds all pardon? It is impoſſible I ſhould avoid the juſt vengeance of heaven for ſhedding of innocent blood! . . . . O cruel Abbaſſah, your revenge would be amply ſatisfied, if you did but ſee the deplorable ſituation into which you have brought your unhappy brother! It was undoubtedly you who inſtigated this ancient ſage to brave my reſentment! But, whatever was his motive, he has convinced me of my fatal errors, and upon this account I command him to be amply rewarded, and that no perſon moleſt him for cenſuring my conduct, or raiſing what monuments he ſhall think proper to injured innocence.—Ah, Sir, replied Mondir, the only reward I demand for exciting this ſalutary contrition in your breaſt, is, that you will follow my directions, which will re-eſtabliſh your former virtues! Avoid the artifices of a malicious woman who is bent on your deſtruction. Be no longer influenced by Zobeide, but permit the queen of Circaſſia to wait upon you, who will inform you of of the fate of Abbaſſah, which the other's perfidy has concealed in order to perpetuate thoſe extravagances into which ſhe has imperceptibly drawn you. You will find from Zeineb .... What, interrupted Haroun, does Zeineb know where the unhappy Zelia .... Run, my good father, and inſtantly bring hither the queen of Circaſſia, and if poſſible Abbaſſah along with her. I hope your compaſſion will be as ſtrong an incitement to oblige me in this as your zeal was in bringing you hither! .... But what am I ſaying! Is it poſſible for me to ſupport the preſence of Abbaſſah, while my hands are even yet reeking with the blood of her huſband! No; I will only ſee Zeineb. In the mean time I will give orders that a guard be placed over Zobeide, and that ſhe be not permitted to come out of her apartment without my leave. Mondir left Haroun with the higheſt raptures, for the ſucceſs of an enterpriſe concerning the event of which he had been very doubtful, though he was at the ſame time greatly affected by the unhappy ſituation of this prince. The queen of Circaſſia expreſſed the moſt exalted ſatisfaction on being informed of that happy revolution in Haroun's breaſt which ſhe had ſo eagerly wiſhed for, and inſtantly obeyed his commands. But the melancholy ſituation in which ſhe found him, ſtriding about his apartment in the utmoſt agonies of horror and deſpair, greatly abated her joy. Come, my good Zeineb, ſaid he, and inſtantly paſs ſentence on a guilty prince, for it is the duty of virtue to puniſh vice. But your deciſions will be probably influenced by clemency, whereas revenge alone ought to dictate my doom. .... Tell me inſtantly where Abbaſſah conceals herſelf, that I may go and preſent her with a dagger to plunge into a heart which a fatal paſſion has hurried into the moſt unparalled barbarity! She will paſs an equitable ſentence on my unprecedented cruelty! . . . . O Zelia, liſten to the voice of that innocent blood which calls loudly for revenge, and let nothing check your reſentful arm! . . . Having thus ſaid, he threw himſelf upon a ſopha, and Zeineb, notwithſtanding ſhe was greatly affected by his melancholy ſituation, thought the preſent a proper opportunity to give the fatal blow which was requiſite for the complete re eſtabliſhment of virtue and reaſon. Alas, Sir, ſaid ſhe, that dear ſiſter, whom you would inſtigate to this revengeful behaviour, is ſolely engaged in offering the ſincereſt prayers for your tranquillity. The ſum of all her wiſhes at preſent is, that you may enjoy that compoſure and unalloyed felicity of which ſhe is in perpetual poſſeſſion. What, exclaimed the Calif, is my ſiſter no more! . . . . Having thus expreſſed himſelf, he was not only deprived of ſpeech, but of every other faculty. As ſoon as he came to himſelf, Zeineb employed every argument, that reaſon and religion ſuggeſted to mitigate the horrors of his ſoul; in which friendly office ſhe was aſſiſted by Mondir, who now no longer reproached an unhappy prince; who was become a rigid judge of his own actions. Inſtead of cenſuring, they judged it proper to extenuate his crimes, in order to calm his agitations; in which they in ſome degree ſucceeded, by frequently repeating to him that repentance atones for the greateſt of ſins, and thoſe actions which they could not prevail on him to think pardonable, they threw the odium of them on Zobeide, when, by a detail of her malevolent proceedings for the deſtruction of Giafar, and to keep him ignorant of the real ſtate of the caſe, they proved to him, ought to bear the principal part of the guilt. They in concluſion related to him the various diſtreſſes Abbaſſah had laboured under previous to that fatal moment which put a period to her woes, and alſo every

every thing that had happened ſince. The tears which this recital drew from Zeineb completely re-eſtabliſhed in Haroun's breaſt thoſe natural ſenſations of ſoul of which he had not for a long time given any ſymptoms, except by violent guſts of rage and deſpair.—I will, ſaid he in a feeble, faultering accent, follow your advice, and ſpend the remaining days of my life in tears and contrition, if you think that will in ſome meaſure expiate my guilt. If I can ſoften the reſentment of heaven, by conſtantly retaining in my mind, that I have murdered my deareſt friend, that I have plunged a dagger into the boſom of my ſiſter, that I ſacrificed a number of innocent victims, and that I have miſtaken the extravagances of paſſion for a juſt and laudable zeal, theſe ſhocking images ſhall always be before my eyes, and I hope they ſhall be inſtrumental in averting thoſe torments I have juſtly merited in that ſtate of eternity beyond the grave, to which my grief will in a ſhort time convey me. But I ought, alas! to make all the reſtitution in my power for the many cruelties I have committed; and with this view I will order a ſuperbe mauſoleum to be erected on the place where Giafar and Abbaſſah were buried, and that the bodies of all the Barmecides be conveyed thither, and their names replaced in thoſe annals of fame in which their exalted virtues claim the firſt rank. And as the inhabitants of Yemen have a great veneration for the family of Zeid, I will give them the ſon of Giafar for their king. What a cruel pleaſure would it give me to receive in my arms that harmleſs cauſe of ſo many woes, if I did not dread that the hands of the vileſt of wretches would ſully his innocence, and make him a partner in my guilt, which would greatly augment my ſufferings; and moreover, what a ſhocking circumſtance would it be hereafter for him to reflect, that he had

been

been embraced by thoſe very hands that had murdered his father! Fatima ſhall govern during his infancy, at the ſame time taking care to inſtill into him thoſe virtues which may render him capable of holding the reins himſelf when he comes to maturity. I pardon Mirza, Rezia and Hormoz, and ſhall for the future be very compaſſionate to all thoſe who by crimes ſimilar to my own, ſhall remind me of thoſe fatal extravagances into which my paſſions have hurried me. As to Zobeide, whom I ought both out of regard to God and man to puniſh in the ſevereſt manner, I from this moment divorce her, and ſentence her to ſpend the reſt of her days in the dungeon deſtined to the vileſt of criminals. I ought, alas! to condemn myſelf to the ſame place, as no perſon can be more deſerving of ſuch a ſentence, if God had not committed to my care a powerful nation, to whom I ought to endeavour to make ſome recompence for my barbarous cruelties. I hope the generous Ruggier will not divulge my conduct in foreign kingdoms, as it will be a perpetual ſtain on the title of Muſulman.

The affectionate concern and cordial congratulations of Zeineb and Mondir gave the unhappy Calif ſome rays of hope and conſolation; and even Mirza, Fatima and Ruggier, were greatly affected by his ſituation: Though Fatima could not make herſelf quite eaſy, which was occaſioned by another conſideration than the loſs of Abbaſſah. She was afraid, that as ſoon as the queen of Circaſſia, who was obliged ſhortly to return to her huſband, had left Haroun, he would again fall into the ſnares of Zobeide, and relapſe into his former cruelties. Upon this account ſhe could have wiſhed that the child, who was more dear to her than any thing elſe, had not been in the Calif's power; but the all-directing hand of Providence brought about an event which diſſipated all her fears.

Ahmed,

Ahmed, with the aſſiſtance Zeineb had obtained from Haroun, and which, notwithſtanding the perplexed ſituation ſhe was in, ſhe had diſpatched with the utmoſt expedition, had over-run the whole kingdom of Turqueſtan, whoſe monarch had commenced an unjuſt war. The capital Caſhgar was the only place that made any reſiſtance, during the ſiege of which he caſually received a mortal wound from an arrow.—How violent was the grief of the affectionate Zeineb on receiving this fatal intelligence! The Calif ſuſpended his own ſufferings to ſhare in her's, and Mondir was again obliged to take upon him the diſagreeable office of comforter. Fatima would have quitted Hakem's tower, where ſhe hourly lamented the unhappy fate of Abbaſſah, and adminiſtered that aſſiſtance to the queen of Circaſſia which ſhe in gratitude owed her, if ſhe had not dreaded Haroun, to whoſe preſence ſhe could not as yet reconcile herſelf.——This prince conſtantly attended Zeineb; and finding her one day a little more compoſed than uſual, he ſaid, O moſt amiable and virtuous of your ſex, may the moſt vile and wretched of men preſume to diſcover a wiſh which will probably fill your breaſt with horror! But as I am aſſured that what I am going to propoſe is not the impulſe of a fatal paſſion, I look upon it as the dictate of heaven, in order to prevent a relapſe into my former errors. If my crimes have not created an unſurmountable averſion in the breaſt of my dear Zeineb, if ſhe will deign to unite her fate with that of repenting Haroun, he will make it the ſtudy of his future life not to ſtray from the paths of juſtice; and it is hoped that the peace of his ſoul may be ſome incitement to this condeſcenſion. You ſeem to be alarmed, continued he, (perceiving thoſe emotions which the reflexion on his late extravagances neceſſarily excited in her breaſt, but which her virtue and generoſity had always ſurmounted);

mounted); if! alas, I make too large a demand on your noble and benevolent disposition, I will for ever renounce the only wish I am capable of entertaining! —I by no means, replied Zeineb, look upon my sovereign with horror: on the contrary, I esteem, nay love him; not indeed with that tender passion which Ahmed alone could excite in my breast, but with that steady constant affection, which nothing has been able to lessen, and the dictates of which I will readily follow, if I can be in the least instrumental to the re-establishment of your virtue and renown.—In short, Haroun was soon after married to the Queen of Circassia, but could not even in her arms obliterate the remorse of his late cruelties. He not only lamented all the days of his life the unhappy fate of Giafar and Abbassah, but endeavoured to repair his crimes by a long series of the most illustrious actions, a detail of which would be much more prolix than that of his vices; and he carried that renown which had attracted the affection of Zeineb to such a pitch, as almost entirely effaced his former cruelties. He permitted the people, without the least molestation, to go in crowds, and pay their adoration at the tomb of Giafar and Abbassah, whom they looked upon as martyrs to conjugal affection; and he shewed himself more truly great by this toleration, than weak in giving occasion for such a custom.

He was lavish of his treasure to Mirza and Fatima, who conducted the son of Giafar to Zabith; and he was not in the least displeased with Ruggier for refusing the rich presents which he had offered him. This young hero soon after returned to France, to assist Charlemain against the Saracens; and the impression Haroun's cruelties had made on his breast was the principal motive for his embracing Christianity, for he reflected that a wise and good man ought to make that religion his choice, whose pure morality puts the ſtrongeſt curb upon the paſſions. At laſt, diſcovering himſelf to be deſcended from illuſtrious anceſtors, he married Bradamante, and obliterated in her arms the pleaſures he had enjoyed with Irene, who continued to experience the common fate of all thoſe women who endeavour to ſecure their lovers by favours and connections not founded in virtue.

As Zeineb was very capable of giving the Calif any future directions that might be requiſite for the ſupport of his virtue, Mondir did not think that there was any occaſion for his remaining at Bagdad; and therefore he accompanied his dear Fatima, whoſe future life was an uninterrupted flow of felicity, which ſhe had the pleaſure of ſharing with Hormoz and Rezia, and they all had the additional ſatisfaction of living to ſee the ſon of Giafar ſupport the dignity of the family of the Barmecides.—Zeineb and Fatima took their final leave of each other at the tomb of Abbaſſah, which, by recalling their part, which they had taken in her misfortunes, freſh to their minds, together with the tragic cataſtrophe of Giafar, and the Barmecide family, renewed their affliction, and ſerved to ſuſpend, or, at leaſt, divide the grief which attended their parting.

Zeineb, with a heart pained by her mournful ſeparation from one, whoſe virtues had left on it the tendereſt and deepeſt impreſſions of friendſhip and eſteem, returned to the Calif, to whom her preſence became more and more neceſſary, to defend him from himſelf, from his violent temptations to deliver himſelf up to ſuch a melancholy deſpair and ſelf-abjection as would have rendered him unfit for the only end he had in view, his making ſome reparation for the ill he had done, by procuring the good of a whole people.

By

By his own fatal experience, of having ſuffered his juſt and laudable horror of a violation of oaths to paſs on him for the principal motive of his wreaking the vengeance of the moſt criminal jealouſy, he was now grown ſenſible of that moſt dangerous of all the perfidious impoſtures of the paſſions, in their lurking behind the fair appearance of ſome virtue, which conceals them from the ſight of thoſe who would otherwiſe deteſt their deformity, and eſcape their rage.

But as his remorſe was ſincere, and his endeavours at all the atonement in his power conſtant and uniform, they found acceptance even with man. His cruelties to his ſiſter, to his friend, and to the Barmecides, came at length to paſs for no more than the ſtain of an illuſtrious reign, and were conſidered as ſpots in the ſun, drowned in a ſea of ſplendor: inſomuch that they did not hinder his being numbered among the greateſt princes of the Abaſſide dynaſty, nor his preſerving the appellation of *Haroun Alrachid*, or HAROUN the JUST.

FINIS.